Lynne Graham was born in Northern Ireland and has been a keen romance reader since her teens. She is very happily married to an understanding husband who has learned to cook since she started to write! Her five children keep her on her toes. She has a very large dog who knocks everything over, a very small terrier who barks a lot, and two cats. When time allows, Lynne is a keen gardener.

Mills & Boon Stars

COLLECTIONS

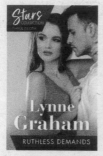

Lynne **Graham** — RUTHLESS DEMANDS

Sharon **Kendrick** — CONVENIENT VOWS

Cathy **Williams** — SINFUL PROPOSALS

January 2019   February 2019   March 2019

Michelle **Smart** — PASSIONATE BARGAINS

Maya **Blake** — SEDUCTIVE NIGHTS

Caitlin **Crews** — SHOCKING SCANDALS

April 2019   May 2019   June 2019

Mills & Boon
Stars Collection:
Ruthless
Demands

LYNNE GRAHAM

MILLS & BOON

First Published in Great Britain 2019
By Mills & Boon, an imprint of HarperCollins*Publishers*
1 London Bridge Street, London, SE1 9GF

MILLS & BOON STARS COLLECTION: RUTHLESS
DEMANDS © 2019 Harlequin Books S.A.

The Sicilian's Stolen Son © 2016 Lynne Graham
The Greek Demand's His Heir © 2015 Lynne Graham
The Greek Commands His Mistress © 2015 Lynne Graham

ISBN: 978-0-263-27542-1

0119

MIX
Paper from
responsible sources
FSC™ C007454

This book is produced from independently certified FSC™ paper to ensure responsible forest management.

For more information visit: www.harpercollins.co.uk/green

Printed and bound in Spain
by CPI, Barcelona

THE SICLIAN'S
STOLEN SON

CHAPTER ONE

LUCIANO VITALE'S LONDON lawyer, Charles Bennett, greeted him the moment he stepped off his private jet. The Sicilian billionaire and the professional exchanged polite small talk. Luciano stalked like a lion that had already picked up the scent of prey in the air, impatience and innate aggression girding every step.

He had tracked her down...*at last*. The thieving child stealer, Jemima Barber. There were no adequate words to convey his loathing for the woman who had stolen his son and then tried to sell the baby back to him like a product. It galled him even more that he would not be able to bring the full force of the law down on Jemima. Not only did he not want his private life laid open to the world's media again, but he was also all too aware of the likely long-term repercussions of such a vengeful act. Hadn't he suffered enough at the hands of the press while his wife was alive? These days Luciano very much preferred the shadows to the full glare of daylight and the endless libellous headlines that had followed his every move throughout his marriage.

Even so, Luciano still walked tall and every female head in his vicinity turned to appreciate his passing. He stood six feet four inches tall, with the build of a natural athlete, not to mention the stunning good looks he had been born with. Not a single flaw marred his golden skin, straight nose or the high cheekbones and hollows that combined to lend him the haunting beauty of a fallen angel. He cared not at all for his beautiful face, though, indeed had learned to see it as a flaw that attracted unwelcome attention.

As it was, it was intolerable to him that in spite of taking every precaution he had almost lost a *second* child. Instantly he reprimanded himself for making that assumption. He could not know for certain that the boy was his until the DNA testing had been done. It was perfectly possible that the surrogate mother he had chosen for the role had slept with other men at the time of the artificial insemination. She had broken every other clause of the agreement they had signed, so why not that one as well?

But, if the baby was his as he hoped, would it take after its lying, cheating mother? Was there such a thing as bad genes? He refused to accept that. His own life stood testament to that belief because he was the last in a long ruthless line of men, famed for their contempt for the law and their cruelty. There could be no taint in an innocent child, merely inclinations that could be encouraged or discouraged. He reminded himself that on paper his son's mother had appeared eminently respectable. The only child of elderly, financially in-debted parents, she had presented herself as a trained infant teacher with a love of growing vegetables and cookery. Unfortunately her true interests, which he had only discovered after she had run from the hospital with the child, had proved to be a good deal less respectable. She was a sociopathic promiscuous thrill-seeker who overspent, gambled and stole without conscience when she ran out of money.

Time and time again he had blamed himself for his decision not to physically meet with the mother of his child, not to personalise in any way what was essentially a business arrangement. Would he have recognised her true nature if he had? He had not expected her to want to see him either, when he came to collect the child from the hospital after the birth, but in the event he had arrived there to learn that she had already vanished, leaving behind only a note that spelt out her financial demands. By then she had found out how rich he was and only greed had motivated her.

'I must ask,' Charles murmured in the tense silence within the limousine. 'Do you intend to tip off the police about the lady's whereabouts?'

Luciano tensed, his wide sensual mouth compressing. 'No, I do not.'

'May I ask...' Choosing tact over frank frustration, Charles left the question hanging, wishing that his wealthiest client would be a little more forthcoming. But Luciano Vitale, the only child of Sicily's once most petrifying Mafia don, had always been a male of forbidding reserve. A billionaire at the age of thirty, he was a hugely successful businessman and, to the best of Charles's knowledge, resolutely legitimate in all his dealings. And yet his very name still struck fear into those who surrounded him and they paled and trembled in the face of his displeasure. His loathing for the paparazzi, and the ever lingering danger of his criminal ancestry making him the target of a hit, ensured that he was encircled by bodyguards, who kept the rest of the world at bay. In so many ways, Luciano Vitale remained a complete mystery. Charles would have given much to know why a man with so many more appealing options had chosen to pick a surrogate mother to bring a child into the world.

'I will not be responsible for sending the apparent mother of my son to prison,' Luciano said without any expression at all. 'There is no doubt in my mind that Jemima deserves to go to prison but I do not wish to be the instrument that puts her there.'

'Quite understandable,' Charles chimed in, although it was a polite lie because he did not understand at all. 'However, the police are already looking for her and notifying them of her location could be done most discreetly.'

'And then what?' Luciano prompted. 'The elderly grandparents receive custody of my son? And the authorities are forced to enter the picture to consider his welfare? You have already warned me that surrogacy arrangements receive a divergent and uncertain reception within the UK court system. I will not take any risk that could entail losing all rights to my son.'

'But the Barber woman has already made it clear that she will only surrender the boy for a substantial sum of money…and you *must* not, you *cannot* offer her cash because that would put *you* on the wrong side of British law.'

'I will find some acceptable and legal way to bring this matter to a satisfactory conclusion,' Luciano breathed softly, lean brown fingers flexing impatiently on his thighs. 'Without damaging publicity or a court case or sending her to prison.'

Warily encountering his client's cold dark eyes, Charles suppressed a shiver and tried not to think about how Luciano's forebears had preferred to clear their paths of human obstacles: with cold-blooded murder and mayhem. He told himself off for that imaginative flight of fancy but he could not forget that chilling look in Luciano's gaze or his notorious ruthlessness in business. He might not kill his competitors but he had never been a man to cross and was known to exact harsh retribution from those who offended him. He doubted very much that Jemima Barber had the slightest comprehension of the very dangerous consequences she had invited when she had reneged on her legal agreement with Luciano Vitale.

Sì, Luciano brooded, he would achieve his goal because he *always* got what he wanted and anything less was unthinkable, particularly when it came to his son's well-being. If the little boy proved to be his, he would take him whatever the cost because he could not possibly leave an innocent child in the care of such a mother.

Jemima tidied the flowers on her sister's grave. Her crystalline blue eyes were stinging like mad, her heart squeezing tight with misery inside her.

She had loved Julie and hated the reality that she had never got the chance to get closer to her natural sibling and help her. Born to an unknown father and a drug-addicted mother, the twin girls had ended up in separate adoptive homes. Julie had briefly been deprived of oxygen at birth and had required major surgery soon afterwards. Her sister had not been available for adoption until her treatment was complete a full two years later. Jemima, however, had been much more fortunate in every way, she thought guiltily. Her middle-aged adoptive parents had adored her on sight, adopted her at birth and given her a wonderfully happy and secure childhood. Julie had been adopted by a much wealthier couple but her developmental delays and problems had disappointed and embarrassed her parents. Ultimately the adoption had broken down when her sister was a wayward teenager and Julie had ended up back in care, rejected by the parents she'd loved. It was no surprise to Jemima that from that point everything in her twin's life had gone even more badly wrong.

The twins had not met again until they were adults and Julie had tracked Jemima down. Right from the outset Jemima and her parents had been captivated by her lively charming twin. Of course that had gone wrong as well for *all* of them, Jemima acknowledged reluctantly. But perhaps it had gone worst of all for little Nicky, who would now never know his birth mother. Her misty eyes rested on the eight-month-old baby in the buggy on the path and predictably brightened because Nicky was the sun, the moon and the stars in Jemima's world. He studied her with his big liquid dark eyes and smiled from below the mop of his black curly hair. He was the most utterly adorable baby and he owned his auntie's heart and soul and had done so since the moment she'd first met him when he was only a week old.

'I saw you from the street. Why are you here again?' a worried female voice pressed. 'I don't understand why you're torturing yourself this way, Jem. She's gone and I say good riddance!'

'Please don't say that,' Jemima urged her best friend, Ellie, whom she had first met in nursery school. She turned to face the taller, thinner redhead with determination.

'But it's the truth and you have to face it. Julie almost destroyed your family,' Ellie said bluntly. 'I know it hurts you to hear me say it but your twin was rotten to the core.'

Jemima compressed her lips, determined not to get into another argument with her outspoken friend. After all, when times had been tough during the Julie debacle Ellie had regularly offered Jemima and her parents a sympathetic shoulder as well as advice and support. Ellie had proved her loyalty and the depth of her friendship many times over. In any case, it would be pointless to argue now that Jemima's twin was dead. Even so, the pain of that loss still made such judgements wounding. Only a few months had passed since Julie had carelessly stepped out in front of a car and died instantly. Julie's adoptive family had refused even to attend the funeral and the cost had been borne by Jemima's parents, although they could ill afford the expense.

'If we'd had more time together, things would have turned out very differently,' Jemima declared with a bitterness that she struggled to hide.

'She ripped off your parents, stole your identity and your boyfriend and landed you with a baby,' Ellie reminded her drily. 'What could she have done as an encore? Murdered you all in your beds?'

'Julie never showed any tendency towards violence,' Jemima argued back through gritted teeth. 'Let's not talk about this any more.'

'Let's not,' Ellie agreed wryly. 'It would make more sense to discuss what you're planning to do with Nicky now. You've got quite enough on your plate with a full-time job and helping out your parents.'

'But I'm more than happy to look after Nicky as well. I love him. He *is* my only living relative,' Jemima pointed out with quiet fortitude as the two women walked out of the graveyard and down the road. 'Obviously I'm not planning to give him up. We'll manage somehow.'

'But what about his father? Surely you have to consider his rights?' Ellie countered impatiently and, seeing her companion stiffen and pale, she groaned. 'My shift starts in an hour—I have to go. I'll see you tomorrow.'

Parting from her friend, who lived in an apartment on the same street, Jemima walked away at the slow pace of someone exhausted—Nicky still only slept a few hours at a time. She had expended a great deal of thought on the worrying topic of Nicky's paternal ancestry. Other than the fact that Nicky's father was supposedly a very wealthy man, she knew nothing about him or, more importantly, why he had chosen to father a child through a surrogacy agreement. Was he a gay man in a relationship? Or were he or his partner unable to have a child? Julie had not cared about such details but Jemima cared about them very much indeed.

There was no way she could ignore the reality that Nicky had a living father somewhere in the world, a parent who had paid for and planned his very conception. But she didn't know his identity because Julie had flatly refused to divulge it and there was therefore nothing that anyone could expect Jemima to do about tracing the man, she reflected with guilty relief. Her sole concern was, and always had been, Nicky's well-being. She wasn't prepared to hand the little boy over to anyone without first seeing the proof that that person would love and nurture her nephew. That was her true role now, she conceded unhappily: to step into the untenable situation Julie had created and try to ensure that Julie's son was not damaged by his mother's rash choices.

Jemima still marvelled that her twin had not even recognised that she was literally agreeing to bring a child into the world for a price. Incredibly at the time she had signed up, Julie had only viewed the surrogacy agreement as a job that paid living expenses at a time when she was short of cash and needed somewhere to live. She had admitted to loathing what pregnancy did to her body and she had not changed her mind about handing Nicky over after the birth. No, Julie had simply decided that she had not been well enough rewarded for suffering the tribulations of nine months of pregnancy followed by a birth, particularly once she had learned that Nicky's father was rich.

And what were the chances that the man would prove to be a caring, compassionate father? The sort of man who would love and cherish Nicky to the very best of his ability? Jemima believed that there was little chance of that being the case when the man concerned had not even wanted to *meet* the mother of his future child. From what little she had read most surrogacy agreements encouraged some kind of contact between the various parties involved, at least initially. After all, Nicky was half Julie's flesh and blood as well. He had not been conceived from a donated egg but from her sister's body, which meant he was very much Jemima's nephew and a part of Jemima's small family, a little connected person whom Jemima felt it was her duty to love and protect.

Jemima let herself into the small retirement bungalow that was her parents' current home. It had two bedrooms and a small garden and she was very grateful that there was enough space for her and Nicky to stay there. Her father was a retired clergyman and her mother had only ever been a clergyman's wife. Sadly, the careful savings her parents had made over the years had gone into Julie's pocket when she had pretended that she'd wanted to rent a local shop and start up her own business. Or maybe that hadn't been a pretence, Jemima conceded, striving not to be judgemental.

Quite possibly, Julie had genuinely intended to set up a business when she'd first floated the idea to Jemima's parents but Julie had been tremendously impulsive and her plans had often leapt enthusiastically from one money-making scheme to the next within days. Her sister might have seemed to have good intentions and might have uttered very convincing sentiments but she *had* told lies. There was no denying that, Jemima reflected unhappily.

Regardless, the Barbers' financial safety net was now gone and her parents' lifelong dream of buying their own home was no longer possible. In fact the only reason her parents still had a roof over their heads was Jemima's decision to come back home to live and help to pay the rent and the household expenses, which were exceeding her father's small pension. Faced with bills they couldn't afford to pay, the older couple had begun to fret and their health had suffered.

With quiet efficiency, Jemima changed Nicky and settled him down for a morning nap. Screening a yawn of her own, she decided to lie down too, having learned that napping when Nicky did was the only sure way to get her own rest. She peeled off her tunic top and winced when she caught an accidental glimpse of her liberally curved bottom in the wardrobe mirror.

'Your backside's far too big for leggings! Always wear a long top to cover your behind,' Julie had urged her.

But then Julie had been thin as a willow wand and tormented by bulimia, Jemima reminded herself ruefully. Her twin had had serious issues with food and self-image. On that unhappy reflection, Jemima fell straight to sleep, still clad in her leggings and vest top.

When the shrilling doorbell wakened her, Jemima scrambled up in surprise because most visitors were family friends and aware that her mum and dad were currently staying in Devon with a former parishioner.

That was the closest her parents could get to a holiday on their restricted income. She peered into the cot, relieved to see that her nephew was still peacefully asleep, his little face flushed, his rosebud mouth relaxed.

From the hall she could see two male figures through the glass.

'Yes?' she asked enquiringly, opening the door only a fraction.

An older man with greying hair dealt her a serious appraisal. 'May we come in and speak to you, Miss Barber? My card…' A business card was extended through the narrow gap and she glanced down at it.

Charles Bennett, it read. *Bennett & Bennett, Solicitors.*

Instantly fearing yet another problem linked to her twin's premature death, Jemima lost colour and opened the door. Julie had left a lot of debts in her wake and Jemima just didn't know how to deal with them. She shrank from the prospect of telling the police that her sister had stolen her identity to the extent of contracting debts in her name, travelling on her passport and even giving birth in Sicily as Jemima Barber. She was very much afraid that revealing that information would make her current custody of Nicky illegal and she was frightened that the minute she admitted that he was *not* her child he would be taken from her and placed in a foster home with strangers.

'Luciano Vitale…' the older man introduced as his companion stepped forward and Jemima took yet another step back from her visitors, all her senses now on full apprehensive alert.

And when she focused on the taller, younger man by

his side she froze, for he was a man like no other. His movements were fast, smooth and incredibly quiet as if he were a combat soldier slinking through the jungle. He was poetry in motion and pure fantasy in the flesh. Indeed he was very probably the most breathtakingly beautiful man Jemima had ever seen in her life. The shock of his sudden magnetic appearance was hard to withstand. Her chest tightened as she struggled to catch her breath and not stare as the compellingly handsome lineaments of his lean bronzed features urged her to do. It made her feel frighteningly schoolgirlish and she hurriedly turned her head away to invite them into the living room.

Luciano couldn't take his eyes off Jemima Barber because she was so very different from what he had expected. His very first sight of her had been her passport photo application in which she had looked blonde, blue-eyed and a little plump, indeed so ordinary he had rolled his eyes at the idea that such a commonplace woman could give him a child. His second view of her two months earlier on security-camera footage from a London hotel had been far more indicative of her true nature. Blonde hair cut short and choppy, she had sported a very low-necked top, a tiny silver skirt and sky-high hooker heels that had showed off her slim figure and the rounded curve of her breast implants. She had been acting like the slut she was, giggling and fondling the two men she was taking back to her hotel room that night.

Now that image was being replaced by another, even more challenging one for evidently Jemima Barber had reinvented herself yet again. Possibly that big change in appearance was a deliberate element of her con tricks, he conceded. The short hair was gone, exchanged for hip-length extensions, which provided her with a glorious mane the colour of ripe wheat in sunlight. Her heart-shaped face seemed bare of make-up, his keen gaze resting suspiciously on the succulent pout of her pink mouth, the faint colour blossoming in her cheeks and the pale ice-blue eyes, an unusual shade that he had initially assumed was a mere accident of the photographic lighting. She wore a drab pair of black leggings and a tight vest top, which accentuated the sumptuous swell of her breasts.

With difficulty he dragged his attention from that surprisingly luscious display, acknowledging that the camera shots of her chest must have been unflattering, because in the flesh she looked much more natural. Even so, she was distinctly curvier. Had she simply put on weight? The plain clothing was a surprise as well but, of course, she hadn't been expecting visitors and it was possible that she dressed more circumspectly in her elderly parents' radius. In fact at this moment she looked ridiculously wholesome and young. It made him wonder who Jemima Barber really was below the surface. And then he questioned why he was wondering about her at all when he already knew all that he needed to know. She was a liar, a cheat, a thief and a whore without boundaries. She sold her own body as easily as she planned to sell her son.

Hugely self-conscious below the intensity of Luciano's appraisal, Jemima could feel her face getting hotter and hotter but, because he unnerved her, she kept her attention on the older man and said, 'How can I help you?'

'We're here to discuss the child's future,' Charles Bennett informed her.

At that news her heart dropped to the soles of her canvas-clad feet and her head swivelled, eyes flying wide as she involuntarily looked back at Luciano. Looked and instantly saw what she had refused to recognise seconds earlier, finally making the terrifying connection that set a large question mark over her hopes and dreams for Nicky. Nicky was like a miniature carbon copy of Luciano Vitale. Luciano wore his hair a little longer than was conventional. It fell below his collar in glossy blue-black curls that flared luxuriantly across his skull. He had a straight nose, spectacular high cheekbones, winged brows and deep-set eyes the colour of tawny tiger's eye stones—eyes as hard and unyielding as any crystal.

Stray recollections of her late sister's remarks on the topic of Nicky's father echoed in the back of her head.

'If he met me, he would want me... Men *always* do,' Julie had trilled excitedly. 'He's exactly the sort of man I want to marry—rich and good-looking and madly successful. I'd make the perfect wife for a man like him.'

And, of course, Luciano Vitale wouldn't be too impressed right now when, instead of the slim, fashionable Julie, he got the fatter, plainer twin, a little voice whispered in Jemima's shaken head. Was that why he was staring? But he didn't *know* that she was Julie's sister and he had never even met her sister. As far as she was aware he did not even know that Julie had an identical twin nor was he likely to know that Julie had stolen Jemima's identity. Did he even know that her sister was dead?

Jemima assumed not. Had he known, surely that would have fuelled the lawyer's first words because Julie's death now changed everything. A cold little shiver shimmied down Jemima's spine at that awareness. As Nicky's mother, Julie had had rights to her son even if those rights could be disputed in court. As Nicky's aunt, Jemima had virtually no rights at all. The only thing that blurred those boundaries was the fact that Julie had given birth in her twin's name and it was Jemima's name on Nicky's birth certificate and not his real birth mother's. It was a legal tangle that would have to be sorted out some day.

But not on this particular day, Jemima decided abruptly as she collided with Luciano's chilling dark eyes, which were regarding her with as much emotion and empathy as a lab specimen might have inspired. Nicky's father was angry, distrustful and ready to make snap judgements and decisions, she reckoned fearfully. He was not visiting in a spirit of goodwill and why indeed would he? Julie had given birth to his child and had then run away with that child, leaving behind an unabashed demand for more money.

Jemima tilted her chin up as if she were neither aware of nor bothered by Luciano's scrutiny and concentrated on the lawyer instead. The tension in the atmosphere was making her tummy perform nauseous somersaults and suffocating her vocal cords. She knew that she needed to get a grip on herself and do it fast because she had no idea of what was about to happen and for Nicky's sake she had to be able to react fast and appropriately. It disturbed her, though, that one major decision had somehow already been made and that was her willingness to pretend to be Julie for as long as she could pretend while she assessed Nicky's father as a potential parent. If she admitted who she really was, her nephew could be immediately removed from her care and her heart almost stopped at the mere thought of that happening. For that reason alone she would lie…she would *pretend*…even if it went against all her principles.

Luciano was very still, his entire attention engaged by the strange behaviour of the woman in front of him. Women did not stick out their chins and ignore Luciano when they were lucky enough to gain his attention. They smiled at him, flirted, treated him to little upward glances calculated to appeal. They never *ever* blanked him. Yet Jemima Barber was blanking him.

'I want DNA testing carried out on the child so that I know whether or not he is mine.' Luciano spoke up for the first time, startling her. His dark, deep accented drawl trailed along her skin like a fur caress and awakened goosebumps.

As the ramifications of what he had said sank in Jemima went rigid at the insult to her sister's memory. 'How *dare* you?' she shot back at him angrily, her temper rising and spilling out without warning and shaking her with its intensity.

His perfectly modelled mouth took on a derisive

slant. 'I dare,' he said levelly. 'There must be no doubt that he is mine—'

'In any case, mandatory DNA testing after the birth was a clause in the contract you signed,' the lawyer chipped in. 'Unfortunately you left the hospital before the test could be completed.'

The reminder of the contract that Julie had signed in Jemima's name doused Jemima's anger and covered her with a sudden surge of shame instead. She was about to lie. She was about to pretend that she was her sister when she was not and the knowledge cut her deep because, in the normal way of things, Jemima was an honest and straightforward person who detested lies and deception. Her desire to look out for Nicky's needs, she registered unhappily, had put her on a slippery slope at odds with her conscience. She should be telling the truth, no matter how unpleasant or dangerous it was, she thought wretchedly. Two wrongs did not make a right. This man was Nicky's father. But *could* she simply stand back and watch Luciano Vitale take her baby nephew away from her?

She knew she could not. There had to be safeguards. Nicky was defenceless. It was Jemima's job to carefully consider his future and ensure that his needs were met. But she had to be unselfish about that process too, she reminded herself doggedly, even if the final result hurt, even if it meant standing back and losing the child she loved.

'DNA testing,' Luciano repeated, wondering if his worst fears were being borne out by her pallor and clear apprehension. Maybe the child *wasn't* his. If that were the case, it was better that he found that out sooner rather than later. 'The technician can visit the child here. It is a simple procedure done with a mouth swab and the results will be known within forty-eight hours.'

'Yes,' Jemima muttered, dry-mouthed, nerves rattling through her like express trains as yet another fear presented itself to her.

All bets were off if he intended to have her tested for DNA. Did twins have the same DNA? She had no idea and worried that she would be exposed as an imposter. She lowered her feathery lashes. Well, she would just have to wait and see what happened. She was not in a position to do anything else. Arguing against the need for such testing would only muddy the waters. It wouldn't achieve anything. It would only increase the animosity and uncertainty about her nephew's future.

'So, you will agree to this?' Luciano said softly.

Involuntarily, Jemima glanced at him and connected with liquid dark eyes surrounded by black velvet lashes as lush as his son's. Her heart went *bang-bang-bang* inside her and she felt incredibly dizzy, as if she stood on the edge of an abyss gazing down at a perilous drop. Something tugged and tightened low in her pelvis and she was unexpectedly alarmingly aware of her body as if her prickling skin had suddenly become too tender to bear the weight of her clothes. 'Yes...'

'In fact you will agree to all my demands,' Luciano told her without skipping a beat while he silently marvelled at the translucent perfection of her pale blue eyes. 'Because you are not stupid and it would be very stupid to refuse me anything that I want.'

Brows pleating, Charles Bennett turned to study his client in astonishment and then his attention skimmed back to the young blonde woman staring back at Luciano as if he had cast a magic spell over her.

CHAPTER TWO

'AND WHY WOULD you think that?' Jemima fired back in sudden bewilderment, shaking her head as though to clear it.

'Because I hold pole position,' Luciano informed her with chilling assurance. 'I have security-camera footage of you stealing credit cards and using one of them in an act of fraud. If I should choose to pass that evidence to the police, I—'

'You're threatening me!' Jemima interrupted in shock.

Stolen credit cards? Was he serious? Was it possible that Julie had sunk that low while she was working in London? Jemima did recall wondering how her sister was contriving to stay at a fancy hotel. She had asked and Julie had winced as though such a financial enquiry were incredibly rude and had sulkily refused to explain.

'My client is *not* threatening you,' Charles Bennett interposed flatly. 'He is simply telling you that he has footage of the theft.'

But Jemima had turned pale as death and did not

dare look in Luciano's direction again. Proof of theft? My goodness, he could have her arrested right here and now! *Forcibly* parted from Nicky! Her lashes fluttered rapidly as she struggled to think.

'So you *will* agree to the DNA testing?' Luciano queried once more.

'Yes,' she agreed shakily.

'We will endeavour to be civilised about this matter.'

In receipt of that unpersuasive statement, Jemima's palm tingled. Never in her life had she wanted so badly to slap someone for lying. But that richly confident, patronising assurance from Luciano Vitale sent violent vibes of antagonism coursing through her and, daringly, she turned her head to look at him again. It was a grave mistake. As she fell into the hypnotic darkness of his gaze shock gripped her, tensing every muscle with sudden bone-deep fear for in Luciano she sensed a propensity for violence that made a mockery of her own softer nature. He was a man of extremes, of dangerous emotions and dangerous drives, and for a split second it was all there in his extraordinarily compelling eyes like a high-voltage electrical pulse zapping her with a stinging warning to back off or take the consequences. Seemingly he hid the disturbing reality of his true nature behind a chillingly polite mask.

'Yes, we must try to be civilised,' she heard herself say obediently while she shrank from the terrifying surge of ESP that had enveloped her in an adrenaline-charged panic mere seconds earlier.

'I can be reasonable,' Luciano declared, smooth as

polished glass. 'But I will do nothing that could put me on the wrong side of British law. Be clear on that score.'

'Of course,' she conceded, wondering why she didn't feel reassured by that moral statement.

He wanted to stay on the right side of the law. She quite understood that. Only, where did that leave her? Julie had committed her crimes in Jemima's name and the only way for Jemima to clear her name was to own up to her sister's identity theft. Unfortunately doing that would also mean that she lost the right to care for Nicky. How could she bear that loss? How could she risk it? All she could do in the short-term, she thought in a panic, was fake being Julie until she was confronted by the police. At that point she would have to come clean because she would have no other choice.

Luciano studied his quarry, his gaze instinctively lingering on her ripe mouth and the porcelain smoothness of the upper slopes of her full breasts. He was a man and he supposed it was natural for him to notice her body, but the pulse of response at his groin and the sudden tightening there infuriated him. He turned away dismissively, broad shoulders rigid below his exquisitely tailored charcoal-grey suit jacket.

'The technician will call to take the sample this afternoon,' he delivered.

'You're not wasting any time,' Jemima remarked gingerly.

Luciano swung back, eyes narrowed and cutting as black razors. 'You have already wasted a great deal of my time,' he told her with brutal bluntness.

Jemima clenched her teeth together and glanced at

his companion, whose discomfiture was unhidden. There was civilised and civilised, she guessed, and Luciano Vitale had no intention of treating someone like her with kid gloves. It was clear that he saw her as inferior in every way. She would have to toughen up, she told herself urgently, toughen up to handle someone who disliked and distrusted her without showing weakness. Weakness, she sensed, he would use against her.

Shell-shocked as Jemima was by Luciano's visit, once he had left she followed her usual routine with Nicky. She had looked forward to spending the long summer holidays with the little boy before she had to make childcare arrangements to enable her to return to work at the start of the new term. Now she was wondering if she would lose custody of him before then. She was down on the floor playing with Nicky when the doorbell went again.

It was the technician from the DNA-testing facility. The woman extended a consent form on a board for her to sign and then asked her to hold Nicky. The swab was done in seconds and Jemima waited for the technician to use the same procedure on her but instead she packaged the swab and departed, her job evidently complete. Heaving a sigh of relief that she herself had not been asked to give a sample, Jemima was in no mood for further company and she suppressed a weary groan when yet another caller turned up at the door.

Her face stiffened when she recognised her ex-boyfriend. Yes, she was still friends with Steven because her parents liked him and she had had to deal with the awkwardness of continuing meetings whether she liked it or not. Steven was a big mover and shaker in the church she attended and ran a young evangelical group to great acclaim.

'May I come in?' Steven pressed when the polite small talk about her parents' little holiday had dried up and she was rather hoping he would take the hint and leave.

'Nicky's still up,' Jemima warned him.

'How's the little chap doing?' Steven enquired with his widest, fakest smile.

'Well, his father may have turned up,' Jemima heard herself say without meaning to. That she had admitted that much to Steven was evidence of how much emotional turmoil she was in because once she had realised how much he disapproved of her taking responsibility for Julie's son she had stopped confiding in the tall blond man.

Steven took a seat with the casual informality of a regular visitor. A handsome dentist with a lucrative line in private patients, her ex was well liked by all. Jemima, however, was rather less keen. She had believed she loved Steven for years and had fully expected to marry him before Julie came into their lives.

'Yes, he's good-looking and he could give me some fun but he's *your* boyfriend. I'm not poaching him,' Julie had told her squarely.

But Jemima hadn't wanted to keep Steven by default and once she'd realised how infatuated he was with her twin she had set him free. Of course, as a couple, Steven and Julie hadn't suited, as Jemima had suspected at the outset. Her sister and her ex had enjoyed a short-lived fling, nothing more, and Jemima genuinely did not hold Steven's defection against him. How could she possibly blame him for having found her colourful, lively sister more attractive? No, what annoyed Jemima about Steven was that he was smugly convinced that he could talk his way back into Jemima's affections now that Julie was gone. Steven had no sensitivity whatsoever.

'His father?' Steven echoed on a rising note of interest. 'Tell me more.'

Jemima told him about her visitors but withheld the information about the stolen credit cards and the underlying threat, reluctant to give Steven another opportunity to trash her sister's memory.

'That's the best news I've heard in weeks!' Steven exclaimed, his bright blue eyes lingering intently on her flushed face. 'I admire your affection for Nicky but keeping him isn't practical in your circumstances.'

'Sometimes feelings aren't practical,' Jemima countered quietly.

Steven gave her an earnest appraisal. 'You know how I feel about you, Jem. How long is it going to take for you to forgive me? I was foolish. I made a mistake. But I learned from it.'

'If you had really loved me, you wouldn't have wanted Julie—'

'It's different for men. We are more base creatures,' Steven told her sanctimoniously.

Jemima gritted her teeth and resisted the urge to roll her eyes. It amazed her that she had failed to appreciate how sexist and judgemental Steven could be. 'I've moved on now. I'm fond of you but I'm afraid that's all.'

'Tell me about Nicky's father,' Steven urged irritably.

'I only know his name, nothing else...'

Steven started looking up Luciano Vitale on his tablet and fired a welter of facts at her.

Luciano was an only child, the son of an infamous Mafia don. Jemima did roll her eyes at that information. He was filthy rich, which wasn't a surprise, but much that followed did take her aback. In his early twenties Luciano had married a famous Italian movie star and had a daughter with her before tragically losing both wife and child in a helicopter crash three years earlier. Jemima was shocked, *very* shocked by that particular piece of news.

'So there you have it...that's *why* he wants a kid... his daughter died!' Steven pointed out with satisfaction. 'How can you doubt that the man will make a good parent?'

'He's still single. How much actual parenting is he planning to do?' Jemima traded stubbornly. 'And maybe Nicky's supposed to be a replacement but he's not a girl, he's a boy and a child in his own right—'

Steven pontificated at length about the immorality of the surrogacy agreement and how it went against all natural laws. Jemima said nothing because she was too busy looking at photographic images of the exquisite blonde, Gigi Nocella, Luciano's late wife and the mother of his firstborn. Luciano had matched Gigi, she reflected abstractedly, two beautiful people combined to make a perfect couple. He had already lost a child, she thought helplessly, and she was filled with guilt at her own reluctance to hand over Nicky. Who was she to interfere? Who was she to think she knew everything when she was already painfully aware that her sister had made so many bad choices in life?

'Vitale *needs* to know what Julie did to you and your family,' Steven said harshly. 'After all, if he'd kept better tabs on her, Julie would never have come here and caused so much grief.'

'That's very much a matter of opinion, Steven,' Jemima said stiffly and, deciding that she had been sufficiently hospitable, she stood up in the hope of hastening his departure.

'You're not thinking this through, Jem,' he told her in exasperation. 'Nicky's not your child and you shouldn't be behaving as if he is. If you pass him on to his father...'

'Like a parcel?'

'He *belongs* with his father,' Steven argued vehemently. 'Don't think that I don't appreciate that that child is preventing us from getting back together again!'

'Only in your imagination—'

'You know how I feel about you keeping Nicky. Why are you trying to do more for the kid than his own mother was prepared to do? Let's be honest, Julie was a lousy mother and not the nicest—'

'Stop right there!' Hot-cheeked, Jemima wrenched open the front door with vigour. 'I'll tell Mum and Dad that you called in when I phone them later.'

She closed the door again with the suggestion of a

slam and groaned out loud in frustration. But grateful as she was to see Steven leave, he had left her with food for thought. She played with Nicky in the bath and stared down at his damp curly head with tears swimming in her eyes. He wasn't her child and all the wishing in the world couldn't change that…or bring Julie back. Luciano Vitale had lost a much-loved daughter. She must have been loved, for that could be the only reason her father had gone to such lengths to have another child. Jemima wrapped Nicky's wet, squirming figure into a towel and hugged him close.

Luciano had searched for eight months to find his child. He wanted Nicky. She had to stop being so self-ish. She had to take a step back. Was she prejudiced against Luciano because he had chosen a surrogacy arrangement to father a second child? She was conservative and conventional and she supposed she was a little bit disposed to prejudice in that line. The admission shamed her. How could she have accepted Julie and Nicky but retained her bias against Nicky's father? Of course, what if Luciano Vitale wasn't Nicky's father?

Two days later, however, she received the results of the DNA testing, which declared that her nephew was Luciano's flesh and blood, and she had barely settled the document down when the landline rang.

'Luciano Vitale…' Her caller imparted his identity with a warning edge of harshness. 'I would like to meet my son this evening.'

Jemima reminded herself that there was no room for her personal feelings in her dealings with Luciano and she breathed in deep. 'Yes, Mr Vitale. What time suits you?'

They negotiated politely for an earlier time than he first suggested because Jemima knew that the later he arrived, the more tired and cross Nicky would be. And she wanted the first meeting between father and son to go well because it would be downright mean and malicious to hope otherwise. The small living room was spick and span by the time she had finished cleaning, but Nicky was teething again and cried pathetically when she tried to put him down for his afternoon nap. Ellie had been texting her constantly with queries since she had told her friend about Luciano and was reacting to his proposed visit with as much excitement as a famous rock star might have invoked.

'Are you sure I can't come round and sort of hover on the doorstep?' Ellie pleaded on the phone. 'I'm gasping to see the guy in the flesh. He looks hotter than the fires of hell!'

'It's not the right moment, Ellie. He has a right to his privacy.'

'Not looking like a walking, talking female temptation, he hasn't!'

'He may look good in photos but he's not the warm, approachable type,' Jemima reminded her friend.

'Well, why would he be? He thinks you're Julie and Julie ripped him off! When are you planning to tell him the truth?'

'When I find the right moment. Not tonight because in the mood he's probably going to be in he's likely to just scoop up Nicky and walk straight out of here with him,' Jemima admitted with a grimace.

'Whether Luciano Vitale knows it or not, he owes you,' Ellie said loyally. 'Julie couldn't cope with Nicky and you've been caring for him since he was only a week old. Your parents will miss him terribly, though, when he goes.'

When he goes, Jemima repeated inwardly, her heart sinking as she was finally forced to face that certainty. Nicky was about to be taken away from her and there was not one blasted thing she could do about it. She was not Nicky's closest relative, Luciano was.

Jemima was very tense while she waited for her visitor. Nicky looked adorable in a little blue playsuit but he was teething and in a touchy temperamental mood in which he could travel from smiles to tears in the space of seconds.

Jemima heard the cars arrive and rushed to the window. The equivalent of a cavalcade had drawn up outside on the street, a collection of vehicles composed of a black limousine and several Mercedes cars, all with tinted windows. As she watched several men emerged from the accompanying cars and fanned out across the street while clearly taking direction from ear devices. All the men wore formal suits and sunglasses and emanated an aggressive take-charge vibe. Finally the rear door of the limo was opened and Luciano slid out, instantly casting everyone around him in the shade. He wore well-washed jeans and a long-sleeved black sweater...and still, he took her breath away.

The well-cut denim outlined long, powerful thighs

and lean hips, while the dark sweater somehow enhanced his blue-black hair and olive skin. Her mouth ran dry while she stared and smoothed damp palms down over her own, more ordinary jeans, wishing she had the same sleek, fashionable edge he exuded with infuriating ease. As she began to back away from the window a movement behind him attracted her attention and she stared as a slim blonde woman climbed out of the car. Instantly, Luciano turned to speak to the woman and a moment later she got back into the car, evidently having thought better of accompanying him. Who was she? His girlfriend?

It's none of your business who she is, a voice reproved in Jemima's mind and she moved through to the doorway and breathed in deep, struggling to bolster herself for what was to come. She opened the door briskly. 'Mr Vitale...'

'Jemima,' he said drily, stepping inside, his sculpted lips unsmiling, an aloof coolness stamped across his lean bronzed face like a wall.

'Nicky's in here...' Jemima pressed the living-room door wider to show off Nicky where he sat on the floor surrounded by his favourite toys.

'His name is Niccolò,' Luciano corrected without hesitation. 'I don't like diminutives. I would also like to meet my son alone...'

Jemima glanced up at him in surprise and dismay but he wasn't looking at her. His attention was all for Nicky, no, Niccolò, and Luciano's lustrous tiger eyes were gleaming as he literally savoured his first view of his son with an intensity she could feel. Jemima stared, couldn't help doing it, noting with relief that the forbidding lines of Luciano's lean dark face were softening, the hard compression of his beautifully sculpted hard mouth easing.

'Thank you, Miss Barber,' Luciano Vitale murmured, deftly planting himself inside the room and leaving her outside as he firmly closed the door in her face.

With a sigh, Jemima sat down on the phone bench just inside the front door. Of course he didn't want an audience, she reasoned, striving to be fair and reasonable. Who was the woman waiting outside for Luciano? If she was his girlfriend, did he live with her? Was it possible that the girlfriend was unable to have children and that she and Luciano had entered the surrogacy agreement as a couple? And what did any of those facts matter to her? Well, they mattered, she conceded ruefully, because she cared a great deal about Nicky's future but ultimately she had no say whatsoever in what came next.

As a whimper sounded from the living room Jemima tensed. Nicky was going through a stranger-danger phase. She could hear the quiet murmur of Luciano's voice as he endeavoured to soothe the little boy. Sadly, a sudden outburst of inconsolable crying was his reward. Jemima made no move but her hands were clenched into fists and her knuckles showed white beneath her pale skin as she resisted the urge to intervene. The sound of Nicky becoming increasingly upset distressed her but she knew she had to learn to step back and accept that Luciano Vitale was Nicky's father and his closest relative.

When Nicky's sobs erupted into screams, the living-room door opened abruptly. 'You'd better come in... He's frightened,' Luciano bit out in a harsh undertone.

Jemima required no second invitation. She scrambled up and surged past him. Nicky's anxious eyes locked straight on to her and he held up his arms to be lifted. Jemima crouched down to scoop him up and he clung like a monkey, shaking and sobbing, burying his little head in her neck.

Luciano watched that revealing display in angry disbelief. Niccolò had two little hands fisted in his mother's shirt, his fearful desperation patently obvious as he hid his face from the stranger who had tried to make friends with him. As Jemima quieted the trembling child Luciano registered two unwelcome facts. His son was much more attached to his mother than his father had expected and Jemima was very definitely the centre of his son's sense of security. It was a complication he neither wanted nor needed. His attention dropped to the generous curve of Jemima's derriere in jeans and he tensed, averting his gaze to the back of his son's curly head as he felt himself harden. So, he liked women to look more like women than slender boys and she had splendid curves, but he abhorred that hormonal response that was so very inappropriate in Jemima Barber's radius.

'He's teething, which always makes him a bit clingy,' Jemima proffered in Nicky's defence. 'And this is the wrong end of the day for him because he's tired and fractious—'

'He's terrified. Isn't he used to meeting people?' Luciano pressed critically.

'He's more used to women.'

'But your parents must've been looking after him for you while you were in London,' he pointed out, momentarily depriving her of breath as he reminded her of the lie she was living for his benefit. After all, nobody could be in two places at once and while Jemima had been teaching and covering Nicky's childcare costs at a local nursery facility, Julie *had* been in London.

'Dad's retired but he's still out and about a lot, so Nicky would've seen less of him,' Jemima muttered in a brittle voice, crossing her fingers at a lie that made her feel guiltier than ever because Nicky adored his grandfather.

Nicky stuck his thumb in his mouth and sagged against Jemima with a final hoarse whimper. 'Sorry about this…' she added uncomfortably. 'But in time he'll get used to you.'

Luciano compressed his lips. He didn't have time to waste.

'Is that your girlfriend outside waiting in the car?' Jemima asked abruptly, keen to know and to change the subject about Nicky's lifestyle in recent months.

Luciano frowned, winged ebony brows pleating above hard dark eyes fringed by lashes as dense and noticeable as black lace. 'No, the nanny I'm hiring.'

Jemima stopped breathing. 'A nanny?' she gasped in dismay.

'I will need some support in caring for my son,' Luciano countered drily, wondering what he was going to do about the problem his son's mother had become.

Well, he certainly wouldn't be marrying her as Charles Bennett had ludicrously suggested after the results of the DNA test had been revealed.

'A paper marriage,' Charles had outlined. 'In one move you would legitimise your son's birth, tidy up any future inheritance issues and gain a legal right to have custody of your son. As an ex-wife you could also give her a settlement without breaking the law. It would be perfect.'

Perfect only in a nightmare, Luciano reflected grimly. No way was he linking his name to a woman who was no better than a thieving hooker, not in a paper marriage of any kind.

He was employing a nanny, Jemima thought wretchedly as panic snaked through her in a cold little shiver of foreboding. Clearly Luciano was planning to remove Nicky from her care as soon as he could.

Luciano surveyed his infant son, who was engaged in contentedly falling asleep against his mother's shoulder. He could rip him away from Jemima as he himself had once been ripped away from his own mother. All right, he had been almost three years old but he had never forgotten the day he was torn from his mother's loving arms. Of course there had been a lot of blood and violence involved and naturally he had been traumatised by the episode. He would not be doing anything of that nature. He despised Jemima Barber but he did not wish her dead for having crossed him. At the same time, however, he deeply resented her hold on his son.

'Nicky's very emotional,' Jemima remarked cautiously. 'He does get upset quite easily.'

'I'm surprised he's so fond of you. You've spent most of your time in London and left other people looking after him,' Luciano condemned.

'I've spent much more time with him than you appreciate,' Jemima protested, tilting her chin. 'Of course he's fond of me...'

'But you always planned to give him away,' he reminded her coolly. 'As long as the pay-off was sufficient. Shouldn't you have prepared him better for the separation?'

An angry flush illuminated her pale porcelain skin. 'I didn't know if there was going to *be* a separation!' she fired back awkwardly.

'I would let nothing prevent me from claiming my son. Since you disappeared there has not been a single day that I haven't thought of him,' Luciano proclaimed, dark honey-rich eyes glittering with challenge. 'He is mine—'

'Yes...' she conceded raggedly, her breath catching in her throat below the onslaught of his extraordinarily compelling gaze. 'But handing him over isn't going to be as simple...er...as I once thought it would be.'

Luciano shrugged a broad shoulder without interest. 'You convinced a psychiatrist that you knew what you were signing up to do and could cope with it.'

Desperation slivered through Jemima's taut frame. 'Things change...' she whispered.

'I want my son,' Luciano told her bluntly.

The germ of a wild idea burst into being inside Jemima and flew straight from brain to tongue without the benefit of any filter or forethought. 'Couldn't *I* be your nanny? Even for a little while?'

Luciano studied her in disbelief. 'My nanny? *You?* Are you crazy?'

'Only until he settles into his new life. You'd be getting a trained infant teacher to look after him. I'm well qualified with young children.'

'But you've never worked with them?'

'Of course I have work experience.'

'Before you decided that you much preferred earning easy money as an escort?'

Jemima froze. 'An...*es-escort?*' Her voice stumbled over the mortifying word. 'That's a dreadful—'

Luciano sighed. 'I know everything about you. You can't lie to me. You were working as an escort in London and you were very popular with older men until you began to steal their wallets. I spoke to the agency that made your bookings for you before deciding to dispense with your services.'

Her lips parted and then closed again. She had turned white as snow, shock thudding through her, her heart thumping loudly in her eardrums. She didn't want to believe him but she did because Julie's love of money had been much stronger than her self-respect. An escort? An escort offering extras? Jemima squirmed, raw humiliation bowing her head. Working as an escort had given her twin the chance to steal. And sadly, the stolen credit cards had only been the tip of the iceberg, she acknowledged wretchedly. Seemingly Julie had been as willing to sell herself as she had been to sell her son.

'It was an exclusive escort service,' Luciano conceded, recognising her mortification and less gratified by it than he had expected to be.

'So I wouldn't be quite what you want in a nanny,' Jemima breathed, stricken, receiving that message loud and clear from his attitude.

'I'm afraid not. My security team will pick Niccolò up tomorrow and bring him up to London for the day. I'll send the nanny with them.' Luciano read her consternation with ease. 'Naturally I want to spend time with my son.'

'Before you do...*what*?' Jemima pressed helplessly.

'Before I take him home to Sicily with me,' Luciano fielded. 'You know how this must end, Jemima. Why make it more difficult for all of us?'

Jemima subsided like a pricked balloon. Julie had accepted payment and signed the agreement. There was no escape clause unless she was willing to run screaming to the media with her sad story. And where would that get her? More importantly, what would it gain Nicky? Notified of the circumstances of Nicky's birth, the social services would probably step in to take charge of Nicky and decide his future and there was no guarantee that Luciano would get him either. In fact there was every chance that Nicky would be placed in an adoptive home and neither Jemima nor Luciano would ever see him again. Seeking outside help would be the wrong thing to do, she decided in despair. The very fact she had lied and faked being

Julie to hold on to her nephew would be held against her by the authorities…and by Luciano if he ever found out the truth.

CHAPTER THREE

'So COULD I have a lift with you up to London?' Jemima asked the nanny cheerfully. 'I assure you that a lift is all I want, but my being in the car will make it easier for you to get to know Nicky and I can run through his routine with you as well.'

'Er... I...' Nonplussed, the nanny, who had introduced herself as Lisa, hovered on the doorstep and looked at the tall, broadly built bodyguard standing behind her for direction.

The bodyguard dug out a cell phone and punched in a number and Jemima got the obvious message: nothing could be done because no plan could deviate in the smallest way without Luciano Vitale's permission and approval. She scolded herself for thinking that she was being clever when she had come up with the idea the night before. Yet she truly wasn't trying to interfere with Luciano's day with Nicky. She simply wanted to be more accessible if anything went wrong.

'I just thought I could take the opportunity to do some shopping,' she fibbed nervously as the bodyguard's conversation in staccato Italian continued at length.

'Mr Vitale makes all the arrangements,' Lisa told her with an apologetic smile. 'I don't want to screw up my first day on the job. It would be handy, though, to know a little more about your son.'

'Miss Maurice?' The bodyguard handed the phone to the nanny.

Jemima watched the woman stiffen, straighten her shoulders and pale as she evidently received her instructions while answering yes and no several times. She then extended the phone to Jemima.

Realising that it was now her turn to receive her orders, Jemima laughed out loud, stunning her companions.

'So glad you've found something to laugh about today,' Luciano drawled, sharp and swift as a stiletto stabbing at her down the line.

'Oh, please don't take it like that,' Jemima babbled in dismay. 'I promise you that you won't see or hear from me today. I just want to be in London…to…er… shop—'

'I can hear the lie in your voice—'

Her blood ran cold in her veins.

'You got a sixth sense or something?'

'Or something. Tell me the truth or I will not consider the idea,' he told her coldly.

'I wanted to be within reach…you know, in case you needed me. That's all.'

At his end of the line, Luciano gritted his perfect white teeth. Where the hell did she get the nerve to bug him like this? He expelled his breath in a hiss of impatience. 'Why would I need you?'

'Not you, *him*,' Jemima stressed. 'And dial back the tension, Luciano. Nicky can be very temperamental. He works best with calm, quiet and soothing—'

Luciano was incredulous. 'Let me get this straight— *you* are telling *me* how to behave?'

'But not in a rude way, in a *helpful* way,' Jemima emphasised.

'You are irritating me,' Luciano growled soft and low.

'Ditto.' Jemima groaned out loud, having forgotten her audience. 'Less of the growly stuff would be nice but not if you replace it with the rave-from-the-grave voice.'

The rave from the grave, Luciano mouthed in silent disbelief. She was actually telling him that he irritated her. How dared she? A thieving whore...but the *mother* of his *son*...

'You can travel to London with them and accompany Niccolò back again at five today. Pass the phone back to Rico...'

Jemima did as she was bid, handing Nicky's baby bag to the second bodyguard who had appeared before tucking her nephew under her arm to lock up the house.

'What a fuss about nothing,' she wanted to remark to the nanny as she climbed into the limousine and the two women together secured the baby into the very fancy car seat awaiting him, but caution silenced her. Luciano was an intractable tyrant supported in his moods and habits by his intimidated employees. Presumably standing up to Luciano meant instant dismissal. Jemima suspected she wouldn't last five minutes working for him because she had too much a mind of her own, so it was probably fortunate that he hadn't jumped on her nanny offer. At the same time, however, she was relieved he had agreed to let her catch a lift to London and travel back with Nicky at the end of the day. She had been a tiny bit afraid that Luciano wasn't planning on letting Nicky return to her again and now that looming fear could be set aside for at least one more day. Having passed her cell-phone number to Lisa, she asked to be dropped at the entrance to a Tube station.

The attraction of browsing round shops where she could not afford to buy anything held little appeal for Jemima. In recent months she had grown accustomed to being stony broke, to questioning every single purchase and asking herself if she really needed the item. And although she would have adored some new clothes and the chance to replace cosmetics that had run out, she was happy to make those sacrifices to keep Nicky and give her parents peace of mind in their retirement. A desire to make the best of whatever life threw at her had always driven Jemima and she took the same approach to her day out, heading to the first of her free attractions—the British Museum—before enjoying a picnic lunch in Kensington Gardens and a walk round the Tate Modern. She was on the banks of the Thames when her phone rang and she snatched it out.

'Nicky's ill… Where are you?' Luciano demanded thinly. 'I'll have you picked up.'

Her frantic questions elicited no adequate response beyond the assurance that the baby was not in danger. Luciano was much more intent on retrieving her as soon as possible so that she could comfort the little boy. Jemima was perspiring with stress and anxiety by the time a limousine lifted her at the agreed pick-up point and drove her across London to an exclusive block of apartments. There, flanked by two enormous bodyguards, she got into a glass lift to be swept up to the penthouse.

'I thought you were going to stay within reach!' Luciano roared at her as she came through the front door.

Jemima was accustomed to dealing with distraught and often angry parents whose child had become upset at school or had suffered injury and at one glance she recognised that Luciano fell into that category. He was a powerful man who controlled everything around him but Nicky's illness had made him feel powerless and that anger was the fallout. She could hear Nicky's distressed choking wails echoing through the apartment and was not in the mood to waste time sparring with his anxious father. 'Where is he?'

'The doctor's with him,' Luciano gritted, closing a managing hand to her spine to herd her in the right direction. He was the most alarmingly dominant man and, even worse, she thought ruefully, it seemed to come entirely naturally to him, as if an autocratic need to trample over the little people had been programmed into him at birth. 'Not that he's been much use!'

Lisa was pacing the floor with a wailing Nicky and looked as though she had been through the wars. Earlier that day she had looked immaculate. Now her long hair was falling down untidily and her shirt was spattered with food stains. An older bespectacled man, who could only be the doctor, overlooked the scene with an air of discomfiture.

'What's wrong with Nicky?' Jemima asked worriedly.

The doctor studied her anxiously. 'A touch of tonsillitis...nothing more—'

'My son would not be making such a fuss over so little,' Luciano began wrathfully.

'Oh, yes, he would.' Jemima threw Luciano a wryly apologetic glance. 'He makes a real fuss when he's sick. He's had tonsillitis a couple of times already and I was up all night with him.'

With a yell, Nicky unglued his reddened eyes and, focusing joyously on Jemima, he gave a frantic lurch in Lisa's hold. The other woman crossed the room in haste to settle him into Jemima's arms. 'It's obvious he wants his mum.'

'Perhaps you could explain to...er...Nicky's father that this is not a serious condition. The baby has a mild fever and a sore throat and possibly some ear pain.' Exhausted, Nicky moaned against Jemima's shoulder, his solid little body heavy against her as he slumped.

'Try to get him to drink some water to keep him hydrated,' the doctor advised with a wary glance in Luciano's smouldering direction. 'Within a couple of days and with the medication he'll soon be back to normal.'

'Thank you,' Jemima pronounced quietly as she

sank down on a comfortable leather seat and accepted the baby bottle of water Lisa helpfully extended. She studied Nicky and glanced across the room at Luciano. So, she finally had first-hand evidence of whose genes had dealt Nicky the theatrics and the fireworks, she thought wryly, ignoring Nicky when he twisted away his mouth from the bottle. 'Do you want your cup?' she asked.

Nicky looked up at her, dark eyes cross and shimmering with tears.

Jemima dug the baby cup out of the bag and proceeded to pour some water into it while still cradling Nicky.

'Seems that he is one little boy who knows what he wants,' Lisa remarked.

'You're spot on.' Jemima watched the baby moisten his lips and then try a tiny sip. Forced to swallow, he grimaced and sobbed again while she praised him and told him what a brave, wonderful boy he was.

Luciano watched the performance unfolding with blazing dark golden eyes, angry frustration assailing him. He knew when he was facing a fait accompli. Jemima handled Nicky beautifully, clearly knew him inside out and responded smoothly to his needs. He himself and the highly qualified nanny had failed utterly to provide the comfort his son had needed. He wondered if little boys were programmed to want mothers over father figures. He wondered tensely how his son would cope without a mother, particularly with her sudden disappearance. Bemused by that flood of concern and the sort of deep questions he normally suppressed, Luciano grated his teeth together in frustration and called someone to show out the doctor.

'It *is* only a mild illness,' Jemima remarked quietly. 'Relax.'

'How the hell am I supposed to relax when my son is suffering?' Luciano lashed back at her in fierce attack.

'Sometimes you *can't* fix things and the normal childhood illnesses fall into that category,' Jemima pointed out gently.

Well, he *cared* about Nicky; he was quite accidentally revealing that with his behaviour. Of course, he had to be aggressive even in that, but then he was an aggressive man. And intelligence warned her that Luciano Vitale would not voluntarily share anything with her that he considered to be private or personal. Obviously his feelings about his son would fall squarely into that territory and it was not for her to pry, she told herself doggedly as Nicky snuffled into an exhausted sleep on her lap.

Luciano strode to the door, raking an impatient hand through his blue-black glossy hair. A dark shadow of stubble outlined his sculpted mouth and strong jawline. He was obviously the sort of man who had to shave twice a day. He had loosened his racy red tie at the collar, unbuttoned the top button of his white shirt. He looked a little more human and a little less perfect than at their previous meeting and she censured her selfish sense of satisfaction that he was finding his son more of a challenge than he had expected. Such a feeling was mean and ungenerous, she reminded herself angrily. Nicky was Luciano's flesh and blood and she should be pleased that he was so keen to get to know his child.

Lisa reappeared and hovered.

'The nanny will put my son in his cot for a nap now,' Luciano announced. 'We have to talk.'

Talk? What about? A frown indented Jemima's brow as she passed her nephew carefully over to the young woman and the door closed in their wake.

'What do you want to discuss?' she asked stiffly.

Luciano shot her a chilling appraisal. 'Oh, please, don't come over all naïve on me now. I prefer honesty. You've made it clear that you want to make the most profit you can from having brought my child into the world,' he pointed out with unconcealed contempt. 'But I simply want what makes my son happy and it is patently obvious that in the short-term at least Niccolò will not be happy if you suddenly vanish from his life.'

Jemima studied him, surprised he was willing to admit that possibility.

'Although there is nothing I can like, respect or admire about you, Jemima…my son *is* attached to you,' he conceded in a grim-mouthed tone of finality. 'I do not want to damage him by immediately forcing you out of his life. He deserves more consideration from me. After all, he did not choose the unusual circumstances of his birth—*I* did.'

His ringing assurance that he did not like, respect or admire her cut Jemima surprisingly deep and yet she was wryly amused by her apparent vulnerability towards his low opinion of her morals. He thought she was Julie and while she faked being Julie she had to own her sister's mistakes and pay the price of them too.

Luciano watched her porcelain-fair skin wash a guilty pink that simply accentuated the ice-blue eyes, which reminded him of very pale aquamarines he had once glimpsed in his mother's jewellery box. Those eyes and that full, soft pillowy mouth were snares that any man would zero in on, he told himself, his attention widening its scope to encompass the full, buoyant swell of her breasts below the simple tee she wore. He wondered what colour her bra was and marvelled at the ludicrous thought. What was he? A randy schoolboy? He had access to many sexual choices and almost any one of those women would be classier, safer and more beautiful than Jemima Barber, he reminded himself impatiently. Even so, it was his son's mother who was making him hard and taut and needy where it mattered, when he was all too often indifferent to female fawning and flirtation.

But then possibly what annoyed him most about Jemima was that he had yet to see any sign that she was making the smallest effort to sexually attract him. She did not appear to be wearing make-up and her plain denim skirt came to her knees while she sat with her pale slim legs neatly and modestly folded to one side. It was like a simulated virginal act, he reasoned in exasperation. Possibly she had already worked out that hooker heels and too much exposed female flesh were not his style.

Sex was no big deal, he thought impatiently. That was a truth he had embraced long ago. He didn't make time for sex, though, and perhaps that explained his reaction to his son's mother. Possibly any reasonably appealing woman would have given him the same response. But the nanny did nothing for his libido, he conceded, and neither did any of the very attractive female staff he employed. No, Jemima Barber had something special about her, something insidiously sexy he had yet to pin down and label, and it drew him like a very strong magnet. And he loathed it, loathed it like poison in his system, because she was everything he despised in a woman.

The silence smouldered like a simmering pot on a gas hob. Jemima could feel heat striking through her, spreading up from the warmth in her pelvis. *He* did that to her. *He* made her tummy fill with butterflies. *He* made an embarrassing hot, slick sensation pulse between her thighs. *He* made her nipples tighten and push against the barrier of her bra.

That reality mortified and shamed her and reminded her of her first crush as a teenager when her body had gone haywire with a physical longing she hadn't understood and hadn't really been ready to embrace. But this was different because those responses were now attacking her adult body. She found herself studying that gorgeous face of his even though she didn't want to stare, didn't want to notice the perfection of his sleek cheekbones, the classic jut of his nose or the strong line of the jaw cradling that superbly masculine mouth. And then she fell into the dark and dangerous enticement of his deep-set eyes that were tigerish gold in the light from the window and once she looked she couldn't breathe, couldn't think, couldn't even function, she thought in bemused dismay.

The door opened and an older woman came in carrying a tray. Coffee was poured. Luciano took his black and without sugar. Jemima took hers milky and sweet, their differences as pronounced in coffee as in everything else.

Cradling his cup in one elegant, long-fingered hand, Luciano murmured, 'I've decided that I want you to accompany us to Sicily as the nanny you offered to be...'

Shock made Jemima's lower lip part from her upper and she breathed again and a little faster, her eyes widening at that bombshell of a suggestion.

'It would ease the transition for my son but it would be on the strict understanding that you would begin stepping back from him while allowing others to step forward to take your place in his little world,' Luciano spelt out coolly. 'He must learn to do without you.'

Jemima tried and failed to swallow as he described the role. He had delivered the killing blow of truth by telling her what he ultimately expected and wanted from her. Sicily and the nanny job would be very temporary for her and would come at a high cost for a woman who loved the child she cared for. She lost colour, pain knotting inside her at the prospect of walking away from Nicky, but at the same time with every word Luciano Vitale spoke she saw that whether she liked it or not he was worthy of her respect as a father. He detested her yet he still recognised the strength of her bond with his son and he was keen to protect Nicky from getting hurt. How could she judge him badly for that? A more gradual process of parting Jemima from her nephew *should* work much better than a sudden break, she reasoned unhappily. Luciano was taking the sensible, cautious approach to the problem.

Her silence perturbed Luciano, who had expected instant eager agreement. Didn't Jemima Barber worship money and the high life? Wasn't she a fish out of water in her parents' modest home? He had assumed that was why she had made the strange offer to take on the role of acting as her son's nanny. After all, only that position would grant her entry into Luciano's wealthy, exclusive and privileged world. She was also broke, in debt and had to be afraid of the police catching up with her, so a trip abroad should have all the appeal of an escape hatch.

'Have you changed your mind about that offer?' Luciano asked in surprise.

'Well, it was an impulse of the moment offer,' Jemima admitted ruefully. 'I didn't really think it through. It was provoked by the prospect of parting from Nicky—'

'Sicily may make the process a little less traumatic,' Luciano commented tongue-in-cheek, reckoning that a few little treats like shopping trips round the fashion houses would quickly improve her attitude. Of course, he knew she wanted more and he was prepared to give her more to oil the wheels of persuasion. 'If you agree, I will naturally settle your debts here in the UK and compensate the men whose credit cards you stole so that they will drop the charges. That would remove the threat of arrest as well.'

In shock at that smoothly outlined proposition, Jemima snatched in a stark breath of astonishment and studied him with frowning eyes. 'But it wouldn't be right to let you pay those bills.'

Luciano raised a cynical brow. 'Of course you will be happy for me to settle your debts,' he countered forcefully. 'That is the sort of woman you are. Why are you trying to pretend otherwise?'

At that direct and unsettling question, Jemima flushed and hurriedly dropped her eyes. Julie would never have argued against such a benefit. In that he was quite correct. Her twin had always happily taken money to settle her problems and fulfil her dreams and not once had she protested or done anything that would have worked against her own natural interests. So, if Jemima was still set on pretending to be Julie, she had to bite her lip and go with the flow. She tried to take a sensible overview of her situation. The debts Julie had acquired in Jemima's name were a major source of worry to both her and her parents. To be free of that pressure would be wonderful, she acknowledged guiltily.

'And quite naturally *I* don't want my son's mother dragged into court over debts or dishonesty,' Luciano pointed out without hesitation.

But I'm *not* your son's mother, she suddenly wanted to tell him, because the web of her deceit was getting thicker and harder to justify. And what would happen if she simply told him the truth now? Would he still take her with them to Sicily? Still offer her the chance to learn how to part gently from the baby she loved? Jemima thought not. She stole a glance at him from below her lashes. She had *lied* to him. If he found that out, he would be so angry he would snatch up his son and walk away. He wasn't a forgiving or understanding or tolerant man. Furthermore the only thing she had to offer on his terms was that she was supposedly the mother of his son. Shorn of that borrowed status, she would have no standing whatsoever in his eyes.

'Obviously not,' Jemima conceded tightly before she could lose her nerve again. 'I'll come to Sicily with Nicky—'

'Niccolò,' Luciano corrected without hesitation.

'He'll always be Nicky to me,' she fielded quietly, refusing to give ground.

Something bright flashed in his dark gaze, lighting his eyes gold like the dawn sky, and she stiffened, like a small animal suddenly faced with a predator.

'Doing what I tell you to do would be a wise move now,' Luciano spelt out softly, his intent gaze raking down over the fullness of her pink lips, the swell of her tantalising breasts and the slim legs on view. He had never lusted after a woman of her ilk before. What did that say about him? But lust was healthy and indifference was not, he reasoned fiercely, all too reluctant to banish the sexual energy infusing him when for the first time in much longer than he cared to recall he felt *alive* again.

Suddenly restless, Jemima uncoiled her legs and stood up. 'You're trying to intimidate me.'

The golden gaze grew ever more intense. 'Am I?'

'I'll do everything that is reasonable but I won't be intimidated and I won't grovel,' she framed tautly, extraordinarily aware of the darker, deeper note in his rich drawl and the warning flare of his brows.

'You *won't*?' Luciano's intonation was soft and slippery as silk brushing her skin as he stalked closer, all predator, all threat.

And she should have backed away, she knew that was what she should do, but a current of inexplicable excitement was quivering up through Jemima and working its own seduction. 'I won't,' she confirmed shakily, her own voice dropping in volume and, to her annoyance, emerging breathily.

'But the idea of you grovelling at my knees is appealing, *piccolo mia*,' Luciano confided huskily, eyes golden and predatory as a raptor's locked to her upturned face. 'The image of you giving me pleasure while you're doing it gives me a high…'

At first, Jemima just couldn't credit that he had said that to her and then she told herself that he couldn't possibly have meant that sexual innuendo. A surge of embarrassment and uncertainty caused a burst of colour to fly into her cheeks and she blinked, trying to close him out, trying to rescue her brain from the sudden erotic imagery he had filled it with. That wasn't something that had ever happened to her before in a man's presence. She didn't imagine doing sexual things with men as a rule, but maybe if she had, a little voice whispered, Steven would not have been so stupefied by her infinitely bolder twin. Something about Luciano Vitale got to her on a primal level she had never experienced before.

'Did you really just say what I thought you said?' she mumbled unevenly.

CHAPTER FOUR

A HUSKY LAUGH escaped from Luciano. 'Is that how you work this spell with men who should know better? You flutter your lashes and blush at will and act naïve? Let's hit the bottom line and save some time. I don't *want* naïve or shy or fake virginal, Jemima. I like women who aren't afraid to be women...just as I am a man unafraid to admit when I feel like sex.'

Jemima was out of her depth and didn't know where to look or what to say. She couldn't admit that she wasn't a fake virgin and she couldn't admit to being naïve or shy when Julie hadn't had a shy or modest bone in her entire body. Julie had treated sexual invitations as ego boosts and had revelled unashamedly in male admiration. For just a moment, Jemima longed for the cool to emulate her late sister, who had taken her looks and sensuality for granted. *He felt like sex?* Involuntarily she glanced up at him again and a tiny little hot frisson ran up from her feminine core to pinch her nipples taut when she collided with his gleaming golden eyes. She felt the pull of his magnetic force then, the potent, compelling awareness of a powerful sexuality.

'And equally unafraid to act,' Luciano imparted, every predatory instinct in his big powerful body fired by her masquerade of innocence as he reached for her, determined to smash that façade that was so very foolish in the circumstances when he knew so much about her true character.

Jemima regained the strength to move a little too late, her paralysed legs moving her clumsily backwards in the unfamiliar room. He had knocked her off her usual calm, rational perch and wrecked her composure with that blunt sexual come-on. He had truly shocked her but he had excited her as well because, on a level Jemima didn't want to examine, she was hugely flattered by the idea that a male as gorgeous as Luciano Vitale could find her attractive.

As he spoke Luciano reached for her and propelled her back against the door she had almost reached, one hand closing round her shoulder, the other rising to curve to her chin. 'I like the chase. You're right about that, *piccolo mia*,' he told her incomprehensibly as if she had spoken. 'But this is the wrong time to run away.'

She was entrapped by his gaze, her chest swelling as she snatched in a needy breath, her throat tight with tension. Luciano Vitale wanted her. *Her?* The very concept turned her inside out because he was drop-dead beautiful in a way she had never dreamt existed. From the crown of his luxuriant black hair to his stunning eyes and flawless bone structure, he mesmerised her.

'Your pupils are dilated...' Luciano breathed, stroking a strand of golden hair back from her brow to tuck it below her ear, shifting closer, bending his dark head.

'Are they?' She was so insanely aware of how much taller and stronger he was, she was frozen with her hips welded against the solid wooden door. The lemony scent of his cologne assailed her nostrils. He smelled amazingly good and a ball of heat warmed in her pelvis.

'I scare you, don't I?' Luciano laughed again, startling her. 'I don't want to scare you...not any more.'

His breath fanned her cheek and she shivered, feeling the press of his long, powerful thighs and the hard, thrusting fullness at his groin against her stomach. Her whole body seemed to overheat at that point of contact. He was aroused and she had made him that way...she, Jemima Barber, without cosmetic witchery or fancy clothes. Who would ever have believed it? She felt like a real woman for the first time since Steven's betrayal. She didn't understand what possible appeal she could have for Luciano Vitale, but she didn't much care during that instant of exhilaration. As he lowered his head a little more and his lips brushed whisper soft across hers, it felt like *her* moment and it felt crazily like something she had been waiting for all her life.

Long fingers laced into her hair to hold her steady and the pressure deepened. She opened her mouth and he took immediate advantage with a dominance that thrilled rather than annoyed. His tongue darted into the moist interior and tangled with hers and she kissed him back with an eagerness she couldn't suppress. Her body took flight on new sensation, excitement rising like a tide inside her, drowning out every objecting voice in the back of her head. Every inch of her was suddenly tender and supersensitive, so that firm brush of his hand across her covered breasts made her straining nipples prickle in reaction and the trail of his fingers up her thigh as he lifted her skirt set her on fire with tingling impatience and longing. That passionate kiss held her utterly spellbound, her senses excited beyond bearing, and the throb of awakening between her thighs was almost unbearable in its intensity.

He stroked a fingertip across the tight triangle of fabric stretched between her legs and her knees turned to water. 'You're wet,' he told her thickly.

She couldn't breathe for shock at the tiny tremors of response quivering through her while the heat at the heart of her stoked higher. She had never in her life before wanted to be touched so badly and she was ashamed of the desire until his hungry mouth found hers again with bruising force and all thought fled in the same instant. One kiss and he dragged her under again while his skilled fingers strummed beneath her panties and stoked the hunger higher, sliding into the moist cleft and caressing the slick tissue before returning to the tiny bud that controlled her entire being.

She trembled and a strangled moan was wrenched from low in her throat as he rubbed her tormentingly sensitive flesh and suddenly her body was racing out of her control and she was jerking helplessly and gasping mindlessly beneath his mouth in a sudden explosive climax that blew her away. Her legs gave way and she would have fallen had he not lifted her and settled her down on the nearest seat.

Limp and shaking, she wrenched her rucked skirt down in a desperate movement. Shock was blasting through her and her heart was still racing. She couldn't believe what had just happened. She couldn't believe that she had let him do that to her…something so intimate, so inappropriate, so wanton…

'You were ready for that,' Luciano purred, staring down at her with smouldering dark golden eyes. 'You're a passionate woman.'

But Jemima had *never* been a passionate woman. Steven had told her that passion was for sluts and she had always been careful not to seem too keen in that line because that had seemed to be what he expected from her. When he had plunged into a wild fling with Julie she had been shattered at how quickly he had changed his attitude. Luciano, however, wanted that passion, *thrived* on it, she sensed in confusion, forcing herself to look at him, her face hot and flushed, her sated body still somehow feeling like a wanton stranger's.

'Let's not…talk about it,' she mumbled unsteadily.

'Let's not… I prefer to *do* rather than talk,' Luciano murmured, wondering why she was still acting so oddly. Touching her had been a mistake. He wanted more. Given the smallest encouragement he would have dragged her off to bed and eased the burn of his libido. He didn't want to wait. He wasn't used to waiting but he was suddenly very conscious of who she was. His son's mother. It would be most unwise to rock the boat before they reached the security of his Sicilian home, Castello del Drogo.

'It shouldn't have happened,' Jemima breathed tightly, rising from her seat and snatching up her bag. 'I don't know how it did—'

Luciano was not amused. 'It's simple. I wanted you. You wanted me—'

'I forgot where I was and who I was with for a moment,' Jemima corrected stiffly, still carefully evading his eyes. 'I was out of control.'

'I liked it.' Luciano could not understand why she was in retreat. With his knowledge of her, she should have been making the most of the situation and trying to please him. And he was very much in the mood to be pleased.

'You were talking about Sicily and…er…settling bills,' she reminded him stonily.

Ah, business first. He perfectly understood her change of focus. 'I will take care of them. You will have to sign a confidentiality agreement first. You will not be free to talk to anyone, and that includes the media, about the surrogacy agreement or about me or my son,' he informed her with forbidding cool.

'That's not a problem. I'll go and see if Nicky is awake yet. It'll be time for us to leave soon,' she said with scarcely concealed eagerness as she checked her watch.

Luciano stood watching the door swing shut on her exit. A black winged brow quirked. Was it some sort of a game she played with men? Give a little and then back off? Some men would want her all the more after that type of will-she-won't-she uncertainty. But Luciano was in no doubt that she would ultimately share his bed and her withdrawal irritated him. He hardened even more at the prospect of spreading those soft, rounded thighs and plunging between them until he had attained his pleasure. One night would probably be enough, he decided with a dark smile. He wanted her horizontal. For that single night he wanted her every which way up he could have her. That would work her back out of his system and possibly by that stage he would grasp what had attracted him in the first place.

At least there would be no complications with Jemima, he reflected as he phoned his housekeeper to make household arrangements. Never mind Jemima's little ploys, she knew the score. He would reward her richly for sex, for sharing physical pleasure without emotion or strings, and she would be quite happy to walk away again.

'I'm a close friend of Jemima's and her family,' Steven Warrington declared smugly as he walked into Luciano's office. 'And with respect, I'd like to know why you think it's necessary for her to accompany you and your child to Sicily.'

Luciano surveyed the smaller blond man with shrewd, unimpressed eyes. 'That's my personal business, Mr Warrington. But I see no reason not to tell you that my son is attached to Jemima and I'd like to minimise his sorrow when she moves on.'

'Taking Jemima to Sicily with you seems a strange

way of letting *her* move on,' Steven opined with another smile. 'I'd prefer it if you simply removed your son now and left Jemima to get on with her life unencumbered.'

'Happily your opinion doesn't count,' Luciano fielded.

'It soon will. She's the woman I intend to marry.'

Luciano almost rolled his eyes at the idea of Jemima, with her decided preference for the wilder side of life, anchored by a wedding ring to the highly conservative male in front of him, but his lean, dark features remained unrevealing. 'Congratulations,' he responded smoothly.

The information he had already requested on Steven Warrington was finally rolling up on Luciano's computer screen as the younger man departed. Had Luciano the patience, he would have received that information *before* agreeing to see Warrington but curiosity had driven Luciano to depart from his habitual caution. So, Steven was an ex and there was a very, *very* long list of exes in Jemima's chequered past. Did she leave them all longing for a raunchy repeat? Although not the ones whose wallets she had lifted, Luciano conceded, while wondering why that aspect of her nature didn't bother him more. She was a thief. Why did he want to bed her? He had never knowingly wanted to bed a deceitful woman before. Having grown up in the shadows of a crime-fuelled household, he was not drawn to the dark side in any way. Unlike his late father he was temperate and controlled.

Maybe he had been too ascetic in his habits for too long, he reasoned in frustration, because he was still struggling to understand the key to Jemima Barber's appeal. Even so, he wanted her and on those grounds he would have her simply because remarkably few things in life gave Luciano genuine pleasure. Steven Warrington's self-righteousness amused him. Jemima had no plans to marry Steven. He was quite sure of that.

But somehow that didn't eradicate an almost overwhelming temptation to smash a fist through Steven's blindingly white teeth. Luciano didn't comprehend the urge and he suppressed it, thoroughly off-balanced by that sudden lurch towards violence. He had felt it before, of course he had, with his very genes drenched in the violence and corruption of his forebears. But never ever had he had that experience where a woman was concerned and that awareness unsettled him. One night. He would have her in his bed for only one night, he assured himself grimly.

In any case, he reflected thoughtfully, it was not as though he could be at any real risk with Jemima, because Luciano didn't do emotional connections with anyone. His son would be the sole exception to that rule. Loving and caring for a child was pure and it wouldn't damage him or anybody else.

'I think it's the best solution for everybody,' Ellie declared bravely while Jemima was trying to console her weeping mother and her deeply troubled father as the four of them sat round the kitchen table over mugs of tea.

Jemima was feeling sick with shame at having hidden so much from her adoptive parents and she still did not feel up to the challenge of telling them the truth. They would have been horrified if they knew that she was pretending to be her dead sister and faking being Nicky's mother. No argument she could make would persuade them that such dishonesty was justified. In any case her parents were already dealing with quite enough. The older couple had returned from Devon only that morning to learn that their daughter and Nicky would be leaving the next day for a trip to Sicily, following which Jemima would be returning home *alone*. Unfortunately Julie's son had become as dear to Jemima's parents as any grandchild. They too had been part of Nicky's life almost from birth.

'Nicky is Luciano's son and the poor guy's been searching for him all these months,' Ellie pointed out, trying hard to support her friend's arguments in favour of the trip to Sicily and the inevitable surrendering of Nicky to his sole surviving parent.

'I believe he'll be a good father. He's only asking me along because he knows Nicky's attached to me and he doesn't want him to be hurt by me suddenly disappearing from his life,' Jemima explained afresh.

'Mr Vitale *is* being responsible,' her father conceded thoughtfully. 'Although I could never condone the agreement he made with Julie. That was rash and she was the worst possible candidate he could've chosen—'

'Yes, but don't forget it wasn't Julie he really picked. He believed he was picking Jemima.' Ellie was quick to remind the older man that Julie had applied to be a surrogate using her twin's identity rather than her own.

'True and you've certainly stood by the little chap,

giving him what he needs to flourish,' Jemima's father said to his daughter with warm approval. 'I suppose we'll simply have to wait until our daughter gives us a grandchild to fuss over, my dear,' he said to his wife.

Jemima paled beneath that look of approbation. She knew just how shocked her parents would be if they ever learned about the deceit she had employed in her dealings with Luciano.

That same morning, Charles Bennett made a return visit with a colleague in tow. He read through the confidentiality agreement with Jemima and explained every clause while his companion informed Jemima that he was there on her behalf to protect her interests. He spoke up on several occasions, pointing out that a lot of money could be made from selling stories to the media but that choosing to abide by Luciano's rules would be financially rewarded by a bonus once she had finished working for him. Jemima signed on the dotted line and was grateful when the lawyers left.

Later that same day, Ellie stood by grinning while Jemima patiently stood and obediently posed while all her measurements were taken and carefully noted down by the middle-aged female tailor and her assistant who had also called at Luciano's request.

'So, he's planning for you to wear a nanny uniform?' Ellie remarked teasingly after the women had departed.

Jemima pulled a face. 'Obviously,' she pointed out ruefully, far from looking forward to the prospect of being dressed in some starchy formal outfit in the Sicilian heat.

'I suppose it's one good way of ensuring that you

don't forget that you're one of the workers rather than
a guest... I mean, it could be a bit awkward with you
supposedly being Nicky's mother,' her friend opined
with a wince. 'When are you planning to tell Luciano
that you're Julie's sister?'

Jemima grimaced. 'Probably not until I'm leaving
Sicily, which will be the end of August at the latest because term starts the following week and I'll be starting teaching again,' she reminded the other woman.
'It would be a bit of a risk admitting my true identity
any sooner than that because Luciano could just ask
me to leave immediately but by late August it's hardly
going to matter to him.'

'Stop beating yourself up about it. You're not doing
anyone any harm—'

'It's not that simple, Ellie. Every time I'm with Luciano I'm *lying* to him,' Jemima pointed out heavily,
wishing she had found it possible to confide in Ellie
about how much more complicated her relationship
with Luciano had recently become. The problem was
that she was too ashamed to admit that their strained
relationship had suddenly—inexplicably, to her—dived
into the kind of intimacy she had always held back
from.

Only three days had passed since that day in London and she still lay in her bed at night unable to quite
accept that she had fooled around with Luciano to the
extent that she had forgotten not only the tenets that
she had been raised by, but also everything she could
not afford to forget about her current predicament.
She was acting as Julie, not herself, and, although she

was convinced that her late sister would also have succumbed to the advances of a gorgeous billionaire, she knew she couldn't grasp at that as an excuse for her behaviour. In reality she had lost control and had allowed herself to be swept away on a roller coaster of sexual sensation new to her. She had acted like a giddy teenager rather than a grown-up, had lived in the moment, had *rejoiced* in the moment without any thought of what it would be like to meet Luciano again or to work for him in an official capacity.

'You're lying *solely* for Nicky's benefit,' Ellie told her with loyal reassurance. 'And by going to Sicily with Nicky you're making all these changes easier for him—'

Jemima gave her friend an anxious look. 'So you think I'm doing the right thing?'

'I always thought that the best solution for Nicky was to be with the father who arranged for him to be born. He's a lovely child, I can see that, but he's not *your* child. I hate to agree with Steven about anything but I do want you to get your own life back,' her friend told her ruefully. 'Be young, free and single again. You deserve that. Nicky was Julie's mistake.'

Jemima compressed her lips and said nothing. She could not think of Nicky's bright, loving existence as a mistake on any terms and being single and free had proved a less fun-filled experience for her than she had been led to expect. Nicky was part of her life now and she loved him. She had not carried her nephew through a pregnancy but the little boy felt as much a part of her as though she had. She knew that walking away from him was going to hurt her a lot, but, if that was truly what was best for Nicky in the long run, she would have to learn to live with that.

The next morning, Jemima, Nicky and their luggage were collected by a limousine accompanied by a car full of bodyguards. The trip to the airport was accomplished in record time and even boarding the private jet awaiting them was a fairly smooth and speedy experience. Jemima was surprised that Luciano was not on board and that, indeed, she and Nicky appeared to be the only passengers aside of the security staff, who took seats at the rear of the plane. The cabin crew made a big fuss of Nicky and were unceasingly attentive.

Luciano boarded in Paris, where he'd had a meeting, and the first thing he noticed was Jemima, curled up fast asleep in a reclining seat with Nicky out for the count beside her in his fancy travelling seat. Her mane of hair was braided when he wanted to see it loose again...even though he knew much of that hair was fake? He shook off that awkward question and scanned the worn jeans and casual washed-out top she sported with a frown of incomprehension forming between his dark brows. Why had she not yet made the effort to dress up for him...even once? No woman had ever been so sure of her hold on Luciano's interest that she would show up garbed almost as poorly as a homeless person! Or was this deliberate dressing down and this avoidance of glamour merely Jemima's highly effective way of ensuring that he bought her a new wardrobe?

Jemima wakened slowly, comfortably rested after having endured a final nervous, sleepless night in her parents' home. Luciano now sat across the aisle. Drowsily she studied his perfect profile, thinking that no man should have lashes that long, that dark or that lush or a nose and a jaw that would not have disgraced a Greek god. Butterflies found wings in her stomach and fluttered. Luciano turned his handsome dark head and she encountered dark golden eyes as lustrous as melting honey. A little quiver ran through her like a tightening piece of elastic, unleashing far less innocent responses that made her squirm with self-consciousness.

'We'll be landing in thirty minutes.'

'Right…er…I'll go and freshen up,' Jemima muttered, sliding out of her seat.

For a split second he gazed up at her, scanning the bloom of soft pink warming the porcelain complexion, which merely enhanced the ice-blue-diamond effect of her unusual eyes and the full softness of the lips he had already tasted. And his body reacted as instantly as a starving man facing a banquet, urgency and hunger combining in a mind-blowing storm of response. His strong jaw line clenching, Luciano gritted his even white teeth angrily and looked away, schooling himself to coldness again.

He didn't like losing control. He had never liked losing control. He had often seen his father lose his head in temper and living through the experience unscathed had been a challenge for everyone around him. Luciano had little fear that he himself would erupt into mindless violence, but he was absolutely convinced that reactions like passion and anger twisted a man's thinking processes and made bad decisions and human errors more likely. She would be in his bed this very night, he reminded himself soothingly. He would have what he wanted, what he increasingly felt he *needed* from her, and then this temporary insanity would be over and done with, decently laid to rest between the sheets. It astonished him, it even slightly unnerved him, that sexual desire could exercise that much power over him.

Jemima concentrated on the mechanics of feeding and changing Nicky while stubbornly denying herself the opportunity to look back in Luciano's direction. He was gorgeous and he had to know he was gorgeous. After all, he saw himself every time he shaved, she thought wildly. But that was not an excuse to stare and blush and act all silly like an adolescent who didn't know how to behave around a man. Absolutely not any sort of an excuse at all, Jemima reminded herself doggedly as she abstractedly admired how much Nicky's glossy black curls resembled his father's and resisted the urge to make another quite unnecessary visual comparison.

Suddenly the thought that she would be in Luciano's vicinity for the rest of the summer was a daunting one. She could never act polite and indifferent in the company of such a dynamic and passionate male. He lit her up like a fire inside but she ought to be fighting that tooth and nail. She was *lying* to Luciano and he was Nicky's father, which meant that there was no possibility of any normal relationship developing between them. Keeping her distance and resisting temptation were what she needed to do. Intellectually she knew that…but knowing and actually doing were two very different things, as she had already discovered. Unfortunately for her peace of mind, Luciano's attraction yanked at her on every possible level…

CHAPTER FIVE

LUCIANO'S PHONE BUZZED into life after they landed, shooting out a string of text messages and missed calls, every one of which hailed from his British lawyer, Charles Bennett. His mouth quirking as he wondered what could possibly have prompted the relaxed Charles to such an uncharacteristic display of urgency, Luciano phoned the older man as soon as he stepped inside the airport.

'I have the worst possible news for you. We've all been conned,' Charles announced with rare drama the instant the call connected. 'Jemima Barber is *not* the mother of your child—'

Luciano froze and waved an impatient hand at his bodyguards to silence their chatter while he listened. 'That's not possible,' he declared.

'I haven't got all the details yet and I won't waste your time with speculation but I believe that the mother of your child was one of an identical set of twins. She died when she was struck by a car a couple of months ago,' the lawyer explained curtly.

Luciano was frowning darkly. 'Which would mean—'

'That at best our Jemima is an aunt to the boy and

a con artist,' Charles framed drily. 'I have a top-flight set of investigators digging into this right now and I expect to have the whole story for you by this evening at the latest.'

'How sure are you of these facts?' Luciano prompted, watching Jemima detach his son's clinging fingers from her hanging golden braid. *Not* Niccolò's mother? How could that be? His brain, usually so fast to adapt to new scenarios, was for some reason still struggling to find solid ground in this shift of circumstances.

'Take it from me—she's definitely *not* the woman who gave birth to the boy. I now have that woman's real name along with a copy of her *death* certificate. She called herself Julie Marshall. Matters are complicated by the fact that from the very beginning of your dealings with Julie, your son's real mother was using Jemima Barber's identity to hide behind.'

'But why? You believe this was a conspiracy from the start?'

'Who can tell? With one of them dead it's doubtful that the full truth will ever be known,' Charles pointed out cynically.

Rage began to shadow Luciano's rational mind as the ramifications for his son began to filter into his thoughts. His son's mother had deceived him and his staff from day one and now she was dead and, as such, untouchable. Luciano was his son's only living relative. He refused to credit that an aunt could possibly have a claim to challenge his own. So, naturally, Jemima had not owned up to the truth. After all, her only way of making a profit through Niccolò was by *pretending* to be his birth mother.

As they climbed into a limousine outside the airport Luciano watched his son nestle trustingly into Jemima's arms and then complain loudly at being placed in the car seat instead. His lean dark features shadowed. He was finally a parent and already he had failed. He had failed to protect his son from hurt. Niccolò had been encouraged to form a bond with his two-faced, duplicitous aunt and would be emotionally bereft when the woman disappeared from his world. Who did Luciano blame for the formation of that deceptive bond? Jemima Barber! She must've known from the outset that her only weapon would be the baby's attachment to her. Niccolò was only a baby but he had already been tricked into bestowing affection where he should not. Luciano, in a rage beyond anything he had ever experienced, ground his even white teeth together while he pretended an interest in the emails on his tablet.

She was a lying, cheating *prostituta* with a stone for a heart! And just like her late sister, the only thing that greased the wheels in Jemima's world was money. There was no other explanation for her behaviour! At any time she could have admitted the truth but she had preferred to lie and stage a scam to ensure that she wielded the greatest power she could and made the biggest possible profit out of her dishonesty. In ignorance Luciano had agreed to settle her debts—her sister's debts?—and had made the mistake of offering her an all-expenses-paid trip to Sicily. And she would

have even more cause to celebrate when she saw what
awaited her at the castle...

Of course he didn't *want* her now, he told himself
fiercely. He wanted nothing more to do with her and
out of sight would be out of mind. How long had it been
since a woman put one over on him? He suppressed a
shudder of all too fresh recollection. What did it say
about him that the women who most attracted him
were thoroughly immoral and unscrupulous charac-
ters? Was that some hangover from his ancestral forebears? Something dark and shady in his blood that slyly
influenced his choices?

Although Jemima was trying not to stare at Luciano she was convinced that something unpleasant had
happened. She had watched his lean, darkly handsome
face freeze into rigidity while he was talking on the
phone at the airport. Had he received bad news? Some
business setback? Or something of a more personal
nature? Jemima acknowledged how very little she actually knew about Luciano Vitale. He was a widower
who had lost a wife and a daughter and that was the
summit of her information. But whatever was amiss,
Luciano's jaw was rock hard with tension and he had
barely acknowledged the existence of Jemima and his
son since the jet had landed. Ironically, Nicky, who
acted up whenever Luciano actively tried to get closer
to him, now chose to stretch out an inviting hand towards his father, who might as well have been on another planet for all the interest he was showing in him.
Still, there was yet another similarity between the two
of them, Jemima reflected helplessly. Neither one of

them could *hear* to be ignored…and ten to one that was exactly why Nicky was vying for attention now.

The limousine came to a halt and Jemima looked out of the window, surprised to see various aircraft parked. 'Where are we?' she asked.

'A private airfield. I use a helicopter to fly to my home,' Luciano divulged, his firmly modelled lips compressing.

Jemima's eyes widened in surprise. She had never been on a helicopter before and yet he evidently regularly used them just to travel home. Nothing could have more easily illustrated the vast gulf between their worlds. While they were boarding the helicopter, there was no further conversation, which was probably just as well because Jemima was concentrating on her exciting new experience.

As the helicopter took off Jemima peered out of the window to watch a slice of sea appear at a crazy angle. Her brow pleated in astonishment when the craft then flew out directly over the water. Where on earth were they going? Naturally she had assumed that Luciano's home was either in a city or in the mountainous interior but as the minutes passed on their seabound journey it was clear that their destination could only be another island.

She watched land appear again with keen interest. A bright patchwork of forested slopes, olive groves and a vast brown building on the shoreline of a long beach appeared. The building had towers and turrets like a castle, and as the helicopter dropped down to land in the manicured grounds enclosed by tall boundary walls she realised that it *was* a genuine castle.

'What's this place called?' she asked as she hopped down onto the grass and approached Luciano to take Nicky back off him.

'Castello del Drogo. The island is named for it. I'll keep him,' Luciano told her, hoisting the sleepy baby against his shoulder in a blatantly protective movement, his eyes as dark and cool as the night sky and about as far from melting honey as eyes could get, she thought ruefully.

Refusing to be quieted by his discouraging coldness, Jemima smiled. 'How long have you lived here?'

'A couple of years. It has the privacy I need. Intruders can only approach by sky or sea and both are monitored. I can walk by the sea here without fear of a camera appearing from the bushes,' he spelt out flatly.

They got into the beach buggy waiting to waft them up to the doors of the castle. Jemima was smiling, her earlier concerns forgotten as she rejoiced in the warmth of late afternoon and the beautiful gardens surrounding them. It would be really interesting to stay in a castle, she thought absently, studying the imposing fortress before her. 'How old is it?'

'The oldest section is medieval, the youngest eighteenth century.'

They mounted shallow steps to the giant porticoed entrance where two women awaited their arrival. Both wore black, one of possibly pensioner age and the other around fortyish.

The hall was an imposing oval shape with a marble

floor and black ebonised furniture inlaid with mother-of-pearl. Jemima was silenced by the sheer splendour of the castle, especially when she compared it to her parents' tiny retirement home. How could she ever have denied Nicky the wealthy lifestyle that his father evidently enjoyed?

'Do you own the whole island?' she whispered, unable to contain her curiosity.

'Yes,' he admitted in the sort of tone that implied that it was not a very big deal to own your own island, and in Jemima's mind the gulf between them stretched even wider.

Luciano introduced the older woman as his housekeeper, Agnese, and the younger as her daughter and Nicky's new nanny, Carlotta. He settled the baby into Carlotta's arms and addressed her in Italian. Jemima reminded herself doggedly of her agreement to step back from Nicky as he was borne off screaming, presumably to be fed and put to bed. As Carlotta mounted the stairs Jemima could hear her talking softly and soothingly to the distressed baby and her concern eased a little.

'Agnese will show you to your room,' Luciano announced.

Agnese's small creased face was as frozen as an ice sculpture. Telling herself that that was still preferable to a dirty look, Jemima followed the older woman upstairs and down a tiled passageway with ancient stone walls. Double doors were flung wide and light flooded across the most amazing bedroom Jemima had ever seen. Tall windows cast sunshine over the sumptuously hung four-poster bed. Gorgeous furniture vied with opulent fabric and a glorious floral arrangement to take her attention. Taken aback as she realised that the palatial room was for her use, Jemima hovered by the little table bearing the magnificent flowers and watched wide-eyed as an actual maid in a uniform appeared through one of the several additional doors to smile and stand back as though waiting to usher Jemima into the room she had vacated.

The housekeeper indicated with her hand that Jemima should take the invitation and Jemima obediently walked into a very large dressing room lined with built-in furniture. And that was when the show began. The maid began opening doors and rifling through hangers packed with garments to display them. Racks of shoes, drawers filled with silky lingerie and a dressing-table unit packed with cosmetics below a mirror surrounded by special lighting were duly shown off. Jemima's jaw dropped while she attempted to work out what all these items could possibly have to do with her. The maid passed her a tiny gift envelope and she slid out the card.

With my compliments, Luciano.

Jemima blinked and looked again, fingers tightening round the card as it slowly sank in on her that she had not been measured up for a nanny uniform as she had assumed but for a new wardrobe. She broke out in perspiration, her jeans uncomfortably warm. Luciano had given her a vast new wardrobe and as she flipped with anxious hands through the nearest selection she realised that it was all designer stuff, filled with famous fashion labels that even she, who didn't follow fashion, had heard of. She was gobsmacked, so gobsmacked that when the maid and the housekeeper departed she simply sank down on the boudoir chair by the dresser and stared back at her own unadorned face. Her face looked weird in the fancy lights, oddly bare and shocked, and she breathed in deep and stumbled upright to peel off her jeans before she could expire from heat exhaustion. In the bedroom she opened the suitcase she had travelled with and yanked out a cool cotton skirt to step into it.

But she still couldn't think straight. Indeed all she could think about was the contents of the dressing room. What on earth had she done to give Luciano the impression that such an extravagant gesture would be welcome? Her tummy gave a nauseous flip and she shut her eyes tight, hot colour burning her cheeks. Oh, yes, she knew what she had done. She hadn't said no when she should've. She hadn't said yes either, she reflected numbly. She had simply let him do what he wished. And evidently that had been sufficient to encourage Luciano to go out and spend thousands and thousands and thousands of pounds to enable her to dress like a queen. Hands cool now with shock, she pressed them to her hot cheeks and groaned out loud. My goodness, what was she going to do?

She was supposed to be Julie and Julie would have been ecstatic. Julie had adored clothes and everything her sister wore had carried a logo. Jemima blinked and wandered back into the dressing room. She trailed an uncertain hand across the soft smooth briefs still visible in an open drawer and sighed heavily. The clothing had been tailored to her exact height and size, but how could she wear it? How could she possibly say thank you and just wear it?

Neither a borrower nor a lender be and being wary of unexpected gifts was how Jemima had been raised. She also knew that old adage about being true to oneself. And accepting such largesse when she had done nothing to deserve it ran contrary to her principles. She swallowed back a heartfelt groan while she surveyed the racks of shoes. If Jemima had a weakness, it was for shoes and she swore her toes tingled like a water diviner's when she saw the cross-strapped green high heels studded with tiny twinkly stones. They called out to her feet and, kicking off her serviceable pumps, she slid her yearning toes into those tempting shoes. Yes, this was the way to be gracious, the only way not to throw all of Luciano's generosity back in his teeth; she would accept one small item to show gratitude. Having bolstered herself with that argument, Jemima tottered downstairs in her wholly inappropriate footwear.

Agnese was waiting for her like a little old witch in the hall.

'I'm looking for Luciano,' Jemima announced with a pleasant smile.

Agnese was eying the frivolous shoes with rampant censure. 'Il Capo is in the library.'

Il capo meant 'the boss', Jemima translated, having watched enough Godfather movies to recognise the lingo. Walking with precise but wobbling care in the direction of Agnese's pointing hand, Jemima wondered if the new wardrobe had given Agnese the wrong idea about the precise nature of Jemima's relationship with Luciano, and then she scolded herself for wondering, reckoning she had more to worry about than the suspicion that the staff had disliked her on sight.

Luciano had had four drinks in succession while he waited for Charles to call. His father had been a drinker and it was very rare for Luciano to drink to excess but his impatience to know the finer details of the scam was literally eating him alive. He couldn't wait to confront Jemima but he would not do it until he knew everything there was to know about her. He was *so* angry with her, so bemused by the strange conflict tearing at him. He was in turmoil and he didn't know why, which simply added another layer of hostile frustration to his mood.

Frowning at the sound of the knock on the library door, Luciano strode across the room to drag it open and discover who had dared to disturb him when he had requested peace. When he focused on Jemima's glowing, eagerly smiling face, he found himself taking a step back because he was initially surprised to see that she was happy. *But then she didn't know yet that he knew.* Of course she was happy, he ruminated bitterly, rage arrowing through him afresh. What else would she be but happy when he'd put her in a bedroom next door to his and given her a fortune in designer clothing? She was a gold-digger; naturally she was happy with her rewards. By bringing in Carlotta, he had even released

Jemima from the burden of constant childcare and very probably she was even happier about the prospect of greater freedom as well...

'Luciano...' she said softly and then her eyes flew off him to dart round the book-filled shelves. 'Oh, my, what a wonderful room! You are so lucky to have so much space for books,' she remarked chirpily.

'Is there a reason for your visit?' Luciano enquired forbiddingly, his attention clinging to her when she lurched a little on her path towards his desk at the centre of the room. His gaze skated down over her back view, lingering with pleasure on the ripe, rounded curve of her bottom shaped by the stretchy, clinging texture of the skirt she wore. His attention was then unwillingly caught by the colourful, glittery and ridiculously high-heeled shoes she wore below the skirt. For some reason she had teamed incongruous party shoes with her drab outfit and she could hardly walk in them, he registered in surprise as she clutched the side of his desk to steady herself.

Jemima studied Luciano and any hint of clear thought wilfully evaded her. No male that extraordinarily gorgeous could possibly encourage rational reflection in a woman, she conceded ruefully. He looked so tense and angry. His cheekbones were starkly defined, the line of his strong jaw rock hard. Yes, something had definitely gone wrong in his life. She was knocked sideways by the sudden realisation that just as Nicky's bad moods made her want to fix things for him, Luciano provoked the same need in her, only she didn't for one moment think that a cuddle and a soothing bottle would provide a magic cure for whatever ailed him.

Yet she still could not resist the temptation to offer. 'Can I help with whatever's wrong?'

'Why the hell would you think there's something wrong?' Luciano demanded harshly, hugely disconcerted by the question when in his experience other people couldn't read him at all well.

'Because there so obviously is,' Jemima pointed out, wishing he didn't have such stunning eyes. So dark and lustrous and sexy and absolute killers when fringed by black curling lashes into the bargain.

Unsettled by that assurance, Luciano gritted his teeth.

'You're so cross,' Jemima pointed out gently.

'I am not cross,' Luciano growled.

'I'll just mind my own business, then,' Jemima muttered, caving into the tension sparking like lightning rods through the atmosphere.

'Perhaps that would be best,' Luciano riposted very drily.

Her face flamed and she roamed restively over to the tall windows that overlooked flower beds surrounded by low box hedges and an ancient mossy fountain. 'I came down to speak to you about the new clothes you bought for me.' In emphasis she lifted a foot to show off the shoe she wore and very nearly fell over. All dignity abandoned, she grabbed at the back of an armchair to stay upright and hastily put that foot back on the floor. 'Er...these shoes are gorgeous... In fact it's all gorgeous, but with the possible exception of these shoes I can't possibly accept an entire wardrobe.'

'Why not?' Luciano shot back at her, startling her with that blunt comeback. 'And turn round and face me when you're speaking to me.'

With great reluctance and carefully slow movements, Jemima turned and straight away registered why she preferred talking to him without looking at him. Face on he was too much of a distraction. She lowered her lashes, blocking him out to some extent, her soft mouth unusually taut with nerves. 'Well, I'm very grateful for your generosity but I don't believe in accepting expensive gifts from people—'

'I'm not *people*!' Luciano cut in with ruthless bite. 'And I would hazard a guess that you have often accepted such gifts from men—'

'Yes…er…but that doesn't mean it was right. Having done it before, I don't have to keep on doing it,' Jemima pointed out, gathering steam in her argument. 'Maybe I think it's time for me to change my ways?'

'Maybe there are two blue moons in the sky,' Luciano incised with ringing derision.

'Being with Nicky *has* changed me,' Jemima argued, setting off on another tack. 'It's made me appreciate what's really important in life.'

'Within hours of his birth you had already decided what was really important to you…more money,' Luciano reminded her cruelly.

Jemima lifted her chin. 'But that doesn't mean I can't develop a different outlook. And I have changed. If you must know, I'm trying to turn over a new leaf.'

His dark eyes glittering like polished jet, Luciano vented a laugh of unholy amusement. 'I assume that's your idea of a joke...'

'No, it's not actually,' Jemima told him tightly, thinking sadly of the number of times her late twin had spoken of that same ambition to her. 'Everybody has to start somewhere when they make changes. I mean, why would you give me all those clothes anyway, for goodness' sake?'

'You're not that naïve.'

Her colour heightened. 'So, obviously it was a gift made with certain expectations, and if I'm not prepared to meet those expectations, I can't possibly accept it.'

'Of course you're prepared to meet my expectations.' Luciano surveyed her with galling assurance, smouldering dark golden eyes roaming over her with a potent sexuality that made her tremble. Her nipples prickled below her clothing and a tiny burst of heat ignited in her pelvis, starting up a nagging throb of awareness.

'I'm only here for a few weeks of summer for your son's benefit,' Jemima reminded him stubbornly. 'His benefit, *not* yours.'

Luciano said a rude word in English that made her flinch.

'I'm trying to be reasonable and honest here to avoid misunderstandings,' she told him in growing frustration.

Luciano stalked closer, silent and graceful as a night-time predator, and said an even ruder word in dismissal of that statement. What did such a woman know about honesty? What had she ever known?

He was so close now that Jemima could have reached out and touched him. Her heart was thudding out a staccato beat of apprehension and her breathing had ruptured into winded audible snatches.

She stiffened her spine and tilted her head to one side. 'I don't like your language.'

'I don't like what you're saying. I get very irritated when those around me talk nonsense or tell lies,' Luciano told her grittily, his Italian accent liquefying every vowel sound. 'You're trying to say that you don't want me and that is a *huge* lie!'

Her pale blue eyes widened. 'Are you always this sure of your own attraction?'

Long brown fingers lifted her braid from her shoulder and detached the tie on the end. He began to unlace the long golden strands. 'I want to see your hair loose…'

A new leaf, he was ruminating in disbelief. Could she really believe that he would be impressed by such drivel? How could she look at him with those luminous ice-blue eyes that seemed so candid and continue to lie and lie to his face? She was a completely shameless and stupid liar. Anger, bitter and jagged as a knife edge, cut through Luciano, burning and scarring wherever it touched. He was all too familiar with the cunning cleverness of female lies.

'This is getting too…too intense,' Jemima muttered uncertainly.

Luciano wound long fingers into the golden mane

of her hair to tug her closer. 'You shouldn't lie to me. If you knew how angry it makes me, you wouldn't do it.'

Her nostrils flared on the scent of him that close. Some expensive lemony cologne overlaid with clean, husky male and a faint hint of alcohol was assailing her and her tummy performed a nervous somersault. 'I'm going back home in just a few weeks,' she reminded him shakily. 'I'm only here for Nicky.'

'Liar...my son was not your primary motivation,' Luciano derided in a raw undertone, thoroughly fed up with her foolish pretences. 'You came here to be with me. Of course you did.'

Her brows pleated in dismay. 'Luciano...you're not listening to me—'

'Why would I listen when you're talking nonsense?' he demanded with sudden harshness.

Jemima looked up at him, scanning the dark golden eyes that inexplicably turned her insides to mush and made her knees boneless. As he lowered his head her breath caught in her throat and her pupils dilated. Without warning his arms went round her, possessive hands delving down her spine to splay across the ripe swell of her hips and haul her close. His mouth crashed down on hers with hungry force and in the space of a heartbeat she travelled from consternation to satisfaction. That kiss was what she really wanted, what her body mysteriously craved.

He kissed her and the world swam out of focus and her brain shut down and suppressed all the anxious thoughts that had been tormenting her. It was simultaneously everything she most wanted and everything she most feared. To be shot from ordinary planet earth into the dazzling orbit of passion and need by a single kiss was what she had always dreamt of finding in a man's arms, but Luciano was by no stretch of the imagination the male she had pictured in such a role. After all, Luciano wasn't for real. She might be inexperienced but she wasn't stupid and she knew that sex would only be a game with him and that he would only play with her without any intention of offering anything worthwhile. A woman needed a tough heart to play such games as an equal and she knew she wasn't up to that challenge.

'You want me,' Luciano grated against her red swollen mouth, his breath warming her cheek and bringing the faint scent of alcohol to her awareness.

Jemima shivered violently against the unyielding confines of his lean, muscular body. She loved the strength and hardness of his well-honed frame. Even through their clothes she could feel him hot and ready against her and the tight ache at the heart of her was like a strangling knot that yearned for freedom. The taste of his mouth was still on hers, nerve cells jangling with the longing for a repeat and the erotic plunge of his tongue. With a receptive shudder that signified the strength the gesture demanded, she brought up her hands and pressed against his broad chest to drive some space between them.

'No, not like this,' she mumbled gruffly, fighting herself as much as she was fighting his attraction.

She wanted him. He was right about that. She had never wanted anything or anybody as much as she wanted Luciano at that moment. Pulling free of him, stepping back, physically hurt as unsated cravings set up a drumbeat of angry dissatisfaction throughout her quivering body. Kicking off the silly shoes that limited her mobility was the work of seconds and her sudden loss of height disconcerted him into lifting his arms off her in surprise. Ducking out of reach and barefoot, Jemima darted round him and pelted out of the door as though baying hounds were chasing her.

Black brows pleating, Luciano swept up the abandoned shoes and looked at them incredulously. Did she think she was Cinderella or something? In bewilderment, because a woman had never before treated him to such stop-go tactics, he poured himself another stiff drink. He didn't get it. He really didn't understand why she was running away. Why would she do that? What possible benefit could she hope to attain by infuriating him?

And then the proverbial penny dropped and he wondered why he had not immediately grasped her strategy. After all, it was an exceedingly basic strategy: she wanted *more*. In fact Jemima or Julie or whatever she and her late twin had chosen to call themselves had been born wanting more. And she knew he was rich enough to deliver a *lot* more. Only he wouldn't, Luciano thought angrily, stoking up his resentment and his hostility. He was determined not to further reward a woman who had lied and schemed to make a profit out of his infant son as though he were a product on sale to the highest bidder.

CHAPTER SIX

BREATHLESS, JEMIMA LEANT back against the door she had slammed behind her in her haste to reach her bedroom. Well, so much for turning down the gift of the clothes with charm and diplomacy! Hadn't that gone well? She grimaced and groaned out loud. Why did she make such a mess of everything with Luciano? What happened to her brain? What happened to tact? Why had she kissed him back as though her life depended on it? Resisting him, acting repulsed would have kept him at bay, but instead she had encouraged him.

The trouble was, she thought ruefully, nobody had ever made her feel as Luciano Vitale did. When she was at college before she'd begun seeing Steven, plenty of men had tried to get her into bed. In fact being constantly badgered for sex had put her off dating. Ironically, though, she had not set out to still be virtually untouched at the age of almost twenty-four. Her parents might believe that she should remain a virgin until she married but Jemima had focused on a more attainable goal. She had believed that she would retain her virginity until she met someone she loved and she had

believed she loved Steven, but Steven had seemed to
prize her virginal state even more than her parents and
had insisted that they should respect church teaching
and wait until they were man and wife. Yet how quickly
he had abandoned that conviction when true temptation had come along in the guise of her much sexier
sister, she reflected wryly.

'You can't turn your back on true love,' Steven had
told her self-righteously before he had gone off with
her twin. 'Julie's the perfect woman for me.'

But Jemima couldn't tell herself the same thing
about Luciano, not least because she didn't believe that
he was perfect. He was arrogant and domineering and
too rich and powerful for his own good. Yet she was
madly, wildly and irrationally attracted to him. In addition she respected his sincere affection for Nicky.
She also liked Luciano on a level she couldn't quite
explain even to herself, for she did not know where
that liking had come from or on what she based it. In
the same way, when Luciano was angry and exasperated as he had been earlier she automatically wanted to
make everything better for him and improve his mood.
Why she felt like that she didn't know because common
sense warned her that Luciano was wrong for her in
every possible way. They were too different as people.

Sex was a pursuit in itself for Luciano, an amusement and not necessarily part of a meaningful relationship. Yet he *had* done commitment in the past. He had
been married and a father before she'd even met him
and at a relatively young age, Jemima reminded herself,
and that suggested that while Luciano might have the

reputation of being a womaniser he had always had a deeper and more caring side to his nature.

Across the room, a door opened and she glanced up. Luciano, his jacket and tie discarded, strolled towards her in his shirtsleeves.

'What on earth are you doing in here?' Jemima exclaimed in consternation.

'Finding you. You ran away,' Luciano condemned. 'Have you any idea how irritating that is?'

'You were being too pushy.'

'I'm naturally pushy.'

'That's not an acceptable excuse.'

'You were trying to pretend you don't want me,' Luciano reminded her with a sudden edge of accusation. 'That was an outright lie!'

'It's arrogant to be so full of yourself.'

Luciano shrugged a broad shoulder sheathed in smooth cotton. 'I'm not the modest type and I know when I'm wanted.'

And he would have had plenty of practice in that line, Jemima reckoned, scanning his lean, dark, flawless features and the intoxicating whole of his fallen angel beauty, which knocked her for six every time she looked at him. That was so superficial of her, she scolded herself, but when she was gazing at Luciano her brain could not concentrate on anything else. In any case her body hummed like an engine raring to go in his radius, making it difficult for her to breathe or move, never mind think.

'Perhaps you're waiting for me to offer you a villa or an apartment in Palermo or Rome or Paris…a less temporary and more rewarding position in my life?' Luciano suggested smooth as glass.

'Why would I want you to offer me a villa or an apartment?' Jemima asked him in genuine bewilderment.

'A mistress has some security. A casual lover has none,' Luciano pointed out.

'I really don't know what we're talking about here. I thought mistresses died out with corsets,' she confided jerkily, unnerved by the dialogue because he could not possibly be asking someone like her to be his mistress, his *kept* woman. That idea struck her as so ridiculous that a nervous giggle bubbled in the back of her throat.

'I don't want to talk,' Luciano breathed with sudden lancing impatience as he met her pale aquamarine gaze. He ran his hands through the thick tangle of hair tumbling round her shoulders. 'I like your hair. It's so long. Are you wearing extensions?'

'No, it's all me,' Jemima muttered breathlessly, because he was standing so close now that she could feel the heat of his body striking hers.

And right there, he knew he had her because he knew for a fact that only a few months earlier his son's mother had had short hair. But he had already accepted that she was a lying fake, hadn't he? Charles Bennett didn't make mistakes. Yet, trailing his fingertips through that lustrous skein of golden silk, Luciano couldn't have cared less about who Jemima was or what she was. He only wanted to see that marvellous hair spread across his pillows and without hesitation he bent and lifted her up.

'Put me down, Luciano!' she gasped.

'No,' he said simply. 'I want you.'

'That's not enough!'

Luciano shouldered open the door between their bedrooms. 'It's enough for me, *piccolo mia*.'

And she was on the brink of telling him why it wasn't enough for her when he kissed her, kissed her long and hard and hungrily until the blood drummed in her head and her toes curled and her mind went blank. Her fingers reached up and delved into his black curls, shaping his proud head, roaming down the back of his neck. The need to touch him was so powerful it overwhelmed every other prompting, even the cautious vibes trying to tug her back to sanity.

Luciano settled her down on his bed and studied her with immense satisfaction. He knew what she was. He knew what she was capable of. But he could not be damaged by a known threat. Her greed was a weakness he would use to control her, he reflected with satisfaction while only dimly questioning what had happened to his belief that one night would be sufficient for him. He knew he wasn't fully in control and it made him feel outrageously free of his rigid rules to do as he liked. She would be his for as long as he wanted her and that was all that currently mattered to him. He bent down and crushed her ripe mouth under his again, one hand closing to the rounded curve of her breast and feeling the race of her heartbeat. His own heartbeat was like thunder in his ears. Her mouth was hot and eager and sweet, so sweet that he couldn't get enough of it.

His kisses were like an addictive drug that Jemima

couldn't resist. Time and time again, she told herself, 'Just one more kiss.' And then what? a little voice piped up at the back of her head. Her spine arched as he lifted her and deftly released the catch on her bra. Before she could react he was peeling her top off over her head and tugging the bra down her arms.

'You're glorious,' Luciano husked, tracing her firm, full breasts with an almost reverent hand, pausing to toy with the protruding tips before bowing his head to lash his tongue across the tender crests.

Jemima huffed, lashes fluttering as sweet, seductive sensation snaked down from her nipples to her feminine core and joined the throbbing heat gathering there. Long brown fingers cradled her bare, rose-tipped curves and his mouth grew a little rougher while he teased the engorged buds, licking and suckling and nibbling with an erotic expertise that made her hips writhe against the mattress. She did not have a single thought in her head, only a sense of shock at the raw intensity of what he was making her feel.

With impatient hands he wrenched her out of her skirt and tossed his shirt on the floor to join it. Jemima gazed up at him with wondering appreciation, her attention lingering helplessly on the sleek bronzed torso composed of lean, hard muscle that swooped impressively down to frame a flat stomach and narrow hips. His shoulders were wide and as rounded with rippling muscles as his biceps. Only then as she reluctantly tore her attention from him did she become conscious of her naked breasts, but as she lifted her hands instinctively to cover herself he caught them in one of his and pinned them above her head.

'No interfering,' he told her in a roughened undertone. 'We only do this my way, *piccolo mia*.'

Colour washed her cheeks because she felt literally shameless lying there half-naked. He used his mouth to torment a straining nipple and she gasped, all self-consciousness wrested from her in the space of a moment. 'Let me touch you…' she pleaded.

He released her wrists. 'Some other time,' he mumbled, kissing a haphazard trail down over her ribcage and her tightening stomach to part her thighs.

Jemima froze, incredulous at his position and mortified, at least until he touched her and it was as if wildfire shot through her veins. Just as quickly there was nothing in her mind but a feverish concentration on what he was doing to her and how incredibly good it made her feel. Pushing her thighs back, he started slow with a long swipe of his tongue and when her hips lifted of their own accord he laughed softly.

'I'm really good at this,' he told her shamelessly.

And he didn't lie. He found every sensitive spot of arousal hidden in her tender folds, traced and teased those places with sleek, skilled fingertips, the glide and dip of his tongue and even the edge of his teeth. She could feel herself growing achingly wet in response, her heartbeat thumping inside her chest as if she were running a race. A fullness like a dam began to gather and build low in her pelvis and she turned this way and that to cope with the rise of heat and the throbbing torture of his electric exploration, restricted by his strong hold on her hips. Fire was burning through her as sensation piled on sensation at mesmerising speed. And then her own response started becoming more than she could contain, tiny spasms rippling through her quivering body and finally growing into a convulsive wave that swept her up and flung her high before sending her sobbing to earth again. She felt as though the top of her head were flying off while her body felt detached and heavy.

'I am burning for you, *piccolo mia*,' Luciano growled, sliding up over her to claim her mouth again.

He tasted of her and that shocked her but she was already in a state of shock so a little more didn't seem to matter. She had stepped out of her safe comfortable world into a far more dangerous one and learned weakness. And it wasn't the incredible allure of what he had made her feel that was her weakness, she acknowledged numbly. Her weakness was *him*. It was the heady joy she experienced when she saw the wicked smile in those lustrous golden eyes gazing down at her with satisfaction. It was knowing that his pleasing her had pleased him, made him feel good, lifted him out of the bad mood he had been in. That gave her a high more powerful than anything she had ever felt and incandescent warmth filled her.

'You do something crazy to me,' Luciano groaned as he rolled back from her to deftly take care of protection. 'I almost forgot to use a condom.'

Long fingers gripped her hips as he tilted her back and shifted against her. And she felt him nudge against her most tender flesh for the first time. It relit the fire that he had only recently sated, sending a frisson of reflexive hunger coursing through her again. Below his tousled black curls the arresting planes of his lean dark face were taut; his eyes blazed scorching gold with need. He took her mouth again with his, unexpectedly slow and gentle until his tongue delved between her lips and tangled with her own in a delicious dance. Nothing had ever been as arousing as that kiss and it fired her adrenaline. Her hands lifted to sink her fingers into his luxuriant hair and hold him to her but he pulled away a split second before he pushed into her.

'You're still so tight,' Luciano growled in frustration, stilling in an effort to accustom her to his girth, raw need driving his big powerful body as potently as a gun to his head.

She could feel her body stretching to accommodate him and apprehension gathered. She couldn't tell him that he would be her first because he believed she had birthed his son. He believed she was experienced and would undoubtedly prefer that to the rather pathetic truth. She squeezed her eyes tight shut and arched up to him in determined welcome, keen to get her introduction over with before the little regretful voices inside her head could gain her attention. And she knew what those little voices were about to tell her and she flatly refused to listen. She wanted Luciano and she wanted to know what all the fuss was about. His every tiny movement sent rippling sensation through her outrageously sensitive body.

Luciano pushed her back another few degrees to get a better angle and thrust home.

A searing flash of pain flared through Jemima and she cried out, eyes flying open filled with tears and surprise. 'That hurts!'

Luciano stilled, staring down at her with brooding, dark disbelief. He knew what his brain was telling him. He knew that his body had met with a resistance that he could not credit existed. While he had known she was not the mother of his son, he had certainly assumed she would be almost as practised with men as her sister had been. The awareness that he had got that badly wrong shook him back to full awareness, clearing his shrewd brain of the fog of alcohol and aggression that had clouded it.

'Are you OK?' he asked rawly.

'Yes, of course I am,' Jemima assured him and she shifted under him, washing wild sensation through Luciano's screamingly taut body while need continued to grip him like a hammer blow to the head. He eased out of the wonderfully tight grip of her and sank back into her with a groan of helpless satisfaction.

The pain diminished to a stinging discomfort closely followed by a jolt of exquisite pleasure. As Luciano moved the pleasure kicked in again and again and Jemima clutched at his arms, her knees rising as she arched to meet his next potent thrust. A wild singing impatience shot with primal need held her firmly in its grip and she lifted her hips in time to his fluid movements. He drove deeper and ground down on her and a helpless moan was torn from her lips as he picked up the pace. He slammed into her and her body clenched round him in excitement, her heartbeat thundering.

Glorious sensation shimmied through her pelvis and set up a chain reaction that sent her out of control when she convulsed beneath him. She plunged over the crest into a climax of intolerable excitement that sent spasms of delight rippling through her satiated body.

Weak as a kitten, Jemima wrapped her arms round Luciano only to stiffen as he literally shook her off. In a fluid movement he withdrew from her and sprang off the bed to stride into the bathroom. There was blood on him, Luciano acknowledged incredulously as he stepped into the shower. She had actually been a virgin. Where did that unexpected little attribute fit into the lying and gold-digging and plotting he had ascribed to her? What the hell had he been thinking? What the hell had he done?

Luciano pulled on jeans. Incredibly the mere thought of her lush, shapely body aroused him afresh and he wanted to punch something in frustration. A virgin? He was in deep shock and feeling ridiculously guilty. He had been so convinced that Jemima was a lying, gold-digging cheat like his son's true mother, *like...* No, he refused to go there, believing that the past was better left buried. But that past had made Luciano a cruel, distrustful cynic with women.

Jemima should have warned him. But how could she have without telling him the truth? Hadn't she appreciated that the first time might hurt? He had never had to think of that possibility before because he had never even come close to being any woman's first lover. He had been the first with Jemima, though, and he found himself savouring that knowledge in the weirdest way.

It shouldn't make any difference to his attitude to her…
but somehow it did. He could no longer confuse her
with Julie the escort or with his late wife, Gigi. Jemima
had been considerably more sexually innocent than
either.

Hearing Luciano's movements in the bathroom,
Jemima emerged from her own reverie and hurriedly
yanked the sheet up over her bare breasts even if the
gesture did strike her as too little too late. Luciano appeared in the doorway. What did he think of her now?
she wondered for a split second before reality finally
came crashing back down on her again. In the storm of
her personal doubts and insecurities she had miracu-
lously contrived to forget the lies she had told and they
were about to catch up with her, she reckoned wretchedly. Luciano knew now, he *had* to know that a virgin
couldn't possibly be Nicky's mum.

Where had her wits been when she'd let him sweep
her off to bed? How had she managed to overlook the
need to protect the one intimate fact that could prove
she was a liar? Of course it hadn't once occurred to
her that she would have sex with Luciano. Fantasy was
one thing, actually *acting* on fantasy something else
entirely. Nor had she calculated the very real danger
of tempting a male as aggressively dominant as Luciano. He was passionate and oversexed. Knowing she
wanted him, he had targeted her and she had been an
easy challenge, she reflected shamefacedly.

'So…' Luciano breathed silkily, leaning back against
the door frame barefoot and bare-chested, wearing only
well-worn jeans. With that much unclad masculine flesh

on view she found it impossible not to stare. 'What price do you put on your virginity?'

Jemima blinked. *'Price?'* she parroted in stricken disbelief.

Luciano raised a well-defined black brow. 'Well, obviously there has to be a price for me to pay because you put a price on absolutely everything else. You put a price on my son's worth, didn't you? Giving away something for free isn't your style.'

Her face had flamed hot as a fire. 'I don't know what you're talking about.'

Luciano shifted an impatient hand and studied her fixedly. 'Quit with the lies, Jemima. Lies only make me angry and you don't want me angry,' he warned her.

Lean muscles flexed below bronzed skin as he changed position. The deep chill in his assurance crept through her like the sudden touch of icicles on too-hot skin. He was scaring her but he didn't need to scare her because Jemima was already fully aware of the wrong she had done. 'All right, I won't tell you any more lies,' she muttered heavily. 'You know I'm not Nicky's birth mother now, don't you?'

'Obviously. So what's the going rate for a virgin these days?' Luciano asked with scorching derision. 'Presumably you gave it up for a good reason and with you the reason will always relate to profit.'

'I'm not like that, Luciano!' Jemima exclaimed in consternation.

His beautiful sensual mouth twisted. 'If you can try to sell a baby, I assume you can put a price tag on virginity.'

'I wouldn't ever have tried to sell a baby!' Jemima argued fiercely. 'I know how wrong that would be!'

'But it wasn't wrong to keep his father from him when his mother was already dead?' he shot at her smoothly.

Jemima flinched at that direct question, sudden tears springing to her eyes and stinging like mad. She could not even blame her late twin for her predicament. Indeed she was all too well aware that she had buried herself in the hole she had dug. After all, *she* had lied to Luciano from the moment she'd met him and compounded her errors by having sex with him. She had done worse than blur the boundaries between right and wrong, she had stepped right over those boundaries.

'My first question should be…*who are you*?' Luciano drawled. 'But then that would make me a liar too because I already knew that you weren't who you were pretending to be before we hit the bed.'

Jemima stared at him in dismay. 'You already knew?' she exclaimed, disconcerted yet again. 'And yet you *still*…' Her voice drained away as she glanced involuntarily at the disordered bedding.

Angry tension pulled Luciano's muscles taut. 'I wasn't expecting a virgin…'

Jemima was still struggling to accept his earlier statement. 'You knew I wasn't Nicky's mother and yet you were still willing—'

'Sex is sex, Jemima, and I had had a lot to drink. When the urge controlled me, I didn't really care who you were,' Luciano told her with derision.

Her tightly controlled face washed pink and then ran pale. She knew she was being punished for not being more careful about who she became intimate with. He was telling her that he had just used her to scratch an itch and that the shock of her true identity hadn't been enough to repel him. 'How long have you known?' she whispered sickly.

'Since we landed in Sicily.'

Her pale eyes widened because she was recalling his change of mood at the airport. 'I know what you must think of me—'

'You have no idea what I think of you,' Luciano cut in with icy bite.

'I love Nicky so much—'

'Of course you're going to say that.'

'I was afraid that if I told you I was only his aunt, you'd just take him away immediately.'

'I expected you to say that too,' Luciano incised, lounging back against the door frame, the light behind him glimmering over his powerful pectorals and the hard slab of rippling muscle below.

'I've been with Nicky since he was only a few days old,' Jemima told him in her own defence while struggling not to sound pleading.

'And you knew all along that your twin had acted as a surrogate mother?'

'Yes, but she wouldn't tell me your name or any details. Julie didn't trust anyone…*ever*,' Jemima completed with feeling emphasis. 'She knew that I wasn't comfortable with the decisions she had made and although she left Nicky in my care she didn't give me any information that I could have used to interfere with her plans.'

Luciano wasn't convinced. Consistent liars told more lies with ease, adding complex layers of falsehood to their stories to make them seem more credible. Been there, done that…visited the graves, he conceded with a sudden deep inner chill of recoil from his own experiences. His dark eyes iced over with a diamond glitter.

'You and your sister grew up in separate adoptive homes?'

'Yes…'

'And when did you first meet her?'

'A couple of months before she got involved in the surrogacy agreement with you and she didn't tell me about that until she turned up again with Nicky.' Jemima dragged her attention from him to study her tightly linked hands. Time was flinging her back almost two years and reminding her of her excitement and joy when she had first discovered that she had a twin sister who wanted to meet up with her.

Jemima had not tried to trace her birth parents because she had been fearful of hurting her adoptive family's feelings. It had not, however, occurred to her that she might have a sibling to find and she had been overwhelmed by Julie's first approach. It had hurt to learn that her birth father was unknown and that their birth mother had died from drug addiction, but it had hurt more to hear about her twin's early health problems, her unsuccessful adoption and unhappy childhood.

'I was so much more fortunate than Julie was. My parents loved me from the beginning,' Jemima said tautly. 'It wouldn't have mattered if I'd been a bit slow at school but Julie's family—'

'I'm not interested in Julie's life story,' Luciano cut in smoothly.

'She's Nicky's mother!' Jemima condemned.

'And I'm grateful she's not here to cause my son any more damage,' Luciano told her truthfully.

'That's an appalling thing to say!' Jemima slammed back at him, sliding her legs off the bed and yanking violently at the sheet for cover.

'Is it?' Luciano rebutted grimly, angry dark eyes hard as obsidian. 'She was his mother and that gave her rights over him but she wasn't a decent, caring person fit to exercise those rights!'

With a final forceful jerk, Jemima dislodged the sheet and wrapped it round her naked body to stalk back through the interconnecting door into her own room. Eyes wet with tears, she was trembling. Her first foray into sex had gone badly wrong and made her feel worthless and rejected. Her late sister was being abused and there was very little she could say because Julie *had* done wrong. But very few people were *all* bad. Jemima blinked back the tears as she dug through her case to extract her dressing gown and dropped the sheet to walk into the bathroom.

She needed to shower, wash away the memory of Luciano's touch and the feel of his body on hers. Shivering, she switched on the water. Her mind drifted back inexorably to her sister and powerful regret filled her because she kept on thinking that if she had only had a little more time with Julie she could have got closer to her and somehow changed things for the better. On another, more rational level, though, she was painfully aware that Julie had never listened to her and had neither respected her opinion nor sought her advice, particularly where Nicky had been concerned.

But Nicky had crept into his aunt's heart the moment she'd met him because he had been a most unhappy baby.

'I don't know how to be a mum!' Julie had complained, becoming almost hysterical because her son had been crying and inconsolable. 'You tell me to cuddle him but I don't feel comfortable with that. He's making *me* feel bad!'

Nicky had suffered from colic and Julie had not been able to cope with him or the sleepless nights. Jemima had tried to help and had ended up taking over. She had blamed herself when Julie had gone back to London to work, leaving her baby in Jemima's care. She had blamed herself too when her twin had failed to bond with her child but she had also been aware of Julie's chequered past history. In truth Julie had had many troubled relationships in her life and rarely settled anywhere for any length of time. Running away from difficult situations had been the norm for Julie.

Luciano had no compassion, Jemima thought wretchedly. Julie had done bad things but her sister had not set out to be a bad person. Tightening the tie on her dressing gown, Jemima walked back to the door that still lay open between the two bedrooms.

'I loved my sister…and I won't say sorry for that!'

Jemima told Luciano defiantly. 'But I *am* sorry I lied to you. That was wrong. I got too attached to Nicky and I was frightened of losing him but I do appreciate that that doesn't excuse my not immediately telling you that his mother had passed away.'

Luciano's full sensual mouth twisted. 'It was a power play, wasn't it?'

Jemima gazed back at him without comprehension. 'Power didn't come into it...'

Somewhere in the distance she heard a thin high-pitched wail and stiffened. 'Nicky's crying,' she muttered, walking to the door.

'Carlotta will take care of him,' Luciano countered.

Wrenching open the door, Jemima listened to the wails drifting down from the floor above and started down the corridor. 'I can't leave him upset,' she called apologetically over her shoulder, sensing Luciano's disapproval and refusing to look back at him.

She would be gone from his fancy island castle soon enough, she reflected wretchedly. He was hardly likely to allow her to stay now that he knew she had lied to him and had no real claim to Nicky. Yet it still stunned her that he had gone to bed with her in spite of that knowledge. He had admitted that he had been drinking. Inwardly she cringed. Had alcohol made her seem more attractive than she was? Why was she even thinking in such a way? What did it matter now? They had had sex and there was no going back from that. It had been a casual thing for him and he had been quick to vacate the bed afterwards. He had actually asked her what price she put on her virginity, she recalled painfully. She felt ashamed and humiliated and blamed him for it.

Why, oh, why had he had to make her feel so bad about their ill-starred intimacy?

CHAPTER SEVEN

CARLOTTA WAS ANXIOUSLY rocking Nicky in her arms. His little face was scarlet with tears and he was sobbing noisily.

'He doesn't like being rocked when he's upset,' Jemima told the brunette in an apologetic tone, thinking that it would have made more sense if she had been given the opportunity to consult with the nanny *before* the other woman started taking care of Nicky.

A voice spoke up in Italian from the doorway and Carlotta gave Jemima a frowning look of surprise before turning rather abruptly to hand Nicky over to her. Although conscious that Luciano was present and had acted as an interpreter, Jemima ignored him and concentrated on his son. Nicky went rigid as he was passed over and then sagged against her, shoving his face into the curve of her neck and whimpering.

'He has nightmares. He's frightened when he wakes up. He only needs to be soothed,' Jemima declared, walking the floor of the elaborately decorated room with Nicky cradled in her arms. She was still alarmingly conscious of the ache at the heart of her body

and hot pink flushed her cheeks as she buried her face
in Nicky's tumbled curls, revelling in the clean baby
scent of innocence. With a heavy sigh she sank down
into the rocking chair beside the cot.

Luciano had paused long enough to grab up a shirt
and don it on his way to the nursery, but nobody seeing
his bare feet and rumpled damp hair could doubt that
he had recently undressed only to get dressed again
in a hurry. Naked below her sensible dressing gown,
Jemima could feel her face burning as if she were on
fire. Their mutual state of undress was noticeable and
embarrassing. She didn't want anyone to know or guess
that she had slept with Luciano. That was her private
disgrace and not for public sharing. Carlotta, however,
simply smiled at Jemima, clearly relieved that the baby
had calmed down.

His son's sobs had subsided almost immediately,
Luciano registered without surprise while he watched.
The baby's fingers clutched convulsively at Jemima
for reassurance. Niccolò had missed her. Obviously he
had missed her. How much of the little boy's misery
had been caused by the sudden change in his routine
and surroundings and the equally sudden absence of
the one person he trusted? Luciano paled beneath his
dark skin, shaken by the reality that he had set down
rules that could well have hurt his son and caused him
unnecessary suffering. He had instructed Carlotta to
deal with the baby alone and to involve Jemima as little as possible in his care.

But how could he love his son and yet deny the child
the one person whom he so clearly loved and wanted?

Shame writhed inside Luciano, a reaction he had not experienced in more years than he cared to count. He watched her smooth the baby's head with a tender hand and read the softness in her eyes.

'He knows his mother,' Carlotta said quietly in Italian to her employer.

It seemed a terrible irony to Luciano at that moment that Jemima was *not* his son's mother because the boy was deeply attached to her and she was equally attached to him. He realised he needed to talk to his lawyer to find out exactly what kind of woman Jemima Barber was. How could he trust his own instincts now? Nor could he have any faith in what Jemima's version of the truth might be. Anyone determined to speak up in defence of Julie Marshall would have failed to inspire Luciano with confidence.

As he stepped unconsciously closer to the woman in the rocking chair Nicky lifted his head off Jemima's shoulder and stared at Luciano with wide dark eyes. And then he smiled with sudden brilliance, freezing his father to the spot in shock for it was the very first positive response Luciano had received from his son. It was significant too that the child had smiled only when he was secure in Jemima's presence, he acknowledged ruefully.

Resting his head back down drowsily again, Nicky fell asleep. Getting to her feet, Jemima lowered him with care into the cot, straightened his sleep suit and covered him up gently. 'He should sleep the rest of the night now,' she whispered.

Luciano stared down at his slumbering son, then

glanced up again and noticed that Jemima was deliberately avoiding looking at him. Annoyance skimmed
along the edges of his sensitised awareness as they left
the room. She tried to step past him out in the corridor
but he rested a staying hand on her arm.

'Jemima…we—'

'I'm really hungry,' Jemima proclaimed in a rush,
jerking her arm back out of reach and addressing his
shirt-clad chest. 'Would it be too much trouble for me
to have something to eat in my room? Even a sandwich
and a cup of tea would do.'

'Put on something in your new wardrobe and come
downstairs to join me for dinner instead,' Luciano suggested, falling into step beside her as she walked down
the corridor.

Her facial muscles clenched tight. 'Thanks but no,
thanks… I'm not in a very sociable mood.'

As she descended the stairs she saw a huge portrait
of an exquisite brunette on the landing and, already
regretting her tart reply to his invitation, she said in
an effort to break the pounding silence, 'My goodness, who's that?'

'My mother, Ambra. It was painted shortly before
she married my father. She probably never smiled like
that again,' Luciano breathed harshly.

His intonation made Jemima wince. 'When did she
die?'

'When I was three years old,' Luciano admitted between gritted teeth, fighting off his terrible memories
with all his might.

'Did your father remarry?'

'No.'

Jemima was already scolding herself for surrendering to her low mood and turning down the dinner invite. She had allowed Luciano to believe that she was the surrogate mother of his son and had used that pretence as a means of staying in Nicky's life. Was it any wonder that he despised her? Or that he had assumed that she was like her sister and after his money? Julie had worshipped rich men and money. Yet no matter how much money Julie had had it had never been enough and money had trickled through her fingers like water.

'We'll talk over breakfast in the morning,' Luciano breathed in a driven undertone as he came to a halt outside his bedroom door, which was mere feet from hers.

'I shouldn't have lied to you,' Jemima began, and then an unfamiliar stab of angry bitterness powered through her regret and she added, 'But you had no right to insult me by suggesting that I would use sex as a means of making money!'

Luciano ground his teeth together and watched her long, unbound mane of golden hair slide off her shoulders and fall almost to her waist as she moved her head. He wanted to run his fingers through that glossy golden hair so badly that he clenched his hand into a fist to restrain himself. So, he liked the long hair? OK, he really, *really* liked the long hair, particularly now that he suspected it was one hundred per cent natural. He also liked her body...and her eyes...and... With a huge effort he focused on what she had said and murmured grimly, 'I've met a lot of women who sell sex like a product.'

Jemima was so shocked by that blunt admission that she turned up her head to stare at him, ice-blue eyes visibly dismayed. 'Seriously?'

Teeth gritted more than ever at such naivety, Luciano nodded and wished he'd kept his mouth shut. Now she was probably thinking that he consorted with hookers and he didn't want her thinking that. *What the hell does it matter what she thinks?* he snarled at himself, thoroughly disconcerted by his loss of concentration and self-discipline. What was wrong with him? Had the few drinks he had imbibed in his bad mood completely addled his brain? Telling Agnese to hold dinner, he strode downstairs to call his lawyer.

Charles did a great deal of groaning and apologising during the lengthy exchange that followed. Nothing about the situation was quite as anyone had assumed or as clear. Charles still couldn't answer all his employer's questions and reluctantly gave Luciano the phone number of his own chief informant. Breathing in deep, Luciano telephoned Jemima's adoptive father, Benjamin Barber. And not one thing that Luciano learned in the subsequent conversation made him feel happier. Instead he came off that call marvelling at the older man's optimistic and forgiving outlook while feeling a great deal worse about his own opinions, suspicions and activities. Knowing that the least he owed Jemima was a polite warning about what he had done, he mounted the stairs again and knocked on her bedroom door.

Half asleep after her delicious meal, Jemima rolled off the bed and lifted her tray, assuming someone was calling back to collect it. Instead she was faced with Luciano, infuriatingly immaculate again in tailored chinos and a black tee shirt. 'Yes?' she said discouragingly, clutching the tray and feeling horribly irritated that she had not known it would be him at her door.

He leant down and took the tray, setting it down on the table to the side of the door. 'I have something to tell you—'

'Can't it wait until breakfast time?'

'I'm afraid not.' Soft pink mouth compressed, Jemima grudgingly stood back to allow him into her room. Since she had no idea what he had to say to her, keeping him out in the corridor where their conversation could be overheard struck her as risky.

'I spoke to your father an hour ago and we talked for quite some time.'

Transfixed by that staggering announcement, Jemima stared back at him in horror. 'I beg your pardon?'

'I phoned your father and he's now aware that you were pretending to be your sister for my benefit,' Luciano divulged.

'Oh, my goodness…how could you *do* that?' Jemima was aghast at the news. 'I just can't believe you told him!'

'The investigators my lawyer employed had already contacted him and it made sense for me to address my questions to your father direct. He was troubled that you hadn't told him what you were doing but he understands why you did what you did and he wants you to know that he forgives you. I had to warn you in case you were planning to phone home.'

Knees weakening, Jemima sank down on the foot of the bed and bowed her head into her raised hands. 'I can't believe you approached Dad... I've tried so hard to keep my parents out of all this!' she exclaimed reproachfully.

'I wanted a clearer picture of what happened and you're too emotionally involved,' Luciano drawled in self-defence. 'It was...enlightening to hear the facts from your father's point of view.'

'I hate you!' Jemima flung at him furiously. 'You had no right to go snooping and interfering!'

'I'm as trapped in the mess your sister left behind her as you are,' Luciano contradicted coolly. 'The legal ramifications of her having stolen your identity will take a long time to unravel. She gave birth to a child using your name. She contracted debts in your name and she broke the law using your name—'

Jemima flew upright in one tempestuous movement. 'Do you think I don't know all that?'

'She took advantage of you and your parents,' Luciano delivered grimly.

'There's no way my father said that!' Jemima accused furiously.

'Your father is a rather unworldly man and I imagine he has had little contact with the criminal element. I'm rather less innocent and much more accustomed to dealing with life's users and abusers.'

'Bully for you!' Jemima snapped back childishly, marching back to her bedroom door and dragging it open in invitation. 'Right now all I want to do is go to bed and forget you ever existed!'

Luciano lifted his hand and a forefinger flicked the full tense line of her lower lip in reproof. 'What a little liar you can be. Without me there would be no Niccolò…and somehow I don't think you'd give him up so easily.'

The touch of his hand against her lip made her entire skin surface tingle. Her breathing quickened and she pressed her thighs together to suppress the tiny clenching liquid sensation low in her pelvis. Her lashes swept up fully to collide with stunning dark golden eyes welded to her every move and change of expression. Her cheeks coloured, her lashes swept down and she backed away from him, furious that without even trying he could still get a physical reaction out of her.

'Goodnight,' she said flatly.

Luciano wanted to scoop her up and carry her back to his bed. It was pure lust, he told himself furiously, the sort of irrational, ungovernable lust that sent a man into cold showers and the depths of neurotic desire. And unlike his late and unlamented father, who had once become obsessed with a woman, Luciano was not the obsessive type. He stayed up late working and by the time he finally fell into bed he was too exhausted to do anything but sleep.

The next morning, Jemima felt more like herself and less traumatised. The truth had come out and she couldn't hide from it. Lying had gone against her nature and weighted her conscience and she was relieved not to be pretending any more. Her parents knew. She chewed her lower lip and decided to phone home that evening, although she dreaded dealing with her father's disappointment in her behaviour. Luciano and Nicky, however, were an even bigger challenge.

Presumably over breakfast Luciano would tell her what he wanted to do next and when she would be flying home. She had lied to him. She might have convinced herself that she had lied for her nephew's sake but in her heart she knew she was lying to herself. In reality, she had not been able to face parting with Nicky and that had been selfish when Nicky's father was available to take charge of his son. While she thought unhappily about her mistakes, she rooted through her suitcase, grimacing at the reality that there was really nothing in her case suitable for a hot day. At least nothing presentable, she affixed ruefully, choosing not to examine why what she wore had to be *more* presentable than usual when Luciano was around. After a few moments, she stalked into the dressing room and skimmed through the hanging dresses. What would he do with them after she had gone? Chuck them out? Pass them on to staff or recycling? She lifted down a fitted blue cotton sundress, plainer in style and less revealing than most of the other garments, and began to get ready.

Seated on the floor in the nursery, Nicky was happily playing with his new toys. Carlotta was friendly, addressing Jemima in broken English to let her know that he had slept well and eaten. A maid met Jemima at the foot of the stairs to show her where she was to go to join Luciano. They trekked across the vast building, mounting stairs and crossing hallways before walking down a long picture gallery that opened to an outdoor area that overlooked the sea and the shore.

The panoramic view and the sunlight blinded her and she had a split-second sizzling snapshot of Luciano, rising with fluid grace from his seat, his lean, powerful body sheathed in an exquisitely cut pale grey suit teamed with a black shirt. *'Buon giorno,'* he murmured smoothly. 'You look amazing.'

Jemima flushed. 'Let's not get carried away,' she told him reprovingly. 'I'm wearing this because it's so hot and I have nothing suitable *and*—'

'Rest assured I will not assume that you are wearing it either to please or attract me, *piccolo mia,'* Luciano incised as drily as though he could read her mind.

Her flushed cheeks turned a solid mortified red and she averted her eyes as she dropped down hurriedly into a seat. Dishes were proffered by one manservant, beverages by another. Her attention briefly falling on the bodyguards standing several yards away, it occurred to her that Luciano lived rather like a king in a medieval court with an army of staff and everyone bowing and scraping and doing their utmost to ensure his protection and his comfort. It was an isolated lifestyle, divorced from normality, and she wondered how it would affect Nicky to grow up like a crown prince in the lap of such indescribable luxury.

From below her lashes she stole a helpless glance at Luciano. He was looking out to sea, his flawless classic profile turned to her. Her heart thumped very loudly in her ears because she was remembering his mouth, that wide, sensually skilled mouth, roaming over her and making her writhe with raw need and then the dynamic flex and flow of his lithe body over hers, driving her to the apex of excitement. Perspiration broke out on her skin and she quickly looked away from him again. No, try as she might to be sensible, she could not forget the intimacy, the first she had ever known and, much like Luciano, utterly unforgettable.

'So, what next?' she muttered in the pulsing silence.

Lustrous dark golden eyes ensnared hers and her breath tripped in her throat. 'That's what we have to decide.'

Jemima tore her eyes free and bit into her fresh fruit. He was using the royal 'we'; she didn't think she would have much actual input into what happened next.

'Tell me how your sister got hold of your passport,' he invited, startling her with that request.

'It happened by accident. The first time we met she showed me her passport because she had worn her hair long then too, and I got out mine and we were laughing and somehow our passports got mixed up.'

'And?' Luciano prompted.

'Julie only realised she had my passport when she was flying out to Italy and she travelled on it because she didn't want to miss her flight.'

'She lied,' Luciano murmured without any expression at all. 'She had already used *your* passport in her application to be the surrogate I hired. And the reason she lied was that she had several criminal convictions in her own name. She probably tracked you down quite deliberately. She set you up to steal your identity, Jemima. Accept that.'

Jemima paled. She was remembering laughing with her sister as they compared unflattering passport photos. 'It was months before I found out about the…er… exchange and when I contacted her about it, she said she'd give it back when she returned from Italy.'

'Only she never did,' Luciano completed.

'Obviously you think I'm very stupid,' Jemima said tartly, burning her mouth on an unwary sip of coffee and swallowing hard, burning her throat into the bargain, tears starting into her eyes at the discomfort.

'No, I think you were scammed. She was a practised, confident trickster and she was your sister and you didn't want to accept the truth,' Luciano said in a surprisingly uncritical tone. 'I can understand ignoring the evidence and wanting to believe the best of someone close to you. It happened to me once.'

'Oh…' Jemima was taken aback by that admission. 'I loved her—I felt an immediate sense of connection with her.'

'Scammers have to be attractive to pull people in.'

Jemima concentrated her attention warily on eating.

'Why didn't you go to the police about your passport when she refused to give it back?'

'I didn't need my passport because I couldn't afford to travel at the time…and I didn't want to get her into trouble. For a long time she made excuses about why she wasn't returning it and I believed her,' she admitted with a rueful roll of her eyes.

A manservant topped up Luciano's black coffee. He rose lithely from his seat and lounged back against the stone balustrade girding the terrace. He surveyed her with satisfaction. She was elegant as a swan in the tailored blue sundress, her hair restrained in its usual braid, only stray little golden hairs catching the slight breeze round her troubled face. She had loved and cared for her sister, contriving to mourn Julie Marshall's passing in spite of all the damage her sibling had done. Jemima had a lot of heart and a generosity of spirit that he admired even though he couldn't emulate it. And he wanted what she had to offer for his son. He sensed that she could be the greatest gift he would ever give him.

For once he wasn't going to be selfish and he wasn't going to remind himself how often he had sworn never to surrender his freedom again. In any case he owed Jemima a debt. In the grip of ignorance and lacerating bitterness at her betrayal of trust he had seduced her and she hadn't deserved that. Virginity had to matter to a woman who had reached almost twenty-four years of age without experimenting and he had taken it from her. Carelessly, thoughtlessly, cruelly.

'I took advantage of you last night,' Luciano breathed in a driven undertone. 'I was angry. I was drunk.'

Her pale blue eyes widened and she set down her cup with a sharp little snap. 'No, nobody took advantage of anyone last night. I'm an adult and I made a choice.'

'You weren't in any fit state to make a choice.'

Anger flared in her mutinous gaze. 'I chose you because I've never been so attracted to anyone before. I'm not proud that I was that shallow but it *was* my decision!'

Silence lay thick and heavy between them in the

heat and she shifted uneasily in her seat, embarrassed by her own vehemence. Had she really had to admit that she had never wanted any man the way she had wanted him? Didn't that sound a bit pathetic?

'The odd thing about decisions is that when you make major ones you're always convinced that you'll never change your mind. After my wife died in the crash I decided that I would *never* marry again,' Luciano confessed tautly, unsettling her with that admission. 'I did not want to share my life with another woman but I was grieving for the child I had lost and I did still want to be a parent. That is why I came up with the idea of a surrogacy agreement. I thought it would be a simple business contract and problem free, but I didn't count on dealing with a woman like your sister.'

Jemima heaved a sigh but said nothing. By running away with Nicky after the birth, Julie had changed everyone's lives and there was no getting away from that. She was, however, far more interested in wondering why Luciano had decided never to remarry. Had that been a tribute to the wife he loved? Gigi Nocella had been a gorgeous and very famous movie star. What woman could possibly follow in such gilded footsteps?

'You have had complete responsibility for my son since he was only a few days old,' Luciano pointed out.

'Yes.' Jemima snapped back to the present and shook irritably free of her futile speculation about Luciano's past. 'Julie went back to London to work. She told me that she earned good money working in PR and I had no reason to doubt her. I continued my teaching job and placed Nicky in a nursery nearby. Julie didn't help with the expense and it was a challenge to afford it on my salary and my savings were soon gone. My parents were struggling too, so it made sense for me to give up my apartment and move home again.'

'You've made sacrifices to look after my son,' Luciano acknowledged grimly. 'And you have looked after him well. I believe that you love him and that he loves you.'

'I couldn't help loving him.' Jemima sighed.

'But he's not your child.'

Jemima grimaced at that unnecessary reminder. 'That didn't come into it for me.'

Luciano continued to study her with brooding intensity. 'My son may not be your child now but he *could* be...'

Jemima stared back at him in bewilderment. 'What on earth are you saying?' she framed uncertainly.

'I'm asking you to marry me to become my son's mother and my wife,' Luciano clarified with silken sibilance, his dark eyes glimmering golden as a lion's in the sunlight. 'It makes sense—in this situation it makes the very best sense. Think about it and you'll see that.'

CHAPTER EIGHT

JEMIMA WAS IN SHOCK.

Luciano Vitale was asking her to marry him. How was that possible? She had joined him at breakfast expecting to be told when she would be flying home and instead he had proposed marriage. Her lashes fluttered down to screen her eyes.

'Nicky's mother?'

'And the mother of any other children that we might have together,' Luciano slotted in smoothly, catching her startled upward glance and looking steadily back at her. 'I'm talking about a normal marriage and a family. Be assured of that.'

Jemima felt rather like a mouse cornered by a cat. His brilliant dark eyes sought out hers, level and direct and forceful, as if seeking assurance that she was listening properly. A normal marriage, a *family*. Shock was piling on shock. Her taut lips parted and she blurted out, 'But you're not in love with me!'

Luciano inclined his arrogant head to one side and compressed his sensual mouth. 'Is that kind of romantic love so necessary to you?'

Jemima went pink. 'I always assumed that I would only marry for love.'

'But love doesn't always last,' Luciano parried wryly. 'It can also encourage unrealistic expectations in the relationship. I can't offer you love but I can offer you respect and consideration and fidelity. I believe there is a very good chance that a marriage created on such practical foundations would succeed.'

She thought he was quite probably the most beautiful man in the world as he leant back against that balustrade, black curls ruffling in the breeze above his darkly handsome features. He was offering her respect, consideration and fidelity. Didn't he believe in love? Or did he still think he was in love with his first wife? She wanted to ask but it felt like the wrong moment. Luciano had proposed marriage. Wasn't that supposed to be special? It was obvious he had thought in depth about marrying her.

'Why me?' she asked baldly.

'Primarily you love my son and he loves you. I grew up without a mother and I want more for him.'

'You could marry anyone,' she cut in helplessly.

'But to any other woman Niccolò would always be second best once she had a child of her own. I don't believe you will react like that but many women would,' Luciano fielded quietly.

'Yet you planned his birth knowing you intended to raise your child without a mother,' she reminded him.

'That was before I saw the strength of the bond between you and him and the happiness that gave him.'

Having heard enough, Jemima forced a smile and

rose from her seat. 'I'm afraid the man I marry would have to want me for more than my child-rearing abilities,' she told him stiffly, struggling to keep the little amused smile in place and mask the deep hollow of hurt opening up inside her.

Luciano dealt her a seething look of frustration and strode after her. 'Jemima!'

Jemima didn't turn her head, she just kept on walking away fast, unable to face any further dialogue. She was so hurt and she didn't really understand why. Surely it was always a sort of a compliment if a man asked you to marry him? Even if you didn't want to say yes. And at that point, she realised what was wrong. She wanted *more*. She wanted him to want her personally and that was downright silly as well as unlikely. So many more beautiful and sophisticated women would have snatched at Luciano's offer with two greedy hands. Who did she think she was to be so finicky?

'Jemima…!' Luciano exclaimed, closing a powerful hand round her shoulder to spin her round in the picture gallery. 'You know very well that I want you for more than that!'

Jemima sucked in a gulp of oxygen and almost lost it again as she clashed with blazing dark golden eyes. 'Do I?' she slashed back in challenge.

'You *do* know,' Luciano told her, crowding her back against the wall behind her.

'How *would* I know?' Jemima flamed back at him. 'Nicky loves me and you think I'm good for him. That's why you're asking me to marry you.'

His white teeth flashed against his bronzed skin. 'Last night, we—'

'No, don't try to drag last night into it,' Jemima warned angrily. 'Your proposal made it clear that providing your son with a mother was your main motivation!'

'*Accidenti*... I was taking a conservative approach. I assumed you would prefer that!'

'Why would a woman want a conservative proposal?' Jemima countered impatiently.

'You would've preferred me to take you to bed again before I proposed?'

Jemima recognised the difference between her outlook and his and almost screamed in vexation. She thought of love and romance while he thought of sex, and wild, raunchy sex at that. Well, he had been upfront about not being able to offer love, so what more could she reasonably expect from him? And did she really *want* to say no? No to being Nicky's mum? No to being Luciano's wife and the potential mother of his children?

Luciano planted his hands squarely on the wall either side of her head, his lean, powerful body effectively imprisoning hers. Her ice-blue eyes widened as she felt his erection push against her belly, his hard readiness formidable even through the barrier of their clothes. Heat coiled at the heart of her rose up and clear thought process broke down. Hunger settled in a tight, hard knot inside her, constricting her breathing.

'No. On bended knee and dinner by candlelight would have been more your style,' Luciano derided.

'I'm not that old-fashioned,' she told him in exasperation.

Lowering his head, he brushed his lips almost teasingly against hers and then lingered to capture and suckle her lower lip, one hand sliding down the wall to close on her hip and jerk her into closer contact. His tongue eased between her readily parted lips and delved in an unashamedly sexual sortie. Her breathing fractured as she came off the wall to wrap her arms round his neck, fingertips sliding into his luxuriant hair.

'So, is this a yes, *piccolo mia*?' Luciano husked sexily against her swollen mouth.

'Are you *always* calculating the odds?' Jemima complained, jerking her head back out of reach.

Luciano gave her a wicked grin that loosed a flock of butterflies in her tummy and left her feeling dizzy. 'I don't switch off my brain very often,' he admitted.

She could have him if she wanted him, Jemima reflected on a heady high. And she wanted him—oh, my goodness, yes, she wanted him. But it would be crazy to make an impulsive decision based on the feelings of the moment. And her feelings just then were overwhelmingly physical and dangerously unreliable. Close to Luciano, her body vibrated like a tuning fork. He made her want to drag him off to the nearest secluded corner. That awareness cooled her heated blood and made her take a mental step back to take stock.

'I have to think about this,' Jemima declared, ignoring the frowning slant of his black brows above his stunning eyes. 'I need to be on my own for a while. I'm going for a walk on the beach.'

Recalling the flight of winding stone steps that led down to the shore from the terrace, she walked back into the sunlight. Round and round and round she went, moving faster and faster in her need to escape until her heels finally sank into the blissfully soft sand at the bottom. With a sigh she slipped off her shoes, closed her fingers through the straps and walked barefoot down to the shore.

The surf dampened her feet as she moved away from the castle. Little white houses straggled up the hillside on the other side of the horseshoe-shaped bay and boats bobbed in the harbour. A church with a bell tower made the village look even more picturesque in the sunshine.

So, how did she really feel about Luciano? Did she want him for the right reasons? Shouldn't Nicky be her driving motivation? Did it matter that she was thinking less about Nicky and more about becoming Luciano's wife? Why couldn't she think about anything but Luciano? Was she infatuated with him? No doubt that would wear off with continued exposure to him and prevent her from behaving like an embarrassing teenager with a crush, she thought with an inner wince. After all, it was obvious that if such a marriage of convenience was to work she would have to be more practical in her outlook.

Could she happily settle for respect and consideration and fidelity? Well, she thought wryly, maybe not *happily*, but, if the alternative was not to have Luciano at all, her choice was being made for her. If the chance was there, she definitely wanted to take it and give it a go. And what about her family, her friends and the teaching career that she loved? Living abroad in Sicily? Could she adjust to that change? Friends and family would be able to visit as she would be able to visit them, she told herself, and, while she would miss her job, raising Nicky and having more children would certainly fill her time.

Registering that she was walking straight for the natural rock formation that cut off the beach at one point, Jemima changed direction in favour of the path running between the shore and the single-track road. She put her shoes back on, relieved she had worn low heels, and only as she straightened did she appreciate that she was not walking alone. Three of Luciano's bodyguards hovered several yards away and she made a shooing motion of dismissal with her hands before turning defiantly on her heel and picking up her pace towards the village. Why on earth were they following her? Were such precautions really necessary for her safety?

Tired and hot, she paused at a café above the beach and walked in to sit down. It was busy. A large group of elderly men sat playing a board game in one corner and several other tables were occupied. As soon as Jemima sat down a bodyguard approached her to ask her what she wanted, acting as a liaison between her and the proprietor, who was viewing them nervously. Freshly squeezed orange juice was brought and she sipped, cooling off from the early-morning heat while watching a handful of children play ball on the beach below.

Nicky would have a whole beach to himself at the castle, she thought heavily. Would he even be allowed to play with other children? Had Luciano the smallest idea of what an ordinary childhood was like? What had his own been like? He had shared so little with her. All she knew about his background and his first marriage had been gleaned from the Internet. Luciano was not a male who willingly opened up about his past.

A sports car purred to a halt outside and Luciano sprang out of it. The proprietor bowed almost double and the waiter copied him. The old men stopped their game, suddenly rigid, their chatter silenced. As he strode in Luciano addressed the owner and then settled down lithely opposite her, seemingly impervious to the apprehensive silence that had greeted his arrival and that of his protection team.

'Why did you have me followed?'

'My father died when his yacht was blown up in the harbour out there,' Luciano volunteered. 'I have lived a very different life but there are still those who hate and fear me because of the blood in my veins. I can't take the risk of ignoring that.'

Jemima had gone very pale. She brushed his hand soothingly with her fingers. 'I'm sorry...'

His lush lashes lifted and dark golden eyes scanned her as a glass of water was brought to the table for him. 'For what? For old history? Nobody grieved for my father, least of all me,' he admitted bluntly.

'Was your childhood unhappy?' she murmured tautly, her eyes on his lean, dark face and the strong tension etched there.

'Is knowing such things about me important to you?'

Amazed that he should have to ask that, Jemima nodded confirmation.

Luciano drank his water. 'It was a nightmare,' he admitted gruffly. 'That's why I want a normal family life for Niccolò.'

Jemima wondered what a nightmare entailed and wasn't sure she could live with further clarification. The haunting darkness in his eyes sent a chill racing down her spine. The old men in the corner were still staring and she glanced away, wondering what it had been like for Luciano to grow up as the son of a man who was loathed and feared and whose reputation for corruption had stretched beyond death to shadow his son's. Frustrated tenderness laced with intense compassion twisted through Jemima. A normal family life. It was not so much to ask. It was not an impossible dream, was it? In fact it was a modest aspiration for so wealthy and powerful a male and that knowledge touched her heart more deeply than anything else could have done.

Luciano wondered why Jemima appeared to be on the brink of tears. He could see moisture glimmering in her ice-blue eyes. He didn't want to talk about his dirty past; he didn't even want to think about such things. It had soiled him for ever—how could it not soil her? Furthermore, he was still reeling from his own behaviour the night before: he had lost control of his temper and acted with dishonour. Even his father had waited to marry his mother before sharing a bed with her. He repressed his troubled thoughts, knowing the futility of regretting what was past.

'I want to marry you,' he told her very quietly.

'I know,' she whispered, her heart beating so fast it felt as though it were in her throat. 'But I'm not sure what that means to you.'

'I wanted you the first moment I saw you,' Luciano ground out in a driven undertone. 'Is that what you want to hear? I thought you were your sister then and I couldn't believe that I could want such a woman, so I fought it. You're a very loving woman, Jemima, and my son needs that. I don't think I'm capable of giving that kind of love, but you are.'

Yes, that was what Jemima had needed to hear. A blinding smile curved her lips and lit up her face. 'OK...you've won me over,' she told him shakily.

Luciano snapped his fingers and the proprietor came running. He spoke in Italian. The waiter scurried around serving everyone in the bar, even Luciano's protection team. The café owner reappeared with a dusty bottle, which he proffered with pride. The wine was poured and toasts were made.

'I bought everyone a drink to celebrate our wedding plans with us,' Luciano explained as her eyes widened.

'We're talking weddings now?' Jemima parroted as he nudged her nerveless fingers with a wine glass. 'You want me to have a drink? But it's only ten o'clock in the morning!'

He groaned out loud and raked impatient fingers through his black curls. '*Santa Madonna!* I forgot to give you the ring!'

In a daze, Jemima moistened her dry mouth with the wine. 'There's a ring?'

'*Certamente*…of course there's a ring!' Luciano withdrew a tiny box from his pocket and flipped it open to a spectacular sapphire ring surrounded by diamonds. Removing it from the box, he lifted her hand and slid it onto her engagement finger. 'If you don't like it, we can choose something else.'

'No…it's beautiful,' Jemima whispered dizzily. 'Where did you get it from? I mean, we only arrived…'

'It belonged to my mother's family…and no, before you ask, it never belonged to Gigi,' he assured her.

Smiles had broken out all around them. Several solemn toasts were made. Luciano seemed taken aback by the warmth of the good wishes offered. Jemima drank her wine and watched the sunlight glitter off her amazing ring while wondering with a little frisson of excitement if Luciano would be sharing a bed with her again that night.

'Why did Gigi never wear this ring?' she asked baldly.

'It wasn't flashy enough for her. She only wore diamonds.'

It was the first time he had voluntarily mentioned his first wife. Jemima supposed that in time she would learn more but she could tell by his tension that, although he was trying hard to be more open with her, it was a tender subject and he was struggling. So much had already changed between them but the biggest alteration in Luciano's attitude had occurred as soon as he'd realised that she wasn't her twin sister, Julie. The awareness that he had fought any attraction to her before he'd known her true identity soothed Jemima's concerns. Luciano was willing to overlook her lies because he respected her attachment to Nicky and her principles. In other words, what was important to her was equally important to him.

'So, when will we be getting married?' she asked as Luciano tucked her into the elegant sports car outside.

'As soon as possible. Draw up a guest list of friends and family.' Curling black lashes shaded Luciano's gaze, his wide sensual mouth relaxed. 'My staff will take care of all the arrangements. We'll have the wedding here.'

Her eyes widened. '*Here* in Sicily?'

'I don't think it would be a good idea to trail Niccolò back to the UK again,' Luciano commented with a frown. 'You would have to stay somewhere where my security people could look after you both because when word of our relationship breaks in the media you will both be a paparazzi target. It will be easier if you remain here on the island, where your privacy can be assured.'

Jemima tried to absorb the realities of her new life and slowly shook her head in bemusement because she could not even begin to imagine being a target for the paparazzi. But, more importantly, a further change of climate and yet another selection of strange faces would not benefit Nicky either, she conceded ruefully. If Castello del Drogo was to be the little boy's permanent home, he should be allowed to settle into his new surroundings without the stress of having to adapt to any additional challenges.

'I have a tour of Asia scheduled and, as I'll be away

for a couple of weeks, I suggest that you invite your family out to keep you company until the wedding,' Luciano remarked, disconcerting her.

He was leaving her. Jemima refused to betray any reaction. Obviously he would travel on business and such temporary separations would be part of their lives. She had never been the clingy type. She was independent and self-sufficient, she reminded herself doggedly. Wanting to climb into his suitcase with Nicky was just plain stupid.

'I'm surprised you're prepared to leave Nicky so soon,' she admitted.

'When the tour of my holdings was organised, actually finding my son still seemed like a fantasy,' he confided ruefully. 'Now that I have found him I have no intention of being an absent parent. Once I'm home again I'll be spending a lot of time with him.'

They returned to the *castello*. 'What made you buy this place?' Jemima asked curiously. 'Was it purely for the private setting?'

'I didn't buy it. I inherited it. It belonged to my mother's family. She grew up here.' His lean bronzed face shadowed.

'Did you stay here when you were a child?'

'No. My mother never returned after she married my father. He first saw her playing on the beach down there as a teenager,' Luciano told her, tight-mouthed. 'When I was older he called it love at first sight. I would call it lust…'

Like what Luciano had felt on first seeing Jemima? Jemima wondered ruefully. An instant attraction, similar to what she herself had felt, so how could she look down on that?

'How did they get together?' she prompted.

'In a decent world they would never have got together. He was a murderer, a thief, a gangster,' Luciano declared without any expression. 'She was the adored only child of a titled, educated man. But that man gambled and got into debt and my father bought his debt and soon my father owned him. My father wrote off the debt in return for my mother's hand in marriage...'

'My goodness,' Jemima said sickly. 'What did she have to say about it?'

'She loved her father and she did what she had to do to save him from the shame of bankruptcy,' Luciano revealed. 'I can't imagine she was happy about the price she had to pay. She married a brutal man.'

Jemima heard the chill in his dark-timbred voice and decided it was definitely time to change the subject. He didn't want to talk about his parents' marriage and in the circumstances that was hardly surprising. As she recalled, his mother had died when he was only three years old and it was unlikely that he remembered much about the beautiful brunette in the portrait on the stairs. It was something they had in common and she commented on the fact.

Luciano turned frowning eyes on her.

'Have you forgotten that I was adopted? I don't remember anything about my birth parents but what I do know now, thanks to Julie's research, is that there's nothing there to be proud of. Our birth mum was a drug addict and I'll never know who our father was.'

The grim edge stamped round his beautiful mouth eased. 'Ignorance could be bliss.'

'Leave it in the past where it belongs,' she urged, closing her hand round his. 'We're not responsible for what our parents did, nor do we have to resemble them.'

Luciano smiled at her simplistic advice and her un-subtle attempt to offer him comfort. He didn't need comfort. He knew who he was and where he had come from and what he had to avoid to achieve a reasonably happy and successful life. Caring too much about any-thing, be that women, work or money, was what he had surrendered to embrace peace of mind.

Nicky was surfacing from a nap when they entered the nursery and he held out his arms to Jemima with a huge smile. She hauled him up and turned to Luci-ano with a grin, wanting to include him, wanting to encourage father and son to get to know each other properly. 'Let's take him down to the beach. He's never seen the sea.'

She changed into her serviceable and rather faded blue racer-back swimsuit, unable to face the challenge of modelling one of the daring 'barely there' bikini sets in her new wardrobe. Luciano joined her in swim shorts, lifting a delighted Nicky high and smiling with satisfaction when the little boy laughed. She watched the long, lithe line of his muscled back flex as he tucked Nicky securely below one arm and strode downstairs. Not an ounce of fat clung to his well-built physique and it showed in his narrow waist and lean hips.

A picnic lunch was delivered and food for Nicky. The baby loved getting his toes wet in the surf. He loved even more being held up in the air and looking down at his father. Jemima watched father and son, relieved at how naturally they could interact in a more relaxed setting. Clearly no longer uneasy in Luciano's presence, Nicky dug his hands into his father's hair and touched his face with growing familiarity.

'That was a good suggestion,' Luciano told her appreciatively as they headed back to the *castello*.

A blonde waved and smiled at them from the terrace as they climbed the steps up from the beach. She surged forward to greet Luciano and kiss him Continental-style on both cheeks. She was a beauty, a tall, slender blonde with dark eyes and great dress sense.

'Jemima, meet Sancia Abate...' Luciano made the introduction casually. 'Sancia, my wife-to-be, Jemima, and my son, Niccolò.'

Sancia barely glanced in Jemima's direction but fussed in a very feminine way over Nicky.

'Who is she? Does she work for you?' Jemima asked as they walked away.

'No. She's Gigi's kid sister,' he confided, startling her. 'I still let her use the guest house here when she needs a break. Nicky gets tired quickly, doesn't he?'

Jemima watched the baby stick his thumb in his mouth and close his eyes against her shoulder and she smiled in spite of her surprise at that revelation concerning the svelte blonde. 'You exhausted him. He's not used to that kind of play. My father's past that stage.'

'But he's very fond of him,' Luciano cut in.

'Yes, he is. Did you have grandparents?'

'No, my grandfather died soon after my parents

married.' His strong jaw clenched, his mouth flattening. 'Agnese was my nurse when I was a child. She was the closest thing I had to a grandparent.'

'I didn't have any either. Mum and Dad met and married later in life,' Jemima told him as she passed Nicky over to Carlotta in the hall and joined Luciano on the stairs. 'You lost your mother young.'

'Yes.'

'How did it happen?'

Luciano strode across the landing without answering her.

'Was she ill?' Jemima persisted, following him down the stone passageway and into his room.

'No,' Luciano gritted impatiently, slamming the door closed behind him with a frustrated hand. 'Don't you take hints? I don't want to talk about this…'

Jemima reddened uncomfortably, feeling like a rude nosy parker for having continued to ask questions even after he walked away. 'I'm sorry…'

His lustrous dark golden eyes glittered. 'No, I don't want to lie but I don't want to tell you the truth either.'

She turned round and smoothed her hands up over his cheekbones in what was meant to be a comforting and apologetic gesture. 'I'm a horribly nosy person,' she confessed guiltily. 'Give me an inch and I'll take a mile. Don't even *hint* at a secret…it turns me into a bloodhound that won't quit!'

Reluctant laughter escaped Luciano. He stared down at her anxious face and a deep hunger for the warmth of her engulfed him in a tidal wave of need. He pulled her into his arms and claimed her mouth with devastating urgency.

Taken by surprise, Jemima laughed and then gasped beneath the savage onslaught of his mouth. Her body caught flame like hay, a burning ache stirring between her legs, a hot, prickling awareness stiffening her nipples.

'*Madonna!* I think I'll die if I don't have you now,' Luciano growled, long fingers closing into the shoulders of her swimsuit to wrench it down and release her breasts.

He tumbled her down on his bed and skimmed off his shorts in an impatient motion, coming up on the mattress to join her unashamedly naked and eager. He knelt at her feet and yanked her swimsuit down her hips to toss it aside while his smouldering gaze wandered at will over her splayed body.

'I love these…so pretty, so lush,' he husked, his fingers cupping the curves of her high, full breasts before rising to stroke the pouting crests. 'And these.' A lean hand travelled up a slender thigh and nudged her legs apart to display a tantalising ribbon of soft, glistening pink. 'And *this* perfect place, *piccolo mia*. I am enslaved…'

He found that feminine perfection with the erotic expertise of his mouth and it was magical and then terrifying to lose control so fast. She clutched at his hair. She sobbed. She gasped. Ultimately she cried his name in an ecstasy of quivering, wanton pleasure, her body weak and heavy with satisfaction as she lay beneath him, too stunned by his passion and the explosive response he had roused from her to move again.

'What was it about me…er…being nosy that set you off?' she whispered helplessly.

Luciano's brow furrowed. He honestly didn't know. He had looked at her and an uncontrollable urge to take her to bed had overpowered him. He couldn't explain it. Her wild response to him had soothed the savage turmoil inside him in a manner beyond his comprehension. He touched her with gentle fingers, put his mouth to a rose-pink nipple, toying with her for a few moments, smiling against her flushed skin as she muttered his name as though she were saying a prayer. He turned her over onto her stomach. She complained about being moved and he ignored it, lifting her up, aligning their bodies and then plunging into the damp, silken heat of her with a raw groan of enthusiasm, swiftly echoed by her boneless cry of encouragement.

Delicious sensation ricocheted up through Jemima's body, building from the hot, aching heart of her into a blaze that consumed as Luciano slammed into her with compelling strength. Her excitement climbed with the sweet, earthy delight of his penetration. And just when she believed that powerful excitement couldn't reach any greater height he sent her flying into an orgasm that snapped taut her every muscle and blew her apart in a sublime surge of drowning, melting pleasure.

'Oh…wow…' Jemima mumbled, flopping down against the pillows.

Luciano flipped her over and gathered her damp, trembling body close. 'Oh…wow…' he teased. 'Well, you have no choice but to marry me now.'

'How's that?' she framed, barely able to think straight.

'I didn't use a condom—'

Her brows pleated in dismay. 'Luciano—'

'Having unprotected sex is a sign of commitment, which I have never risked before with a woman,' he announced above her head.

'You want a brass trophy or something?' Jemima looked up at him with wry amusement.

'No, I want a repeat...' Luciano growled, treating her full lower lip to a tiny carnal nip swiftly followed by a soothing stroke of his tongue. 'That was the best sex I ever had, *piccolo mia*.'

'Good, because you won't have got me pregnant,' Jemima told him with assurance. 'It's the wrong time of the month for that.'

Luciano stared down at her with brooding intensity, his lean, darkly handsome features set in unsettlingly serious lines. 'Don't be too curious with me.'

Jemima had become very still and her eyes were troubled. 'Why not?'

'Unlike you, I'm not the sharing type. I have too much stuff to hide.'

'Red rag to a bull, Luciano,' Jemima warned. 'And if we're getting married there's nothing you should need to hide from me.'

Luciano sat up, his dark eyes veiled, his lean, strong body taut with tension. 'My father killed my mother when I was three,' he breathed in a constrained undertone. 'She was trying to take me and leave him... He threw her down the stairs and she broke her neck. I saw it happen.'

Jemima froze and then consciously unfroze again to

close her arms protectively round him. 'How horrible for you to be forced to live with a memory like that.'

Luciano was rigid in the circle of her arms. 'It's my past.'

'Yes...*past*,' Jemima stressed, stringing a line of haphazard kisses along the clenched line of his strong jaw until some of his tension eased.

He frowned down at her. 'Doesn't it bother you, knowing what I just told you?'

'Not as much as it bothered you telling me.'

'I've never told anyone before,' he breathed into her hair. 'I used to have nightmares about it.'

'And who comforted you then?' she whispered.

'Agnese...she was always there for me. She saw it happen too.'

'And nobody went to the police?'

'My father had too many friends in high places and corrupt connections within the police. My mother's death was written off as a tragic accident and he got away with it. By the time I was old enough to do any different he was dead. But he would have killed anyone who stood as a witness against him, even if I had been the witness,' he explained heavily. 'That was his life. That is the kind of environment that I grew up with and it is exactly those experiences that made me swear that I would never ever be like my father in any way.'

'And you've lived up to that promise,' Jemima reminded him quietly. 'Haven't you?'

'Yes, *piccolo mia*.'

'So, you should be proud of what you have achieved and celebrating your success,' Jemima told him, shifting her hips in the hope of giving his thoughts a different direction.

Being highly suggestible, Luciano lifted his tousled head with a sudden smile and kissed her again with all the pent-up fire of his hot temperament. She smiled up at him, satisfied that she had finally got behind his barriers, broken through the hard shell to the real man within. He didn't have to love her to confide in her. Somehow at that instant it seemed more than sufficient compensation.

CHAPTER NINE

'COME FOR TEA, said the spider to the fly,' Ellie mocked with a grimace. 'I don't like Sancia.'

Jemima wrinkled her nose. Her best friend, Ellie, was very quick in her judgements but Jemima tried to give everyone a fair hearing. And that included Sancia Abate, the gorgeous blonde who had stepped unannounced and unforeseen out of Luciano's past. After all, Jemima would have been the first to admit that the main source of her unease about Sancia was the other woman's close blood tie to Luciano's celebrated first wife. Luciano, however, had been so casual about the continuing friendship that only an extremely jealous and possessive woman could have been suspicious of the relationship. Sancia was evidently still accepted as family and Jemima was happy to respect that.

In any case, she had to admit that Sancia had proved to be an almost invisible guest over the past two weeks while Luciano had been abroad. For the past three days, Jemima had been entertaining Ellie and her parents' friends and relatives, all of whom Luciano had had flown out for the wedding that was scheduled to take place in forty-eight hours' time. Her parents and their closest friends had already settled into a comfortable routine of strolls on the beach and visits to the village café, while Jemima had whiled away many a happy hour trying on wedding dresses and relaxing with Ellie.

'I mean, what's a blonde that looks like that doing hanging round here on a very quiet island without even a boyfriend in tow?' Ellie remarked suspiciously.

Jemima had learned that Sancia was not only gorgeous to look at but also multitalented. Sancia had written a bestselling biography on her much-loved sister's life and currently seemed to drift between stints as a well-known fashion model and a less-well-known actress. The guest house was situated beyond the castle gardens above the beach, a former boathouse that had been renovated to offer extra accommodation. Bearing in mind the sheer size of the castle, the cottage was virtually never used.

Jemima was wryly amused that she had found it necessary to dress up to visit Sancia. More and more she was making use of the wardrobe Luciano had bought for her, recognising that the garments might be more fashionable and form-fitting than she was accustomed to wearing but were also more flattering in style and shape. To enjoy tea with the glamorous Sancia, she was wearing a lilac skirt and top with an unmistakeable designer edge.

'Oh, you haven't brought Nicky.' Sancia sighed in disappointment as soon as she opened the door. 'Come in.'

'He always has a nap straight after lunch.'

'*Porca miseria!* You sound like one of those rigid English nannies people joke about!' the blonde commented with a teasing smile.

'I hope not...' Jemima stilled on the threshold of a spacious reception room that was dominated by photos and portraits of Gigi Nocella.

'Oh, didn't you know that the guest house is where Luciano keeps his stash of memorabilia?' Sancia remarked in apparent surprise. 'I thought you would have guessed. I mean, there's nothing at all to be seen up at the castle.'

'No, nothing,' Jemima agreed, having naturally noticed that, surprisingly, Luciano had not a single photograph on display anywhere of his late first wife or their little daughter.

'I know. He had the place stripped...the poor guy.' Sancia sighed. 'Once Gigi was gone, he just couldn't live with even the *smallest* reminder of her. It was too painful for him. Haven't you noticed that he never ever mentions her?'

Jemima was not very practised at female games of one-upmanship but she knew enough to know when she was being targeted and she murmured quietly, 'Are we having tea?'

'I'm not very domesticated but I do have the tray ready for us.' Sancia gave her a wide grin, unperturbed by Jemima's cool intonation, and stepped out into the room that Jemima assumed held a kitchen.

Jemima hovered by the window overlooking the fabulous view of the beach before succumbing to a curiosity that she simply couldn't suppress. The room she stood in was ironically both her worst nightmare and her most precious discovery. All around her sat the means to satisfy her curiosity about Luciano's first wife. Giving way to temptation, Jemima wandered around peering at the photos and the paintings.

There was no denying that Gigi Nocella had been superbly photogenic and immensely gifted in the genes department. The brown-eyed blonde, of whom Sancia was but a pale, more youthful copy, was exquisite to a degree very few women were and had reputedly been mesmerising on-screen. And here she was represented in all her earthly glory in various attitudes that ran from young and naïve to sexy and smouldering to pensive and mysterious. But the photos that Jemima paid most heed to were the ones that also contained Luciano.

The first she noted was their wedding photograph, in which he looked ridiculously youthful, reminding her that he had been very young when he married and that Gigi had been several years older.

'He worshipped the ground she walked on,' Sancia murmured from behind Jemima, making her flinch.

'Oh, my goodness, you gave me a fright!' Jemima spun and fanned the air, refusing to react to the blonde's provocative statement.

In any case, she didn't need the verbal commentary when she could see the adoration etched in Luciano's lean dark face as he looked intently at the mother of his daughter. It hurt Jemima to see that light in his eyes. She knew that he would never look at her with that depth of caring and concern. She would never be that important to him or that perfect in looks and figure that every head would turn to watch her walk by. No, she conceded sadly, she was in a totally different category from Gigi and, whether she liked it or not, Luciano would probably not have looked twice at her had his son not looked at Jemima with love first.

But she would have to learn to live with that reality, wouldn't she?

'After the crash, Luciano said he would never ever love a woman again,' Sancia delivered.

'Ah, well, life moves on and now he's getting married and he's starting another family,' Jemima responded with deliberate insensitivity before adding, 'It's different for you, though, as her sister. You'll never be able to replace her and you must miss her terribly.'

Red coins of colour accentuated the blonde's cheekbones. 'You have no idea.'

'I do actually. I didn't know my sister for very long before I lost her but there was a special bond there... at least on my side,' Jemima confided.

With hindsight she had begun to accept that her twin had not had the capacity to care for others in the same way as she did. She could not argue with the evidence and it was surely better for her to remember her sibling as she had been rather than idealise her memory.

'Gigi was irreplaceable,' Sancia told her a tad sharply.

'But I'm not trying to replace her,' Jemima responded quietly. 'How could I? And why would I even want to? Luciano and I have a completely different relationship.'

As Jemima walked back from the beach through

the castle gardens her pale blue eyes were overbright
with tears. She didn't want to let the tears fall, not with
her usual bodyguards bare yards from her, silent and
watchful of her every move. Furthermore she had not
the slightest doubt that anything unusual she did would
be reported straight back to Luciano, who seemed to
worry a great deal about her while he was away from
her. He phoned her several times a day and questioned
her right down to asking what she ate at mealtimes.
And when she had asked him why he bothered when
she had so little news to relate, he had told her teasingly
that he liked the sound of her voice and could listen
to her reciting an old phone book just as happily. The
minutiae of Nicky's day were of equal interest to him
and it was obvious to Jemima that Luciano really did
miss seeing his son. His conversations with her, however, were just polite and sort of flirty, she reasoned
ruefully. He wasn't a teenager, after all, he was a man
of almost thirty-one with sufficient experience to know
exactly how to charm a woman.

Especially if that woman wasn't Gigi Nocella,
Jemima thought, her throat closing over convulsively
on a sob. He wouldn't have had to make a special effort to say the right thing to a woman as perfect as Gigi
had been. So, how often did he go down to visit that
personal shrine in the guest house? If Jemima hadn't
existed and Luciano hadn't been away on business,
would he have been with Sancia right now happily
reminiscing about the old days when his first wife and
child had still been alive? It was hardly any wonder that
Sancia resented Jemima and clearly felt threatened by

her appearance on scene. Nothing could put Gigi more effectively back into the past than her once-besotted widower having another child and taking a second wife to put in Gigi's place.

Well, it wasn't Gigi's place any longer, Jemima told herself urgently. In less than two days Jemima would be Luciano's wife and she could hardly wait! She wasn't so silly as to allow Sancia's mean outlook to affect her personally, was she?

As her mobile phone rang she dug it out, grateful for an interruption that would hopefully give her thoughts a new and more positive direction. When she heard Steven's familiar badgering tones she almost groaned, however, for she had thought she had heard the last from her ex-boyfriend when he had phoned her to say he wouldn't be attending the wedding—he hadn't been invited!—because he knew she was making a dreadful mistake.

'Luciano has turned your head with his wealth,' Steven told her, merely starting a new angle of attack.

'His wealth doesn't matter to me. His kindness does,' Jemima parried, thinking of the generosity of Luciano's invitation to her parents and their friends, who were all enjoying a wonderful holiday in the run-up to their wedding. And by bringing her family and Ellie out to join her, he had ensured that she wasn't lonely and without support.

'You may not see it but I see very clearly that you are paying me back for what happened with Julie.' Steven sighed. 'You weren't able to forgive me.'

'I *did* forgive you, Steven. I simply didn't want to

take back up again where we'd left off and I think that's fair enough,' Jemima fielded. 'I saw you in a different light when you were with my sister.'

'I made a dreadful mistake, Jemima,' Steven groaned. 'But I *do* love you.'

'Not the way you loved her,' Jemima told him without heat.

'That wasn't genuine love and you don't love Luciano either. You're marrying him to keep Nicky,' Steven protested.

Jemima sat down on a stone bench surrounded by glorious rose beds and stared out blindly at the magnificent view of the bay. 'That's not true.'

'Marriage is a sacrament and it shouldn't be used.'

'But I *do* love him,' Jemima heard herself say and her whole mental view of the world lurched as she made that belated discovery. She was thinking about the male who had chilled her at first meeting and travelling at supersonic speed through the whole history of their relationship, ranging from his laughter in bed with her to the brutal background that he had triumphed over.

And there at the very heart of all her turmoil was the love she had neither acknowledged nor understood. She loved Luciano with all her being and easily zeroed in on every kind and caring thing he did for her from his hesitant tendering of his mother's ring for their engagement to his patient, undemanding love for Nicky in which he was willing to wait and earn his son's trust and affection. In the same moment she recognised why her encounter with Sancia and Gigi's shrine in the guest house had distressed her so much. It had hurt to see Luciano's love for her predecessor. It had hurt even more to frankly admit that she could never emulate such a woman to win that level of appreciation. With Luciano, she would always be Nicky's loving stepmother first and his wife second. Second best, second best for all time...

Could she truly live with that?

'Sorry, Steven. I have to go,' she said, cutting the call on Steven's expostulations with relief.

Her face was wet with tears. She had been crying without knowing it and she mopped her face, praying her mascara hadn't run. There could be no pleasure in appreciating that she would always be inferior in her future husband's eyes and heart to his first wife, but she was a practical, realistic woman and there really wasn't much she could do about that hurt. Was there?

She wouldn't even consider abandoning Nicky, for he felt as much her child as if he had been born to her rather than her sister. She saw no advantage to refusing to marry Luciano either. What would that achieve? She didn't want to be Nicky's nanny for the rest of her days or merely Luciano's lover. And if she didn't choose to marry him and give him more children, some other woman eventually would.

Not on my watch, Jemima conceded fierily.

CHAPTER TEN

SOMETHING VERY LIKE panic sent chilling tentacles travelling deep to pierce Luciano's usually rock-solid sense of security. He completed the phone call to his future relative, which had been preceded by one from Agnese. He had made a mistake, a *serious* mistake, he acknowledged with a sinking heart, and now he had to pray that he had sufficient time and the opportunity to put it right. And if he didn't?

Santa Madonna, that option could not even be considered!

Why the hell had he valued his pride above every other thing in his life for so many years? How on earth had he allowed a past bad experience to cast such a dangerous shadow over the present and potentially destroy his future?

And you thought you were so cool, so clever, he reasoned in a daze of growing shock at the mess he had created. But the creed of silence as a form of protection had been bred into his very bones at his father's knee. Never tell, never explain, never apologise. And before he had experienced that one weak moment with

Jemima he had *never* broken that rule. He had kept his secrets. He had kept them from the media too. Indeed he had buried those sleazy secrets deep and had refused even to think about them, for that was the safest, wisest way to hold on to sanity.

He had never dwelt on his mistakes because he was a rational man and it came naturally to him to move on past and not look back at car wrecks. Even so, those mistakes had seriously influenced the choices he had made, he conceded belatedly. Furthermore, Jemima didn't have his conditioning or his inhibitions and she would not understand...

The helicopter came in over the bay while Jemima was having breakfast with everyone in the shaded loggia on the ground floor. Nicky dropped his toast as he waved his hands with excitement, straining in his high chair to get a better view of the craft as it dropped down out of sight to land in the castle grounds.

'Is that Luciano coming back?' Ellie asked uncertainly.

'I doubt it. He's not due until tomorrow,' Jemima said a little tiredly because she had not slept well. 'And he's a stickler for his schedules.'

'I suspect,' her father murmured warmly as he stared over her shoulder, 'that your bridegroom missed you more than you know because here he is now...'

Jemima twisted her head round so fast she risked a whiplash injury and she thrust her chair back and stood up to stare in surprise at the male striding through the gardens towards them. It was, without a doubt, Luciano.

Sheathed in a dark business suit teamed with a white shirt and silvery tie, he looked both formal and formidable. His lean, darkly handsome face was taut, the line of his beautiful mouth forbidding. A jolt of dismay ran through Jemima and quite instinctively she found herself wondering if she had done something wrong.

His stunning dark golden eyes immediately sought hers as though he was looking for something and then he quickly turned his attention on to their guests and his first physical meeting with her parents. To a backdrop of Nicky's squeals of excitement and loud vocal appeals to be noticed, Luciano responded smoothly and pleasantly to the tide of introductions before stooping to detach Nicky from his harness and lift him into his arms.

'Hush,' he said softly to his son while ruffling his hair. 'You can't always be the centre of attention.'

'Well, when he isn't he likes to let us know he doesn't like it!' her father quipped cheerfully. 'He's a terrific little scene stealer.'

'Let me take him,' Jemima's mother urged, holding out her arms. 'You and Jemima should have some time together in peace.'

Nicky complained loudly at the transfer, demanded Jemima with pleading arms and then sobbed. Carlotta came out of the house to help while Jemima hovered, her attention anxiously pinned to Luciano, for all her nervous antennae were still telling her that something was badly wrong. His long, lean, powerful body was incredibly tense, his movements less fluid than usual and his lean, strong face taut with self-discipline.

Oh, my goodness, she thought in sudden consternation. Maybe he had returned early because he had changed his mind about marrying her! It was a nightmare scenario with the wedding guests and her family already staying at the castle, but it was perfectly possible that he had got cold feet and come back early to tell her. Jemima was quite convinced that such disasters had occurred to better women than her and it was surely more likely to happen when a man wasn't in love with the woman he had asked to marry him.

Luciano shot another veiled glance at Jemima. She was pale and there were shadows below her beautiful pale eyes and he could see that she looked nothing like a happy bride on the brink of her wedding. Inwardly he cursed himself again and he reached for her hand.

'Will you come for a walk with me?' he intoned in a roughened undertone. 'We have a visit to make.'

Her brow furrowed as he deftly walked her away from the breakfast table. 'A visit?'

'I believe you had tea with Sancia yesterday—'

'My goodness, the grapevine around here is positively supersonic!' Jemima countered while she thought fast.

'I like to keep an eye on events when I'm unable to be present in person,' Luciano assured her with a perfectly straight face.

Controlling...*much*? But Jemima said nothing because she knew that he was upset and she couldn't bear that. Glancing up at him, she could see the haunted look she had seen before was back in his eyes and she could see that, for all that he looked spectacular, he must have been travelling all night and lines of strain were etched between his classic nose and even more perfect mouth. Of course, if he wanted to cancel the wedding, he would be feeling awfully guilty about it, she thought painfully.

'What did you think of Sancia?'

'We don't have much in common,' Jemima replied mildly.

'She was a bitch to you, wasn't she?' Luciano growled within sight of the guest cottage above the beach.

Taken aback, Jemima came to a halt and stared up at him. 'I—'

'I can be selfish but I'm not stupid…most of the time,' Luciano tacked on, compressing his hard mouth. 'I've been foolish—'

'It's all right…whatever you decide to do, it's all right. Just don't be upset about it,' Jemima mumbled helplessly, resisting the urge to wrap both arms around him and offer him comfort. Even in the overly emotional mood she was in, she knew that was not the normal way to behave when a man dumped you and that the very last thing she should be worrying about was how *he* felt. And yet that urge was engrained in her when he was around, she thought painfully as he closed his hand firmly round hers and urged her on towards the cottage.

'Why are we going to see Sancia?' she prompted uncomprehendingly. 'I admit she wasn't the kindest hostess but I have nothing more to say to her.'

'But I have plenty to say,' Luciano incised, banging on the door with his fist.

Sancia opened the door little more than three seconds later. It was barely nine in the morning but she was wearing a pristine white sundress and had a full face of make-up on, so she had evidently been expecting visitors. 'Luciano…' she said, wreathed with welcoming smiles.

'Sancia…' he grated, moving past her to stare in shock at the array of photographs and paintings decorating the cottage living room. 'What is all this?' he breathed.

'Well, you should know,' the blonde said archly. 'You insisted on giving it to me.'

'You asked me for it—you wanted it for your book,' Luciano reminded her.

Only moments into their visit and Jemima was already feeling better, for she could already see that Luciano had had no part in creating the shrine in the room to his late wife. That, it seemed, had been solely Sancia's doing.

'It's been like this ever since the year she died,' the blonde fielded, playing it for all she was worth.

'You're the only person who has ever used this place.' Luciano released Jemima's hand and swept up a book from the coffee table. 'Wasn't the book enough for you?'

'I don't know what you mean?'

'Sancia, I was married to Gigi for five years. This isn't a biography, it's a work of fiction. You gave her fans what they wanted to read, not the truth. The truth would have been too ugly,' he breathed, his deep, dark drawl roughening along the edges.

Sancia switched to Italian and spoke at length.

'No, we will discuss this in English so that Jemima understands,' Luciano decreed grimly. 'I want to know what Sancia told you yesterday.'

'Nothing that was untrue,' Sancia trilled, sweetly saccharine. 'That you don't like to talk about Gigi and that you *said* you'd never love a woman again.'

Luciano grimaced. 'Sancia! Where is your compassion? Your sister almost destroyed me!'

'There is no need for you to tell—' Sancia began urgently.

'A couple who are about to marry should have no secrets from each other,' Luciano declared, and as Jemima stiffened in surprise he smiled ruefully. 'A very wise woman once told me that but I wasn't listening.'

'But you have never wanted the truth to come out!' Sancia was still arguing. 'You were happy for me to write a whitewash!'

'I've matured.' Luciano tossed the book back down on the table and looked at Jemima. 'Gigi was not the glowing star and wonderful woman described in this book. I married her because she told me I was the father of the child she carried. She was repeatedly unfaithful to me with the leading men in her movies, and the day she died she was leaving me for another man.'

'Oh, no...' Jemima mumbled, pained by the look in his eyes.

'That man, Alessio di Campo, is a famous producer and he was the love of Gigi's life—well, as much as she could love anyone, she loved him,' Luciano revealed doggedly. 'He was a married man with a wife and only when his wife died were the two of them willing to go public about their relationship. Their affair had, however, apparently continued throughout our marriage. I told her that she was welcome to leave but that I would not let her take our daughter, Melita, with her.'

'How can you trust her? She could go to the press with all this!' Sancia screeched accusingly.

'Jemima won't and even if the story was to get out, so what?' Luciano shrugged a broad shoulder with fluid fatalism. 'It's all done and dusted now. To finish the story, Gigi told me that Melita was *not* my daughter but Alessio's,' he revealed heavily. 'I had stayed in a bad marriage for years for my daughter's sake and suddenly she wasn't my child any more. That truth was more devastating than Gigi's departure with Melita that day.'

'It was a cruel lie,' Sancia swore, desperate to be heard again. 'I never believed that!'

'Testing was carried out after the crash,' Luciano cut in flatly, his lean, masculine face unrelentingly grim. 'Melita was *not* my child but I loved her as though she was and had she survived I would have kept her with me had I had the choice. As it was, both mother and child died instantly when the helicopter Alessio had sent to pick them up crashed on the flight to Monaco.'

Jemima's eyes were stinging. Only Sancia's sullen, resentful presence prevented her from saying what she really felt because her heart was bleeding for him. He had been hiding the truth from her all along and she was deeply shaken by the true version of what his marriage had entailed. It had not occurred to her that Gigi could have been anything less than perfect. In reality, though, Gigi had been a horribly disloyal and dishonest partner and Jemima was no longer surprised that Luciano had required DNA testing before he had been prepared to accept Nicky as his son.

'Let's go...' Luciano breathed, curving a protective arm to Jemima's spine.

'I could sell Gigi's *true* story for a fortune,' Sancia remarked quietly.

'Go ahead. I no longer care,' Luciano responded almost cheerfully. 'But if you go naming names you will probably make a lot of dangerous enemies amongst the very people whom you still want to employ you. But that's your business now that I will no longer be settling your bills. My pilot's waiting for you at the helipad. I'm sure I don't need to add that you're no longer welcome here.'

And with that final withering speech they were both back out in the fresh air and sunshine again. Shell-shocked, Jemima leant against Luciano for a few seconds, revelling in the strength of his tall, powerful body and the gloriously familiar scent of him. All she could think about was that Gigi had been a dreadful liar and then Julie had lied to him and cheated him and then Jemima had lied to him as well! How could he ever fully forgive her for having lied to him after what he had had to endure in his first, unhappy marriage?

'You know... I thought you'd got cold feet about the wedding,' she told him dizzily. 'I believed you were back early to dump me—'

'No, I was too scared I was losing you. I didn't know

what Sancia had done but I always suspected she could be poisonous.'

'But how could you even find out that I was seeing her yesterday? The bodyguards?'

'No, Agnese. She's like a bloodhound. She phoned me to tell me that Sancia had invited you and informed me that that was suspicious because Sancia is not friendly towards other women.'

'Why were you paying Sancia's bills?'

'At first I felt sorry for her because she was always overshadowed by Gigi. Of course, she knew all her sister's dark secrets because she worked as Gigi's assistant on the Palermo estate we lived on in those days.' He hesitated. 'With the timing involved, nobody guessed that Gigi had been in the act of leaving me when she died and I told myself that it was my private business. But, more honestly, I chose to save face rather than tell the truth. The paparazzi had dogged us obsessively throughout our marriage because, of course, there were always rumours about Gigi's behaviour but she was never caught out.'

'I can understand you not wanting people to know that she had affairs,' Jemima murmured ruefully. 'It hurt your pride and Sancia played along with that because it suited her to do so.'

'She made a killing on the book because she wrote what Gigi's fans wanted to read. They didn't want to hear about the man-eater with the monstrous ego who seduced me when I was twenty-two and too rich and naïve to smell a rat. Of course, she was already pregnant when she first slept with me.'

'And you didn't even suspect?'

'I was infatuated with her. It was probably a little like the way you reacted to your unknown twin when she first turned up. I only saw what I wanted to see in Gigi and I was flattered by her interest.'

'But the marriage only lasted because of Melita?'

Luciano could not hide his sadness. 'The marriage died within months of Melita's birth. I loved that little girl and she loved me. Gigi had no interest in her daughter but she wouldn't have given up custody of her because she said that would damage her reputation as a mother.'

'And *did* you say that you would never love a woman again after her?'

'Yes,' Luciano admitted freely. 'Because loving Gigi was a horrendous experience and I couldn't forgive myself for being such a fool. I sincerely believed that it would only be safe to love a child, which is why I planned the surrogacy arrangement.'

'You do think in some seriously screwy ways sometimes,' Jemima told him gently.

His nostrils flared as he thrust open a side door into the castle. 'It seemed perfectly logical to me at the time. Gigi did a lot of damage and I didn't want to be burned again.'

'It was still a little over the top,' Jemima criticised. 'You may have decided to live without love but most children want two parents.'

Luciano shot her an impatient look. 'All right, I'm selfish...and maybe I didn't think it all through the way

I should have done. But look how it turned out,' he said with a sudden grin. 'I got you… Have I still got you?'

'It would take more than Sancia to scare me off.'

'Yet you actually thought I could be about to dump you?' An ebony brow quirked in wonderment. 'What makes you so modest? I cut my trip short a day and travelled all night to get to you because I heard that you were upset.'

Jemima stiffened. 'Who *said* I was upset?'

'I promised not to name names,' Luciano revealed.

'I wasn't upset yesterday,' Jemima insisted out of pride. 'I was just working through some stuff and thinking a lot. Getting married is a big challenge.'

'Especially when the groom is someone like me,' Luciano slotted in without hesitation. 'Someone too proud and private to admit that his first marriage was a disaster and that his first child wasn't his child.'

Jemima wrinkled her nose as he walked her up the rear staircase she had never used before. 'But I sort of understand you keeping quiet about that, although that doesn't mean I approve of you being that secretive.'

'And the prospect of marriage must become even more challenging for a woman when the bridegroom refuses to admit that he loves you,' Luciano told her in a rush shorn of the smallest eloquence. 'That wasn't just secretive, that was stupid, because if you'd known how much I love you yesterday you would have laughed in Sancia's face and I wouldn't have been panicked into rushing halfway across the world to assure myself that you weren't going to desert me.'

'I wouldn't desert you…or Nicky,' Jemima added,

still working very slowly through what he had said. 'You love me?'

'Insanely.' A flood of dark colour accentuated his high cheekbones. 'The thought of life without you downright terrifies me. A couple of weeks being without you has proved a chastening experience. I've never missed anyone or anything so much in my life...'

Jemima suddenly realised that they were having a very private conversation in the corridor and she walked on a few steps and thrust open his bedroom door. 'Never missed anyone...'

Luciano leant back against the door to close it fast behind him. 'Jemima, does it take a hammer to knock an idea into your head?' He groaned. 'I phone you every hour on the hour and you think that's normal? I invite your whole family here to keep you company so that you can't even look at another man while I'm away. Don't you ever get suspicious, *piccolo mia*? You think I don't realise that wet blanket, Steven, is sitting out there waiting for you, hoping like hell that I'll screw up and lose you?'

'But I don't fancy Steven...and even when you upset me or I get annoyed with you, I still fancy you,' Jemima confided a little desperately, because he was smiling that wicked smile of his that made her heart beat crazily fast.

'Is that a fact?' Luciano teased, shifting off the door to shed his jacket and jerk loose his tie. 'I had this unrealistic fantasy where I came home and everything would be all right and we would go straight to bed... Don't know what I thought we'd do with all our guests.'

'Everything *is* all right. Our guests are also remarkably good at entertaining themselves,' she opined. 'Oh, by the way, I love you…loads and loads…and it's got nothing to do with your money like Steven thinks.'

'Honestly…you love me?' Luciano growled. 'But why?'

'That's the weird bit… I truly don't know. One minute I was fancying you like mad and the next I was wanting to make your life perfect for you,' Jemima confided with an embarrassed wince.

'Equally weird for me from the very first moment. Took me a long time to realise that not wanting to love again was basically a fear of being hurt again, which is cowardly,' he declared with disdain. 'And then you were there and I liked just about everything about you and it wasn't only sex. I should've told you the truth about Gigi sooner but I suppose I didn't want you to think less of me.'

'How could I think less of you for her bad behaviour?'

Luciano shrugged. 'I love the way you are with Nicky because she was so cold with Melita. Comparisons are tasteless but…'

'So, don't make them.' Jemima unzipped her dress and shimmied out of it while he watched.

'Your parents…' Luciano began, slightly shocked.

'I think everyone will mind their own business rather than ours,' Jemima whispered sagely. 'But you do realise that you still haven't told me who told you that I was upset?'

Luciano expelled his breath on a slow hiss. 'Your father.'

Taken aback, Jemima blinked. 'Say that again?'

'He thinks I make you happy and he likes the fact that I'm honest with him,' Luciano told her guiltily, as if he had been consorting with the enemy. 'I was grateful that he called me.'

Jemima was secretly pleased that the father she loved so much clearly liked and trusted the man she was about to marry. 'I've got no complaints either. We love each other and that's special.'

'Simply finding you was special, *piccolo mia*,' Luciano told her as she unbuttoned his shirt, undid his waistband, sent her fingers roaming over the prominent bulge at his groin with a daring new to both of them and even more thrilling. '*Dio mio*, I love you...'

'Me too...*so much*,' she managed to say just before his mouth came crashing down on hers with all the passion she adored.

Jemima walked down the aisle of the little village church in her lace wedding dress and with her hand on her father's arm. Off the shoulder and styled with tight sleeves and a fitted bodice, her wedding gown made the most of her hourglass figure and the exquisite lace fell to the floor, showing only the toes of the extravagant shoes she wore.

Luciano was so entranced by the sight of her that he couldn't look away and play it cool. His son, Nicky, sat on his grandmother's lap near the front of the church and began to bounce and hold out his arms when he laid eyes on Jemima, the closest thing to a mother he would ever know. Luciano smiled, the happiest he had ever been in his chequered life and far happier than he had ever even hoped to be.

Jemima focused on the man she loved and her heart jumped behind her breastbone. All hers at last, officially, finally, permanently hers. As if a wedding ring were the equivalent of a padlock, she scolded herself. It was the love she saw in his beautiful dark eyes that would hold him and she rejoiced in the thought of the future that awaited them and their son.

EPILOGUE

'IL CAPO!' AGNESE SIGNALLED Jemima from the door of
the castle with a beatific smile that said that all was now
right with the housekeeper's world because Luciano
was finally home again after a week away on business.

Jemima thought back four years to the days when
the elderly Agnese, Luciano's fiercest admirer, had
still been unsure of her former charge's second wife.
She and Agnese had started out being excruciatingly
polite to each other while Jemima had become friendlier with the housekeeper's daughter, Carlotta, whose
English had come on as quickly as Jemima's Italian
during the first year of her marriage. And then Concetta, their first child, had been born and Agnese had
crumbled like a meringue at first sight of Il Capo's
daughter to reveal the kindly, loving woman she hid
behind her tough little image.

After Concetta, the nursery had got even busier and
had had to expand because two children had been born
to swell the family. Jemima's second pregnancy had
produced twin boys, Marco and Matteo, and she had
decided to take a break from the production line for

a year or two at least. Three little boys ranging from
Nicky, who was almost five, and the twins, who were
two years old, had proved quite a handful. Concetta
was three, clever and well behaved, certainly easier to
control than three rumbustious little boys. Jemima's
daughter was very fond of raising her brows in the
boys' direction and mimicking her father with an air
of female superiority.

Jemima's life had changed so rapidly from the moment she had become a mother for the first time after
Nicky that she sometimes could hardly recall the period before she had met Luciano. Real life and fulfilling
happiness had begun for her in Sicily at the *castello*.
Occasionally she had thought sadly about the job she
had left behind, but caring for Nicky had kept her very
busy and Concetta's arrival had persuaded Jemima that
she was perfectly happy shaping her routine round her
husband and children. Such an existence might not be
perfect for everyone, but it was perfect for her.

She adored Luciano and she adored her kids and
her home and the staff who looked after them so well.
She never ever forgot either to be grateful for her good
fortune. Luciano had bought a comfortable house for
her parents back in the UK, but they remained regular visitors to the island, most often staying in the cottage by the beach. Her husband had become almost
as fond of his in-laws as his wife. He appreciated the
retired couple's loving interest in their grandchildren
and rarely went to the UK without taking them out to
dinner. Jemima's friend, Ellie, was a regular visitor as

well, but there had been no further contact from Steven, who had married a couple of years back.

Now awaiting Luciano's arrival, Jemima smoothed her hands down over the elegant blue dress she wore with the most ridiculously high heels in her wardrobe. He bought her shoes everywhere he went without her because he knew that, even though she preferred to spend most of her time at home rather than shopping or partying as she could have done, she got a kick out of wearing that kind of footwear. It was the type of thoughtfulness and all the little caring touches that accompanied it that made Jemima such an adoring wife.

The shouts of three little boys backed by the far more muted tones of her little daughter warned Jemima that Luciano was in the hall. She grinned as he raised his voice to be heard above the hubbub and then there was silence, the sound of quick steps across the tiles as he made his escape and the door opened.

And there he stood, her beautiful Luciano, who still thrilled her as much at first glance as he had five years earlier. 'You look very beautiful, Signora Vitale,' he told her teasingly.

She encountered his stunning dark golden eyes and her heart sang as she surged across the room to throw herself into his arms. 'I missed you.'

Luciano gazed down at her with smouldering appreciation. 'The kids are waiting in the hall.'

'They want to see you too.'

'Can't be in two places at once, *amata mia*,' he husked, claiming a passionate kiss with raw, hungry enthusiasm.

'Carlotta will distract them,' Jemima mumbled.

'We're being selfish,' he groaned, lean brown hands worshipping her generous curves. 'But I can't… Bedtime's hours away,' he muttered defensively.

'So it is… I love you,' Jemima confided, enchanted by the level of passionate appreciation in his smouldering scrutiny, for it was wonderful to feel that desirable to the man she loved.

'Not one half as much as I love and need you,' Luciano countered. 'It isn't possible, *amata mia*.'

'What have I told you about that negative outlook of yours?' Jemima censured, backing down on the sofa in what was a decidedly inviting way with happiness and amusement and passion all bubbling up together inside her and making her feel distinctly intoxicated on love.

* * * * *

THE GREEK
DEMANDS HIS HEIR

CHAPTER ONE

'OH, YES, I should mention that last week I ran into your future father-in-law, Rodas,' Anatole Zikos said towards the end of the congratulatory phone call he had made to his son. 'He seemed a little twitchy about when you might...*finally*...be setting a date for the wedding. It has been three years, Leo. When are you planning to marry Marina?'

'She's meeting me for lunch today,' Leo divulged with some amusement, unperturbed by the hint of censure in his father's deep voice. 'Neither of us has any desire to sprint to the altar.'

'After three years, believe me, nobody will accuse you of sprinting,' Anatole said drily. 'Are you sure you *want* to marry the girl?'

Leo Zikos frowned, level black brows lifting in surprise. 'Of course I do—'

'I mean, it's not as if you *need* Kouros Electronics these days.'

Leo stiffened. 'It's not a matter of need. It's a matter of common sense. Marina will make me the perfect wife.'

'There is no such thing as a perfect wife, Leo.'

Thinking of his late and much-lamented mother,

Leo clamped his wide sensual mouth firmly closed lest he say something he would regret, something that would shatter the closer relationship he had since attained with the older man. A wise man did not continually look back to a better-forgotten past, he reminded himself grimly, and Leo's childhood in a deeply troubled and unhappy family home definitely fell into that category.

At the other end of the silent line, Anatole made a soft sound of frustration. 'I want you to be happy in your marriage,' he admitted heavily.

'I will be,' Leo told his father with supreme assurance and he came off the phone smiling.

Life was good, in fact life was *very* good, Leo acknowledged with the slow-burning smile on his lean, darkly handsome face that many women found irresistible. He had just that morning closed a deal that had enriched him by millions, hence his father's phone call. His father was quite correct in assuming that Leo did not need to marry Marina simply to inherit her father's electronics company as a dowry. But then Leo had never wanted to marry Marina for her money.

At eighteen, a veteran of the wretched warfare between his ill-matched parents, Leo had drawn up a checklist of the attributes his future wife should have. Marina Kouros ticked literally every box. She was wealthy, beautiful and intelligent as well as being a product of the same exclusive upbringing he had enjoyed himself. They had a great deal in common but they were neither in love nor possessive of each other. Objectives like harmony and practicality would illuminate their shared future rather than dangerous passion and horrendous emotional storms. There would be no nasty surprises along the way with Marina, a young woman Leo had first met in nursery school.

It was forgivable for him to feel just a little self-satisfied, Leo reasoned as his limo dropped him off at the marina in the French Riviera where his yacht awaited him. Exuding quiet contentment, he boarded *Hellenic Lady,* one of the largest yachts in the world. He had made his first billion by the age of twenty-five and five years on he was enjoying life as never before while at the same time ensuring that, although the cutthroat ambiance of the business world was where he thrived, he still took time off to recuperate after working eighteen-hour days for weeks on end.

'Good to have you on board again, sir,' his English captain assured him. 'Miss Kouros is waiting for you in the saloon.'

Marina was scrutinising a painting he had recently bought. A tall slender brunette with an innate elegance he had always admired, his fiancée spun round to greet him with a smile.

'I was surprised to get your text,' Leo confided, giving her a light kiss on the cheek in greeting. 'What are you doing in this neck of the woods?'

'I'm on the way to a country house weekend with friends,' Marina clarified. 'I thought it was time we touched base. I believe my father has been throwing out wedding hints—'

'News travels fast,' Leo commented wryly. 'Apparently your father is becoming a little impatient.'

Marina wrinkled her nose and strolled restively across the spacious room. 'He has his reasons. I suppose I should admit that I've been a little indiscreet of late,' she remarked with a careless shrug of a silk-clad shoulder.

'In what way?' Leo prompted.

'I thought we agreed that until we got married we wouldn't owe each other any explanations,' Marina reminded him reprovingly.

'We may have agreed to go our separate ways until marriage forces us to settle down,' Leo agreed, 'but, as your fiancé, I think I have the right to know what you mean by "indiscreet".'

Marina shot him a bright angry glance. 'Oh, Leo, don't be tiresome! It's not as if you *care*. It's not as if you love me or anything like that!'

Leo remained silent, having long since learnt that listening was by far the best tool to use to calm Marina's quick temper and draw her out.

'Oh, all right!' Marina snapped with poor grace, tossing her silk scarf down on a luxurious sofa in a petulant gesture. 'I've been having a hot affair…and there's been some talk, for which I'm very sorry, but, really, how am I supposed to stop people from gossiping about me?'

His broad shoulders squared below his exquisitely tailored jacket. 'How hot is hot?' he asked mildly.

Marina rolled her eyes and burst out laughing. 'You don't have an atom of jealousy in your entire body, do you?'

'No, but I'd still like to know what's got your father so riled up that he wants us to immediately set a wedding date.'

Marina pulled a face. 'Well, if you must know, my lover is a married man…'

Leo's stunning clean-cut bone structure tautened

almost infinitesimally, his very dark eyes shaded by lush black lashes narrowing. He was taken aback and disappointed in her. Adultery was never acceptable in Leo's book and he had made the fatal mistake of assuming that Marina shared that moral outlook. As a child he had lived with the consequences of his father's long-running affair for too many years to condone extra-marital relations. It was the only inhibition he had in the sex department: he would never ever get involved with a married woman.

'Oh, for goodness' sake, Leo!' Marina chided, her face colouring now with angry defensiveness in receipt of his telling silence. 'These things always burn out—you know that as well as I do!'

'I won't pretend to approve. Furthermore that kind of entanglement will damage your reputation...and therefore mine,' Leo reproved coolly.

'I could say that about the little lap-dancer you were sailing round the Med with last summer. You could hardly describe that slutty little baggage as adding lustre to your sophisticated image!' Marina remarked cuttingly.

Predictably, Leo did not even wince, but she flushed uncomfortably at the look he shot her. But then very few things put Leo Zikos out of countenance and regular sex was as important to him as ordered meals and exercise and indeed rated no higher than either by him. He was a very logical male and he saw no need to explain himself when he and Marina had yet to share a bed. The very fact that they had both chosen to retain the freedom of taking other lovers during their long engagement had convinced them that it would be much more straightforward just to save the sex for when they were married.

There is no such thing as a perfect wife, his father had said only an hour or so earlier, but Leo had not expected to be presented with the definitive proof of that statement quite so soon. His high opinion of Marina had been damaged because it was obvious that she saw nothing inherently wrong with sleeping with another woman's husband. Had his own views become so archaic, so unreasonable? Was he guilty of allowing childhood experiences to influence his adult judgement too much? He was well aware that he had friends who engaged in extra-marital affairs, but he would never accept such behaviour from anyone close to him or indeed within his own home.

'I'm sorry but I've had Father on my case. He's not ready to retire and let you take over yet but he's terrified that I'll scare you off,' Marina confided ruefully. 'As I supposedly did with your brother—'

Leo tensed, disliking the reminder that until today Marina's single flaw in his judgement was the reality that she had once enjoyed an ill-judged one-night stand with the younger half-brother whom Leo loathed. That Bastien had treated Marina appallingly in the aftermath was another thing Leo never forgot for, more than anything else, Marina was virtually Leo's best friend and he had always trusted her implicitly.

'Perhaps we should set a wedding date to keep everybody happy,' the brunette suggested wryly. 'I may only be twenty-nine but Father's already getting scared we're getting too old to deliver the grandkids he wants.'

Leo frowned, barely contriving to suppress the need to flinch when she mentioned children. He still wasn't ready to become a father. Parenting required a level of maturity and unselfishness that he was convinced he had yet to attain.

'What about fixing on October for the wedding?' Marina proposed with the sort of cool that implied she had not the faintest idea of his unease. 'I'm no Bridezilla and that would give me three months to make the preparations. I'm thinking of a very boho casual do in London with only family and our closest friends attending.'

They lunched out on deck, catching up on news of mutual friends. It was very civilised and not a single cross word was exchanged. Once Marina had departed, Leo reminded himself soothingly that he had not lost his temper. Even though he had agreed to the wedding date, however, his strong sense of dissatisfaction lingered. Even worse, that reaction was backed by an even more unexpected feeling, because suddenly Leo was astounded to register that what he truly felt was...*trapped*.

'Nonsense, Grace. Of course you'll go to Turkey with Jenna,' Grace's aunt, Della Donovan, sliced through her niece's protests in her usual brusque and bossy manner. 'A free holiday? Nobody in their right mind would turn their nose up at that!'

Grace gazed out stonily at the pretty garden behind her aunt and uncle's substantial house in north London. Her thoughts were in turmoil because she was trying to come up fast with a polite excuse to avoid the supposed treat of a holiday with her cousin.

'I mean, you've sat all your stupid exams now, haven't you?' her cousin, Jenna, piped up from the leather sofa in the snug beside the kitchen where Grace was seated with Jenna's mother. Mother and daughter were very similar, both of them tall, slender blondes in stark contrast to Grace, who was small and curvy with a fiery mane of red hair and freckles.

'Yes, but—' Her pale green eyes troubled, Grace bit back the admission that she had been planning to work every possible extra hour at a local bar so that she could save up some money to cushion her when she returned to university at the end of the summer. Any overt reference to her need for financial support was always badly received by her aunt and regarded as being in poor taste. On the other hand, although her aunt was a high-powered lawyer and her uncle a very well-paid business executive, Grace had only ever been given money when she worked for it. From a very early age, Grace had learned the many differences between her standing and Jenna's within the same household.

Jenna had received pocket money while Grace had received a list of household chores to be carried out. It had been explained to her when she was ten years old that she was not their *real* daughter, would never inherit anything from her aunt and uncle and would have to make her own way in adult life. Thus, Jenna had attended a fee-paying school while Grace had attended the comprehensive at the end of the road. Jenna had got her own horse and riding lessons while, in return for the occasional lesson, Grace had got to clean the riding-school stables five days a week after school. Jenna had had birthday parties and sleepovers, which

Grace had been denied. Jenna had got to stay on at
school, sit her A-levels and go straight to university
and at twenty-five years of age worked for a popular
fashion magazine. Grace, on the other hand, had had
to leave school at sixteen to become a full-time carer
for Della's late mother, Mrs Grey, and those years
of care and the strain of continuing her studies on a
part-time basis had swallowed up what remained of
Grace's far from carefree teenage years.

Complete shame at the bitterness of her thoughts
flushed Grace's heart-shaped face. She knew she had
no right at all to feel bitter because those years of
caring for an invalid had been payback to the family
who had cared for *her* as a child, she reminded herself
sternly. The Donovans, after all, had taken Grace in
after her mother's death when nobody else had wanted
her. Without her uncle's intervention she would have
ended up in the foster-care system and while the Donovans might not have given her love or equality with
their own daughter they *had* given her security and
the chance to attend a decent school.

So what if she was still the modern-day equivalent
of a Victorian charity child or poor relation within
their home? That was a comparatively small price to
pay for regular meals and a comfortable bedroom, she
told herself firmly. She always reminded herself of
that truth whenever her uncle's family demanded that
she make herself useful, which generally entailed biting her tongue and showing willing even if she didn't
feel willing. Sometimes though she feared she might
explode from the sheer effort required to suppress her
temper and watch every word she said.

'Well, then, I suppose I'm going to be stuck with

you,' Jenna lamented, sounding far younger than her years. 'I can hardly go on a girlie holiday alone, can I? And none of my mates can get time off to join me. Believe me, you're my very last choice, Grace.'

Grace compressed her soft full mouth and pushed her rippling fall of fiery hair back from her taut brow where a stress headache was beginning to tighten its grip. Her cousin's best friend, Lola, who had originally planned to accompany Jenna, had broken both legs in a car accident. Sadly that was the only reason that Grace was being invited to take Lola's place and, equally sadly, Grace didn't want to accompany Jenna even though it was a very long time since Grace had enjoyed a holiday.

The unhappy truth was that Jenna didn't like Grace. Jenna had *never* liked Grace and even as adults the cousins avoided spending time together. A much-adored only child, Jenna had thoroughly resented the arrival of another little girl in her home and Grace wasn't even sure she could blame her cousin for her animosity. The Donovans had hoped that their daughter would see Grace as a little sister, but perhaps the fact that only a year separated the two girls in age had roused competitive instincts in Jenna instead and the situation had only worsened when Grace had unfailingly outshone Jenna in the academic stakes and eventually gone on, in spite of her disrupted education, to study medicine.

'I'm afraid at such short notice Grace is your only option.' Della directed a look of sympathetic understanding at her daughter. 'But I'm sure she'll do her best to be good company.'

Jenna groaned. 'She barely drinks. She doesn't

have a boyfriend. She doesn't *do* anything but study. She's like a throwback to the nineteen fifties!'

Della sent Grace an exasperated look. 'You will go with Jenna, won't you?' she pressed. 'I don't want to go to the expense of changing the name on the booking only for you to drop out.'

'I'll go if Jenna really wants me to…' Grace knew when to beat a strategic retreat because crossing Della Donovan was never a good idea.

While she continued to live below the Donovans' roof and paid only a modest amount of rent, Grace knew she had to toe the line in any family crisis, regardless of whether or not it suited her to do so. As a child she had learned the hard way that her compliance was taken for granted and that any kind of refusal or reluctance would be greeted with the kind of shocked reproach that screamed of ingratitude.

For that reason the cash fund she had been hoping to top up to help her through term time would have to take a setback. More worryingly though, could she even hope to still have a job to return to if she took a week off at the height of summer when the bar was busy? Her boss would have to hire a replacement. She suppressed a sigh.

'We're so lucky I thought to renew your passport when I was still hoping to take Mum away for a last holiday…' Della's voice faded and her eyes filmed over at the recollection of her elderly parent's passing.

'I haven't really got any clothes for a beach holiday,' Grace warned mother and daughter, conscious that Jenna was extremely snobbish about fashion and very conscious of appearances.

'I'll see what I can find you from my cast-offs,' Jenna remarked irritably. 'But I'm not sure my stuff will stretch to your big boobs and even bigger behind. For a wannabe doctor, you're very laid-back about having a healthy body image.'

'I don't think I can fight my natural body shape,' Grace responded with quiet amusement, for she had grown past the stage where Jenna's taunts about her curves could inflict lasting damage. Yes, Grace would very much have liked to be born able to eat anything she liked and remain naturally thin but fate wasn't that kind and Grace had learned to work with what she had and exercise regularly.

A door slammed noisily and Grace came suddenly awake, sitting up with a start and swiftly realising with a sinking heart where she was.

'I am sorry but it is forbidden for people to sleep here. It is a reception area,' the young woman behind the desk told her apologetically.

Grace threaded unsteady fingers through her tousled mane of hair and rose to her feet, glancing at the clock on the wall with relief. It was after ten in the morning and hopefully she could now return to the apartment she was supposed to be sharing with her cousin.

The blazing row she had had with Jenna late the night before returned to haunt her. So far, the holiday had been a disaster. Possibly it had been rather naïve of Grace to assume that her cousin would not be on a holiday man hunt when she already had a steady boyfriend back home. Unhappily Grace now knew differently. Jenna had only wanted her cousin for company until she found a suitable holiday fling and now that she had found him she simply wanted Grace to vanish. And unfortunately for Grace, Jenna had met Stuart the very first day. He was a banker, loud-spoken and flashy, but her cousin was really keen on him. For the past two nights, Jenna had told Grace that she could not come back to the apartment they were sharing because she wanted to spend the night there with Stuart. Grace had sat up reading in Reception that first night but when Jenna tried to throw her out a second time she had stood her ground and argued.

'I've got nowhere else to go,' she had pointed out to her cousin. 'I don't want to sit up all night in Reception again!'

'If you were halfway normal, you'd have found a man of your own by now!' Jenna had snapped. 'Stuart and I want to be alone.'

'It's a one-room apartment, Jenna. There isn't room for anyone to be alone in a one-room apartment. Couldn't you go back to *his* place tonight?' Grace had dared to suggest.

'He's sharing with a crowd of six blokes. We'd have even less privacy there. In any case, my parents *paid* for our apartment. This is *my* holiday and if it's not convenient for me to have you staying with me, you *have* to get out!' Jenna hissed with a resentful toss of her head.

Recalling that final exchange, Grace grimaced and knocked on the apartment door rather than risk utilising her key because she did not want to interrupt the lovebirds. It was a surprise when Jenna opened the door. Her cousin was already fully dressed and, astonishingly, her blonde cousin smiled at her. 'Come in,' she urged. 'I was just having breakfast. Do you want a cup of tea?'

'I'd kill for a cup.' Grace studied the bathroom door. 'Is Stuart still here?'

'No, he left early. He's off scuba-diving today and I don't know if I'll be seeing him tonight. I thought you and I could go to that new club that's opening up.'

Relieved by Jenna's friendlier attitude while being irritated that Stuart's elusiveness had caused it, Grace nodded. 'If you like.'

Her cousin clattered busily round the tiny kitchen area. 'Stuart wants to cool it...thinks we're moving too far too fast—'

'Oh...' Grace made no further comment, knowing how touchy Jenna could be, confiding in you one moment and snapping your nose off the next.

'There's plenty more fish in the sea!' Jenna declared, slamming the fridge door and straightening, blonde hair flying round her angry face. 'If he comes calling again, he won't find me waiting for him.'

'No,' Grace agreed.

'Maybe you'll meet someone tonight,' her cousin mused. 'I mean, it's past time you leapt off the old virgin wagon and got a life!'

'How do you know I haven't already?' Grace enquired.

'Because you always come home at night and never that late. Know what I think? You're too fussy.'

'Possibly,' Grace conceded, sipping her tea while wondering how soon she could make her excuses, strip off and get into bed to catch up on her sleep.

Jenna's entire world seemed to revolve around the man in her life and she got terribly insecure if she didn't have one. Grace's world, however, revolved round her studies. She had worked incredibly hard to win a place at medical school, was currently at the top of her class and was convinced that men could be a dangerous distraction. Nothing was going to come between Grace and her dream of becoming a really useful person with the medical knowledge and the skills to help others. After all, she had been raised with the warning story of how her mother had screwed up her life by relying on the wrong man.

On the other hand, Grace also knew that sooner or later she would have to find out what sex was all about. How could she possibly advise her future patients if she didn't have that all-important personal experience? But she had yet to meet anyone she wanted to become intimate with and thought it was very sad that something more than logic was required to fuel attraction between a man and a woman. After all, if only logic had ruled, Grace would have become involved with her best friend and study partner, Matt.

Matt was loyal, kind and thoughtful, exactly the sort of man she respected. But if Matt, in his wire-rimmed spectacles and the sweaters his auntie knitted for him, had threatened to take his shirt off she would have run a mile. There was not even the smallest spark on her side of the fence but she kept on trying to feel that spark because she knew that Matt would make a wonderful partner.

Leo stood in the rooftop bar admiring a bird's-eye view of Turunc Bay. By night the busy resort of Marmaris encircled it like a multicoloured jewelled necklace. Flaring scarlet lights in the night sky announced the grand opening of the Fever nightclub. Leo smiled. Rahim, Leo's partner in Fever, knew how to publicise such events and attract the attention of the tourists.

'You've done an amazing job here,' Leo commented approvingly, gazing down through the glass and steel barriers at the packed dance floor.

'Let me give you a *proper* tour,' Rahim urged, keen to show off his masterpiece. A renowned architect and interior designer, he had good reason to want to show off the sleek contemporary lines of his creation. Having delivered exactly what he had promised, Rahim was keen to interest Leo in making another, even larger investment.

Almost a week of solitary introspection on board *Hellenic Lady* had driven Leo to the edge of cabin fever. He was fed up with work, sick of his own company but in no real mood for anyone else's. He strolled down the illuminated staircase with Rahim, his bodyguards surrounding him. The noise of the music was such that he caught only one word in two spoken to him. Rahim was talking about an exclusive hotel complex he wanted to build further along the coast but Leo was not in the right mood to discuss the project. From the landing he gazed down at the crowded floor and that was when he saw her standing by the corner of the brilliantly lit bar, light shining off hair an eye-catching shade of metallic copper...

Her? Just another woman, his brain labelled while his brooding gaze clung to her triangular face. He tore his attention from the fey quality of her delicately pointed features. *Fey?* he silently repeated to himself. Where had he got that strange word from? He noted a lush full pink mouth and the curling mass of glorious red hair snaking down her narrow spine. More red than copper, it also looked natural. His attention lingered, positively drinking in the swooping curves lovingly delineated by a pale lace dress. She had the figure of a fertility goddess with high full breasts, a tiny, highly feminine waist and a voluptuous bottom. His long brown fingers curled round the guard rail, a spooked sensation making the hair rise at the nape of his neck even as the throbbing pulse at his groin reacted and swelled with a very male lack of conscience or morality.

He couldn't remember when he had last been with a woman, an acknowledgement that almost shocked Leo back to reality. Of course, when he was working he would never waste time seeking out a woman... and when he *wasn't*? The necessity of explaining his engagement and specifying no-strings-attached up-front had unequivocally cooled his libido. But now, without the smallest warning, he was recalling Marina's married lover and he was angrily asking himself why he had bothered to halt his high sex drive. After all, Marina didn't care what he did as long as he didn't interfere with her pleasures. And was that truly what he wanted from his future wife? A woman who would never question where he went or what he did? Or demand that he *love* her?

Of course it was what he wanted, he reasoned with growing impatience, particularly when the alternative was jealous, debilitating scenes. Marina's affair had put him on edge but did that affair offend him so much that he intended to break off the engagement and start looking for a more puritanical bride? That would be nonsensical, he decided squarely. He would never know any woman as well as he knew Marina Kouros.

Struggling to suppress his unusually troubled and uneasy thoughts, Leo focused on the redhead's glorious shape. Hunger filled the hollow inside him and it was the sort of hunger he hadn't felt in years, gnawing powerfully at him with painful persistence, ignoring his rigorous efforts to pursue a functional conversation with Rahim. In an abrupt movement of rejection, he looked away from the redhead, but every muscle in his big well-built body snapped taut. Nerves he hadn't known he had jangled like alarm bells until Leo was forced to glance back to the corner of the bar lest he lose sight of the woman. What was it about her? Perhaps he should find out.

In receipt of a chilling glance from Jenna, who was standing at the bar with Stuart, Grace hurriedly turned her head away, colour sparking high over her cheekbones. Stuart had gatecrashed their night out. Jenna had been overjoyed and within minutes of Stuart's appearance had made it clear that Grace was a gooseberry. Clutching the drink that Stuart had insisted on buying her, Grace sipped the sickly sweet concoction and wondered what she was going to do with the rest of her evening. Where was she to go? At least in a crowd she was virtually invisible and attracting no particular attention.

Jenna pushed her way through the crush and settled impatient blue eyes on Grace. 'Why are you still here? I assumed you'd have left by now.'

Grace straightened. 'I'm coming back to the apartment tonight,' she warned her cousin. 'I've spent two nights sitting up in Reception and I'm not doing it again.'

'I can't believe how selfish you're being!' Jenna complained. 'You wouldn't even be having a holiday if it wasn't for me!'

'Change the tune,' Grace advised ruefully, weary of the constant battle to restrain her own nature and simply wanting to be herself. 'The "be grateful, Grace" one is getting old. You asked me on this holiday and I'm afraid you're stuck with me until we go home.'

As Grace averted her attention from her cousin's furious face she noticed a man standing on the stairs watching her. He was drop-dead beautiful, Mr Fantasy in the flesh with black hair, gypsy-gold skin and stunning symmetrical features. He was also tall, broad-shouldered and surprisingly formally clad in a business suit, as were his companions. Somehow, though, she couldn't drag her eyes from him for long enough to scrutinise the other men. His brows were dark and straight, his eyes deep set, glittering in the flickering lights, his nose a classic arch, his mouth a sensual masterpiece.

'*Please* don't come back to the apartment tonight,' Jenna pleaded. 'I haven't got much time left to be with Stuart...'

Stuart lived in London too and Grace marvelled at her cousin's lack of pride. He'd already spelled out the message that he wanted nothing more than a fling. Jenna flung her a last look of angry appeal before turning on her heel to return to Stuart. As Grace turned away, intending to leave the club and find a quiet café where she could read the book in her bag, she almost tripped over the large man in her path.

'Mr Zikos would like you to join him in the VIP section for a drink.'

Involuntarily, Grace raised a brow as she glanced back at the stairs. Mr Zikos? He nodded acknowledgement and suddenly he smiled at her and in the space of a second he went from stunning to downright breathtaking, the clear-cut austere lines of his darkly handsome face slashed by an almost boyish grin that was utterly and incredibly appealing. Later, Grace swore her heart, always the most reliable of organs around men, leapt in her chest and bounced with enthusiasm, leaving her feeling seriously short of breath and oddly dizzy.

A drink? The VIP section? What did she have to lose? A bouncer undid the ceremonial velvet rope cutting off the stairs and Grace unfroze, moving forward with the strangest sense of anticipation.

CHAPTER TWO

LEO EXTENDED A lean tanned hand with unexpected
formality. 'Leos Zikos. My friends call me Leo.'

Grace touched his fingers in a glancing collision
that made her teeth grit at her own ineptitude. But up
close, he was so tall, so dark, so strikingly handsome
that he unnerved her and given the smallest chance
to scamper back down the short flight of stairs without making a fool of herself she would have fled.
'Grace Donovan,' she supplied a little gruffly, her
heart beating very fast in what felt like her throat as
she hurriedly sat down on the seat he indicated and
nodding belated recognition of the presence of a second, smaller man.

'Irish?' Leo quirked a brow.

'My mother was but I'm from London.'

Leo asked her what she would like to drink.

'Something plain and simple. This…' Grace indicated the glass in her hand with its elaborate green
concoction and umbrella with a faint wrinkling of her
nose '…is like a sugar bomb.'

After introducing her to Rahim, Leo informed her
that they owned the club. Grace told him that she was
a student on holiday with her cousin. A waiter ar-

rived with a tray and champagne was served with a flourish. The first waiter was closely followed by two more, who presented plates of delicate little snacks. Leo asked her what music she would like and within the minute the DJ himself was surging upstairs and standing right in front of her while she told him.

At first Grace was entranced by the heady assault of Leo's full attention and she sipped and she nibbled, leaning closer to politely listen to the two men discuss the couples-only complex that Rahim wanted to design. By the time the older man had extracted a plan from an inner pocket along with photos of the site and its superb beach, Grace was getting bored and, what was more, by then her favourite song was playing and she scrambled up off her seat to stand at the rail, her feet shifting in time to the throbbing beat of the music.

'Dance?' she directed hopefully at Leo, who was welded to the spot by the luscious view of her swaying hips.

He grimaced. 'I don't,' he told her without apology, fighting the swelling at his groin.

'No problem,' Grace told him with an easy smile and a glint in her green eyes as she headed back down the stairs to the dance floor. Just for one night, she thought rebelliously, her thoughts still dwelling on Jenna's humiliating attacks, she was going to be herself, her *real* self that she never dared to show at home. And that meant that she would do and say what she wanted, rather than maintaining her usual quiet role in which she worked to politely conform and meet other people's expectations.

Leo was stunned by her departure. There had been no fuss, no drama, just an unobtrusive determination to do as she liked rather than try to please him. She hadn't flirted or flattered either. His straight brows pleated in frank bewilderment. Women didn't behave like that around Leo. Even Marina, who liked her own way, tailored herself to a neat fit of his preferences while in his company.

'I believe you have met a woman with a mind of her own,' Rahim remarked. 'And talking about such women, I am married to one and if I am not home soon, I will be unpopular.'

Leo stood at the rail, broad shoulders straight as an axe blade and rigid with tension until he relocated Grace again. He noted that she was dancing just at the edge of the floor and he wondered if she planned to join him again. Or was she expecting him to chase after her? Leo didn't chase: he had never had to go to that much effort with a woman. Consequently, he should've been irritated by her behaviour but he was not and he didn't understand that.

What was it about her? She had extraordinary eyes, he recalled, as pale and translucent a green as a piece of sea glass he had once picked up off a beach as a boy. And just as the sea fascinated him, she did as well. He was down the stairs before he even knew he was planning to retrieve her.

'Can't...' he informed her with a wry look when she studied him expectantly. 'No sense of rhythm.'

Leo stood there in front of Grace like a very large statue frozen in place. Her breath hitched in her throat as she looked up into his exotically dark eyes, noting the luxuriance of his black lashes. He was gorgeous. Did he really need to dance? a little voice enquired wryly inside her head.

'Anyone can dance,' Grace told him softly.

He bent his arrogant dark head, his big body still infuriatingly rigid in stance. 'I don't do anything that I can't do superlatively well.'

Grace grinned at that Alpha male excuse and planted her hands on his lean hips. *'Move,'* she urged him, amused against her will by his frozen stance. *'Feel* the beat...'

The only thing Leo felt as she tugged him to her to demonstrate that elusive rhythm was the punch of lust that almost left him light-headed as he looked down into her laughing sea-glass eyes. Women didn't ever laugh *at* Leo. They laughed *with* him. He shifted his lean hips in response to her guidance, but only to take advantage of the opportunity to yank her closer and line up that teasing, tantalising mouth of hers with his own.

In the space of a heartbeat, Grace travelled from amusement to another place entirely and it was a shockingly unfamiliar place. She had no experience of passion and suddenly there it was, shamelessly smashing down her defences and powered solely by the hungry, scorching demand of his mouth. For a split second she stiffened in shock and then she turned boneless, liquid heat rolling through her veins. His tongue plundered the semi-closed seam of her lips and she parted them for him, head falling back on her shoulders as he took immediate advantage. He plundered the moist, tender interior of her mouth with an acute sense of the rhythm he had denied, sending an electrifying shudder of piercing sexual pleasure travelling through her.

Leo lifted his head, closed a hand firmly over hers

and urged her back up the stairs. Grace blinked like a sleepwalker suddenly forced awake, astonishment rising inside her that a man could actually make her feel like that…all shaky and molten and needy, her nipples tight and aching, warmth and dampness gathering between her thighs. Her own response was a revelation to her. Yes, he did kiss superlatively well, she acknowledged dizzily, and didn't that make him the perfect man for her sexual experiment? Presumably if he was that good at kissing he would be reasonably proficient at the rest of it as well.

'Another drink?' Leo proffered the glass and extended the snacks, willing to do just about anything to ensure that he was able to keep his hands off her for long enough to get back in control of his unruly body. Leo did not like to lose control but he was still hard and throbbing almost painfully, his libido all too eager to continue what he had begun. But haste wasn't cool and Leo was never hasty. He didn't do one-night stands either, at least not since he was a teenager. But Grace drew him like a bee to a hive of honey.

Grace clasped the champagne flute gratefully in one hand, astounded to realise that her hand was trembling slightly. But then it wasn't really Leo still having that effect on her, she told herself urgently, it was more probably the distinctly daunting knowledge that she had decided that, given the opportunity, she would make love with the man she was with. She glanced uncertainly up at him, her gaze drinking in the height and slant of his cheekbones, the strong angular jut of his classic nose, the mobile expressiveness of his wide, sculpted mouth. He was absolutely beautiful in the way only a very masculine man could be without the smallest hint of prettiness, although the jury was still out when it came to the ridiculous length of the long curling black lashes framing his remarkable eyes.

'Are you single?' she checked a tad abruptly.

'Yes. Will you spend the night with me?' Leo murmured sibilantly, his accent underscoring the syllables with a rasping edge. 'I've never wanted a woman as much as I wanted you on that floor.'

His directness disconcerted Grace but pleased her as well because she valued candour. She laughed. 'It's all right. You don't have to say stuff like that. I made up my mind to say yes when you kissed me.'

It would be a completely *practical* sexual experiment, Grace reasoned nervously, striving to reassure herself about a spontaneous decision that was unusual for her. Here she was far from home and she would never see him again, so there would be no lingering embarrassment, no further meetings, and no lasting connection. She had always believed in calling a spade a spade and the two of them were both after the same thing: a complication-free hook-up. He was as close to perfect for her purposes as it was possible to get.

Relief gripping him at her immediate agreement shorn of any prevarication, Leo closed a powerful arm round her narrow waist and gazed down at her with an intense sense of satisfaction and anticipation. Her nose turned up a little at the end and there was a scattering of freckles across the bridge but he discovered that he found those flaws endearing rather than noticeable deficiencies. 'It *wasn't* flattery.'

'If you say so,' Grace fielded, unconvinced, utterly challenged by the concept that she had sufficient sex appeal to tax the restraint of so sophisticated and good-looking a male. 'But outside a serious relationship sex is only a recreational pursuit.'

Taken aback by that prosaic comment and struck by an outlook that came remarkably close to his own, Leo elevated an ebony brow. 'But a most enjoyable one.'

Grace almost hit him with the shocking survey figures on the level of female sexual dysfunction and dissatisfaction in society but decided to keep wannabe-Dr-Grace firmly under restraint. 'I certainly hope so,' she said, her face heating at the very thought of what she had already agreed to do with him. She fretted that alcohol could be affecting her judgement although she had only had two drinks and hadn't finished the first.

But no, she wasn't drunk, not even tipsy because she always got giggly if she drank too much. Yet in retrospect her agreement to spend the night with him seemed so cold-blooded that she agonised over it for a nerve-racked few minutes of insecurity. Yet wasn't that attitude more sensible than waiting in the naïve hope that someone would eventually offer her both romance *and* commitment? She was almost twenty-five years old and she had waited long enough for a man to offer her a picture-book perfect solution to the loneliness she worked hard at hiding from the outside world. It wasn't going to happen in the foreseeable future and she had to be level-headed about her prospects. Matt was a great study mate and friend but sadly not lover material.

In any case she was an intelligent adult woman and free to do as she liked if she found a suitable attractive partner, she reminded herself stubbornly. By tomorrow she would finally know what sex was all about and at least she wouldn't have to spend another night trying to stay awake in the reception back at the apartment block. In truth, even the offer of a bed for the night was ridiculously welcome.

Leo traced a strong brown forefinger along her slim freckled arm, lingering on the fine skin of her wrist. Her skin was very soft and satin smooth and much paler than his own. 'I will please you,' he insisted.

A slight shiver racked Grace as if, after that kiss, her entire body had become super sensitive to his touch. She badly wanted him to kiss her again and the strength of that craving unsettled her. Never until that moment had she appreciated how powerful sexual hunger could be. Oh, she had read about it, heard about it, talked intellectually about it but all of those stories and assumptions were meaningless when set next to the actual experience. Leo Zikos would be like her personal science project, she told herself soothingly, and in the process of her research she would learn much that she needed to know.

She asked Leo when Rahim had left and for a few minutes they discussed the hotel scheme.

'You were getting bored,' Leo commented. 'I should apologise for that.'

'Is your business based on nightclubs?'

'No, this is my only investment in that line. I started out as a corporate trader and built a property empire with my investments. Now I have hotels, mobile phone and transport companies...' Leo shifted a hand to indicate the breadth of his interests with an elegance of movement that was compelling. 'I believe very strongly in diversification. My father once went bust because he concentrated all his energies in one field. What are you studying at university?'

'I'm about to go into my final year.' Grace responded as if she had misheard his question because she was in no hurry to tell him that she was a medical student. More than one male had backtracked from Grace in the past once they had discovered how clever she was. It was surprising how many men were turned off by her high IQ.

She met his riveting dark eyes and discovered that below the lights they weren't really dark at all. They were tawny gold and vibrant with power and a tiny shiver of naked awareness snaked down her taut spinal cord.

Leo stared down at her, a brooding quality tightening his lean dark features. He had read about pheromones and he was wondering if it was possible that she put out some strange invisible chemical message that turned him on hard and fast in a way that seemed to make no sense. After all, even if he was reacting like one, he wasn't a teenager at the mercy of his hormones any more.

He bent his head and the coconut scent of her shampoo filtered appealingly into his nostrils but he wasn't thinking about that when he looked at her ripe pink mouth. He moved nearer, his breath fanning her cheek. Almost imperceptibly she swayed closer. His arms tautened round her and without the smallest forewarning of what he was about to do he devoured the voluptuous promise of her lips with a passionate intensity that sent arousal roaring through him like an out-of-control fire.

The second kiss was even hotter than the first, Grace acknowledged dizzily, and she'd known it was coming, forewarned by the glitter of his eyes, the tensing of his arms round her and the quickened thump of his heartbeat beneath her palm when she was forced to plant a hand against his shirtfront to retain her balance on the edge of the seat. She had no thought of avoiding that kiss. In fact, excitement was zinging through her as an astonishing surge of awareness travelled through every nerve ending in her body, supersizing her every response.

Leo dragged his mouth from hers with the greatest of difficulty. 'Let's go,' he husked.

She had only been with him a little over an hour, Grace acknowledged in dismay. I'm a slut, I'm a slut, she reflected in mortification. Maybe sometimes sluts have more fun, said another voice inside her head and she almost laughed, registering that she was on a kind of mindless adrenalin high as if she had just reached the top of a ski run. She looked up at him, her gaze skimming over the already familiar lines of his breathtakingly handsome face and her tummy turning over even as heat leapt through her lower body in a disturbing wave of reaction. 'Go where?'

'Back to my yacht,' Leo advanced, urging her to her feet while carefully avoiding the scrutiny of his bodyguards. Making out with an audience was not cool and he had never done it before. What was he? A hot-under-the-collar kid? A dark flush had scored his strong cheekbones.

'You're here on a yacht?' Grace frowned, surprised by the news.

'I've been cruising the Med for the past week.' Leo

walked her down the stairs, but not before one of the men seated at the table across the way cleared their path. When she turned her head she saw the other two falling into step behind them. One of them was talking into one of those security earpieces she had only previously seen worn in films and the men backed into the dancers to impose a barrier around her and Leo and ensure their smooth passage across the crowded dance floor.

'Are those men bouncers?' she asked.

'My security team.'

'Why do you need a security team?' Grace enquired nervously.

'Protection. I've had a security presence in my life since childhood,' Leo confided evenly, as if it was the most normal thing in the world. 'My mother and her sister were Greek heiresses. Sadly, my aunt was kidnapped and held for ransom as a teenager.'

'Good grief,' Grace whispered in the comparative quiet of the club foyer. 'Was she freed? I mean, did she come home again?'

'Yes, she came home but she never fully recovered from her ordeal,' Leo replied grimly.

Grace stiffened, registering that something pretty horrible had happened to his aunt while she was being held and she suppressed a shiver.

'It makes more sense to guard against such risks,' Leo declared in a lighter tone as a car drew up by the kerb and one of his guards hastened to open the door for them.

Grace was nonplussed, out of her depth and feeling it. He had to be very rich to feel the need to take such precautions. She was with a man who inhabited a totally different world from her own and she breathed in slow and deep while she wondered if she had made a rather foolish decision.

'This is a little unnerving for me,' Grace admitted abruptly, watching one man climb in the front with the driver while the others climbed into the second car behind them.

'Ignore them…I do,' Leo asserted, recognising that she was not impressed like most women but instead ill at ease with the trappings of his lifestyle.

On the drive to the marina, her breath feathered in her throat while Leo chatted easily about his recent travels and stroked the back of her hand with a lazy forefinger. The car stopped and the passenger door sprang open. In her high heels, his hand cupping her elbow to steady her, she walked a few steps and stopped dead when Leo stepped into a motorboat and extended his hand to her.

'I… I… Where's your boat?' Grace demanded uneasily.

'There…'

Grace followed his gesture and further out in the bay saw a ship's silhouette etched against the moonlit sky. 'It looks like the *Titanic*!' she gasped because it was huge.

'An unfortunate comparison. I can assure you that *Hellenic Lady* is seaworthy and safe.' Leo stepped back onto the marina and bent down to scoop her up into his arms before stepping back into the launch with her.

He had acted so fast Grace hadn't had a moment to do more than utter a startled squeak of protest. Then he set her down again, settling her into a padded seat

by his side. The speedboat was racing across the sea
before she could even catch her breath. A night on a
yacht, she thought ruefully. Well, that might be fun,
she conceded, and fun had been in very short sup-
ply since she'd arrived in Marmaris as Jenna's pretty
much unwelcome guest.

'OK?' Leo prompted as the launch reached the yacht.

'I'm fine.' Grace swallowed back her worries and
allowed him to guide her up a gangway.

Leo didn't know what had come over him. He
wasn't the caveman type but as soon as he had seen
her anxious expression he had panicked, deeply unaccustomed at the idea that she might be changing her
mind, and he had snatched her off the marina and got
her into the launch as fast as he could. Grace Donovan brought out something in him that he didn't like,
something very basic and elemental and essentially...
unnerving. Possibly once he figured out what that
mystery something was he would feel better about it.

A man in a peaked cap greeted Leo, and Grace
didn't know where to look because she was embarrassed, convinced that their plans for what remained
of the night had to be obvious. Leo wafted her away
up another staircase and down a corridor. He spread
open the heavy carved doors and invited her to pre-
cede him.

Her sea-glass eyes widened to their fullest extent,
stunned appreciation etched on her lovely face as she
slowly executed a circle to take in the full effect of the
gorgeous bedroom. Huge windows looked out on the
starry sky and the dark rippling water so far below.
Leo hit a button and blinds buzzed into place to seal
them into privacy. Blinking, she turned, eyes skating

hastily over the opulent bed with its perfectly draped oyster silk spread. There were paintings on the walls, honest-to-goodness oil paintings, at least one of which looked sufficiently classic and imposing enough to be an Old Master.

'Would you like a drink? Something to eat?' Leo enquired, wondering why he had brought her to the master suite when he usually took his lovers to one of the guest cabins for the night. He had always been a very private man.

'No, thanks. I'm sorry, I'm a bit out of my depth with all this,' Grace confessed, hands shifting to shyly indicate the unbelievable luxury of her surroundings.

And yet she looked as if she belonged, Leo thought suddenly, her hair a river of fire across her shoulders, framing her astonishingly vivid little face, light green eyes flickering with uncertainty against a pallor that only made her freckles stand out. She truly was a beauty in a very natural way that was entirely new to a male much more accustomed to women groomed to a high standard of artificial perfection.

'It's only money.'

'Only someone with pots of it would say that,' Grace quipped, straightening her slim shoulders. 'We're from very different backgrounds, Leo.'

'There are no barriers here.' Leo stalked closer, surprisingly light and quiet on his feet for so large a male. He reached for her hand and drew her towards him. 'I wasn't exaggerating when I told you how much I wanted you, *meli mou.*'

'What did you call me?'

'Meli mou?' His mouth quirked as he brushed a stray red strand of hair back off her cheekbone.

Her hair felt like silk against his fingers and she was much smaller than his women usually were, the top of her head barely reaching his shoulder in spite of her fantastically high heels. Her diminutive stature gave him the oddest protective feeling. 'It's Greek for "my honey".'

'I'm more tart than sweet,' Grace warned him.

'Sugar cloys,' Leo husked and he wondered if that was the very basic truth that explained his reaction to her. She was independent and outspoken and he had never met anyone quite like her before.

He stroked a finger across the pulse flickering madly at her collarbone and her breath tripped in her throat. 'You keep touching me...'

His eyes glowed potent gold. 'I can't keep my hands off you. Is it a problem?'

Grace's lashes screened her eyes. She wasn't used to being touched and he did it with such ease and spontaneity. Her mother had been physically demonstrative, when she had been sober, and their brief time at the commune in Wales had been almost happy. But, after her mother's death, her uncle's family had been much more reserved and Grace had received little physical affection from them. 'No, not a problem,' she said in a low voice, thinking she had better watch herself with him because somehow he was getting under her skin in a way she had not foreseen.

'*Thee mou*, it is as well because I'm not sure I could stop.' Leo slid off his jacket and tossed it on a nearby chair, a lean brown hand tugging roughly at the knot on his silk tie and casting it aside.

I'm only with him to have sex, to lose my virginity and gain a little experience, Grace reminded herself

doggedly. No other feelings should enter the equation.
If she kept it simple and straightforward, she wouldn't
get hurt as her mother had been hurt, putting her future in a man's hands and learning her mistake too
late. She had only been a little girl when she had first
found out about her father's betrayal but the memory
of her mother's pain had lingered.

'Hey...' Leo turned her head back to him to stare
down into her haunted eyes. 'Where did you go just
now? Bad memories?'

Grace reddened with chagrin. 'Something like that...'

'Another man?' Leo gritted, appalled by the rage
that flooded him at the idea that she might be thinking of a lost lover while she was with him.

'Not that it's any of your business, but no,' Grace
countered succinctly, lifting her chin. 'I don't allow
men to screw with my mind.'

'Only your body?' Leo breathed, reaching for both
her hands to tug her to him.

Her copper lashes lowered and she glanced up at
him from beneath their spiralling cover. 'Only my
body. I hope that's a deal?'

'We're talking too much,' Leo gritted, on fire from
that provocative upward glance of hers, scarcely able
to credit that *she* was warning *him* off wanting anything more than sex. Wasn't that his line? Hadn't that
always been *his* line? It made him feel curiously insecure, not a sensation he enjoyed.

His mouth enveloped hers again and the piercingly
sweet thrust of his tongue made her shudder, heat
surging up from her pelvis, sending fingers of flame
to make her nipples tingle and swell.

'I'm going to undress you very, very slowly...' Leo asserted, 'revealing only one tiny piece of you at a time.'

Her tummy performed a somersault, consternation filling her as she wondered if she would be up to that sophisticated challenge.

CHAPTER THREE

LEO'S LIPS WERE aggressive and smooth on Grace's as he lifted her and laid her down gently on the bed, breaking contact only to flip off her shoes and let them fall.

Grace breathed in deep, mastering her nervous tension, terrified of letting it show. Of course she could have told him the truth that she was a newbie in the bedroom, but she was convinced that it would seriously dent her desirability in his eyes. And being treated as if she were rather more beautiful and seductive than she was felt especially good to her at that moment. She wondered where the bathroom was, knew she would have preferred diving in there to undress before reappearing casually wrapped in a towel or something. But wouldn't that be aping a fifties bride on her wedding night? Shyness and inhibitions were not sexy, she told herself impatiently.

'I love your hair,' he told her, stroking the tumbled strands as he sank down on the bed at the same time as he removed his cufflinks and unbuttoned his shirt. 'It's a gorgeous colour.'

'I got called "Carrots" at school and hated it for years,' Grace recalled with a rueful grin.

'When you smile, *meli mou*, your whole face lights up,' Leo said softly, lowering his head to claim another passionate kiss that rocked her even where she lay, her body behaving like a Geiger counter detecting radiation, strange new reactions awakening inside her.

His shirt parted, giving her a glimpse of broad, strong pectoral muscles and washboard abs that made her mouth run dry. He was excessively good to look at, what one of her friends would term 'man candy'. The pool of warmth at her pelvis spread. He turned her over, ran down the zip and gently spread the edges back, kissing one slim white freckled shoulder and then the other and tugging her back against him.

'Do you always go this slow?'

No, he didn't and, considering that he was already hugely aroused, Leo had no idea why he was determined to be the perfect lover for her. 'Depends on my mood... I want to savour you...'

He slid the sleeves down her arms and paused to appreciate the full globes filling the cups of her bra before he succumbed to temptation. With a soft little sound of impatience, he snapped loose the catch on the bra and raised his hands to cradle her superb breasts, massaging the creamy flesh, pressing her flat to explore them with his mouth and lingering over her straining rosy nipples.

'You have amazing breasts,' Leo muttered thickly as he dallied there, employing both his tongue and the glancing edge of his teeth to tease the straining buds.

Grace was rather more amazed at the effect he was having on her ignorant body. A hungry ache stirred at the heart of her. All of a sudden catching her breath was a challenge and she ran her fingers through his luxuriant black hair, surprised by how soft it was and how right it felt to touch him. She had thought she might have to steel herself to respond to him, genuinely hadn't expected to be quite so caught up in the process as she was, had even believed that throughout the process some part of her quick and clever brain would be standing back assessing and judging. Instead as he lifted her to find her mouth again Grace was engaging in some exploration of her own, hands sliding below the open shirt to trace his wonderfully honed muscular torso, skimming over the flat male nipples and the etching of crisp dark hair sprinkled there before sliding down to stroke the flexing muscles of his taut stomach.

'*Don't*…not this first time,' Leo urged, pulling back from her to slide off the bed. 'I'm too close to the edge.'

Grace blinked, bemused, having assumed he would be as eager to be touched as she was. And, 'not this *first* time'? Was that simply his prodigious self-assurance doing the talking for him? Her body all aquiver about even the thought of a single experience and the unlikelihood of her wanting a second, Grace watched him strip off his clothing with something less than the laid-back cool she had come to expect from him.

Everything came off at once, ensuring that she had little time to be curious about what her first aroused male looked like. He was larger than she had assumed he would be, but that was only a point of academic interest, she assured herself nervously, surveying the prodding length and breadth of his bold shaft. She knew she would stretch and she envisaged neither pain nor anything else that might reveal her inexperience. After all she had gone horse riding from an early age and believed any physical barrier would be long gone. With the same focused intellectual interest, Grace wondered why she literally felt overheated when she looked at Leo naked, her body hot, her breath catching in her throat as if she lacked oxygen.

'You're very quiet,' Leo remarked, coming back down to her, dropping several foil-wrapped contraceptives on the bedside cabinet, soothing Grace's instinctive terror of what had happened to her mother also happening to her.

For a split second she was almost tempted to tell him the truth about herself but innate reserve, learned growing up in a household where she had never belonged, kept her silent.

'I'm used to women who chatter,' Leo admitted with a slanting grin that was irresistible.

'I'm quiet,' Grace admitted, sliding for purchase on the slippery surface of the bedspread and flipping it back to scramble beneath the sheets, still clad in her panties, which she whisked off under cover.

'Someone so beautiful could never be shy,' Leo assumed, sliding in beside her in one lithe movement to reach for her. 'But you are a cheat... I wanted to see you...*all* of you.'

Grace knew she wasn't beautiful. She had grown up with the belief that tall, thin and blonde was the epitome of beauty and all the most popular girls at school had fitted that blueprint. But when Leo studied her with wide wondering eyes she felt beautiful for the

first time in her life and, even though she was convinced it wasn't true, it made her feel special. 'I have
to admit I liked seeing you,' she confessed tensely,
striving to reward his appreciation.

'Really?' Leo laughed, amused by that little mor-
sel of flattery when he was accustomed to a positive
barrage of compliments in the bedroom. He admired
Grace's restraint and lack of drama even while he
could hardly wait to shatter her defences and see her
lose herself in the throes of passion.

He kissed her and it was like the first time all over
again, his tongue thrusting into her mouth to set her
alight, tiny little spasms of excitement igniting afresh
to clench her womb. He pushed her legs apart, ran
a forefinger along the seam there and she stiffened,
knowing she was damp and knowing it was absolutely
crazy to get into bed with him and be embarrassed
about such a natural thing but unable to overcome
her self-consciousness. What on earth had happened
to her belief that she could make him a science project? she asked herself suddenly, dismayed to be losing her detachment. She closed her eyes tight while
he played with the most sensitive spot on her entire
body, pleasure and longing traversing her in steady
waves. She gritted her teeth, suddenly terrified of getting too carried away and losing control as her hips
rose involuntarily.

She made no effort to evade him when he pushed
back the sheet. In fact she braced herself to tolerate
the intimacy as he tipped her legs over his shoulders
and homed in on the most private part of her.

'You're beautiful here too,' Leo purred with a lack
of inhibition that shook her and she studied the ceiling

in disbelief, struggling to retain some distance from the leaps and jerks of her feverishly aroused body. Then the tip of his tongue touched her and circled her and a rolling wave of pleasure gripped her. Her eyes closed, teeth tightening to hold back a gasp but her control was broken within moments because she had never ever experienced that much pleasure. Sounds were wrenched from her parted lips and her fingers knotted in his hair as the screaming ache for fulfilment inside her built and built and she was lost in the storm of it with her heart thundering and her body writhing. And when she reached a climax, it *was* explosive and mind-blowing and all the superlative exaggerated words of description that once would have made her roll her eyes in disbelief.

'You're incredibly responsive, *meli mou*,' Leo husked, finding his every expectation mirrored in the dazed pleasure in her wide eyes and the closing of her arms round him in the aftermath.

Grace was dimly aware of him reaching for a foil packet. Her body might still be leaping with pleasure but her brain was firing back on all cylinders because he had blown *her* expectations out of the water with his very first move.

He shifted over her, lithe and confident as a jungle cat on the hunt, and she shut her eyes tight again against the intrusion of his. It was going to happen, it was *finally* going to happen and she would be like almost every other woman, no longer in the dark, no longer ignorant. But it had never occurred to her before that any man could make her want him so desperately that nothing else seemed to matter. His hands cupped her hips to tilt her boneless body back into a better position and then she felt the crown of him at her entrance and she tensed at the exact same moment he thrust deep and hard. The tender tissue of her channel burned and then a sharp little sting sliced through her, provoking a cry of discomfort from her lips. Leo froze.

'What the hell…? I *hurt* you?'

Forced by the unexpected to open her eyes, Grace knew her face had to be redder than a ripe apple. 'I was a virgin,' she admitted belatedly.

'A *virgin*?' Leo yelled, as if she had jabbed him with a red-hot poker. 'And you're telling me that *now*?'

'It was private,' Grace told him succinctly, her lush mouth folding into a compressed line. 'Now that it's done, can we just go back to where we were?'

Go back to where we were? In a different mood, Leo would have laughed at that wording. But he was in the grip of angry astonishment, his every assumption about her wiped out. He didn't like surprises, but as Grace shifted up to him in reminder that he was still inside her he discovered that his body was much less particular. He stared down at her with stunning dark golden eyes. He was her first and there was something mysteriously satisfying about that discovery. She was so tight and warm and wet. Struggling to control his every move, he sank deeper and a breathy little sigh that certainly wasn't a complaint escaped her.

Grace shut her eyes again, ripples of pleasure reclaiming her, that momentary stab of discomfort forgotten. She could feel his girth stretching her and his hips ground into hers with every slow, heavy thrust. He was being *so* careful.

'It's OK…you're not hurting me at all,' she mumbled guiltily.

His pace quickened and a deep guttural moan was torn from him as her body clenched around his. He felt so good Grace couldn't believe it, couldn't believe she had lived so many years without realising what she was missing out on. A sense of wonder seized her while her heart rate began to race with enjoyment as he pushed into her harder, faster and deeper. She couldn't speak, she couldn't breathe for excitement; she felt as though she had stolen a ride on a comet. The excitement rose and rose to breaking point when without her volition her body jerked into another intense orgasm. Ecstatic cries broke from her lips as the white-hot heat exploded in her pelvis and left her lying limp and utterly drained but with a glorious feeling of satisfaction that was new to her.

'Care to tell me why?' Leo demanded, shattering her idyll. 'Why did you pick me?'

'You did the picking,' Grace reminded him without hesitation, lifting her arms to break his hold on her to enable her to roll away. 'There's no agenda here, if that's what is worrying you. I found you attractive and I decided it was time that I took the plunge.'

'I would have preferred a warning,' Leo told her drily.

'I wasn't expecting that jab of pain. After years of horse riding I assumed there'd be nothing there…my mistake,' Grace pronounced with dignity. 'But thanks for the experience. You were very good.'

Prior to his engagement, Leo had been a legendary womaniser but he felt quite ridiculously put down by Grace's comment. He sprang off the bed and then a much more pressing matter came to his attention before he could reach the bathroom and he uttered a single crude expletive.

Grace froze at the sound of that word. When she was a child she hadn't known it was a bad word because her mother had used it all the time. Unhappily when she had used that word in Jenna's home, her aunt had screamed at her and put a soap bar in her mouth. She had still been throwing up when her uncle came home. The couple had had a massive row and Grace had never ever used that word again.

Impervious to her reaction, Leo had strode into the bathroom to dispose of the evidence. He reappeared, bronzed and stark naked in the doorway. 'The condom broke…'

Grace sat up in horror. 'What?'

'Breaking you in probably strained it,' Leo retorted with deliberate curtness because it was just one more unexpected development that he didn't want.

'It…*burst*?' Grace whispered. 'But I'm not on the pill—'

Leo grew even more rigid in his bearing. 'Shouldn't you have taken that precaution before you embarked on a one-night stand?'

Grace just ignored him; she didn't have to talk to him just because she had slept with him. In fact now that the main event was over she decided that she should ask for a boat back to the marina. Or would that be running away?

'May I use the bathroom?' she asked with careful politeness. 'And then possibly you could organise me a lift back to the marina?'

Leo moved to let her into the bathroom but his temper was now on a short fuse. Wham, bam, thank you, sir. Well, a woman had never treated him like that before but there was always a first time and maybe that was healthy for his ego. But the recollection that it had been *her* first time stopped his building aggression in its tracks. She didn't know what she was doing. She wasn't as much quiet as she was secretive and, flipping mentally back through the time he had been with her, he reckoned she had to be as innocent as a newborn lamb when it came to the nastier things in life. Perspiration beaded his upper lip when he thought of what might have happened to Grace had she gone off so casually and trustingly with some of the seedier individuals he had met on his travels.

'I want you to stay the night. I'll take you back tomorrow,' he stated.

'This is a one-night stand...you don't get to tell me what to do!' Grace flamed back at him with spirit.

'You're not doing so well right now when it comes to looking after yourself,' Leo pronounced drily.

In the space of a moment, Grace travelled from a mood of silent resentment to one of raging rancour and sooner than betray herself by spitting out something inappropriate, she slammed the bathroom door on him. Who did he think would look after her but her own self if she was unlucky enough to conceive after that contraceptive accident? It was none of his business that she had come on holiday without planning to have sex with anyone and she wasn't taking the pill because she hadn't wanted to bombard her body with hormones before she was even sexually active. On the other hand, should she have foreseen the possibility that she might suddenly change her mind as she had done this very evening? Grace stood below the shower in a daze counting the days of her cycle, soon realising that the condom could not have failed at a worse time.

Leo swore vehemently beneath his breath and went off to use another shower. Why was she angry with him? Accidents happened, although it was the first time he had found himself in such a situation. Even as a teenager, Leo had never had unprotected sex because he knew all too well the cost of such carelessness. His half-brother's birth to his father's mistress had been a painful lifelong commitment for Anatole Zikos *and* his wife and son.

Grace emerged from the bathroom wrapped in the white towelling robe she had found hanging there. It was huge on her but she had rolled up the sleeves and wasn't sorry to be covered to her ankles. The intimacy she had naively sought suddenly struck her as having come at too high a price and she was more self-conscious in the aftermath than she had been beforehand.

'I thought you'd be hungry,' Leo remarked with a casual movement of his hand pointing out the catering trolley that had appeared. 'I don't know what you like so I ordered a selection.'

'You have someone in a kitchen cooking for you at *four* in the morning?' Grace exclaimed in astonishment while being grateful for the distraction provided by the food. Wandering barefoot over to the trolley, she lifted the covers to inspect the mouthwatering options on offer. Her tummy gave a hungry growl, hopefully concealed by the clatter of the coffee jug lid she lifted and dropped again. In silence she helped herself to coffee and a plate of elaborate supper bites.

It was ironic though that since meeting Leo she had never been more aware of his compelling presence than she was in that charged silence. He had changed into jeans and a blue T-shirt, his black hair tousled, shiny and damp from the shower, his lean, darkly handsome face shadowed by dark stubble. Apprehensive though she was about the risk of consequences, she had to admit that Leo still looked amazing and the epitome of every fantasy she had ever had about a man.

'I have a doctor on call, if you want—'

'*No.*' Grace leapt straight in before he could say it because the morning-after treatment that could stop a pregnancy developing was not a choice she was willing to make. Even though a pregnancy would damage her chances of qualifying in medicine. 'That's not an option for me.'

'I had to make the option available,' Leo murmured without any perceptible reaction. 'When are you flying home?'

'The day after tomorrow.' Grace sat down in an opulent armchair.

'I will want your address and phone number. This is not a situation I would treat lightly.' Leo served himself with coffee, betraying all the awkwardness of a male who wasn't used to waiting on himself and who had rather expected his companion to take on the role of hostess.

Grace allowed herself to look at Leo for only the second time since she had left the bathroom. Whether she liked it or not, he had gone up in her estimation.

'If you give me your contact details, we won't need to discuss this any further. I only need to add the assurance that if there is any…er…development, I will provide you with my full support.'

'Yes.' Grace almost shrugged because she knew words were cheap. Leo was saying the right things but only he and his conscience could know how reliable he would be in such trying circumstances as those of an unplanned pregnancy. After all, her own father had talked her mother out of the termination she had decided on when she had fallen pregnant as a student. Grace's father had promised her mother that he would marry her and help her raise their child and then he had run off with another woman and left Keira Donovan literally holding the baby. That had been in the days when being an unmarried mother had still been a real stigma and a source of family shame.

Leo settled a notepad and pen down on the table beside Grace. She printed her address and phone number and returned the pad to the table. As she did so, she yawned. 'I'm sorry, I'm very sleepy…'

'It's late…go to bed,' he murmured quietly.

Grace thought of the hassle of arriving back at the marina before dawn, finding her way back to the apartment block and then sitting in Reception until Stuart took his leave. 'I'll stay…at least you have a bed.'

'A bed?' Leo queried, recognising her exhaustion in her pale face and heavy eyes.

Grace climbed into the bed still clad in the robe.

'I wasn't going to touch you again,' Leo remarked drily.

'Obviously I've offended your ego and I'm sorry,' Grace mumbled.

As she closed her eyes Leo peeled off his own clothing, although he retained his boxers and slid into the other side of the bed, dousing the lights. 'What did you mean about having a bed?'

'Our apartment is only one bedroom and my cousin met a man the first day,' she whispered. 'I've been sitting up in Reception most nights so that she can be with him—'

'That's outrageous!' Leo cut in.

'No, it's not. Jenna's family paid for her to go on holiday with her best friend.' Briefly she explained. 'Now that she's met Stuart, I'm surplus to requirements.'

'Surely her parents would be furious if they knew how she was treating you?'

'What Jenna wants, Jenna gets,' Grace muttered drowsily, her voice trailing down in volume. 'It's always been that way. She's the daughter, the little princess...I'm the niece they took in out of the kindness of their heart.'

'But to make such distinctions between two children in the same family!' Leo began angrily until it dawned on him that Grace had fallen asleep.

A moment later, the echo of his own words still ringing in his ears, he realised that there were remarkable similarities between Grace's situation with her cousin and his own non-relationship with the half-brother he hated. Yes, in his home too, the *same* distinction had been made in favour of the legitimate firstborn son, Leo. For the first time Leo was recognising an angle that he had never even considered before: Bastien's side of the story. Was it really so surprising that Bastien had always seemed to seethe with resentment as a child and had matured into a fiercely competitive and aggressive male? He was sobered by the unfamiliar thoughts afflicting him, and it was a long time before Leo fell asleep.

CHAPTER FOUR

'No, PLEASE DON'T tell me it's been great!' Grace urged
Leo with a rueful laugh as, ever gracious, he saw her
into the speedboat that would whisk her back to the
real world, rather than the fantasy in which she had
ordered her own personal perfect breakfast directly
from Leo's personal chef.

'Why not?' Leo demanded, strangely unsettled by
her apparent good humour at leaving him.

'Because you *know* it's been a disaster for you from
start to finish but you're too polite to say it. I was absolutely not what you expected,' Grace pointed out
bluntly, taking a seat in the launch.

Leo, rarely put out of countenance, felt heat sear his
cheekbones and thought that she really was extraordinarily unusual for her sex, when she said exactly
what she thought and felt without chagrin, revealing
not an iota of the vanity he had believed that every
woman possessed. 'I will be in touch—'

'Not necessary,' Grace cut in briskly as if he were
a five-year-old importuning a busy teacher.

His strong jaw line clenched. '*I* will decide what's
necessary,' Leo delivered, losing patience.

From the upper deck, Leo watched the launch convey Grace back to the marina. He was assailed by a vague sense of something unfinished...of regret? His jaw set hard as granite. He had almost asked her to stay with him until it was time for her to fly home. *Why?* She had spoken the truth, after all: it *had* been a disaster. Instead of an experienced woman and a sexual marathon he had landed a virgin and then there had been the mishap with the condom. His teeth gritted together. When he had registered that for some inexplicable reason he was in no hurry to see Grace leave, his blood had run cold on the suspicion that he was feeling more than he was willing to feel for any woman, and from that point on he had been keen to see her depart. Yet the sound of her sobbing his name in orgasm still echoed in his ears and his body hardened as he remembered all too well the tight, hot feel of hers. From his point of view, although there had been too little of it, the sex had been stellar. In fact there had been something oddly, dangerously addictive about Grace Donovan and getting rid of her fast had been absolutely the right action to take!

Three weeks after that day, Grace did a pregnancy test in the bathroom of her aunt and uncle's home.

Her nerves were shot to hell and her mood had been on a steady downward slope for days when her menstrual cycle had failed to kick in on the expected date. Unfortunately pregnancy tests were very expensive and Grace had forced herself to wait until there was little risk of the test providing her with a potentially false result that would require yet another test to be done. And now she was bracing herself for the moment of truth even while her training had already

provided her with good reason to be afraid. The very
last thing she had required earlier that week was a blatantly impatient text from Leo Zikos asking for news
that she did not yet have, so she had simply ignored it.

Her breath hissed in her dry throat when she studied the result: positive. Hell roast the wretched man,
she thought ridiculously, why couldn't he have been
sterile? Instead they were both young and healthy and
the odds had not been in their favour. *Pregnant!* Fear
and no small amount of horror made Grace break out
in a cold sweat because nobody knew better than her
how very hard, if not impossible, it would be for her to
complete her medical studies with a child in tow and
no supportive partner. Suddenly she was furious with
herself for not having protected her own body better
simply because she had failed to foresee the need. She
had assumed that she would always be in total control
and Leo Zikos with his stunning dark eyes had shown
her different. But at what cost?

Leo…stray thoughts and recollections of Leo had
littered the past weeks while Grace had struggled to
put the entire episode behind her and continue as normal. She had discovered that she had a softer, dream-
ier side to her character that she had never suspected.
Well, so much for that, she thought cynically, stuffing
the pregnancy-test paraphernalia back into the plas-
tic bag to be discreetly dumped. Would she tell Leo?
Undoubtedly she would tell him…*eventually* but not
until she had decided what to do. Right at that minute she had more to worry about than taking time out
to contact a male who had nothing other than money
to offer her in terms of support. She suspected that
Leo would expect her to have a termination and when

she refused to give him a 'tidy' conclusion to the development he would be furious and resentful of her decision.

Would he be the exact opposite of the father she had never met? Grace wrinkled her nose, not wanting to think along those lines. She was too intelligent not to be aware that her mother had fed her daughter a steady diet of her own martyred bitterness. Sadly, Grace had been too young to be told such things, too innocent to be anything other than deeply hurt by an absent father who had never felt the need to look for his eldest child. Her father had other children now; she knew after finding him on Facebook that she had half-siblings with the same red hair, the children of the woman he had married after deserting her mother. Yet her father had pleaded for Grace to be given the chance of life before she was even born and how could she do any less for her own baby?

Grace adored babies, but she had believed that the opportunity to have children lay far, far away in her future. And now that everything had changed she was struggling not to think in either personal or sentimental terms about the baby. After all, after her own chequered experience as a child she knew that the best possible option for her baby would be an adoption by two parents with a stable home and everything Grace herself was currently unable to provide.

Didn't she owe her child the very best possible start in life? What on earth could she give in comparison? Her own mother had frankly struggled to cope with the weighty responsibilities of being a single parent. Keira Donovan had often resented her daughter, blaming her for the loss of her youthful freedom. There had always been a shortage of money for necessities and Grace had often been left in the care of unsuitable babysitters. Most telling of all, Grace was painfully aware of how much she herself had longed to have a stable father figure when she was a child. She was terrified of failing her own child the way her mother had failed her. But while her brain reminded her of all those distressingly practical facts, a more visceral response to motherhood deep down inside her was agonised by the concept of handing her baby over to someone else to raise.

The locked door rattled. 'Grace? Are you in there?' It was her aunt's voice, sharp and demanding.

Lifting the bag, Grace unlocked the door and prepared to step past the older woman.

Instead Della Donovan laid her hand on Grace's arm to prevent her from walking away. 'Are you pregnant?' she demanded thinly.

Bemused by the question when she had not shared her concern with anyone, Grace stiffened, her brows lifting in a startled arc. 'Why are you asking me that?'

'Oh, that could be my fault.' Jenna sighed with mock sympathy, pausing at the top of the stairs. 'I was behind you in the checkout at the supermarket and I couldn't help noticing the test...'

Grace lost colour. 'Yes, I'm pregnant,' she admitted stonily.

Her aunt, always a volatile woman, immediately lost her temper. By the time she had finished shouting, threatening and verbally abusing her niece for her morals, Grace knew where she stood and that she could no longer remain in her aunt and uncle's home. Della had said things about Grace and her late mother that Grace knew that she would never forget. White as paper and numb with shock in the aftermath of that upsetting confrontation, she went into her room, phoned Matt and pulled out her suitcase; there was nothing else she could do. Her life, the life she had worked so hard to achieve, was falling apart even faster than she had feared, she acknowledged with a sinking heart.

At the outset of that same week, Leo had texted Grace but she hadn't replied and he was tired of waiting and waking up in the middle of the night *wondering*…

In little more than two months' time he was getting married and Marina had made him more than aware of that fact by calling him to ask his opinion on various questions of bridal trivia that he couldn't have cared less about. Nothing more important had entered those conversations and it had convinced him that he was the only one of them with doubts.

Sadly, even the smallest doubt had not featured in Leo's original blueprint for his future. He fixed on a goal, made decisions, brought plans to fruition and that was that. He didn't do wondering about *what if*! He understood perfectly why he had ended up with Grace Donovan that night. He had been angry with Marina and full of misgivings about what their future together might hold. Regrettably, however, that still did not explain why Grace had hit him like a torpedo striking his yacht below the waterline. It did not explain why she had given him the most incredible sexual experience of his far from innocent life to date or why given the smallest excuse he would have repeated that night.

Consequently, he had checked out who Grace Donovan was while he waited to hear from her and what he had learned from that comprehensive investigation had only made him more confused. Her early childhood had been appalling and her adolescence not much kinder. It was a credit to her strength of character that she had achieved so much, regardless of those disadvantages. Yet there was still so much he didn't understand. Why would a young woman as well-informed as a fifth-year medical student not take extra contraceptive precautions? And why had she avoided telling him what she was studying? He had also taken on board the reality that an unplanned pregnancy would probably wreak greater havoc on her life than it would on his.

When the curiosity, the unanswered questions and the need to know whether or not they had a problem rose to a critical level, Leo refused to wait to hear from Grace any longer. He gave his driver her address and compressed his lips, annoyed that Grace was forcing him to confront her. How *could* he walk away and hope for the best? How could he possibly risk marrying Marina without knowing for sure? The answer to both questions was that Leo could not ignore the situation, being all too well aware of the likely repercussions should Grace prove to be pregnant. On a deeper level, however, Leo could simply not believe that his legendary good fortune with women would crash and burn over something as basic as a sperm and an egg meeting in the wrong womb.

An hour later, Leo was considerably less naïve, having struck a blank at Grace's former address. The frigid blonde in her forties who accepted his business card changed her attitude a little once she noticed his limousine and became more helpful but Leo still couldn't get away fast enough. He really wanted nothing to do with a woman who had thrown out the mother of *his* future child—a phrase with a shocking depth he could not quite digest at that moment—like some pantomime little match girl and who had earlier in the dialogue referred witheringly to Grace in unjust terms that had implied she was some high-living veteran slut.

Thee mou, he was going to be a father...whether he liked it or not. Leo breathed in slow and deep, traumatised by the concept, and rang Marina straight away.

'Oh, dear,' Marina sighed with what he rather suspected was bogus sympathy. 'That rather tops my misbehaviour with my married man, doesn't it? What do you want to do?'

'We'll meet up and talk.'

'No, I suspect that right now you need to be doing that with the baby's mother, *not* with me,' Marina remarked heavily. 'What a ghastly mess, Leo!'

Leo ground his teeth together but there was nothing he could say in his own defence. He felt as though his smooth, perfectly organised life had been violently derailed without warning. Were all his carefully laid plans about his future domestic life to come to nothing now because his contraception had let him down? he questioned bitterly. He swore under his breath and gave the driver the second address he had acquired while wondering exactly who Matt Davison was and what his connection was to Grace. It was not that he was possessive, of course, it was solely the unpleasant awareness that Grace Donovan was very probably going to be the mother of his first child and the nature of her character mattered much more now than it had the night they had met.

Was he already travelling down the destructive path his father had trodden before him? His bitterness hardened. No, he was not going to marry one woman for her wealth while another, poorer one carried his child and thankfully love didn't enter the picture in any way. Anatole Zikos had married Leo's mother while loving his mistress and had never conquered that craving. Leo prided himself on being infinitely more down-to-earth and less emotional than his father. While his situation with Grace might be starting out as a mess, he would swiftly organise the threatening chaos into something more acceptable that both he *and* Grace could live with.

Grace was humming under her breath while she cooked supper, grateful that the smell of the chicken and vegetables didn't stir up nausea the way the scent of anything fried seemed to do. At least her studies hadn't started yet. She was at the start of a reading week, set aside for home study.

The doorbell went and she wondered if Matt had forgotten his key. Her friend's parents had died when he was eighteen, leaving him with the means to buy his own apartment. She was comfortable living in Matt's guest room but, concerned that she was taking advantage of his good nature, she had taken over the cooking and the cleaning to demonstrate her appreciation of his hospitality.

Barefoot, she padded out to the hall, a slim, casually clad figure in skinny jeans and a striped navy and white sweater, her vibrant long hair restrained in a braid that hung halfway down her back.

'Leo...' she pronounced numbly, shattered to find the leading character in her daydreams in the flesh on the doorstep.

'Why didn't you answer my text?'

'I'm afraid I didn't have an answer for you at the time.'

Leo was so close to Grace that he could tell she was wearing no make-up and the sheer glow of her creamy cheeks and bright pale green eyes knocked him flat. She was even more beautiful than he remembered and a fleeting memory of her pale hands stroking down over his stomach gripped him, resulting in a stirringly strong surge of lust that he very much could have done without.

'Your aunt threw you out.'

'So, that's how you found out where I was living! My uncle came to see me the day before yesterday. He asked me to come home with him but I don't want to cause trouble between them, so I can't,' Grace admitted, distinctly overpowered by Leo's proximity because she wasn't wearing heels and without them Leo towered over her, all broad shoulders and long powerful legs, arrogant dark head tipped back to gaze down at her. And looking up at that moment seemed a definite mistake because his brilliant dark golden eyes were framed by black curling lashes as long and striking as any she had ever seen on a man. He had absolutely gorgeous eyes that froze her to the spot and made her stare while her heart rate accelerated, her mouth ran dry and a knot of undeniable excitement tightened and then unfurled in her chest.

It's just attraction, you dummy, she scolded herself a split second later, her skin already cooling with dismay at the strength of her reaction to him. But Leo Zikos was an extraordinarily handsome man and it was hardly surprising that she was reacting to that reality, particularly when she had already slept with him and knew that below his business suit he was even more incredibly fanciable and impressive than he was clothed. That last inappropriate thought struck Grace with such effect and so much embarrassment and self-loathing that her pale skin flamed scarlet, mortified heat crawling over her entire skin surface.

'I've never seen anyone blush that deeply,' Leo confided in wonderment, watching the flush trail down her long white throat and dapple that fine skin with a warmer colour.

'You're supposed to pretend you didn't notice, not embarrass me about it further,' Grace told him roundly. 'I used to go through agonies blushing when I was a kid. It's the fault of my fair skin—it's very conspicuous.'

Leo didn't know where the conversation had gone, but then he hadn't come with a prepared script, and as she strolled back into the kitchen to tend a steaming wok a key sounded in the front door and someone else arrived. Leo wheeled round to inspect a fresh-faced young man in his twenties with brown hair and bright blue eyes behind earnest spectacles.

'Matt…meet Leo,' Grace said quietly.

'Oh, right…er…' The hapless Matt managed to smile at Grace and then deal Leo a very different look of angry disapproval. 'Of course, you'll want to talk. Take him to the living room. I'll take charge of whatever you're cooking.'

'Thanks, Matt,' Grace said comfortably, pressing open a door off the hall and waving a guiding hand in Leo's direction.

Leo's talent had always been reading other people and he clearly saw Matt's suppressed hostility and Grace's complete unawareness of it and probably of its most likely source.

'What's Matt to you?' Leo asked the instant Grace closed the door.

'A good friend...and thank goodness for him. At such short notice the university couldn't find me decent accommodation anywhere but a hostel, so I was grateful for Matt's invite,' Grace proffered truthfully. 'Matt and I are on the same course.'

'Why did your family throw you out?' Leo enquired baldly, stationing himself by the window of the small room, which was cluttered with books, many of them lying half-open.

Grace gave him a wry glance. 'I think you already know why.'

'But that news should have come from you directly to me,' Leo told her grimly. 'I had a right to know first!'

'And perhaps you would've done were we in a relationship,' Grace countered quietly. 'But since we're not, the situation is rather different.'

Even greater tension filled Leo, stiffening the muscles in his broad shoulders, his clean-cut strong jawline hardening at her stubborn reminder of facts he considered to be more destructive than helpful. 'If you're pregnant, we definitely *have* a relationship,' he contradicted.

Grace wrinkled her nose. 'Well, I am having your baby,' she conceded reluctantly. 'But we don't have to have *any* kind of a relationship!'

'And how do you work that out?' Leo gritted, becoming steadily more annoyed by her dismissive attitude.

'I can manage fine on my own. I'm very independent,' Grace informed him. 'I'll continue with my studies, hopefully have the baby during the Easter term break and give it up for adoption.'

'Adoption?' Leo was thoroughly disconcerted and stunned by her solution, that being a possibility he hadn't even considered. 'You're planning to have our child adopted?'

Grace pleated her slender fingers together to conceal the fact that her hands were trembling while she battled to tamp down her distress. 'I know it won't be an easy decision to make when the time comes, Leo. I don't want to give my child up but I was brought up by a single parent until I was nine years old and my mother really did struggle to meet the demands of that role.'

'But—' Leo clamped his lips shut on an instinctive protest while he fought to master emotions he had never felt before. Of course her reference to adoption had taken him very much by surprise. Even so, the very thought of never knowing his own child and not even having the right to see him or her genuinely appalled Leo. Even his own instinctive rejection of her proposition was a revelation that shocked him. 'I don't think I could approve that option.'

'As far as I know you don't legally have any say in the matter,' Grace retorted in an apologetic rather than challenging tone. 'Only married fathers have those kinds of rights.'

'Then I'll marry you.'

Grace groaned at that knee-jerk reaction. 'Don't be silly, Leo. Strangers don't get married.'

Leo lifted his dark head high and surveyed her with glittering golden eyes that were mesmeric in their intensity. 'I don't care how we go about it but while you may not want our child, I *do* and I am prepared to raise that child, should that become necessary.'

It was Grace's turn to be thrown off balance and she paled. 'When it comes to my preferences, it's not a matter of my wanting or *not* wanting the baby…it's much more a matter of what *I* can offer my child and how best *I* could meet my child's needs. And the truth is that as a student with no home of my own or current earning power, I've got very little to offer.'

'While I on the other hand have a great deal to offer and could help you in any way necessary,' Leo cut in succinctly. 'And in the short term I think it would be best if you came to live in my London apartment.'

'*Your* apartment?' Grace echoed in disbelief. 'Why on earth would I move into your apartment?'

'Because that's *my* baby you're carrying and I intend to be fully involved in giving you whatever support you need until our child is born,' Leo declared without hesitation.

'I'm perfectly comfortable here with Matt.' Grace groaned, her brow tightening with stress because Leo was saying things and offering options she had not anticipated and she had already spent several days anxiously worrying over her alternatives before coming to the conclusion that adoption was the most sensible answer to all her concerns. Now Leo was demanding a share of that responsibility and complicating the situation with his own ideas.

'Staying here with Matt is unwise,' Leo murmured drily.

'In what way? He's a very good friend.'

'But that's not all he wants to be,' Leo incised. 'Matt is in love with you.'

Grace was aghast. 'That's complete nonsense!'

'A friend would be relieved when the father of your child arrived to take an interest in your predicament. But a would-be lover feels threatened and annoyed and that's what he is,' Leo spelled out impatiently. 'You're not stupid, Grace. Your very good friend wants you living here with him because he's in love with you.'

'That's completely untrue.' Strikingly taken aback by his contention, Grace turned away in an uncoordinated half-circle. She was picturing Matt, his behaviour and his caring ways while wondering if it was possible that she could have been so blind that she had not noticed the depth of his feelings for her. 'What would you know about it anyway?'

'I only know what I saw in his face once he realised who I was,' Leo said grimly. 'You're really not doing him any favours staying on here…unless of course you're planning on returning his feelings?'

'Er…that would be a no,' Grace muttered guiltily while recognising the terrible unwelcome truth in Leo's arguments. If it was true that Matt wanted more than friendship from her, it was equally true that there was no prospect of her offering it. The intensity of her attraction to Leo had concluded for ever any prospect of her trying to make more of her relationship with Matt. From the instant Leo had taught her of her own capacity to feel so much more mentally and physically than she had ever dreamt she could feel, her former conviction that she and Matt would make a great couple had died.

'Then move into my apartment where you will not be under pressure,' Leo advised softly.

Grace wanted to slap Leo for cutting through all her possible protests by employing the one credible argument calculated to make her think again. Matt spent a lot of time with her. Matt was always there for her, eternally helping her and discussing her worries, but she was doing Matt a disservice by living with him if he was hoping for more than friendship from her. In that scenario the sooner she got out of Matt's home and put some distance between them, the better, she reasoned guiltily.

'When?'

'I see no point in wasting time. Why not now? You can't have that much stuff to pack. You've only been here a couple of days,' he pointed out smoothly, reining back any hint of satisfaction in his demeanour.

Matt was threatening to get involved in a situation that was none of his business and Leo wanted him eliminated before he interfered and caused trouble.

Waiting in the small reception room, he listened to Matt raise his voice and Grace mute hers as she explained that she was moving out. The mother of his child, historically not a happy role in his family experience, but if adoption was in the offing he needed to come up with a viable alternative. Grace hadn't even paused to consider the idea when he'd suggested marrying her. Cynical amusement filled Leo because he was too clever to cherish illusions about what made him so appealing to the female scx in general: first and foremost his great wealth followed by his looks and his sexual prowess. Yet Grace had thumbed her nose at that winning combination, doing what no other woman had done before in rejecting him. Although she had not rejected him the night when it all began, Leo savoured with an appreciation that was yet to pall in spite of the news he had received earlier.

A battered suitcase, two boxes of files and a pile of books now littered the hall. Matt insisted on helping them transport Grace's possessions out to the waiting limousine and Leo's driver climbed out in consternation to whisk the case out of his employer's grip while two of his bodyguards grabbed up the boxes.

'Look after her…don't hurt her,' Matt breathed in a charged and warning undertone before Leo could climb into his limousine.

'I won't,' Leo countered, his accented drawl curt and cool, his ego challenged by the tone of that advice.

'I can't believe I'm doing this,' Grace lamented, because she was already suffering second thoughts. Leo had extracted her from Matt's flat at the speed of light.

'Right now, you need time out to decide what you want to do next,' Leo told her levelly. 'A few days…a few weeks, whatever it takes. You shouldn't be trying to make life-changing decisions virtually overnight.'

'You don't want me to go for adoption?' Grace said, her slim frame tensing, her fingers folding together tightly on her lap.

'Adoption entails you cutting me out of the situ-

ation entirely. *Why* would you want to do that?' Leo
queried softly. 'I am willing to help in every way possible. There are other options and I think you should
consider them.'

Grace breathed in slow and deep, fighting the sense
that he was putting her on the spot because she knew
that was unjust. She was in a highly stressful situation and any decision she made would put her under
pressure. 'This year of my degree I have to spend a
lot of time working long unsocial hours in hospitals.
Coping with that while pregnant will be a challenge.'

'We can find some way to work around the problems. I've made an appointment for you with a doctor,
who's a friend of mine,' Leo told her quietly. 'We're
calling in with him first—'

'A doctor? Why, for goodness' sake?' Grace demanded
impatiently.

'I want confirmation of your pregnancy and the
reassurance that you are in good health,' he admitted quietly.

Grace breathed in deep, suppressing her frustration. He had a right to that official endorsement, she
reasoned ruefully.

Leo's friend was in private practice and her pregnancy test was processed at supersonic speed before
the suave, smoothly spoken doctor gave her a brief
physical check-up and the usual advice offered to
pregnant women.

Having satisfied Leo's request, Grace was quiet
when she slid back into his limousine and thinking
about her baby. Possibly she had been a little too quick
to consider the avenue of adoption, a solution that
would enable her to continue her life after the birth

as though she had never been pregnant. Obviously the idea of reclaiming normality had appeal but what sort of normality would it be when she had to live for ever after with the awareness that she had given up her baby? A cold chill clenched Grace's spine at the prospect of that ultimate consequence. Adoption was final and could well sentence her to live with a secret heartbreak and sense of loss for the rest of her days. Suddenly, the chance to think at her leisure, while not having to worry about where or how she lived or what other people thought, shone like the most luxurious indulgence in front of her. Leo, she dimly appreciated, could talk a lot of good sense when it suited him to do so.

When they arrived at the block of exclusive apartments where Leo lived, his guards and her luggage went in the service lift, imprisoning her with Leo in the opulent confines of a far smaller and less utilitarian lift. She met his stunning eyes once and her heart stuttered as she immediately turned her head away, only to be greeted with a mirrored reflection of him instead: the luxuriant blue-black hair she wanted to tousle with her fingers, the arrogant angle of his head and the firm jut of his jaw, the sheer blazing confidence that inexplicably drew her like a magnet. Her mouth drying, she swallowed with difficulty. She felt out of step with herself, challenged to recognise the stranger she became in Leo's presence, a stranger with random, often inappropriate thoughts and no control over her own body.

'Stop fighting it,' Leo growled soft and low, his abrasive accent purring along the syllables.

Grace glanced up. 'Fighting what?'

'This...'

And he reached for her, pulling her up against his big powerful frame with easy strength. In unmistakeable contact with the long, hard length of his erection Grace's tummy flipped and her knees turned to water. Dangerous heat shimmied between her legs.

'It's crazy—'

'The most powerful craving I've ever felt,' Leo sliced in. 'I felt it the first time I saw you. I fought it to let you walk away. But I'm done being sensible.'

Completely disconcerted by that blunt admission, Grace parted dry lips. *'But—'*

'No...buts, *meli mou,*' Leo husked against her cheek, his breath fanning her parted lips. 'The words you're looking for are *Yes, Leo.*'

A strangled little sound of amusement escaped Grace. 'I hope you're the patient type?'

'Not even remotely.' Strong arms banding round her, Leo lifted her up against him and claimed her mouth with a voracious driving passion that curled her toes and made her nails dig into his shoulder. When she made a half-hearted attempt to evade him his arms merely clamped tighter round her while he delved deeper into her mouth to send a current of fire arrowing through her quivering length. He tasted spicy and sweet and so unbelievably good she couldn't get enough of him. She was barely aware of the lift doors whirring open or of the momentary separation of their mouths as he cannoned into a doorway with a muffled Greek expletive. Indeed the entire experience was like a time out from her brain because a hunger she couldn't fight had taken control.

CHAPTER FIVE

LEO LAID HER down on a wide bed. 'I want you to know that I didn't bring you here for this,' he breathed rawly. 'I didn't plan it.'

His lean, darkly handsome features were taut with hungry frustration and the strangest hint of vulnerability, and for a split second Grace almost raised her fingers to trace the compressed line of his lips. Instead she got a grip of herself and let her hand fall back from his shoulder to lie by her side. Her body was singing a very different message, all revved up like a racing car at the starting line. She was startlingly aware of every erogenous zone she possessed and his pronounced effect on her. Her breasts felt swollen while a hollow ache throbbed at the very centre of her. It was sexual need, plain sexual need, she repeated carefully to herself, as if by acknowledging that she could minimise the effects and suppress them.

'I intended for us to sit down over a civilised dinner and talk,' Leo grated impatiently, stepping back from the bed as if he didn't trust himself that close to her. 'But I can't keep my hands off you!'

He made Grace feel totally irresistible and she marvelled at the sensation and the new buoyancy it gave to her sadly depleted ego, battered by her aunt's abuse, her cousin's scorn and Matt's heartfelt and apologetic, 'How could you be so stupid?' There Leo stood, breathtakingly beautiful, rich and charismatic and he still wanted her when she was sure he had to have many more lovely and laid-back female options.

'I think it cuts both ways,' she admitted not quite steadily, just looking at him and wanting him so much it almost hurt while telling herself that was entirely and unforgivably superficial.

Leo came down on one knee on the edge of the bed. 'You...*think*?'

'Know,' she conceded breathlessly, stinging arousal assailing her nipples as she collided with his spectacular dark golden eyes. She thought she would die if he didn't touch her, told herself that she deserved to die if she let him, but she couldn't lie about the overwhelming surge of hunger that lit her up like a firework.

'I want you so much it's driving me insane,' Leo husked, coming down to her in one driven movement to seal her to the mattress with his weight. 'I don't like the feeling that I'm not in control...'

Grace didn't like it either and was taken aback that they could be so similar in outlook. Her fingers lifted involuntarily and laced through the blue-black hair falling across his brow. Rain lashed the window across the room and a smouldering silence fell indoors. Her heart was racing and against her breast she could feel the quickened thump of his. Dense black lashes lifted on his stunning eyes and she forgot to breathe, registering that somewhere along the way, and without ever pausing to think it through, she had begun developing feelings for Leos Zikos that went way beyond what she had once envisaged.

For a split second fear grabbed her, fear of being hurt, humiliated and rejected, but she pushed the reactions away and buried them deep. Just for a few hours, she promised herself, she would live only for the moment in a little safe pool of non-judgemental peace because soon enough she would be forced to deal with the consequences of her accidental pregnancy.

Leo smoothed a stray strand of red hair behind her ear, noting how small her ear was and that at their last encounter he had miscounted the freckles on her nose. There were five, not four, tiny brown speckles that only accentuated the clarity of her luminous porcelain skin. He sank his hands beneath her, lifting her up to peel off her sweater. She was pregnant, he reminded himself in a daze, for that awareness was still so new to him that it felt unreal. He would have to be careful and that would be a challenge when his raw need for her was threatening to explode out of restraint.

'Is it all right for us to do this?' he murmured a tad awkwardly.

'Good grief, Leo, I'm as healthy as a carthorse!' Grace countered, reddening hotly as his appreciative gaze dropped down to the bountiful swell of her breasts in a lace-cupped bra.

'But infinitely more beautiful and sensual,' Leo purred, fighting an impractical urge to stay welded to her and finally sliding off the bed to strip off his suit. 'So delicate...and yet voluptuous.'

A reluctant grin slanted Grace's mouth. 'You really do have the gift of the gab, as my Irish mother used to say. Women must drop like ninepins around you in receipt of all that flattery.'

In Leo's experience women were infinitely more aggressive in their desire to catch his eye and share his bed. His sculpted mouth quirked at her innocence. He dropped his shirt on the floor, ropes of abdominal muscle flexing across his torso below her admiring gaze. Grace dragged her attention from him in embarrassment and shimmied out of her jeans, blushing at the schoolgirl knickers she sported beneath. She had never had the money to buy prettier underwear. That random thought took her brain off the disturbing truth that she was succumbing to Leo's magnetism all over again. Was that wrong?

She wanted him; she wanted him every bit as much as he seemed to want her. He was the father of the baby she carried and he was neither irresponsible nor uncaring and there was absolutely no reason why they should not be together again...was there? Did she have to be sensible Grace all the time? She recalled the end result of rebelling against her sensible self the night she had met Leo. But then that axe had already fallen, she reminded herself doggedly, quickly talking herself into staying exactly where she was.

'You've got that thinking-too-hard look on your face again,' Leo chided, pulling her into his arms. 'It makes you look incredibly serious.'

His body was so hot against the faintly chilled coolness of her own, so hot in temperature and so deliciously different. He was rough where she was smooth, hard where she was soft. Desire snaked through her like a sharp-cutting knife, clenching low down in her pelvis. Her fingertips grazed across his muscular torso as he leant over her. The kiss he stole was explosive. He sucked and nibbled at her lower lip, all teasing and sex, stirring her up with the occasional plunge of his tongue.

Grace scored her fingers down a powerful hair-roughened thigh and circled his throbbing hardness before pushing him back against the pillows with her free hand. Startled, Leo began to raise his shoulders off the pillows while Grace zeroed in on her objective. Her soft sultry mouth closed over him like a glove and any resistance he had faded fast. Dangling strands of red hair danced across his skin with her every movement.

'OK?' she said, looking up at him, her face as red as a ripe apple.

'Better than…way better,' Leo admitted unevenly, mesmerised by the way she was touching him, craving it more with every passing second.

As she took him deep, his hand tangled in her tumbled hair and excitement filled her as he arched his hips up to her for more. A low groan sounded in his throat, an almost animalistic purr, while her fingers toyed with him and her tongue glided over him. Her pace quickened, her mouth moving over him faster and faster.

'Bloody spectacular…' Leo grated between clenched teeth as she took him up and over in the longest, hottest release of his life.

Grace lay back, feeling vindicated, feeling empowered, no longer the shy, ignorant virgin in need of guidance or instruction. He had really enjoyed that and she knew it. Leo turned her flushed face towards him, dark eyes still tawny gold with arousal. 'You always surprise me.'

Her bra came adrift, his hands kneading her aching flesh while his thumbs skimmed her distended nipples. She closed her eyes, losing herself in a world of sensation while he licked his way down over her body, tugging her knickers out of his path to discover the warm, wet welcome already awaiting him because nothing had ever quite excited Grace as much as her view of Leo shedding his smooth sophistication and crying out from the pleasure she was giving him.

With a hungry growl he eased over her, his recovery rate exceeding her expectations when the heated probe of his engorged shaft pushed against her most tender flesh. A surge of excitement made her inner muscles clench tightly round him. Her heart was hammering. She wanted this, she wanted *him* so much she was trembling and breathless, on a high of such joyful anticipation she could hardly contain it.

'You feel amazing,' Leo rasped, struggling for control as he worked his way gently into the depths of her glorious body when he didn't feel remotely gentle.

Grace tilted up her hips and locked her slim legs round him in acceptance. 'I'm not made of eggshell,' she whispered teasingly.

With a groan of relief, Leo surrendered to the raw need riding him, easing out of her tight channel to slam back in again with a glorious sense of satisfaction.

Grace couldn't catch her breath as he moved with animalistic power, powering into her with a hard driven sensuality that filled her with splintering excitement. Her whole body was reaching for and craving the ultimate crest and when it reached it she soared high as heaven. The intense pleasure radiated through her in an astonishing crescendo of sensation that left her trembling with little aftershocks of delight for several minutes afterwards.

On another level, she was conscious of Leo leaving the bed, doubtless to dispose of the contraception he had employed. She waited for him to return and then heard the shower running, slowly and unhappily realising that there would be no cosy togetherness in the aftermath of intimacy. That surprised her, for Leo was very prone to affectionate touching, not stand-offish in any way. Was he afraid of giving her the wrong message? Apprehensive that a little cuddle might make her assume that he felt more for her than he actually did?

Grace shifted uneasily in the bed, her brain now clear of the overwhelming pleasure that had left her mindless. She was painfully aware that she was developing feelings for Leo Zikos, far beyond the boundaries of those she had first envisaged. Considering how insanely attractive Leo was, she supposed her reaction to him was fairly normal and naturally there was something even more attractive about his insatiable desire for her ordinary self, never mind the fact that he was the father of her baby. Obviously she didn't want to get hurt by falling for someone who didn't feel the same way. But then, nobody wanted to get their heart broken and this was not only a time for her to consider her future as a mother, but also a time in which they could get to know each other better and explore their feelings.

By the time Leo came back to bed, Grace was

sound asleep. Around dawn she shifted up against Leo and the sheer novelty value of being in bed with another person was probably what awakened him. In the darkness, he lay still, listening to Grace's even breathing. He frowned and very gently removed the arm he had inexplicably draped round Grace before quietly easing out of the bed to pull on jeans and a shirt. He padded through to the vast expanse of the main reception room and checked his phone for messages.

There was a text from his father: Anatole would be in London on Saturday and wanted to know if Leo would still be around. Leo almost groaned out loud. He would be on the other side of the world by then but he now needed to move Grace to another location because the London apartment was used by both his father and his brother. Leaving Grace in residence would entail explanations that Leo was not yet ready to make.

He raked impatient fingers through his tousled black hair. What was he playing at? What the hell had he been playing at when he took Grace back to bed again? That was no answer to the mess they were both in and had probably only complicated everything more. He was maddened by his sudden unprecedented loss of restraint and discipline the night before and exasperated by what he saw as his own irrational behaviour.

Sex had always been a purely physical exercise for Leo. Anything even one step beyond simple sex was dangerous in his view because it could open him up to the risk of destructive attachments and desires. He had not had to worry about that before because he had never connected in any more lasting way with a woman he had been intimate with.

He swore under his breath, grasping that it was a little late in the day to acknowledge that he was getting in too deep with Grace Donovan. Hadn't they enough of a connection in the child she had conceived? Getting involved in an affair with Grace would be foolish because when it finished relations would inevitably sour between them and potentially damage his future relationship with his child. Why hadn't he thought about that reality? Why hadn't he thought about what he would be encouraging if he had sex with her again? Most probably raising expectations he was highly unlikely to fulfil?

As Leo poured himself a whiskey from a crystal decanter it seemed to him that his libido had been doing all his thinking for him. That shook him inside out. In fact he broke out in a cold sweat at that knowledge while he paced the pale limestone floor. He drained his glass and set it down with a definitive snap. Was he more like his father than he had ever suspected? Too weak and selfish to behave honourably? More likely than most men to succumb to a sexual obsession? After all, Anatole Zikos had promised repeatedly to end his relationship with Bastien's mother but somehow he had always ended up drifting back to Athene while coming up with one excuse after another. In truth Anatole had been too obsessed with Athene to ever give her up and her death had devastated him.

Leo was all too well aware that he was the son of almost neurotically volatile parents, who had remained locked in an emotional triangle of high drama throughout their marriage. His home life had been a nightmare and when he had visited his friends' homes he had marvelled at the quiet normality that they took for granted. When it came to what he viewed as his dodgy genes, Leo had always been relieved that he appeared to have skipped that over-emotional inheritance and was far too cold-blooded and logical to become obsessed with any woman. Indeed since his troubled childhood had taught him to mask his feelings and rigorously suppress or avoid any more intense reactions he had struggled to deal with any strong emotion.

But that approach wasn't likely to work for a male who had conceived a child with another woman in the run-up to his own wedding, Leo conceded bleakly. Everyone concerned had a right to strong emotions in a scenario like that. He had made the same mistake his father had—he had got the wrong woman pregnant. Wilfully or accidentally—did it matter which? Unlike his father, however, he would not compound his error by marrying a different woman and dragging her into the same shameful chaos. He had some tough decisions to make, he acknowledged grimly. It was no longer a matter of something as self-indulgent as what he *wanted*, but more a matter of honour. Such an old-fashioned word, that, Leo conceded ruefully, but if it meant that he accepted the need to put logic and fairness at the top of his list, it perfectly encapsulated his duty. And unlike his father, Leo planned to put his child first and foremost.

Around seven that same morning, Grace emerged from the shower, wrapped a fleecy towel round her nakedness and wondered ruefully where her cases

were. Their frantic charge to the bedroom the night
before had left no time for such niceties as unpack-
ing. Her face burned and she glanced in one of the
many mirrors, angry and ashamed of herself because
she was still acting out of character and letting her
life go off the rails. One mistake did not need to lead
to another, so why had she slept with Leo again last
night? Waking up in bed alone in the silent apartment
with her brain awash with unfamiliar thoughts of self-
loathing had unnerved her. Leo, she had decided mis-
erably, Leo was *bad* for her.

She crept out to the hall where her luggage still
awaited her and she was about to lift a case when she
heard a sound from another room and stiffened uncertainly.

'Grace…is that you?'

It was too late to retreat with any dignity but the
discovery that Leo was still in the apartment and had
not yet gone off to work as she had dimly assumed
was unwelcome. She moved to the doorway of a large
ultra-modern room flooded with light from a wall
of windows and saw Leo. Her breath hitched in her
throat. Barefoot, clad in only a pair of jeans unfastened at the waist and an unbuttoned shirt, Leo looked
heartbreakingly gorgeous with his messy black hair,
stubbled jawline and stunningly unreadable dark eyes
gleaming in the sunlight.

'I thought you were out,' she confided. 'I need to
get dressed.'

'No hurry… Housekeeping doesn't get here until
nine.' Leo stared at her, his eyes eating her alive in the
pounding silence. With her red hair rippling damply
round her narrow shoulders, her triangular face warm

with colour and her sea-glass eyes bright and eva-
sive, she reminded him of a pixie. She was tiny and
her curves were gloriously feminine. He wanted to
tell her to drop the towel. The swelling at his groin
was more than willing to bridge an awkward moment with sex.

'I have things to do.'

'Come here…I want to show you some properties,'
Leo urged.

Grace moved reluctantly forward, one hand clutching the towel to her breasts lest it slip. She was wasting
her time with the modesty, Leo thought helplessly. It
only made him want to rip it off her more. 'Properties?' she questioned, dry-mouthed.

Leo sank down on the sofa he had abandoned and
swung out the laptop he had been using. 'I've been
looking for somewhere suitable for you to live.'

'But I'm here…er…I thought…'

'This is a company apartment, used by my father
and my brother as well. It's serviced, convenient for
me,' Leo explained. 'Until now I haven't spent enough
time in London to warrant the purchase of separate
accommodation.'

'And that's changing?' Grace took a seat uneasily by his side and the faint but awesomely familiar scent of him assailed her nostrils, an intoxicating
hint of sandalwood and citrus fruit with a foundation
note of warm, musky masculinity. Below the towel
her breasts beaded into straining points and warmth
pooled in her pelvis.

'Obviously it will. If my child's going to be here, I
will be too,' Leo countered carelessly, as if that truth
was so obvious he shouldn't have to say it out loud.

'But fortunately I do own quite a few investment properties here and I've made up a small selection of the ones that are currently available for you.'

Grace was frowning in bewilderment. 'For...*me*?'

'You're homeless. My most basic responsibility should be ensuring that you have a comfortable and secure base.'

'I wasn't homeless until you persuaded me to move out of Matt's spare room,' Grace said shortly, disliking the label as much as his take-charge attitude that suggested she was a problem to be tackled and solved. 'And I assumed I was staying *here*.'

'You need your own space.'

No, Leo wanted *his* space back, Grace suspected. Just then she recalled that he hadn't still been in bed with her the morning after their first night together on the yacht either. 'You should've left me where I was.'

'I'm not going to argue about this with you. It's futile,' Leo spelt out, flipping up the first of three luxury properties, chosen for proximity to her university campus.

Her lungs inflated while she listened to his spiel and watched the screen flip up properties that only someone wealthy could have afforded to rent. Her hands curled into fists and her soft mouth flattened over grinding teeth long before he reached the end of his running commentary and turned the laptop over to her for further perusal. It was the last straw. Grace sprang up and settled the laptop squarely back down on the coffee table. 'Thanks but no, thanks,' she said curtly.

Leo leapt up, his shirt flying back from his corrugated abdomen, his unsnapped waistband giving her a glimpse of the little black furrow of silky hair that arrowed down to his crotch. As she remembered how intimate she had been with him the night before the bottom seemed to fall out of her stomach and she felt positively ill with mortification.

'What the hell is that supposed to mean? That's *my* baby you're carrying and from now on until the finish line you're both *my* responsibility!' Leo shot back at her impatiently.

'No, I'm my own responsibility and I don't need a domineering, controlling man telling me what to do!' Grace flared instantly back at him, light green eyes glittering with the blistering anger she had been holding back. 'I understand that you want to stand by me to show me that you're a good guy but you're handing out very mixed messages and I prefer to know exactly where I stand.'

One look at her and Leo wanted her so badly at that moment that he physically hurt. Her passion called out to him on the deepest level of his psyche even though he had deliberately avoided that kind of passion all his life. She was having an emotional meltdown and that was all right, only to be expected, he told himself soothingly. 'If you were to stay with me, we'd end up in bed again and that's not a good idea when you don't yet know what your plans are.'

'I am not going to end up in bed with you again. I am *never* going to go to bed with you again!' Grace swore vehemently.

Far from comforted by that news, Leo groaned. 'Grace, you're a nice girl and I don't get involved with nice girls. I don't do love and romance. I can't be what you want if you want more.'

'I'm not going to be some kept woman in some house you own either, living off you like a leech because we had a stupid contraceptive accident!' Grace raked back at him furiously, infuriated to be called a 'nice girl' because that tag only suggested dreary, conservative and needy to her. In addition, although she refused to allow herself to dwell on her sense of rejection, she was horribly crushed by his cool, cynical disclaimer of any deeper feelings where she was concerned. 'I may be poor but I have my pride. You're interfering in my life far too much, Leo.'

Leo shocked himself by wanting to shout back at her. He wanted her to do what he told her to do, which was, after all, what ninety-nine per cent of the people in his life invariably did. Consequently, he very rarely, if ever, raised his voice. He was proud of his self-control but then he had always avoided emotional scenes, swiftly ditching women who specialised in them. Of course he had been raised by the ultimate of scene-throwers: his mother, whom he recalled staging dramatic walkouts, outrageous suicide threats and sobbing herself into hysterics.

'You have to have peace and quiet to continue your studies and decide what to do next. I'm *trying* not to interfere with that. If you weren't pregnant, you wouldn't be in this situation now. I only want what's best for you and the baby.'

'And the easiest thing for you to give is money,' Grace completed with reluctant comprehension, her troubled green eyes scanning the opulence of the furnishings and a view of the City of London that had to be next door to priceless. 'Isn't it?'

His lean, darkly handsome face tensed. 'Yes, so will you view the property you like the best? I'll have you moved in by the weekend. I think we should have dinner tonight and talk future options.'

'No, I have a student thing to attend,' Grace lied, freshly determined to dull her intense attraction to Leo by seeing less of him.

'Tomorrow night, then.'

'No, sorry.'

'Grace, I'm trying hard here,' Leo growled in warning.

'I have a check-up with the doctor booked.'

'I'll come with you and we'll eat afterwards,' Leo pronounced with satisfaction.

That wasn't what Grace wanted at all. She felt like a ball being rolled down a steep hill in a direction she didn't want to go. Leo was getting much too involved in her life but by sleeping with him again hadn't she encouraged that? Torn in two by inner conflict, Grace lifted her chin. 'When do you want me to see this property?' she prompted.

'I have a board meeting this morning but late afternoon around four would suit me. I'll pick you up then.'

Grace wanted to tell him that she didn't need his escort either but it was *his* property and she could hardly object. All too frequently in life, Grace had discovered that necessity and practicality overruled any personal preference. Barring a return to Matt's guest room, she *was* technically homeless and in no position to dismiss an offer made by the father of her unborn child. She didn't like that truth but she had to live with it, she told herself unhappily.

When she emerged from the unused bedroom she had taken her case into, fully dressed and composed, Leo had left and Sheila, the friendly older woman washing the kitchen floor, asked her what she would like for breakfast. 'Housekeeping' Leo had labelled Sheila with the casual indifference that spoke volumes about his privileged status in life. Grace ate cereal and toast at the kitchen table and learned all there was to know about Sheila's four adult children, grateful for the pleasant chatter that took her mind off her problems.

There was a tight, hard knot inside Grace's chest and it ached like mad. Over and over again she was still hearing Leo say, *I don't do love and romance... you're a nice girl.* Last night Leo had sung a very different tune, making her sound irresistible, giving her the heady impression that she meant more to him than she did while he smoothly talked her into an act of monumental stupidity. Of course, he had said all those things, demonstrated all that thrilling impatience *before* he got her into bed, and that told her all she really needed to know, didn't it? she scolded herself with newly learned cynicism. He had fooled her, manipulated her, got what he evidently wanted and then withdrawn behind boundaries again. There was a lesson to be learned there and she had learned it well.

A light knock sounded on the bedroom door while she was repacking her case. 'Grace...you have a visitor,' Sheila told her.

Bemused by the announcement when even Matt didn't have her address, Grace followed Sheila down to the hall to see a tall, very attractive brunette with a wealth of mahogany hair and dressed in a very fashionable outfit, who frowned at Grace in apparent astonishment. 'My goodness, you're not at all what I expected!' she exclaimed, extending a slim beringed hand. 'I'm Marina Kouros…and you can only be… *Grace*?'

CHAPTER SIX

'Yes. Am I supposed to know who you are?' Grace asked the tall brunette awkwardly.

'Leo didn't mention me?' Marina Kouros prompted.

'I'm afraid not.'

'Coffee, Miss Kouros?' Sheila proffered from the kitchen doorway.

'No, thanks…we'll be in the sitting room,' the brunette said with easy authority, strolling confidently ahead of Grace, making it clear she knew her way around the apartment before she paused for an instant to firmly close the door.

'Why should Leo have mentioned you?' Grace asked stiffly as she hovered by the wall of windows, insanely conscious of her worn jeans and plain chain-store sweater when compared to her companion's expensive separates.

Marina's discomfiture was, for an instant, too obvious to be misinterpreted. 'Because Leo and I have been engaged for the past three years and we're getting married in six weeks' time…or, at least, we were until you came along.'

Grace's jaw felt frozen and unwieldy as she struggled to speak through underperforming facial muscles. *'Engaged?'* That single word was literally all she could squeeze out of her deflated lungs because her whole body felt as if it had gone into serious shock.

'I'll keep this brief. I'm not here to see you off… well, I suppose that's a lie. If you were to vanish into thin air right now, it would suit me very well, but I know you're pregnant and that it's not quite that simple.'

'Leo *told* you that I'm pregnant?' Grace whispered in even greater shock.

'He's very upfront like that but I must say you are a surprise. I was expecting a blonde bombshell with a pole dancer's wardrobe,' Marina admitted with a distressing candour that suggested Leo's infidelity was more normal than worthy of note. 'But look, I won't prevaricate. I'm here for one reason only. I don't want you to screw up Leo's life and mine and I was planning to offer you money to go away.'

Like an accident victim, Grace was frozen in place, her face as pale as milk, her eyes wide with consternation and haunted by too many powerful reactions to enumerate. Marina evoked so many different reactions in Grace; anger, mortification, guilt and pain were assailing her on all levels. Leo had lied to her. Leo had pretended to be single and unattached, and an engaged man on the brink of his wedding was anything but unattached. He had been engaged for *three* years? That was not a recent or a casual commitment.

'If Leo had told me he was engaged this wouldn't have happened because I would never have been with him in the first place,' Grace framed with desperate dignity. 'I'm genuinely sorry that anything I have done has upset you and that this situation is affecting you as well, but there is no way I would accept money from you.'

'I've known Leo all his life. He had a horrendous childhood and, because of it, he will never turn his back on his own child,' Marina informed her grimly. 'But I don't think he should have to sacrifice his whole life and all his plans *because* of that child. Somewhere, somehow there has to be a happy compromise for all of us.'

'I don't know what to say to you,' Grace framed sickly, her mind glossing over that reference to Leo's childhood because she could barely cope as it was with the overload of information and thoughts already bombarding her. 'I don't know what I can say…other than, how can you still care about a man who cheats on you?'

'I think that's my business.'

'Just as the baby's mine,' Grace countered quietly. 'I don't know what you want from me, Marina. But I won't be staying on in this apartment.'

'I only want you to think about what you're doing. *If* you have that baby…' Marina breathed with unmistakeable bitterness, her well-mannered mask slipping without warning '…you're wrecking *all* our lives!'

'But that's my decision to make,' Grace pointed out with wooden precision as she battled her churning inner turmoil to walk back to the door Marina had closed. She opened the door again in unapologetic invitation. 'If you're finished, I don't think we have anything else to say to each other right now.'

Across the city, Leo said a very bad word below his breath when he read the warning text from Marina.

For the first time ever he was really furious with his ex, his quick and clever brain instantly envisaging the potential fallout from what Grace had just discovered about him. Grace already had quite enough on her plate without that and Marina had absolutely no right to interfere. Had Marina hit out at Grace in revenge? Having always trusted his oldest and most loyal friend, Leo was taken aback by the suspicion, but the timing of Marina's visit spoke for itself and could hardly be deemed an accident. His handsome mouth twisted and he stood up at the board table to excuse himself from the meeting; he *had* to see Grace before she did something stupid.

That was the most surprising thing about Grace, which he had quickly registered. She might have a very clever brain and a steel backbone of independence but both were combined with an alarming tendency to make very sudden decisions and execute moves that were not always wise. It was that deeply buried vein of spontaneous passion and adventure in Grace that worried Leo the most. How else did he explain that night on his yacht? After almost twenty-five years of being a virgin she had just picked him like a rabbit out of a hat? A man about whom she knew nothing? Leo was still appalled by the risk she had taken on him that night until it occurred to him that he had never expended a similar amount of anxiety on any other casual sex partner. Only then did he crack down hard on his undesirable feelings of concern and the vague suspicion that Grace was much more fragile and vulnerable than she liked to pretend.

Well, once they were married, he wouldn't need to worry about her any longer. He would know where she was, what she was doing…in short, once he had control of Grace, *full* control, the horrible sense of apprehension that had gripped him since he first learned of her pregnancy would die a natural death. His anxiety was undoubtedly focused on the baby, he told himself consolingly. The baby was only a speck barely visible to the naked eye at this stage of his or her development—Leo had looked it up on the Internet—but it was *his* future son or daughter and he knew that baby was virtually defenceless and utterly dependent on the health and well-being of its mother's body for survival. What the hell had Marina been thinking of when she had deliberately approached a woman in Grace's condition to break such bad news? Hadn't she appreciated how dangerous that could be?

Grace was stacking her luggage in the hall when the front door opened again. She had been frantically struggling to get herself out of the apartment as fast as possible while accepting the demeaning truth that she could not afford to call a taxi to ferry her and her possessions away in one go. No, she would have to leave stuff to be collected at a later date. But most threatening of all was the awareness that she had absolutely no place else to go because a return to Matt's flat, Matt, who had been constantly texting her with revealing urgency since her departure, was definitely not an option.

As Grace straightened Leo stepped through the door and snapped it shut behind him without removing his glittering dark eyes from her once. 'Going somewhere?' he asked shortly.

Grace hadn't seen Leo leave earlier. In a navy pinstripe suit that screamed designer elegance and a plain white shirt teamed with a jazzy red tie, Leo looked absolutely stunning. Her heartbeat quickened as she remembered running her fingers through his black hair the night before and the unforgettable taste of his mouth. Heat was beginning to stir inside her when she shut down hard on that response, fighting that potent physical pull with all her might, reminding herself of what he was and denying it until she was back in control again.

Grace lifted her chin. 'Yes, somewhere as far as possible from you,' she answered.

'Marina told me she'd come to see you.' His beautiful shapely lips compressed, a muscle pulling tight at the corner of his unsmiling mouth. 'She shouldn't have done that.'

'Oh, I don't know,' Grace fielded in a tremulous driven undertone that mortified her, frankly bemused by a relationship that crossed the expected boundaries. It was inconceivable to her that Marina would've told Leo she had been to see Grace. 'Considering the way you've behaved I thought she was remarkably restrained in what she had to say.'

'My relationship with Marina is not as straightforward as you probably assume it is. Nor does what it entailed matter now because I *broke off* our engagement earlier today.' Leo studied her with screened intensity, expecting an immediate lessening of the tension in the atmosphere.

Grace refused to react in any way because that announcement did not lessen her sense of betrayal in the slightest. 'You said you were single…you *lied*,' she condemned with quiet simplicity.

'Let's move this out of the hall and talk like grown-ups,' Leo suggested grittily.

'I've got nothing to say to you, Leo, so I suggest we stay where we are and you let me leave.'

'*Diavelos...*' Leo ground out, his frustration finally bubbling over in response to her pale composed expression and cold light green eyes. He had expected to find Grace distraught. Somehow he had expected her to shout and sob because he knew, or he had thought he knew, that like some chocolates she had a soft inner centre and would be hurt about what she had learned about him. Instead he was looking at a disturbingly controlled young woman, who refused to either shout or sob, and he didn't know how to deal with that at all. 'In the circumstances you *must* have something to say to me.'

'But I doubt very much if you want to hear it.' So great was the strain of maintaining her tough, unfeeling façade, Grace could barely speak. Pain and disillusionment sat like a massive block inside her chest, radiating toxic, wounding rays of insecurity, hurt and rejection. He had devastated her, shattered her heart into a hundred pieces, but on another level she was grateful for Marina's visit because at least she had found Leo out for the rat he was before she became any more deeply involved with him.

Leo thrust the door of the sitting room so wide that it bounced back noisily. 'I *do* want to hear it!' he challenged.

Reckoning that he was going to make it difficult for her to leave without a muck-raking confrontation and marvelling that he could even want that, Grace trudged into the big room where Marina had faced her with the truth that had destroyed her dreams. Silly, sentimental, romantic dreams, utterly inappropriate dreams for a woman of her age, intelligence and background to have cherished: the dream that a man could be decent and honest and trustworthy.

With her parents' history before her, she should've known better, Grace thought painfully. Even her own father had lied and cheated rather than keep his promise to marry her mother. Soon after Grace's birth, her father had begun working with the woman who would eventually become his first wife and he had kept his infidelity a secret while continuing to live with Grace and her mother. She had the vaguest possible memory of her father because he had walked out on her mother before Grace reached her second birthday.

Grace spun round to face Leo, her arms folded defensively across her slightly built body. 'Right, exactly what do you want from me? Forgiveness? Understanding? Well, sorry, you're not getting either!' she told him roundly.

'I want to explain.'

'No, I don't want to hear any explanations…a bit pointless at this stage!' Grace pointed out curtly. 'You lied to me and there's no getting round that. Don't waste any more of my time, Leo. Let me go.'

'To go where?'

'I don't know yet.' Grace was distracted by the buzzing of her mobile phone in the back pocket of her jeans and she dug it out and switched it off, noticing in forgivable surprise that it was her aunt calling her. Considering her aunt had told her never to bother her family again, what could she possibly want? Unless her uncle Declan, who had visited Grace at Matt's flat, had persuaded his wife to soften her attitude.

'You can't leave when you don't have anywhere to go!' Leo argued fiercely. 'You have to take care of yourself now that you're pregnant!'

'Oh, please, don't pretend you actually *care*,' Grace countered with withering sarcasm, her bitterness licking out from below the surface before she could prevent it from showing.

'If you would just listen to me and stop being so unreasonable,' Leo bit out.

'I don't need to listen. I already know what you are and that's a dirty, lying, cheating scumbag without an ounce of integrity!' Grace shot at him, green eyes suddenly flaring bright as angry stars because he had dared to call *her* unreasonable.

'I broke off my engagement so that I could come back here and ask you to marry me!' Leo launched at her in outrage, fury surging up inside him like lava inside a volcano about to erupt. He had never felt so angry in his life and it was an unnerving experience. He didn't get angry; he didn't *do* angry. Nothing and no one had ever been capable of sending him over that edge because to get angry you had to care and he was not supposed to care.

Grace slowly shook her head at him in apparent wonderment, an attitude that enraged Leo even more because no woman had ever dared to look at him like that. 'Well, the answer to that proposal would've been a very firm no once I found out what you had been hiding from me. Honesty and reliability are hugely important to me, Leo, and you score nil on both counts. I saw today what you did to Marina and I'm afraid that was quite enough to convince me that you're a very arrogant, selfish personality with very few saving graces…no pun intended.'

'Is that all you've got to say to my suggestion that we get married?' Leo growled, hardly able to credit what he was hearing because nobody, least of all a woman, had ever found him wanting on *any* score. So prejudiced against him was Grace that it almost felt to him as though she saw some mirror image of him that was another person entirely. And then he remembered her history and somewhere inside his head an alarm bell clanged, putting him right on target.

'Yes, that's all I've got to say. Once the baby's born, I'll get in touch with you at this address,' Grace assured him flatly. 'But be warned…I have no plans to hand my child over to you or anything like that because you're not my idea of a father in any way.'

Leo could literally feel himself freezing into an ice pillar while still wanting to strangle her into silence. Did he deserve such a character assassination? Well, so much for the winning power of a marriage proposal and a rich and powerful husband! But offended and infuriated as he was by Grace and the awareness that he had seriously underestimated her temper, he was more fixated on where she planned to go when she appeared to have neither money nor any suitable friends or family to live with. Recognising that Grace needed to cool off before he could even hope to reason with her, he reached into his wallet to withdraw a card and extended it.

'I own the hotel. It's small and discreet and you only need to show the card at Reception to be accommodated. My driver will take you there…'

In the grip of frantic thought and the blistering emotional turmoil that their encounter had provoked, Grace accepted the card. She had to go somewhere and she had no place else, she thought wretchedly, and ditched her pride. 'OK.'

A shard of relief speared through Leo's almost overwhelming sense of rage and raw frustration. She wouldn't listen to him, she refused to listen, refused to let him talk...how fair was that? He hated feeling powerless, an unfamiliar sensation because she was the only person who had ever had that effect on him. Even so, it was of paramount importance to Leo that he knew where she was and that she was safe and well looked after. She had got him wrong, *so* wrong, he thought bitterly.

In Leo's limo, Grace dug out her phone to check it and called back her aunt.

'I need to see you urgently,' Della Donovan said in an unusually constrained voice.

Grace wondered what on earth had happened to make her aunt approach her because she was fairly certain that Jenna's dislike of her had initially been learned from her mother. Compressing her lips, she agreed to meet up for coffee that afternoon. Had her uncle pressured his wife into burying the hatchet and healing the breach? The suspicion worried her. Declan Donovan was a kind man but, sadly, such feelings couldn't be forced.

The hotel was small, unassuming from the outside but the last word in elegant opulence and service on the inside. Within minutes of her presenting the card, her luggage was collected and she was settled in a large and beautiful room complete with every possible luxury. The bathroom was a dream and as soon as she had unpacked Grace laid out clean clothes for her meeting with her aunt and went for a bath in an effort to relax her sadly frayed nerves.

She felt so unhappy. In all her life, Grace had never felt quite so unhappy. She had always been alone but she had never felt lonelier than she did at that moment, cut off from everything familiar and at her third change of address in the space of a week. The following week term started and she would be back in class and facing hospital placements. But for the first time ever Grace wasn't looking forward to getting back to her studies. The events of the past worrying weeks had taken their toll and she was exhausted.

Leo had broken off his engagement so that he could ask her to marry him. A sudden involuntary surge of tears stung Grace's gritty eyes. Only now was her brain calmed enough to consider that truth. He was trying so hard to do the right thing even though he had started out doing the wrong thing by not telling her that he was engaged. Did she give him points for that? Grace heaved a heavy sigh. She had been falling in love with him, weaving dreams, seeing a future that might include him, and then Marina had blown that fantasy out of the water. Marina had spelt out the reality that Leo had not only lied to Grace, but was also a regular playboy. That crack Marina had made in which she admitted having expected Grace to be a blonde bombshell in a pole dancer's outfit had lingered longest with Grace. Evidently Leo had betrayed his fiancée more than once. He was a liar and a cheat just like her father, who had also turned out to be a great deal less interested in raising his own child than he had first pretended to be.

Della Donovan was seated in a corner of the busy coffee shop when Grace arrived. She was immaculate in a smart suit, her blonde hair in a chignon; her critical gaze scanned her niece in her trademark jeans. And for the first time ever, Grace felt like picking up on that faintly scornful appraisal and asking when she had ever had the money to dress as smartly as the rest of the family. She suppressed the urge, recognising that now that she had moved out of her aunt's home, where she had always had to watch every word to keep the peace, such humility no longer came naturally to her.

'Grace...' Della murmured with a rather forced smile. 'How have you been?'

And to Grace's astonishment, her aunt engaged her in polite small talk.

'You said this was urgent,' Grace finally reminded the older woman, wondering what the heck was holding her aunt back from simply saying whatever it was she wanted to say.

'I'm afraid I have to ask you a rather personal question first.' Her aunt pursed her lips. 'Is Leos Zikos the father of your child?'

'That's private—' Grace began.

'Oh, for goodness' sake, I wouldn't be asking if it wasn't important!' Della snapped, for the first time sounding like her usual self.

'Yes...he is,' Grace confirmed grudgingly.

The older woman paled. 'I was hoping I was wrong because I was very rude to him and even ruder when he asked for you.'

Grace was unsurprised. 'I'm sure he'll get over it.'

'A man that rich and influential doesn't have to get *over* anything!' Della Donovan argued in a fierce undertone. 'Leos Zikos owns the company your uncle works for. He channels work for that company through the legal firm *I* work for. You're far from stupid, Grace. The father of your baby has a huge amount of power over your family and if you don't keep him sweet, he could punish *all* of us.'

It was a bittersweet moment for Grace, hearing herself described as part of the family for the very first time, but she was thoroughly disconcerted by the genuine apprehension she could see in Della's anxious face. 'You're seriously worried about that risk?'

'Of course I am. Zikos has a name for being hard, ruthless and unforgiving and I'm asking you to smooth things over with him for your family's sake.'

Grace realised why she was being temporarily promoted to family status and almost laughed. 'Della, Leo hasn't ever mentioned either you or Declan.'

Unimpressed, Della curled her lip. 'We looked after you when you were a child, Grace. Now I expect you to look after us and ensure that there is no reason for Leo Zikos to sack your uncle from his job or withdraw business from my legal firm. After all, it's *your* fault that I was brusque with him... I know I offended him but he arrived in the middle of a family crisis... Make sure he understands that.'

Grace was astonished by the entire tenor of the conversation. Della was scared that her comfortable life was under threat. Only genuine anxiety on that score would have persuaded the older woman to meet up with her despised niece and ask her for help to smooth over any offence caused. Grace thought it best not to mention that she was currently at serious odds with Leo herself, having called him a lying, cheating scumbag without integrity.

'I'll check out the situation for you and, if necessary, explain things,' Grace promised to bring the uncomfortable meeting to an end. 'But I really don't think you have anything to worry about.'

'Grace, you have about as much idea as to how the very wealthy *expect* to be treated as a farm animal!' her aunt told her with raw-edged impatience.

Back at the hotel, Grace ordered a meal from room service and lay on the bed, pondering that strange encounter. She believed that her aunt was panicking without good cause. But hadn't she already discovered that she did not know Leo as well as she had assumed? It was not a situation she could ignore, was it? Leo could well be the vengeful type when people crossed him. Della had probably been very rude to him: Della in a temper didn't hold back. As Grace thrust her tray away, she lifted her phone, her conscience twanging. She couldn't simply ignore her aunt's fears simply because she herself did not want to speak to Leo.

'Grace...' Leo growled down the phone like a grizzly bear, apparently not in any better a mood than when she had last seen him.

'I need to talk to you,' Grace advanced stiffly.

'I'll be with you in an hour.' At the other end of the phone, Leo smiled with a strong sense of satisfaction. Clearly, Grace had calmed down and finally seen sense. Nobody was perfect. He had made *one* mistake. And she needed him, of course she did; he was the father of her baby…

An hour later, a knock sounded on the door and Grace used the peephole, recognising one of Leo's bodyguards before opening the door. 'Yes?'

'The boss is on the top floor waiting for you,' she was told.

Grace grabbed her key card and followed the man into the lift. Of course, if Leo owned the place he would have an office or something in the building, she guessed. She breathed in slow and deep at the thought of seeing Leo again. She could handle it; she could handle him without letting herself down. Couldn't she? She had never been one of those girls who was a pushover for a good-looking, smooth-tongued male, although to be honest, she reasoned, she had met none before Leo, which meant that Leo kind of reigned supreme in her imagination as the ultimate player.

She smoothed damp palms down over the denim skirt she had teamed with a green T-shirt. Dressing up for him? That suspicion was a joke when she re-called how Marina had looked, all glossy and glitzy with wonderfully smooth straight hair and amaz-ing make-up. No bad fairy had cursed Marina at birth with red curly hair and freckles, not to men-tion breasts and hips that would have suited some-one much taller.

She walked into a beautifully decorated large room. It had a bed like hers but there the similarity ended because it was much more of a five-star suite. Leo was by the window, broad, straight shoulders taut with a tension she could feel, and in spite of her inner strictures her heart leapt even before he swung round to face her.

'Grace…' he said and his dark deep drawl shimmied down her spine with the potent sexual charisma that was so much a part of him.

Leo felt a hard-on kick in as he focused momentarily on the swell of Grace's high, full breasts below the thin top and the slender perfection of the thighs he hadn't had a good look at since they first met. *Diavelos*, he loved her body, he really, *really* loved her body. It just did it for him every time the way no other woman's ever had. He looked and he simply wanted to touch, taste, *take*.

'I wanted to see you to discuss something…probably something you'll consider quite silly,' Grace warned him uncomfortably, striving to not quite focus on his lean, darkly handsome features with a mouth running dry and a tummy turning somersaults. But there he was, gorgeous, no denying that, she conceded helplessly while she fought to concentrate on what she had to say.

Leo had the celebratory champagne standing by on ice. He knew she was pregnant but was convinced that one little sip would do no harm simply to mark the occasion, because of course she wanted to see him to tell him that she was ready to marry him. The true celebration would be taking her back to bed again, knowing she was his…*finally*. When it dawned on him that Grace was burbling on for some strange reason about her uncle's job and her aunt's legal firm, he was perplexed, until the proverbial penny dropped and he made the necessary leap of understanding. Of course, what else would a lying, cheating scumbag do but throw his weight around through threats and intimidation?

'And you're afraid that I took offence?' Leo prompted, taking very much more offence from what she was saying than from anything her shrewish aunt had thrown at him.

'Yes, of course, I know you're not really like that...' Grace assured him.

No, you don't know. They wouldn't be having this conversation if she knew him and without warning a scorching tide of rage was washing over Leo like a dangerous floodtide.

Grace stared at Leo, noticing that his big powerful body had gone very, very still. His dark eyes shone as bright as gold ingots below his lush black lashes.

'They're my family...I do *care* about what happens to them,' Grace framed in uncertain continuation. 'They really don't deserve to be dragged into this mess between us.'

'I won't adversely affect their lives in any way *if* you agree to marry me,' Leo delivered in a tone that brought gooseflesh to her bare arms.

'I beg your pardon?'

'I think you heard me, Grace. If you do what I want and marry me, I will promise not to interfere with your uncle and aunt's continuing employment.'

Before his shrewd, hard gaze, Grace turned white. 'You can't mean that, not that you would seriously threaten their livelihoods just because *I'm* not doing what you want?'

'I *mean* it,' Leo asserted with fierce emphasis. 'I've run out of patience. I want to marry you and I want that child you're carrying. So, think very carefully about what *you* decide to do next.'

'But that's complete blackmail!' Grace shot back at him, trembling like a leaf in shock and barely able to credit what he was telling her.

'I never pretended to be a knight on a white horse, Grace. You and that baby are *mine* and the sooner you acknowledge that, the happier we will all be.'

'I don't belong to anyone. I belong to myself,' Grace argued through gritted teeth, battling a terrifying sense of panic as hard as she could because Leo had just trashed the faith she hadn't known she still cherished in him.

Leo stalked closer, well over six feet of powerfully built and determined masculinity. 'That was before you met me, *meli mou*. Everything's changed now. We'll get married on Friday.'

'Fri-Friday is only three days away,' Grace stammered, utterly thrown by Leo's controlling behaviour.

'I know and I can't wait to sign on that official dotted line,' Leo grated impatiently. 'Then I'll know *where* you are and *how* you are.'

'You're out of your mind,' Grace breathed in a daze. 'We can't just get married. You were engaged to Marina!'

'Marina's the past, you're the present,' Leo cut in with ruthless bite. 'And at this moment I'm only interested in the future and it starts here, *now* with your answer…'

Grace pinned tremulous lips together in the terrible stretching silence. Her heart seemed to be hammering in her eardrums. He was threatening her aunt and uncle's comfortable life and she couldn't just stand by and do nothing after all they had done for her, she thought wretchedly. They had brought her up, supported her at school, kept her safe. All right, it had been far from perfect but they were still the only family she had and she didn't want them to suffer in any way by association with her. Leo held all the cards: her uncle's employment, Della's legal firm's dependency on the business Leo sent their way. Della had worked long and hard for a partnership and if she had been rude to Leo—well, she was pretty rude to a lot of people, never having been the type to tolerate fools. Grace's mind and her thoughts were in turmoil.

'You could explain now about Marina,' she proffered tersely.

'No, that ship's already sailed,' Leo slammed back at her coolly. 'Are you marrying me on Friday or not?'

Grace wanted to say not, to puncture his carapace of arrogant strength and challenge him, but her character was grounded very firmly in compassion and the risk of her relatives having to pay a high price for her mistake in getting pregnant by the wrong man was not one she could ignore. She snatched in a wavering breath and damned him with her pale green defiant gaze. 'I'll give you an answer in the morning.'

'Why drag this out?'

'Because it's a very big decision,' Grace countered quietly. 'I'll tell you what I've decided tomorrow.'

Impatience assailed Leo and he gritted his strong white teeth. Her eyes were luminous pools of pale green but he noticed the dark circles etched below them and her general pallor. 'You look very tired.'

Grace coloured in receipt of that unflattering

comment. 'I'm going back downstairs to go straight to bed.'

'Have you eaten?' he shot at her as she reached the door.

'Yes,' she said.

'I'll meet you here for breakfast at eight in the morning,' Leo decreed.

How could she marry a man who had been planning to marry another woman for three long years? How could she surrender to blackmail? Would Leo really damage her aunt's and uncle's livelihoods and careers? Or was he bluffing? And if bluffing was a possibility was she prepared to light the fuse and wait and see what actually happened if she said no?

Grace lay in bed mulling over those weighty questions. Although she had completely dismissed the idea, Leo had mentioned marriage the very first day he'd discovered she was pregnant, she recalled ruefully. It seemed that marrying the mother of his child was important to him, *so* important he had immediately recognised it as a necessity. Not that that excused him in any way for employing threats when persuasion had failed, she reasoned.

Grace had so many unanswered questions that she was now wishing that she had listened to what Leo had had to say for himself earlier that day at his apartment. Clearly, Leo's relationship with Marina was unusual. When Marina had introduced herself to Grace, she had been fairly polite and remarkably composed for a female whose fiancé had just dumped her for another woman. Even so, Marina had repeatedly said that Grace having Leo's child would wreck *all* their lives. It was possible that Marina was simply a good actress but even that didn't explain the peculiarity of Marina visiting Grace to try and buy her off and then freely admitting that embarrassing fact to Leo.

Her head beginning to pound with the strain of her anxious reflections, Grace acknowledged that had Marina not existed she would've agreed to marry Leo. After all, it was best to be honest with herself: she did *want* Leo in spite of the shocks he had dealt her. It wasn't sensible, it wasn't justifiable but she had pretty much been infatuated with Leo from the moment she'd met him. On those grounds and bearing in mind the reality that she would very much like her baby to grow up with a father, shouldn't she give marriage a chance?

Only, how did she marry a male willing to blackmail her into agreement? That was wrong, that was *so* wrong. And the best of it was, she was convinced that Leo *knew* it was wrong but he had still put that pressure on her in an effort to get what he wanted. She did owe a debt of care to her uncle and aunt and if their lives were blighted because of something she had done she would be gutted, which didn't give her much in the way of choice. On the other hand, Grace reflected as she swallowed another yawn, she could agree to marriage with certain provisos attached.

Leo studied Grace as she joined him for breakfast, her face blank, her eyes uninformative. He reckoned he would make a good poker player and the challenge of that talent in a potential wife amused him. 'Well?' he prompted grimly, still annoyed that she had forced him to wait for her answer.

Grace sipped at her tea, wishing that Leo didn't

look quite so amazing first thing in the morning when she felt washed out and weary. There he was with his dark golden eyes alive with potent leaping energy, his blue-black hair still damp from the shower and his hard jawline close shaven. He wore yet another one of those remarkably well-tailored suits that beautifully defined his lean, muscular build. 'I'll say yes because you really haven't given me a choice.'

'Choice is a very much overrated gift,' Leo declared, pouring himself a cup of fragrant coffee with a steady hand, determined not to react in any way to her capitulation. 'People don't always make the *right* choice. Sometimes they need a little push in the relevant direction.'

'This was more than a little push,' Grace censured. 'I don't know why you're doing it either. You can't want me as a wife that much.'

'Why not?'

'I'm just ordinary.'

'I don't see you that way, *meli mou*,' Leo countered. 'I see you as different, as special.'

'Leo, you just blackmailed me into marrying you. Ditch the flattery!' Grace said very drily. 'And I may be saying yes but there would have to be certain conditions attached.'

Leo tensed again and flung back his arrogant head, shapely mouth flattening back into a tough line. 'Such as?'

'As the term hasn't started yet, I'm considering taking a year out while all this is going on but I would want to return to my studies in London next year. You would have to support that.'

'Naturally I would support that arrangement,' Leo

asserted, the tension locking his lean bronzed features into tautness evaporating.

Grace went pink and gathered her strength. 'And it would have to be a platonic marriage.'

Leo went rigid again and studied her with incredulous dark eyes as if she were insane. 'You can't be serious?'

'Of course, I'm serious. We don't have to be intimate to be married and raise a child together.'

His dark golden gaze rested on her resolute face. 'I'm afraid you do if you're married to me. I refuse to look outside my marriage for sex. That would degrade both of us and I couldn't live with it. I have strong views on fidelity,' he completed with finality.

Grace groaned out loud, not having expected him to be quite so set against what would in effect have been a marriage only on paper. 'I really did think that that would be the sensible option.'

'No, it would be a recipe for disaster.' Leo stared at her with his black-lashed dark eyes glittering like stars in a lean, angular face that was so handsome it made the breath trip in her tight throat. 'And I speak from experience. My father was persistently unfaithful to my mother and their unhappiness poisoned life for both them and their children.'

'My goodness...' Taken aback by that unexpectedly frank admission, Grace regrouped as she finished eating. 'But it wouldn't be quite so personal with us. For a start, we're not in love with each other or anything like that.'

'But I still want you, Grace, as a man wants a woman,' Leo delivered with savage candour. 'I won't pretend otherwise. I want a normal marriage with all that that entails, not some unnatural agreement that increases the odds of divorce. I also *want* to be there for our child as he or she grows up.'

'You've made your point,' Grace conceded grudgingly, willing to admit that she had not thought through the consequences of a platonic marriage. It had been naïve to assume that Leo might be willing to live without sex while the alternative of her having to turn a blind eye while Leo sought sexual consolation elsewhere was even less appealing to her. But how could he say that he had strong views on fidelity after what he had done to Marina?

As she pushed her plate away and stood up, her curiosity still fully engaged on the mystery of Leo's thought processes, Leo stood up as well.

'So, we're getting married in forty-eight hours?' Leo mused huskily, resting a hand on her arm.

'I think that's a yes.' Still striving to keep her distance, Grace tried to gently detach her arm from his hold but she didn't act fast enough because his other arm just closed round her spine to entrap her slim body against his lean, powerful frame. He was hard... *everywhere*. Hard-packed with muscle, tense and... fully erect. Her face burned in the split second before his mouth came crashing down on hers, nibbling, licking, tasting in a carnal assault on her senses that absolutely no other man could have contrived. Her head fell back and her mouth opened, treacherous excitement lighting her up like a shower of fireworks inside. It was so incredibly sexy. In a mindless moment she was convinced it was the sexiest kiss ever.

A knock sounded on the door and he pulled back from her. A waiter brought in champagne. Flustered by the power of that compellingly provocative kiss and shaken by the thought that she was actually going to marry Leo, Grace backed away to the window to practise breathing again.

Leo extended a champagne flute to her. 'To our future.'

'I shouldn't drink.'

'One sip for the sake of it,' Leo suggested.

Grace touched the flute to her mouth, moistening her lips.

'I'll set up a shopping trip for you today. You need clothes.' Unusually, Leo hesitated. 'Marina has offered to help out.'

'Marina?' Grace exclaimed, wide-eyed.

'We're still good friends. She's probably feeling a bit guilty that she approached you yesterday to buy you off because that sort of behaviour really isn't her style,' Leo remarked with a wry roll of his eyes. 'What you see is what you get with Marina. But if you would feel uncomfortable with her, I'll make a polite excuse…'

In the taut silence, Grace swallowed with difficulty, her mind functioning at top speed. Leo's ex-fiancée was offering to assist her in preparing for their shotgun wedding out of a genuine desire to be helpful? Grace's curiosity about the unconventional nature of Marina's relationship with Leo literally shot into the stratosphere at that revelation. Evidently their ties of friendship had withstood the breaking off of the engagement and the bitterness that Marina had briefly revealed, and that more than anything else impressed Grace and made her want to know more.

'No, don't make an excuse. It's an unusual situation but I think that Marina's kind gesture should be met with equal generosity,' Grace pronounced, hoping that she was making the right decision and not setting herself up as a target for the sort of spiteful comments of the type her cousin and her aunt had specialised in.

CHAPTER SEVEN

'FROM A PRACTICAL point of view, I've been up to my throat in wedding arrangements for the past few weeks, so I know exactly what I'm doing and who to contact,' Marina proffered as she sat beside Grace in the back of Leo's opulent limousine an hour later.

'But there isn't enough time to organise anything fancy.'

'When a man is as rich as Leo is, there are always people willing to meet a challenge for a substantial bonus,' the brunette told her drily.

'But why should *you* help us?' Grace asked baldly, no longer able to swallow back that burning and obvious question.

'I have my pride. First and foremost, I would prefer our friends to believe that the break-up was amicable rather than inspire a pity party,' Marina fielded wryly. 'I've also since had a radical rethink about my own future. Yesterday when I went to meet you I was fighting to preserve the status quo but, having cooled down, I'm now more inclined to think that Leo and I were just treading water and never meant to be. My father is deeply disappointed that he's not getting his dream whiz-kid son-in-law but I'm afraid I want to do what's right for me.'

'You're being very understanding.'

Marina laughed. 'Not as understanding as you probably think. To be frank, I have someone else in my life too and I believe that eventually Zack will make me happier than Leo ever would have done.'

Grace absorbed that unexpected admission without visible reaction. Yet it was undeniably a relief for her to learn that the svelte brunette was not the innocent and cruelly betrayed fiancée Grace had initially assumed she was. 'Even so, you and Leo still seem to be very close.'

'But there was always a flaw in our relationship.' Marina turned to look at Grace with a self-mocking light in her lively dark eyes. 'Although most men consider me attractive Leo never wanted me the way he wanted you.'

'I can't believe that,' Grace said uncomfortably, her face burning with sudden heat.

Marina grimaced. 'It's true and his detachment was bad for my ego. However, because we were friends from a young age, Leo believed we were an ideal match.'

'But you must've loved Leo as well,' Grace incised, cutting through the brunette's frustratingly guarded comments.

'Oh, yes, when I was younger I was absolutely mad about Leo! He was the full package—gorgeous, successful, strong—everything I wanted in a future husband,' the other woman admitted with a rueful laugh. 'Unfortunately, though, when it mattered I never made the girlfriend cut: Leo kept me firmly in the "friends" category. And when he suggested that we get married, I refused to listen to what he was saying and chose to assume that I meant more to him than he was willing to admit.' Her expressive lips compressed. 'Only I couldn't have been more wrong. He didn't mislead me, but any romantic feelings I once cherished for Leo were withered by his indifference.'

'He hurt you and yet you've forgiven him,' Grace commented in surprise.

Marina shrugged as she led the way into a designer bridal boutique. 'Life's too short for anything else. Just be sure you know what you're getting into with Leo because I doubt very much that he'll change.'

A small posse of assistants were waiting to greet them. Grace was extracted from her coat while Marina spoke to the designer, an effervescent blonde. Grace posed like a small statue while she was measured and wondered if she did have the slightest idea what she was getting into in choosing to marry Leo. Evidently he hadn't ever been in love with Marina. Furthermore Marina had ultimately found someone else to love as well, which was what made it possible for the brunette to civilly accept the bride Leo was taking in her place.

'Surely it doesn't matter what I wear to a civil ceremony?' Grace whispered to Marina.

'It will be your first appearance as Leo's wife and you'll feel more confident if you're properly turned out,' Marina asserted sagely. 'Being badly dressed won't impress anyone.'

'I don't really care about impressing people,' Grace admitted.

'But in our world, whether you like it or not, appearances *do* matter,' Marina traded without apology. The designer remarked that white and cream drained Grace of colour and tested less orthodox shades against her skin. Even Grace recognised *the* dress when it was held against her, an unconventional choice that provided an amazingly flattering background for her vibrant hair and pale complexion.

And as the seemingly endless day wore on with a lengthy trip to Harrods and the additional services of a very helpful fashion stylist, Grace discovered that she liked, possibly even *loved*, expensive, well-made clothes. Her fingers smoothed the softest cashmere, stroked silk and traced the delicate patterns of lace and exquisite embroidery. Astonishment and growing awe gripped her when those pricey designer garments shaped her figure and made her look so much better than she had ever dreamt she could look. When the overwhelming shopping experience was finally finished she slid her feet into comfy little pumps teamed with a short black skirt and a zingy sapphire-blue jacket and studied her sleek and elegant reflection in positive stupefaction. For the first time ever Grace thought she looked pretty and that maybe a spot of cosmetic enhancement would help even more.

'Thanks for everything,' she murmured with heartfelt gratitude to Marina, who had waved a magic wand over her like a fairy godmother bent on transforming Cinderella.

'Tomorrow you hit the beauty salon for some treatments and you won't be thanking me then. You haven't ever even plucked your eyebrows, have you?' the brunette prompted in a mixture of amusement and fascination.

Grace winced. 'Is it that obvious?'

Marina laughed. 'Comfort yourself with the knowledge that, in spite of your laissez-faire attitude in the grooming stakes, Leo admitted he couldn't take his eyes off you the first time he saw you.'

'He actually *told* you that?' Grace prompted, colour flaring in her pale cheeks.

Marina nodded confirmation. 'At least he was honest.'

Back at the hotel, Grace went straight up to the suite Leo was using. A stranger opened the door and two others were hovering round the desk at which Leo sat, his jacket off, his tie loosened, broad shoulder muscles flexing below a white silk shirt as he turned his head and stared fixedly at Grace where she hovered, uncertain of her welcome.

He sprang upright. 'Marina did good,' he quipped, brilliant dark golden eyes sliding over her slim figure in a look as physical as a touch. 'In fact, she did brilliantly.'

'She was a tremendous help.' Grace's colour was heightened by his scrutiny and the disturbing reaction of her body to that unashamedly sexual appraisal. Her nipples had prickled into taut sensitivity while a drenching pool of heat settled between her thighs. She was shaken by the intensity of her desire for him to reach out and touch her.

'My staff...' Leo introduced the three men before swiftly dismissing them. The trio swiftly gathered up laptops, briefcases and jackets and filed out. 'I need to have a word with you about the guest list for the wedding,' he told her levelly.

When asked earlier, Grace had put down Matt and

her uncle's family but could think of no one else to include and she studied him enquiringly.

'I take it, then…that you've decided not to invite your father?' Leo pressed, sharply disconcerting her.

'How could I? I've never met him, n-never had any contact with him.' In confusion and shock at the unexpected question, Grace stumbled over her words, wondering how he even knew that she had a father alive.

'Never?'

'Not since I was a baby anyway,' she completed tersely. 'Why are you asking? And how do you even know that I *have* a father living?'

'I had your background investigated while I was waiting for you to get in touch with me,' Leo confessed with a nonchalance that astounded her.

An angry flush illuminated her cheeks. 'You did… *what*? You had me investigated? What gave you the right to go snooping into my background?' Grace launched at him in a sudden fury.

'I needed to know who you were and where you were from…in case you were pregnant,' Leo responded levelly. 'It's standard business practice to check out people before you deal with them.'

'But I *wasn't* business and my life is private!' Grace snapped back at him, outraged by his invasion of her privacy. 'You had no right to pry!'

'I may not have had an official right but I did have good reason to want to know exactly who Grace Donovan and her family were,' Leo retorted unapologetically. 'But to return to my original question—when I found out about your father, it wasn't clear whether or not you had had any recent contact with him.'

Still furious with him, Grace clamped her lips into

a tight line of control. 'No, none and I don't want any either!'

His stunning dark golden eyes narrowed in apparent surprise. 'That seems a bit harsh in the circumstances.'

'He let my mother down badly and I'm quite sure he could have traced me years ago if he'd had any real interest in finding me,' Grace declared thinly.

'Only that would have been a considerable challenge for him when your mother had already taken him to court for harassment, had threatened to accuse him of assault and then changed her name to shake him off.'

Sheer rage roared up through Grace's rigid body like a forest fire running out of control. It convulsed her throat muscles, clenched her hands into fists and burned in her chest like the worst ever heartburn. She didn't know what Leo was talking about; she truly didn't have a clue! Wasn't that the ultimate humiliation? How could it ever be right that Leo should know more about her past than *she* did? Harassment? Assault? Court cases?

Reading her shuttered and mutinous face and the pale sea-green eyes blazing at him, Leo returned to the desk and extracted a slim file from the drawer, which he settled on the desk top. 'The investigation. Take it if you want it.'

Trembling with reaction, Grace studiously averted her eyes from the file, too proud to reach for it.

'I didn't intend to upset you, Grace. But naturally, I assumed that nothing in that file would come as a surprise to you...you were eleven years old when you lost your mother.'

Having Leo study her in that cool, even-tempered manner when she herself was so shaken up simply made Grace want to thump him hard. 'You really do have no finer feelings, do you? You suddenly drag up my father and reveal that you know more about him than I do? Didn't it occur to you that that was inexcusably thoughtless and cruel?' she condemned with angry spirit.

'I didn't realise that it would still be such a sensitive subject for you. But you're right—I should've done. I'm not particularly keen to discuss my own background,' Leo conceded with a wry twist of his sensual mouth.

'I have to go. I have an appointment to see my tutor in an hour,' Grace fielded, spinning on her heel and walking fast out of the room before she exposed herself any more.

Leo lifted the investigation file and then slapped it back down hard on the desk in frustration. He had upset her and he hadn't intended to do that. Grace was sensitive. Grace had hang-ups about her past. But didn't he as well? And since when had he worried about such delicate details? Or reacted personally to someone else's distress? The answer to that last question came back and chilled Leo to the marrow: not since he was a child struggling to comfort his distraught mother. Any desire to follow Grace and reason with her faded fast on that note.

Still struggling to master her powerful emotions, Grace leant back against the wall in the lift. What was it about Leo Zikos that brought her inner aggression out? The very first night she had met Leo she had resolved to be herself rather than act like the quieter, more malleable Grace she had learned to be to fit in with her uncle's family. That version of Grace had never freely expressed herself or lost her temper and had certainly never shouted at anyone. So, what was happening to her now? She was unnerved by her own behaviour and by the sheer strength of the emotions taking her by storm. It was almost as though that one night of truly being herself with Leo had destroyed any hope of her either controlling or hiding her emotions again for ever. Suddenly she was feeling all sorts of things she didn't *want* to feel.

Hell roast Leo for his interference, she thought in a simmering tempest of resentment. He had made her curious, made her burn to know what *he* knew about the father she barely remembered and that infuriated her when she had always contrived to keep her curiosity about her father at a manageable, unthreatening level. Now all of a sudden she was desperate to know everything there was to know. But that was yet another betrayal of her self-control, in short a weakness, and she refused to give way to it. After all, she knew everything she needed to know about her father. Those bare facts could only be interpreted in one way. Her father hadn't cared enough to stay around. That was *all* she needed to know, she told herself impatiently.

She met with her tutor and her decision to take a year out from her studies was accepted. While she negotiated the stairs back down to the busy ground floor of the university building, Grace was thinking resolutely positive thoughts about the seed of life in her womb. She was facing huge changes in her life, but the sacrifices she was making and the adjustments that would follow would all benefit her baby, she told herself soothingly.

Marrying Leo would give Grace the precious gift of time. She would have time to come to terms with the prospect of motherhood and time to enjoy the first precious months of her baby's life without the stress of wondering how she was to survive as a new mother. She would also have Leo's support. Any male that keen to marry her for their baby's sake would be a hands-on father and she very much wanted that male influence in her child's life. She had never forgotten how much she herself had longed for a father as a little girl. In every possible way her life would be more settled when she returned to her studies the following year, she reflected with relief.

But as she went to bed that night her mind was still in turmoil over her personal, private reactions to Leo. Leo, always Leo, who had dominated her thoughts from the first moment she laid eyes on him. How had that happened? Grace had always prided herself on her discipline over her emotions but Leo Zikos had blasted through her defensive barriers like a blazing comet, awakening her to feelings and cravings that she had barely understood before. Was it infatuation? Was it simply sexual attraction? Or did her need to understand him, note his gifts as well as his flaws, indicate a deeper, more dangerous form of attachment? Theirs would be a marriage of convenience, after all, and even Marina had warned Grace not to expect more from Leo than he was already offering her.

But in the dark of the night Grace was facing an unsettling truth: she was beginning to fall in love with Leo, hopelessly, deeply in love with a male who had never uttered a word of interest relating to any connection with her more meaningful than sex. A male, moreover, who had virtually blackmailed her into marrying him and who, while declaring respect for fidelity, had still been rampantly unfaithful to his fiancée.

CHAPTER EIGHT

'I CAN'T HELP being curious to know what you know about my father,' Grace admitted stiffly to her uncle on the drive to the register office.

Declan Donovan studied his niece in surprise. 'Virtually nothing, I'm afraid. Your mother refused to talk about him. Initially she said she was getting married but when that failed to transpire Keira had a huge row with our parents and cut us all off. I think she felt she'd lost face with everybody and it hurt her pride.'

"So, you never met him?'

'No, they had a bad break-up and after that we lost track of your mother for years.' The older man shook his head with unhidden regret. 'Keira was a troubled woman, Grace. I never understood her. Luckily she still had my address in her personal effects when she died, so the social worker was able to get in touch with me to tell me about you.'

Grace flushed and looked away, wishing she had asked that same question years sooner. But she had been too proud to ask about the father who had deserted her and her mother. 'It's not important,' she said with forced casualness.

'It's only natural that you would be thinking of

your parents on your wedding day,' her uncle completed gruffly and patted her hand.

Leo stared as Grace entered the room and he wasn't the only one. Their few guests copied him, their expressions ranging from admiration to awe and disbelief. Anatole, however, dealt his son an appreciative nod as if the stunning appearance of his son's bride had set the seal on his approval. But then Anatole, Leo acknowledged wryly, had never wanted his son to marry Marina and had instead talked a lot of nonsense about Leo needing to seek a soul mate rather than a practical life partner.

Her wedding dress was the colour of bronze with a metallic gleam, a long simple column that flattered Grace's curves and small stature. In her vibrant hair, which was swept up to show off her slim white throat, she wore only a tawny-coloured exotic hot-house bloom. The pulse beating at Leo's groin flared into disturbing activity, lust flaring when he least welcomed it. A primal surge of desire assailed him as her pale sea-glass eyes collided anxiously with his. She looked incredibly sexy and disturbingly vulnerable.

'Money definitely talks, doesn't it?' Grace's cousin, Jenna, remarked sourly. 'That dress transforms you. It's not very bridal though.'

Grace pasted a smile to her tense lips, determined not to react. It had not escaped her attention that her aunt and her cousin resented the reality that Grace was becoming the wife of a very wealthy man. In any case, Grace's attention had already strayed to Leo, tall and dark and devastatingly handsome in a dark designer suit. Her heart hammered, her tummy flipped. She sucked in her breath, striving to stay calm as he strode across the room, his irresistible smile slashing his beautiful shapely mouth.

'You look stunning,' Leo told her with a dark deep husky edge to his resonant drawl that sent a responsive shiver travelling down her spinal cord. 'Let me introduce you to my father, Anatole.'

'And your brother, Bastien,' the older man slotted in hurriedly as a tall dark male with coldly amused dark eyes strolled up and disconcerted Grace by leaning down to kiss her on both cheeks Continental fashion.

'Enough, Bastien!' Leo grated, startling Grace with that eruption even more.

'Was I trespassing?' Bastien quipped, devilment dancing in his mocking gaze. 'Leo never *did* like to share his toys.'

Leo planted an impatient hand to Grace's spine and spun her away from the other man. 'Some day soon I'll knock his teeth down his throat!' he swore in a raw undertone.

Upset that Bastien had described her as one of Leo's 'toys', Grace flushed and murmured with quiet good sense, 'Shaking hands would have been a little formal when I'm about to join the family.'

'I only count my father as family.' Angry colour scored Leo's high cheekbones.

In answer to his hostility towards his half-brother, Grace simply said nothing and instead turned back to politely address Leo's father, who had been left hovering in discomfiture while his two sons squared up to each other.

Matt approached her almost shyly. 'I hardly recognised you,' he admitted, and they talked about her decision to take a year out until it was time to go into the room next door for the ceremony.

During the ceremony, Grace focused on the handsome flower arrangement on the table while listening carefully to the words. She would have preferred a church service but would not have dreamt of telling Leo that. He slid a ring onto her finger but he had not given her one to return the favour with and there was a small embarrassing pause as the registrar allowed them time to complete what was usually an exchange of rings. Clearly, Leo wouldn't be wearing a ring, announcing to the world that he was 'taken', Grace reflected ruefully, wondering why that small detail should make her feel so insecure. Many men didn't like wearing rings, she reminded herself.

A light meal was served to the wedding party at an exclusive hotel. Grace glimpsed her reflection in one of the many gilded wall mirrors in the private function room and barely recognised the refined image of the woman clad in the sleek bronze sheath. At the beauty salon the previous day every part of her had been primped and polished and waxed and trimmed, all her rough edges smoothed away. She had seen Della and Jenna's frowning surprise at her new image and she knew she no longer looked incongruous by Leo's side. The cringeworthy fear that her lack of grooming could embarrass Leo had made Grace tolerate the various treatments and she accepted the need to at least *try* to fit into Leo's world as best she could. Grace had always believed that if something was worth doing, it was worth doing well and that was the outlook she intended to embrace in her role as Leo's wife.

'If we're leaving soon I should get changed,' Grace

whispered after she had drifted once round the small
dance floor in the circle of Leo's arms, every inch of
her treacherous body humming at the hard stirring
contact with his.

'There's no need for you to change. We should head
to the airport now,' Leo told her calmly. 'I'm determined to be the one to take that dress off you, *meli
mou.*'

Ready colour warmed Grace's cheeks and within
minutes they were walking out to a waiting limousine,
having thanked their guests for sharing their day. Travelling with Leo was, she discovered, very different
from going on a package holiday trip. There were no
queues to slow them down. They were rushed through
the airport and waited for the flight call in a private
lounge where they were served with refreshments.

'You still haven't told me where we're going,'
Grace reminded him.

'Italy...I have a house there. It's very private,' Leo
murmured huskily, running a finger across the tender
skin of her inner wrist where a blue vein pulsed below
her fine white skin, sending a current of awareness
snaking through her veins. 'Perfect for a honeymoon.'

They boarded Leo's private jet. The cabin crew
greeted her. Grace studied the opulent leather seating
and stylish fixtures with wide eyes before she took a
seat. She glanced down at the ring gleaming on her
wedding finger and breathed in deep and slow. She
was Leo's wife now but *only* because she was pregnant, she reminded herself staunchly as the jet took
off. It didn't do to forget that salient fact.

A moment later, she was very much taken by surprise when Leo settled the file about her background

down on the table in front of her. 'I'm sorry my investigation into your background distressed you but you should know what's in it and I'd like to get it out of the way now.'

Grace paled, tense as a bowstring. She had planned to work up the courage to ask him for the file and she was relieved he had not pushed her to that point. Flipping it open, she began to read. It very quickly became clear that when she was a child she had only been told *one* side of her parents' story—her mother's. And her father's side of the story was strikingly different.

'Were you aware that your mother was an addict?' Leo asked curiously.

'Yes, of course, but I was told to never mention it again once I moved in with my uncle and aunt. They were ashamed of it,' Grace confided ruefully. 'Mum got into drugs when I was a baby but I didn't know that she'd gone into rehab before I was a year old.'

'Your father got her onto a drug rehabilitation programme but it didn't work.'

No, indeed it hadn't, Grace recalled, her disturbing memories of her late mother including many of her lying comatose or doing inappropriate things because she was out of her head on drugs.

'It must've been challenging for him as a doctor to live with an addict, who was the mother of his child.'

'Yes, and of course he inevitably met someone more suitable, another doctor he worked with, and deserted us.'

'But he did take your mother to court first in an effort to gain custody of you…'

That fact was news to Grace. The story she had grown up with had ended with her father Tony's departure from their lives and his marriage to another woman. Now she bent her head over the file and learned that her father had failed to win custody of her from her mother because Keira Donovan had impressed her social worker with her apparent desire to turn her life around. Although her father had been granted access visits to his daughter, there had been continual cancellations and arguments, which had prevented his visits from taking place. By that stage her father had got married and Grace reckoned that her mother's bitterness over that reality would have known no bounds. In an obvious effort to stop the visits, Keira had accused Grace's father of assault and that accusation had plunged Tony into a damaging slew of investigations by the police, the social services and even the General Medical Council. During that period Keira had disappeared and changed her name to ensure that she couldn't be tracked down.

Having failed to trace Keira and their daughter, her father had eventually given up the search. By then he had become a father for the second time and had had a new family to focus on.

'Your mother took you to live in a commune in Wales,' Leo remarked. 'What was that like for you?'

'Ironically it was better than living alone with my mother,' Grace admitted a shade guiltily. 'There were other people around to look out for me and make sure I went to school and had regular meals.'

'You had it tough.'

'I wish my father had found me. I wish he hadn't stopped looking but he was probably afraid that Mum would make more allegations against him and that that might wreck his career.' Grace sighed as she finished reading up to the point where her uncle and aunt had given her a home after her mother's death from an overdose. 'I can't really blame him. Mum was incredibly difficult. She hated him with a passion and she was very bitter.'

'And how do you feel about your father now?' Leo asked levelly.

'That he probably did the best he could and obviously he didn't deliberately abandon me. At least you were lucky enough to have both your parents growing up,' Grace reminded him, closing the file and replacing it on the table with finality. Yet a little burst of warmth had touched the cold, hollow place in her heart where her belief in her father's lack of interest had lodged in childhood. It was good to know that he had cared enough to fight for her even though he had ultimately lost out. For the first time ever, she wondered if she should try and contact her father.

Leo's expressive mouth quirked in receipt of her innocent comment. 'Having both parents never felt lucky to me. Anatole married my mother, who was a very spoiled Greek heiress, primarily for her money.'

Grace gazed back at him in shock. 'That's an awful thing to accuse your father of!'

'But regretfully true. Although he married my mother he was actually in love with a waitress called Athene. He set Athene up as a mistress and she became pregnant with Bastien only a few months after my mother conceived me,' he confided grimly. 'Eventually my mother found out that she wasn't the only woman in her husband's life. I must've been about six by then. I still remember her screaming, sobbing and throwing things and the drama went on for days.

Anatole duly promised to give up Athene and we lived in peace for a while. But of course Anatole was lying and the truth came out again. That same destructive pattern just kept on repeating and repeating—'

'That must've been devastating for your mother. She must've really loved your father to keep on forgiving him.'

'But *he* loved Athene and obviously Bastien was almost the same age as I was, so in a sense Anatole had *two* families. It was a hideous triangle.' His lean dark features were bleak. 'Anatole couldn't walk away from Athene and my mother refused to let him go. Once when he tried to leave her she took sleeping pills and that scared the life out of him.'

'Of course it did,' Grace said with a shiver.

'When I was thirteen, Athene died in a car crash and Bastien came to live with us. My mother was so relieved that her rival was dead that she agreed to the arrangement. Naturally, Bastien and I didn't hit it off,' Leo said drily, his lean, darkly handsome features grim. 'However, the volatile nature of my parents' marriage convinced me that I didn't want an atom of that obsessive passion in my own marriage...'

Grace sipped at her soft drink and searched his lean, strong face, recognising the gravity etched there. 'Meaning?'

'I have never wanted any part of the possessiveness, the jealousy, the arguments or the overly high expectations that most married couples have of each other.'

'That's the down side of attachment. Love is the upside,' Grace told him gently.

'Not for me, it isn't,' Leo countered with cool conviction. 'I'm not looking for love in our marriage, Grace.'

In spite of the sinking sensation in her stomach, Grace threw him a brilliant smile. 'Neither am I, Leo, but I *will* expect you to love our child.'

'That's a different kind of love,' he declared.

'A less selfish love certainly,' she conceded, wanting to ask him about his relationship with Marina and biting her lip to restrain herself while she was uncertain of her ground. 'You forgave your father for his mistakes, didn't you?'

'He's a good-hearted man but weak at the core. He dug himself into a hole and he couldn't get out of it. He didn't want to hurt anyone by making a choice and the result was that he hurt *all* of us.'

Her lashes dipped over her sea-glass eyes, which were clear as jade in the light filling the cabin. 'If you feel so strongly about your father's infidelity, how could you cheat on Marina?'

'But I didn't...*cheat* on her,' Leo contradicted with a flare of distaste in the brilliant dark eyes narrowed below the lush canopy of his lashes. 'Marina and I got engaged and then agreed to go our separate ways until we got married.'

Her lashes fluttered up in disbelief. 'That's weird.'

'Why? Neither of us was in a hurry to marry and we weren't lovers either, so it wasn't the unsavoury agreement you are obviously imagining,' Leo derided.

We weren't lovers. That phrase repeated inside Grace's brain and stunned her. 'You mean, you and Marina...er...*never*—?'

'Never, but that is confidential.'

Grace was shocked into silence, recalling Mari-

na's comment about Leo's indifference and finally
understanding its source. That Leo had been content
to stand back and allow Marina to do as she liked
during their engagement spoke volumes about the
chilling level of his detachment and it was hardly surprising that the brunette had ultimately decided that
she would be happier with another man. And Marina's statement that Leo was bad for her ego? Oh, yes,
Grace finally understood that and the significant part
it might well play in her own future. Would Leo be so
detached with her that he froze her out too?

The jet landed in Tuscany and they transferred into
a helicopter for the last leg of their journey. By that
stage Grace was fed up bundling her long dress round
her legs to cope with steps and looking forward to
being free of its confines, not to mention her peril-
ously high heels. She stole a tentative glance at Leo's
hard bronzed profile, recalling his declared intention
to remove her dress. Steamy warmth engulfed her
treacherous body, anticipation as potent as an electrical storm at its core. But then desire shimmied like
intoxicating alcohol through her veins when Leo was
close. A heady combination of memory and the physical craving he evoked put her on edge, mortified by
her weakness and ill at ease with her own physical
reactions.

Leo lifted her out of the helicopter when they
landed and she straightened to look in wonder at the
building a hundred yards from them. 'It's a castle!'

'Yes, but a small one. Built by a wealthy eccentric
in the nineteen twenties and bought by my mother.
She owned a lot of property round the world. I turned
the most promising into businesses and sold the rest,'

he volunteered, walking her towards the curiously elegant castle fashioned of cream-coloured stone and set in the midst of beautiful gardens. 'At one time I planned to turn the castle into a small exclusive hotel but once I had renovated it I decided to keep it as a bolt-hole.'

'It's hot for this time of year,' Grace remarked in pleasant surprise, moving into the cool shadow of the tree-lined stone path that led to the castle entrance. Back in London late summer was fading into evenings with steadily dropping temperatures while here in Tuscany the roses were still blooming and the bite of autumn's approach had yet to register.

A cheerful housekeeper chattering in Italian met them on the doorstep. Leo introduced her as Josefina and responded smoothly in the same language before escorting Grace across the highly polished floor tiles in the hall and up the stone staircase. A selection of doors led off the wide landing but Leo headed straight for the set of double doors in the centre and into a massive bedroom with a turret at either corner. 'Wow,' she whispered, pulling away from him to explore the turrets, finding a bathroom in one and a fully furnished dressing room in the other.

An ebony brow lifted, Leo watched in amusement, enjoying the expressions crossing her mobile face while their cases were being stashed behind them. 'You like?'

'I *love*,' Grace confided, kicking off the high heels, which pinched. She brushed the petal of an exquisite white lily in a dramatic floral arrangement, trailed an admiring finger along the gleaming wooden surface of an antique chest of drawers and studied the big bed

with its snowy white linen and ice-blue silky throw.
'It's so romantic.'

'I don't do romance,' he reminded her, unbutton-
ing his shirt, having long since discarded his jacket
and tie.

'Bite the bullet, Leo,' Grace advised in amusement.
'This is a very romantic setting.'

Leo stiffened, but looking away from Grace at that
moment wasn't an option; she looked so impossibly
appealing. She had taken her hair down during the
flight and the brilliantly colourful strands tumbled
luxuriantly round her slim shoulders, glinting like
her metallic dress in the sunlight coming through the
windows. He moved forward, stepped behind her and
ran down her zip, peeling the fabric back slowly from
her shoulders while planting a kiss on the pale flesh
he exposed.

Grace held her breath, watching their reflections
merge in a tall mirror with the faint blurry quality of
antique glass. As he bent over her, the brush of his
lips made her shiver. His hair was so black against
hers, his hand so dark against her white shoulder.
The dress slid down her arms and then dropped in a
pool at her feet.

'My turn to say wow,' Leo growled, flipping her
round to take in the full effect of her curves sheathed
in a dainty white balcony bra and knickers teamed
with lace hold-up stockings. 'I like…I *love*.'

'Th-thought you would,' Grace stammered, her
face burning with colour because standing in front of
him clad in provocative lingerie filled her with stupid
self-consciousness.

'I'm very easy to please,' Leo husked, tipping her

breasts gently free of the silk to massage her pointed pink nipples between finger and thumb, lowering a hand to slide a fingertip beneath the edge of her panties and probe the wet heat she would have hidden from him.

An arrow of stark hunger shot through Grace and she gasped, wanting, needing, pierced by so many sensations at once she couldn't vocalise or think. He crushed her parted lips below his, nibbling and teasing with erotic expertise, and then lifted his head again.

'I want you so much I'm burning with it,' Leo breathed, dropping to his knees to tug down her knickers and spread her thighs. 'And I want you to burn along with me, *hara mou*.'

Grace shivered in sensual shock as he closed his mouth to the most sensitive spot on her entire body. She couldn't believe she was standing there, letting him... All too quickly her knees shook with weakness as she drowned in the intoxicating flood of pleasure he was wrenching from her. Little breathy cries parted her lips, sounds punctuated by a low keening moan. Suddenly it was more than she could bear and it took his hands curving to her hips to keep her upright as the excitement pent up inside her surged high and took her with it in an orgasm that almost tipped her off her feet.

But no, that was Leo's doing as he caught her weak body up into his arms and pinned her down on the bed, leaning over her as he yanked off his clothes with an impatience she could feel in every fibre of her still-humming body.

'Seems to me you're always promising to do this slowly,' Grace whispered.

'I'm not going to deliver slow tonight either,' Leo warned, coming down to her again naked and urgently aroused. 'I'm too damned excited.'

It thrilled Grace that she had the power to unleash such impatience in him. She felt the push of him against her tender flesh and lifted her legs to lock her thighs round his lean hips in welcome, the wanting building again like some monster she couldn't sate because, even when she was fresh from a mind-blowing climax, Leo could somehow make her want him again. Her heart was hammering, her body slick with perspiration and every skin cell was on fire for him so that when he thrust deep into her, she cried out with the hot pleasure of that powerful invasion. He withdrew and sank into her again, choosing a potent rhythm that sent heat pulsing through her pelvis as her greedy body began to strain and burn and reach for the heights again.

'Oh, please, don't stop!' she heard herself gasp in anguished excitement.

She was soaring by then, her body jerking and convulsing with the sheer raw intensity of the pleasure washing over her. Bliss enclosed her like a warm soft cocoon when it was over but a little buzzer also went off in her head, reminding her of how Leo pulled away from intimacy in the aftermath of sex. In a sudden movement, Grace dislodged him and snaked out of the bed to head straight for the bathroom. The very knowledge that she wanted to hug him and stay close had sent her into swift retreat for fear of what she might reveal. There was no room for such sentimental behaviour within the narrow limits Leo had set for their marriage.

A few minutes later, Leo stepped into the spacious wet room to join her. 'What was that all about?' he asked.

'What was *what* all about?'

'You pushed me away,' he reminded her, angry dark eyes spelling out how he had reacted to her conduct.

'That's what you've always done with me afterwards,' Grace pointed out innocently. 'Shouldn't I have done that?'

Leo knew when he was being played, but then he had also never been on the receiving end of such a careless dismissal before. It had stung, it had felt ridiculously like rejection, he reasoned in confusion at his own thoughts. Before he could think any more, he reacted on instinct and closed Grace's dripping body into his arms below the falling spray.

'Things change. We're married now. I think we can afford to be a little more affectionate,' he declared in a rasping undertone, tugging her even closer.

Grace hid a smile against a broad muscular shoulder. He wasn't an irredeemable rat, she decided ruefully. Damaged by his parents' toxic marriage, he had avoided the softer emotions all his life to date. But he could learn by example, yes, and he was one very fast learner, Grace conceded as the embrace became an unashamed hug.

A couple of hours later, they lay naked in a tangle of fur throws in front of the gas-fired logs in the massive fireplace in the main drawing room. As night fell they had become hungry and had raided the fridge to savour the delicacies prepared by Josefina, the housekeeper, who had gone home hours earlier.

'I thought pregnant women suffered a lot from nausea,' Leo said abruptly. 'But you still have a good appetite.'

'I haven't felt sick once,' Grace admitted. 'A little dizzy a couple of times but that's all.'

'I've signed you up to see one of the local doctors while we're here.'

'That's unnecessary this early in my pregnancy.'

Leo dealt her a warning glance. 'Humour me. I have a very strong need to know that I'm looking after you properly.'

But Grace was worried that if she gave an inch, Leo would take a mile. She wondered if he had taken the same managing, controlling attitude to Marina and asked.

Leo rested back thoughtfully on his hands, the hard muscular lines of his chest and stomach flexing taut and drawing her involuntary gaze. 'I never felt the need to interfere...offer advice occasionally, yes, veto or demand, no. You're different.'

'How am I different?' Grace asked baldly.

'You're pregnant,' Leo pointed out, disappointing her with that comeback.

'So, if I'm allowed to ask one awkward question... exactly why *did* you want to marry Marina?'

'Because I thought she was perfect...'

Grace froze, the colour leaching from beneath her fair skin.

'Of course, nobody is perfect,' Leo continued wryly. 'But I did believe Marina was as near to the ideal as I could get because we had so much in common and were close friends.'

Never ask a question if you aren't tough enough to

accept the answer and live with it, Grace told herself wretchedly. How on earth could she compete with his ideal of the perfect wife? Most especially when that ideal woman was still walking around? Was it possible that Leo felt more for Marina than he had ever appreciated? And that losing her might make him finally realise it? Not a productive thought train, Grace scolded herself, and she suppressed her crushing sense of insecurity with every fibre of willpower that she possessed.

'So, why don't you want these blood tests the doctor has recommended?' Leo demanded impatiently.

Grace wrinkled her nose. 'Because there's nothing wrong with me.'

'But the doctor—'

'Dr Silvano is nice but he is a little old-fashioned, Leo. Why should he wonder if there's something wrong with my hormone levels just because I'm not feeling sick all the time?' Grace prompted impatiently. 'A lot of women get morning sickness but there are a lucky few who *don't* and I don't plan to start fussing over myself and worrying without good reason. He's one of those doctors who prefer to treat pregnancy as an illness and I don't agree with that.'

Leo surveyed her with unhidden annoyance. Grace went pink and looked across the cobbled square to the playground where small children were running and shouting. In a few years she would have a child of around that age, she ruminated fondly, wishing Leo would not make her pregnancy so much *his* business. Yet how could she fault a man for caring about her well-being?

'I'll go back first thing tomorrow for the tests,' Grace surrendered with a grimace. 'Will that make you happy?'

The tightness of his superb bone structure eased and the hint of a smile softened the hard line of his sculpted mouth. They had been in Italy for four incredible weeks and even when Leo annoyed her, Grace still never got tired of simply looking at him, admiring the proud flare of his nose, the downward frown of his brows when anything annoyed him, the pure silk ebony luxuriance of his lashes when he looked down at her with eyes of pure gold in bed.

'Yes, that will make me happy,' Leo told her without apology and pulled out his phone to immediately book the appointment.

Grace sipped her bottled water, reflecting that Leo had taught her a master class in the art of compromise and negotiation. His forceful personality and strong views made occasional clashes between them inevitable. He was much deeper and more of a thinker than he liked to show. Clever, shrewd and over-protective as he was, he was also wonderfully entertaining and her every fantasy in bed. He was willing to make an effort as well. Since their wedding night there had been no further flights from intimacy post-climax. She wouldn't let herself think negative thoughts around him, wouldn't let herself dwell on the awareness that she loved him and he did not love her. Unlike him, she wasn't expecting the perfect marital partner.

And in any case, Leo might say that he didn't do romance but it was remarkable how often their outings were drenched in romantic views, surroundings and meals. He had taken her to see a candlelit religious procession in the streets of Lucca one evening and topped it off with dinner in a rooftop restaurant with the stars shimmering far above them. They had enjoyed a picnic below the ancient chestnut trees that overlooked the vineyards in the valley. With no road noise, no people around and virtually nothing in view to remind them of the twentieth century, it had been timeless and peaceful and she had dozed off, probably because she had eaten far too much from Josefina's fantastic picnic dishes. There had been sightseeing trips and scenic drives and a couple of casual dinner engagements with friends Leo had, who lived locally.

And then there were the shopping trips and the gifts. Grace tilted her chin, green eyes reflective as she glanced at the gold watch on her wrist and thought about the pearls in her ears and at her throat, not to mention the gorgeous handbag she had foolishly admired in a shop window. Leo was very generous and his giving wasn't soulless or showing off. If he noticed she lacked something like jewellery he provided it without fanfare and so smoothly it was impossible to politely refuse. No, she couldn't fault his intellect, his company, his generosity or the high-voltage excitement of his sexuality.

Furthermore after a month of living with Leo round the clock she could no longer credit the belief that he had blackmailed her into marrying him.

'When you threatened my uncle and aunt's careers, you were bluffing, weren't you?' Grace condemned very drily.

Leo rocked back in his chair, lashes low over gleaming dark eyes. 'I was wondering how long it would take you to work that out.'

Temper hurtled through Grace like a rejuvenating blast of oxygen. 'You mean you wouldn't have done it?'

'Of course I wouldn't have done it. I'm not an unjust man. Your uncle gave you a home when you needed one and I respect him for that because I doubt very much that he received much support from your aunt.' Leo studied her. 'But from certain things you have let slip quite without meaning to, I think your aunt should be burnt at the stake as a witch...and possibly your cousin with her.'

That cool rundown of her upbringing snuffed out Grace's annoyance as though it had never been and provoked an involuntary laugh from her lips. 'Oh... dear.'

'But in one sense you have done me a favour. Your position in your uncle's family closely resembled Bastien's when my half-brother and I were children and that has enabled me to see that Bastien was often excluded, set apart from my parents and I by his birth and parentage and made to feel like an outsider,' he imparted grimly. 'It was wrong when that was done to you and it must follow that it was equally wrong when it was done to him.'

Grace nodded, impressed by that deduction and his willingness to admit fault on that score. The level of animosity between Leo and his brother had disconcerted her. She suspected they never met without one trying to score points off the other.

'Sadly, that reality won't make me *like* Bastien but it is why I was ready to allow you to believe that I would blackmail you into marriage. I was prepared to use any weapon you put within my reach,' Leo confessed wryly. 'I could not bear our child to experience the isolation which you and Bastien suffered as children. I don't ever want a child of mine to feel like an outsider. And if you and I hadn't married that is what he or she would have ultimately been.'

'So, I'm supposed to forgive the blackmail threats because your goal was the greater good?' Grace fielded very drily although grudging amusement was tugging at her lips. 'With that kind of reasoning you could excuse murder, Leo.'

A wolfish grin slashed Leo's darkly handsome face. 'But you *like* being married to me?'

Grace rested her chin down on the heel of her hand and gave him an enquiring look. 'And why do you assume that?'

'You sing in the shower, you smile at me a lot...you even jump me in bed occasionally,' Leo husked soft and low, dark golden eyes pure burnished gold with wicked amusement and that innate bold assurance that she found so outrageously compelling.

Grace didn't quite know how to react to that unexpectedly personal list of her mistakes. For smiling at him all the time was a dead giveaway of the kind of feelings he didn't want her to have and she didn't want to reveal. But it was a challenge to hide the simple truth that he made her happy, indeed happier than anyone had ever made her feel in her entire life. Because while he might not love her, he did *care* and he seemed to find her irresistible. Did she really need more than that from him? All that lovey-dovey stuff and wedding rings proudly worn on male fingers would really just be the icing on the cake, she reasoned: lovely to have but not strictly necessary.

'You won't be getting jumped tonight,' she warned him, her lovely face flushed and self-conscious.

And Leo laughed uproariously as he so often did with Grace, who teased him and came back at him verbally in a way no other woman ever had and who was nothing short of dirty dynamite in his bed. Oh, no, Leo had no complaints on the marriage front. In fact, Leo was delighted with his bride.

He walked her back to the car and noticed a guy on a motorbike twisting his head rather dangerously to get a second look at the figure Grace cut in a pale pink cami top that showed rather more cleavage than Leo liked and a clinging white skirt that enhanced her curvy behind and show-stopping legs. His mouth flattened while he wondered when Grace would start *looking* more pregnant and less curvy and sexy. He could hardly wait for the day. It offended him when other men studied his wife with lascivious intent.

Grace was glad of the breeze that cooled her as they walked into the castle because she was feeling uncomfortably warm. 'I need a shower,' she sighed, starting up the stairs.

'Me too,' Leo husked with a roughened edge to his dark deep drawl.

Grace was moving towards the bathroom when Leo spoke again and in a sudden tone of urgency. 'Grace... your skirt...you're *bleeding*!'

CHAPTER NINE

COLD SHOCK AND dismay filled Grace as she looked down at herself. In the bathroom she frantically peeled off her clothes.

'You can't have a shower now...you should lie down!' Leo tried to remonstrate with her.

'Don't be silly,' Grace argued shakily. 'If I'm having a miscarriage there's nothing anyone can do to stop it.'

Leo stepped out of the bathroom to call Dr Silvano and then went back in, battling an angry, aggressive urge to snatch Grace bodily out of the shower and force her to lie down but very much afraid that coming over all caveman would only upset her more. He tried to wrap a huge towel round her when she came out, hovering even when she shouted at him to leave her alone. Grace rebelled by stepping back out of view to take care of necessities but he was still waiting with the towel when she emerged again.

'You're so cold,' he groaned.

'Shock,' she said, teeth chattering while she struggled to make herself face what felt like an impossible challenge and slid her arms into a towelling robe. 'You know one in four pregnancies end in miscarriage during the first trimester and I'm only eight weeks and a bit along…'

'*Hush,*' Leo incised, bundling her up into his arms and carrying her over to the bed before rattling through drawers in search of the nightdress she requested. 'Are you in a lot of pain?'

She winced. 'None…whatsoever.'

'You'll still have to go into hospital. *Diavelos*… I should've taken you straight there!' Leo breathed, pacing the floor at the end of the bed, rigid with tension and regret.

'No hospital, Leo. I think I'd freak out on a gynae ward surrounded by pregnant women and newborns.'

'You'd be in a private room and don't be so pessimistic,' Leo censured. 'It may not be what you fear.'

Grace said nothing. She lay as still as an upturned statue staring up at the ceiling. Crazy thoughts tormented her. Was this to be her punishment for thinking that she could give her baby up for adoption? Was this her punishment for not properly valuing the gift she had been given? It seemed that Dr Silvano had been right when he'd expressed the opinion that a mother-to-be suffering from nausea and sore breasts could indicate a more stable pregnancy. Her eyes prickled. It was inconceivable to her that only an hour earlier she and Leo had been laughing and carefree, utterly unaware of what lay ahead.

She was moved from the limo into the small hospital in a wheelchair and taken to a small side ward. Somewhere in the background she could hear Leo talking in low-pitched urgent Italian and thought numbly of how useful his gift with languages could be. A few minutes later she was moved yet again and this time she was transferred to a room where there were no other patients. Leo helped her into bed and the fraught silence between them worked on Grace's nerves until a radiographer entered with a portable scanner. Grace lay still while the gelled probe moved back and forth over her tummy, her attention locked to the small screen, her hopes and dreams slowly dying as what she prayed for failed to appear. The operator excused herself and reappeared some minutes later with a doctor, who spoke English. He broke the news that the machine had failed to detect the baby's heartbeat but that the procedure would be repeated the following day to ensure that there was no mistake.

'I don't see why we should wait twenty-four hours to get a confirmation.' Leo breathed harshly, his bone structure rigid below his bronzed skin.

'It's standard procedure to wait twenty-four hours and check again,' Grace chipped in.

'I'll organise an airlift to a city hospital, somewhere with the latest equipment,' he began.

The doctor said that it would not be a good idea to move Grace again and that air travel at such an early stage of her pregnancy only heightened the likelihood of miscarriage.

'I'm not going anywhere,' Grace declared, turning her face into the wall because she could not bear to continue looking at Leo.

It was over. Why was he making everything more difficult by fighting the obvious conclusion? Most probably she had miscarried and everyone in the room with the exception of Leo could accept that. A second check tomorrow was very probably only a routine precaution.

But then she was not cut from the same cloth as her husband, she acknowledged heavily. Leo was rich and powerful and accustomed to his wealth changing negatives into positives but sadly there was no way to do that in the current situation. Her baby had died without ever learning what it would be like to live. A great swell of anguish mushroomed up through Grace and a choked sob escaped her as she gasped for breath and control.

Leo sat down on the side of the bed and gripped her clenched fingers. 'We'll get through this,' he rasped, his eyes burning and pinned to her pale, pinched profile as he flailed around mentally striving to come up with words of comfort.

'It just wasn't meant to be,' Grace said with flat conviction.

'Some day there'll be…another chance,' Leo completed tightly.

'Not for us.'

Leo ignored that assurance. He wasn't about to get into an argument. Grace was devastated, probably barely aware of what she was saying and Leo, struggling to master the tightness in his chest and the yawning hollow opening up inside him, was realising that he was devastated too, much more devastated than he had ever expected to be in such circumstances. 'Let's not be pessimistic. Tomorrow…'

'It will only hurt me more to hold onto false hope!' Grace snapped back at him, her head flipping, vibrant red hair spilling across the pillows, pale sea-glass eyes distraught and accusing.

Leo's eyes stung, frustration flaring through his lean, powerful frame because he wanted so badly to fix things and knew that he couldn't. 'It was my baby too,' he murmured in a roughened undertone.

'I know…that's *all* you ever cared about. Believe me, I don't need reminding,' Grace framed jerkily, turning away again to present him with her slender back.

Leo paled and sprang off the bed to head for the chair in the corner. 'Try to get some sleep. I'll stay with you.'

Grace sat up with a sudden start, grief and regret weighing her down to the extent that she felt as if she were drowning in inner turmoil and unhappiness. She pushed the pillows back behind her and studied him in his pale grey exquisitely tailored suit that glimmered like dull silver below the stark hospital lights. His blue-black hair was tousled, his strong jawline rough with dark stubble, his stunning eyes unusually bright with emotion. Of course he was upset; she *knew* he was upset. After all, much as he might wish to be, he *wasn't* a block of unfeeling wood. Unfortunately, Grace had already looked beyond their loss to become painfully aware of exactly what her miscarriage meant to them as a newly married couple.

'There's no point in you staying.'

Predictably, Leo argued. He needed to be with her. That was non-negotiable in his mind. He had to see that she was fed, properly cared for and that if things were to get any worse he was on the spot to provide immediate support. His sense of responsibility was too strong to be denied.

'Why would you stay?' Grace whispered, fighting her desire for his presence, fighting her longing for him to come close again, fighting all those softer feelings with the sure knowledge at that moment that she was doing what *had* to be done. She was facing up to reality, struggling to move forward and step away from the lure of a future that could no longer be hers. How could she feel any other way when that future had been so inextricably linked to their baby?

'You're my wife, *hara mou*. I belong by your side,' Leo countered with fierce conviction. 'You're upset, we're both upset but together we're stronger.'

'Maybe that would've been true had we been in love…but obviously we're not.' Grace closed her restive fingers into a tight ball of self-restraint, her deep sense of hurt tamped down. 'Us…as a couple, that's *over*. Of course it is. How could it be anything else after what's just happened?' she asked shakily, anger at the tumultuous emotions she was crushing arrowing through her trembling frame because with every word she spoke she was going against her own heart.

But how could she do anything else? she asked herself in despair. They had come together for the baby's sake and without the baby there was nothing to keep them together. She had to face that, deal with it, *live* with it whether she liked it or not. She loved him but he did not love her. She was too proud and too fair-minded to cling to him and make him feel that he somehow owed it to her to stay with her.

Leo welded long tanned fingers to the rail at the foot of her bed, every muscle in his lean, powerful body pulling dangerously tight. 'I don't know what you're talking about,' he said in a harsh undertone.

'I'm just saying what needs to be said. You're *free*, Leo.'

Leo lost colour, the exotic slant of his cheekbones

pronounced. There was a lurch in the region of his gut as though he had been punched. He didn't want to be free. Naturally he had got used to being married and he was content to stay married and eventually try for another baby. Grace suited him. He didn't know how she did it or why she was so important to him but she matched him in all the ways that mattered. Indeed he had become so accustomed to Grace being around that he could not imagine his life without her. Obviously he was more of a creature of habit and routine than he had ever appreciated because within a short time Grace had become astonishingly necessary to his comfort.

'And what if I don't want to be free?' he grated, soft and low.

'If that's what you *think* you feel right now you're *lying* to yourself,' Grace told him with astonishing conviction. 'And why are you lying to yourself? Because you feel sorry for me and you think it's your job to look after me. You have a very strong sense of responsibility and that's a noble trait but don't let it blind you to what you really want out of life. And what you really want, Leo, is *not* me.'

Leo wondered why *she* was telling *him* how he felt. Did she really think he was so inadequate that he couldn't work out his own feelings for himself? Annoyance slashed through him and he wanted to express it but he was horrendously aware of the experience she had undergone and that it was his duty not to make the situation worse.

'Our marriage was all about the baby and everything you have ever shared with me related to the baby and the baby's future needs. Without our baby...'

Grace framed unsteadily, tears glinting in her over-bright eyes '...we don't have a marriage. We don't even have a relationship. We can get a divorce now.'

'Are you insane?' Leo heard himself snap back at her, all self-discipline vanquished by her use of that bombshell word. *Divorce?* How was he supposed to listen to that in polite and understanding silence?

'I'm looking at a guy who doesn't even wear a wedding ring!' Grace shot at him equally out of the blue and Leo looked down at his bare hand in bewilderment, wondering what wedding rings had to do with anything and whether simply leaving the room would be wiser than remaining.

'You never bothered to ask but I would've liked to get married in a church. But then you never really wanted to be properly married to me, so obviously you didn't bother to ask my preferences. You didn't *choose* me,' Grace condemned heatedly. 'You married me because I was pregnant, so why would we stay together now?' she demanded emotively.

Leo lifted stunned dark golden eyes from the offending hand that lacked a wedding ring and thought how sneaky women could be. She had never mentioned his omission or the church thing. She had never by so much as a hint let him know how she felt about him not wearing a wedding ring and now he was being hung out to dry for a sin he hadn't known he had committed. How fair was that?

'I can buy a wedding ring,' Leo pointed out gruffly.

'That's not the point!' Grace exclaimed in seething frustration because he was not giving her the reaction she had expected: he was not looking guiltily relieved.

'Then why did you mention it? And could we have

this conversation at some other time when you're not emotionally overwrought and we're both feeling calmer?' Leo pressed grittily. 'Because right now is not working for me.'

Grace lifted her chin. 'I thought it was better to say it and get it out in the open. I don't want you faking what you don't feel. You felt things for the baby, not for me.'

'That is untrue,' Leo grated, losing patience. 'You're my wife and I made a serious commitment to you.'

'But I don't want your cold sense of commitment... I want love!' Grace flung back at him helplessly.

'I warned you that I couldn't put that on the table,' Leo breathed harshly.

'Oh, you could if you wanted to,' Grace fielded with unmistakeable bitterness. 'But you don't want to. And do you know why? It's not because you had an unhappy childhood, it's because you're an emotional coward.'

His nostrils flared, his eyes kindling like flames. 'Let's not descend to that level.'

'But it's true. You don't get involved because you're scared of getting hurt. Nobody wants to get hurt, Leo, but most of us still *try* to make a relationship that goes further than practicality and convenient sex. You're too busy protecting yourself to even give it a go.' Exhausted by telling him what was wrong with their marriage, Grace fell back against the pillows, drained by emotion. 'Go back to the castle.'

'To start planning our divorce?' Leo challenged darkly.

'It's inevitable now,' she whispered numbly, her heart heavy as lead inside her tight chest. 'There's nothing left to keep us together.'

'If you really want me to leave, I'll leave and come back first thing in the morning,' he bit out grimly, his darkly handsome features bleak with constraint.

'There's no point you coming back for the second scan.' Grace knew she would cry then because, no matter how hard she was striving to be realistic, a little spark of hope still flourished inside her. She would be shattered when she received the confirmation that, yes, she had miscarried and lost their baby and she didn't want Leo to witness that emotional breakdown and start feeling sorry for her again. 'I could handle that better alone. I'll be able to leave the hospital straight after it.'

'To do what? Fly back to London?' Leo demanded bitterly. 'You're in no fit state for that. At the very least you need to spend a couple of weeks recuperating. If it makes you happier, I'll leave and you can have the castle all to yourself. At this moment I feel that getting fully back to work would be a welcome distraction.'

'I didn't want it to be like this, Leo,' Grace muttered wretchedly. 'I know you're upset as well.'

'I'm not upset.' Leo swung round and left the room, walked down the corridor and settled in the waiting room. He wasn't just upset, he was furious. She was his wife and she was shutting him out, dismissing him as a husband as if he were of no account.

Did he really deserve a wife who had such a low opinion of him? Did she think he had been faking it with her for the whole of the past month? Faking the passion, the laughter, the enjoyment? Without warning he badly wanted a drink and he wanted to punch something hard. He leapt upright again and paced.

Grace was stubborn and rigid in her views. That wedding-ring jibe? How could she be so petty?

Unfortunately, her prejudice against her father for the way she had believed he had treated her late mother had ensured that Grace had not had a very high opinion of men even to begin with. And how much had Leo's own behaviour since their first meeting contributed to her continuing distrust? The casual one-night stand? The engagement he had neglected to mention? The blackmail he had used to persuade her to marry him? His conduct had been less than stellar.

But Leo had always had a can-do approach to problems. Grace wanted him to love her? He could lie and tell her he loved her. Was he willing to do *anything* to keep her? Leo winced, shocked by the concept. What had she done to his brain? His brain clearly wasn't working properly. Shock and sorrow had temporarily deranged his wits because for the first time since childhood he felt helpless and almost panicky.

It felt wrong not being with Grace although maybe she genuinely needed time alone to deal with what had happened. He couldn't help wishing she had turned to him, *leant* on him. He spoke to the nurse in charge, asking her to contact him if Grace's condition changed, and then he breathed in deep and fought his reluctance to leave the hospital. Perhaps if Grace slept a while, she would be more normal in the morning, a little less worked up and fatalistic, although it was hard to see how a confirmation of the miscarriage would do anything to improve her outlook.

Leo helped himself to a whiskey in his limousine. He would get stinking drunk and stop agonising over a situation he couldn't fix, he decided despondently.

He checked his phone to see if Grace had texted him; she had not. He embarked on a second whiskey while wondering if a wedding ring could really mean that much to a woman and he thought about texting Grace to ask to have that mystery explained. But there was a yawning hole stretching ever wider somewhere inside his chest. He thought about the baby, the baby that wasn't going to be, and his eyes burned and prickled, deep regret engulfing him.

He lifted his phone again, needing to talk to Grace, wanting to share his thoughts with a woman for the first time ever. He'd probably wake her up or upset her by saying the wrong thing, he conceded heavily. And the last thing she needed was a series of drunken maudlin texts asking silly questions. But the phone, the only link he had with the woman he so badly wanted to be with, was a terrible temptation. After a moment's reflection, Leo extracted his SIM card, buzzed down the window and flung his phone out of the car. There, now he couldn't be tempted to do or say anything stupid.

Grace tossed and turned restively in the bed, tears trickling from below her lowered eyelids. She wanted Leo, she wanted him back so badly, but he had never really belonged to her in the way a *real* husband would have done and now she needed to learn not to look for him and not to rely on him. She had to accept that this phase of her life was over. There would not be a baby with Leo. He had been so angry when he'd left her and she knew she had provoked him. He had tried to be there for her and she had rejected him, needing him to see that honesty was now the best policy. Their shotgun marriage no longer had a reason to exist and she had recognised that reality long before he did. Wasn't that better than Leo waking up some day about a year from now and questioning why he was still married to a woman so far removed from his ideal of a wife?

Yet the prospect of life without Leo, life *after* Leo was unbearable to Grace. She couldn't sleep and it was mid-morning before she was taken to be scanned. This time the scanner was a bigger, more complex machine and the doctor was present. Grace lay still, all hope of good news crushed by a wretched sleepless night and an irredeemable tendency to expect only bad things to happen to her. So, when the doctor urged her in heavily accented English to look at the screen, she was reluctant and glanced up, startled to see that the small medical team surrounding her were all smiling.

And they showed her baby's heartbeat and switched on the sound so that she could listen to that racing beat that quickened her own. An intense sense of joyous relief filled her with a wash of powerful emotion and tears flooded her eyes. 'I was so sure I'd lost my baby...'

The obstetrician sat down by her side to enumerate the various reasons why bleeding could occur in early pregnancy, pointing out that her blood loss had already stopped and that her baby's heartbeat was strong and regular.

The minute she got back to her room, Grace snatched up her phone to text Leo, but what on earth was she to say to him? What an idiot she had been! Panicking and distraught at the conviction she had lost their baby, she had flung their marriage on the bonfire of her hopes as well. It would be her own fault if

Leo received the news that he was still going to be a father with a new sense of regret because she had blown their relationship apart with all her foolish talk about wanting love. She laboured long over the text she sent him, apologising profusely for the way she had behaved and the things she had said before sharing the fact that she was still pregnant. She was a little surprised that there was no immediate response and rather more disconcerted when a nurse came to tell her that a car had arrived to collect her and she was wheeled out expecting to see Leo and instead saw only his driver and two of his bodyguards. Had she expected Leo to rush hotfoot to the hospital to greet her?

Perhaps that had been a little unrealistic after what she had slung at him the evening before, she conceded wretchedly. She sent him another text, hoping to elicit a response, but it was not until the evening that Leo phoned her and the conversation they shared was brief and stilted. He asked how she was, made no reference to the baby or their marriage and told her that he was in London on business and that he would be away for about a week.

'When you get back, I suppose we'll talk,' Grace said uncomfortably, disappointed that he hadn't once mentioned the baby.

'Great...won't that be something to look forward to?' Leo derided, silencing her altogether.

Had Leo ignored her text because he had decided that there was a lot of truth in what she had said at the hospital? Had he reached the conclusion that the fact they were going to be parents wasn't a good enough reason to stay married to a woman who wasn't his ideal? Was that why he had made no comment? And was the divorce she had suggested what he would be discussing when he reappeared?

Five days later, Grace sat out on the terrace below the twining vines that were slowly colouring to autumnal shades and dropping their leaves. She had thrown up before she made it down to breakfast and her breasts were painfully sensitive. It was as if every possible side effect of pregnancy was suddenly kicking in all at once. She had gone for her blood tests with Dr Silvano and he had reassured her that the results were normal.

Her nerves though were all over the place because Leo was due back that very evening and she was stressed out at the thought of seeing him again because he had been so polite and distant when he phoned. In addition, he had mentioned dining with Marina, who was also in London, and Grace had had to battle an innate streak of jealousy and tell herself that she was relaxed about his friendship with his former fiancée. But even so, Grace feared comparisons being made and knew it would always hurt that Leo should believe that Marina would have made him the ideal wife.

Josefina popped her head out of the French windows that led out to the terrace. 'Signora Zikos? Visitor. Meester Robert,' she pronounced, utilising her tiny English vocabulary.

Her brow pleating in surprise, for she didn't recognise the name, Grace stood up and stared at the man walking towards her, a chord of recognition striking her so hard that she froze and her eyes widened. The man was in his forties and of medium height with red hair as bright as her own. She had studied his photos on Facebook on several occasions and she knew who he was even though she couldn't quite credit that he could be in Italy to visit her.

'You're...' Grace began breathlessly.

'Tony Roberts, your father. I wanted to phone and warn you that I was coming but Leo was convinced it would be better if I simply surprised you,' he explained tautly. 'I hope he was right on that score...'

'Leo? You've *met* Leo?' Grace exclaimed, inviting the older man to sit down at the table she had vacated.

'He came to see me at the surgery last week and told me that you'd only recently found out what happened between your mother and I. By the way, I'm very sorry for your loss,' he told her with quiet sympathy. 'I wasn't sure this was the best time for me to meet you but your husband thought it might cheer you up.'

'My loss?' Grace repeated uncertainly, her brow indenting as she struggled to work out how such a misunderstanding could have taken place. 'But I didn't have a miscarriage...I'm still pregnant.'

Her father gave her a perplexed look, clearly confused.

'Did Leo tell you I had miscarried?' Grace asked abruptly and when he nodded, everything fell into place for Grace and she finally realised that she had totally misinterpreted Leo's silence about her health and threatened miscarriage. Evidently, her text had gone astray and, having failed to receive it, Leo had assumed the worst and had then tactfully avoided any reference to pregnancy or babies. 'My goodness,' she whispered in shock, appalled to appreciate that Leo had been walking round London in ignorance of the reality that he was still going to be a father.

She explained the misunderstanding to her own

father while trying to come to terms with the knowledge that, even divided as they currently were, Leo had still sought out her father and gone to see him for what could only be for her benefit.

'Are you saying that your husband *still* doesn't know that you didn't lose the baby?' he commented in consternation. 'You should go and phone him right now!'

'Leo's due back tonight and I'd prefer to tell him face to face,' Grace admitted with an abstracted smile, hoping that he would believe it was the very best news. 'I gather it was Leo who persuaded you to come to Italy and meet me?'

'I needed very little persuasion. I have waited over twenty years for this opportunity,' Tony Roberts pointed out with a wry smile. 'I assumed that you would hate me because your mother did. I didn't even know Keira had a brother in London. I never met any of her family because she didn't get on with them. I also had no idea that your mother had died when you were eleven. Had I known I would have asked if you could come and live with me instead of your aunt and uncle.'

Josefina brought out a tray of coffee and biscuits and Grace chatted to her father, satisfying her curiosity about his side of the family tree and asking about his three children and his wife. Tony had been so excited about the chance to meet his long-lost daughter that he had gone straight to his partners in the surgery where he worked and requested time off to fly straight out to Italy for the weekend. Grace was doubly touched, overwhelmed by her father's eagerness to meet her and stunned by the effort Leo had gone to on her behalf. Leo *cared* about her happiness, she realised, warmth filling her heart. Only a man who cared about her would have taken the trouble to set up such a meeting.

Morning coffee stretched into a leisurely lunch out on the terrace and the sunny afternoon sped past fast as father and daughter got to know each other, registering their similarities in outlook and interests with acceptance and pleasure. As the daylight faded, Tony took his leave, only then confiding that his wife, Jennifer, was waiting for him back at his hotel. Grace invited the couple to come for dinner the following evening and she watched the older man drive off in his hire car with genuine regret. She suspected that he would have been a lovely supportive father to have when she was younger and then she told herself off for concentrating once again on the negative rather than the positive. She decided it was wiser to be grateful for the enjoyable day she had spent in her father's company and was already looking forward to meeting her three younger half-siblings when she returned to London.

She prepared for Leo's return with care, donning a green dress with elaborate beadwork round the neckline and elegant heels. Hearing the helicopter come in to land, she breathed in deep and crossed her fingers for luck. He would probably still be angry with her because he hadn't received her text and she *had* behaved badly at the hospital. She was still brushing her hair when Leo entered the bedroom.

'I phoned Josefina and asked her to put dinner back an hour because I knew I was running late,' he told her, pausing directly in front of her to gaze down at her with shrewd dark golden eyes. 'How have you been?'

'Good, really good. Leo…I sent you a text from the hospital but I don't think you got it,' Grace said uncomfortably. 'I owe you an apology for some of the stuff I threw at you.'

'You were very distressed.'

'It wasn't the right time or place to spring all that on you,' Grace muttered guiltily. 'I was in a bad frame of mind.'

'Understandably,' Leo cut in, stroking a long soothing forefinger along the taut line of her compressed lips. 'You're very tense. What's wrong?'

Grace backed away a few steps to clear her head. That close to Leo, her very skin prickling with awareness and the familiar scent of his cologne teasing her nostrils, she found it impossible to concentrate. 'If you'd got that text you'd have known that there's nothing wrong,' she told him with a wary half-smile. 'You were right and I was mistaken. I *was* being too pessimistic. The second scan picked up our baby's heartbeat the following morning.'

Leo froze, his ebony brows pleating in bewilderment. 'You mean…you're *saying*…?'

'That I'm still pregnant and everything looks fine. Feeling a bit sicker, mind you,' she burbled, suddenly shy beneath the burning intensity of his appraisal.

'You haven't lost the baby? *Truly?*' Leo pressed, striding forward, dark eyes alight like flames.

'Truly,' she whispered shakily as his arms closed tightly round her and she leant up against him for support. 'Sometimes I'm a terrible negative thinker, Leo. I only realised you didn't know about the baby when my father came to see me today. I thought possibly you hadn't mentioned the baby on the phone because you had changed your mind about certain things.'

'Well, I have changed my position on some stuff,' Leo stated in a driven undertone and then he startled her by swinging her up into his arms and spinning her round in a breathless rush. His charismatic grin lit up his lean dark features. 'That's the most wonderful news, *meli mou*! I didn't quite grasp how much I wanted our baby until I believed he was lost.'

'You're making me dizzy…put me down,' Grace urged, perspiration beading her short upper lip. With a groan of apology he settled her down at the foot of the bed where she lowered her head for a minute to overcome the nausea and dizziness the sudden spinning motion had induced.

'Are you all right?' Leo demanded, crouching at her feet and pushing up her face to see it. 'You are pale. I was an idiot. I just didn't think about what I was doing.'

Grace's nebulous fears about how Leo would react to her news had vanished. Leo was being so normal. There was no distance in him at all and he had been genuinely overjoyed to learn that she was still pregnant. That was not the reaction of a male who was considering the possibility of reclaiming his freedom with a divorce. Relief quivered through her slim, taut frame.

'I'm fine, Leo. I just get a little dizzy if I do anything too quickly. I've also been sick a couple of times,' she explained prosaically. 'It's like my body's finally woken up and realised it's pregnant.'

'It'll settle down,' Leo forecast cheerfully. 'How did things go with your father today?'

'What made you go and see him?' Grace asked instead.

'Well, I knew you wanted to meet him and I thought it would give you something else to think about,' he paraphrased a shade awkwardly. 'Grace—I've never felt so helpless in my life as when I believed you were losing our baby...'

'Me too...it wasn't something we could control.' Grace's fingertips stroked soothingly down his cheek-bone to his strong jawline. 'All my worst instincts went into overdrive.'

Leo sprang lithely upright. 'No, I saw your point once I thought over what you'd said to me. I *did* make it all about the baby rather than about us. You could even say I used the baby as an excuse. Considering that I wanted you the very first moment I laid eyes on you and never stopped wanting you, I wasn't being honest with either of us.'

Her eyes widened at that admission. 'The very *first* moment?'

'It was like sticking my finger in an electrical socket,' Leo quipped. 'The attraction was instant and very powerful. I *had* to know you and then I *had* to have you. When I found myself wanting to hang onto you the morning after our night together, it freaked me out.'

'You did?' Grace was frowning. 'But we were only together one night.'

'One night with a very special woman who made me want much more from her than any woman I'd ever met,' Leo completed huskily. 'Why do you think I was too impatient to wait to hear from you afterwards? I was obsessed. I couldn't think of anything but seeing you again. It's a wonder I wasn't boiling bunnies...'

Grace was in shock but hanging onto his every word. 'Can't imagine that...but you said—'

'I said I didn't do love and then you threw me out of that hospital room when I badly needed to be with you and I had to get by without you for a week.'

'During which you suffered some sort of brainstorm?' Grace framed shakily.

'No, it finally hit me that I was *very* deeply attached to you and that it had just happened, regardless of all my doubts about such feelings.'

Grace finally stood up and approached him. '*Very* deeply attached?'

'Hopelessly,' Leo told her with his irresistible smile. 'Somewhere along the way I fell in love with you but I didn't recognise it. I knew I liked you, wanted you close and needed to look after you. I knew I was jealous of your friendship with Matt and very relieved when you didn't succumb to Bastien's legendary appeal. But I honestly did think that I was feeling all those things because it was natural for me to feel protective towards you when you were pregnant.'

'Easy mistake to make,' Grace told him breathlessly, unknotting his tie, yanking it free of his collar before embarking on his shirt buttons. 'You've just told me you love me and, since I love you too, we *should* be celebrating.'

'You love me? Even after all the mistakes I've made?' Leo pressed, stunning dark golden eyes locked to her flushed face and her huge beaming smile.

'Yes. Unlike you,' Grace murmured in unashamed

one-upmanship, 'I never expected the man I married to be perfect.'

'But I *do* think you're perfect,' Leo argued heatedly. 'Absolutely perfect for me. You're beautiful and clever and warm and loving and you will make an absolutely brilliant mother.'

'Tell me more. My ego loves this,' Grace urged, laughing. 'I really should've guessed you loved me when you tracked down my father for me and got him out here. Instead I was too busy worrying about you dining out with Marina.'

Leo tensed. 'Why on earth would you worry about that?'

'Because you thought *she* was perfect and you were with her for *three* years.'

'If she'd been perfect for me I'd still have been with her and my sex drive would have centred on her,' Leo pointed out levelly. 'And Marina isn't perfect. Not only did she once have a one-night stand with my brother...'

'Bastien?' Grace pressed in surprise.

'Yes. She's also currently having an affair with a married man, although it is not quite as bad as it sounds,' Leo conceded reluctantly. 'His wife has been suffering from early onset dementia for years and is currently in a care home and recognising neither him nor his children. He's been living in limbo for a long time. You won't ever have to worry about my relationship with Marina. We're good friends and would be even better friends had we just settled for that.'

Grace smiled, accepting his explanation, putting those fears to rest. 'Why didn't you tell me that you were planning to look up my father?'

'I had to check Tony out first. He could have been hostile to an approach from you. He could have hurt your feelings and I couldn't have stood by and let that happen to you,' Leo assured her without apology. 'As it was I met him, liked him and saw quite a bit of you in him.'

'I did feel very comfortable with him.' Involuntarily, Grace's eyes flooded with tears and she rested her head down on Leo's shoulder with an apologetic sniff as she fought to regain control. Leo was so protective of her and after a lifetime of always having to look out for herself the depth of his caring and kindness meant a great deal to her. Yet once his managing ways had irritated the hell out of her, she acknowledged, marvelling at how much her outlook and his had changed since their first encounter. 'In the same way I've always felt comfortable with you.'

Leo lowered her back down to sit at the foot of the bed. 'Now for something very important that I skipped the first time around...' he husked, dropping down gracefully on one knee and lifting her hand. 'Grace Donovan...will you marry me?'

'Aren't we already married?' Grace breathed, taken aback and utterly mystified as he lifted her hand.

'Are we? Father Benedetto in the chapel in the village quite understands that you don't feel quite married after a civil ceremony and he has agreed to do the honours for us again,' Leo explained, deftly threading a ring onto her wedding finger. 'All we need to do is book our day.'

Her face the very picture of wonderment, Grace extended her hand, splaying her fingers the better to admire the breathtaking diamond cluster he had given her, and then she glanced down at the startling picture of Leo at her feet in romantic mode. 'I love the ring. Everything's happening backwards for us. We're getting engaged after we got married!'

'Better late than never,' Leo growled, springing back upright. 'You still haven't said yes—'

'Yes…yes…*yes*!' Grace carolled without hesitation, her sheer happiness bubbling over. 'Yes to marrying you, yes to another wedding, yes to loving you for the rest of my life!'

Leo tugged her gently up the bed and flattened her to the pillows. 'Do you think you can do that, *agapi mou*? I'm very far from being perfect.'

'Now that you know that, the sky's the limit in the improvement stakes,' Grace teased, wriggling as he skimmed her hair out of his path and claimed a scorching kiss that she felt all the way down to her curling toes. 'But you definitely don't need to improve at *this*…'

And Leo laughed and thought how shallow and empty his life had been before Grace and how much richer and more interesting it had become with her. As for Grace, she was much too busy getting Leo out of his shirt and admiring his muscular chest to think about anything.

Four years later, Grace stood on the deck of *Hellenic Lady*'s successor while her daughter Rosie played on deck with the family dog, a fluffy pug called Jonas. Grace was relaxed as she always was on such trips. She worked long hours as a doctor in the paediatrics department of a busy London hospital and cherished every day of her time off.

'Daddy...Daddy!' Grace spun round to watch her daughter throw herself boisterously at her father as he emerged from the main saloon.

Leo looked amazing in swim shorts, his lean, powerful body well-honed by exercise, black hair blowing in the breeze. They had enjoyed an incredibly busy four years together. Raising Rosie without a team of nannies would have been impossible with the hours Grace had been working while she trained in various hospitals, but since then, having attained a more settled working day, she had had the time to become a more hands-on mum. Rosie had Grace's red hair, Leo's rich dark eyes and skin that didn't burn in the sun the way her mother's did. She was a lively, affectionate child, happily attending nursery school.

Leo lowered his daughter to the deck and fought off the energetic advances of the dog. 'We'll be docking soon,' he reminded her with a lazy grin, stunning eyes straying appreciatively over the lush curves Grace had showcased in a blue bikini.

The heat of the Turkish sun was already beating down on Grace's bare shoulders and she lifted a towel to drape it round her and cover her skin, which never took a tan. They were returning to Marmaris to celebrate her twenty-ninth birthday at the Fever nightclub where they had first met. Anatole and her father's entire family were on board with them. She got on very well with her two adult half-brothers, who were students, and her little half-sister, who was still at school. From her stepmother, she had received the warm family acceptance that she had tried and failed to win from her uncle's family.

'I'll go and get changed.'

Leo banded an arm round her on the way down the stairs. 'How much of a hurry are you in?'

'It'll take me more than an hour to do my hair and get ready.'

Her husband dropped a kiss on the slope of her shoulder. 'Do you have an hour for me?'

Heat and anticipation shimmied through her. 'I've always got time for you,' she declared with an impish smile. 'You're a very demanding man.'

'But you like that about me, *agapi mou*,' Leo told her teasingly, closing the door of the master suite behind them.

And Grace had to admit, she did like that about him. They were very well-matched in the bedroom department, she acknowledged as he claimed a lingering blatantly sexual kiss that made her body hum and her heart thump with awareness. Being married to Leo was never bland or boring. He was everything she had ever dreamt of in a husband and she was blissfully happy with him.

'I was thinking...' Leo purred, extracting her from her bikini with skill while pausing to worship her full breasts and the sleek curve of her hips. 'Since we're on holiday and you're all mine night and day, do you think we should consider working on extending the family?'

'Jonas would probably love some company.'

Leo found the most ticklish spot on her entire body and punished her for that crack until she dissolved into laughter. 'You know very well I wasn't thinking of the dog!'

'Well, maybe I don't like you describing the conception of another child as work,' Grace countered tartly.

'Work I love, work I can never get enough of, you maddening woman,' Leo groaned into the fall of her hair. 'You know I'm crazy about you, don't you?'

Grace fingered the flawless diamond pendant at her throat, which he had given her for her birthday, and smiled. 'The suspicion has crossed my mind once or twice.'

'Rosie is like a mini you and I'd love another one.'

'I'll put my pills away,' Grace murmured with amusement, linking her arms round his strong brown neck, appreciating his lean, darkly handsome features and his gorgeous eyes. 'I love you, Leo.'

'Nowhere near as much as I love you, *agapi mou*,' Leo countered.

'You're always so competitive,' she complained without great heat as she arched into the hard strength of his body and let her senses sing to the sensual magic of his demanding mouth.

* * * * *

THE GREEK
COMMANDS HIS
MISTRESS

CHAPTER ONE

'It's over, Reba,' Bastien Zikos pronounced with finality.

The stunning blonde he was addressing flashed him a pained look of reproach. 'But we've been great together.'

'I've never pretended that this is anything more than it is...*sex*,' Bastien traded impatiently. 'Now we're done.'

Reba blinked rapidly, as though she was fighting back tears, but Bastien wasn't fooled. The only thing that would reduce Reba to tears would be a stingy pay-off. She was as hard as nails...and he was no more yielding. Indeed, when it came to women he was tough and cold. His mother, an eighteen-carat-gold-digging promiscuous shrew, with a polished line in fake tears and emotion, had been the first to teach her son distrust and contempt for her sex.

'You got bored with me, didn't you?' Reba condemned. 'I was warned that you had a short attention span. I should've listened.'

Impatience shivered through Bastien's very tall, muscular frame. Reba had been his mistress, and terrific entertainment in the bedroom, but it ended now.

And he had given her a small fortune in jewellery. He took nothing for free from women—not sex, not anything.

Bastien turned on his heel. 'My accountant will be in touch,' he said drily.

'There's someone else, isn't there?' the blonde snapped.

'If there is, it's none of your business,' Bastien told her icily, his dark eyes chilling in their detachment as he glanced back at her, his lean, extravagantly handsome features hard as iron.

His driver was waiting outside the building to ferry him to the airport for his scheduled flight north.

A very faint shadow of a smile softened the tough line of Bastien's mouth as he boarded his private jet. *Someone else?* Maybe...maybe not.

His finance director, Richard James, was already seated in the opulent cabin. 'Am I allowed to ask what secret allure—evidently known only to you—exists in this dull northern town we're heading to, and about the even more dull failed business enterprise you have recently acquired?'

'You can ask. I don't promise to answer,' Bastien traded, flicking lazily through the latest stock figures on his laptop.

'Then there *is* something special at Moore Components that I haven't yet picked up on?' the stocky blond man prompted ruefully. 'A patent? A new invention?'

Bastien dealt the other man a wryly amused glance. 'The factory is built on land worth millions,' he pointed out drily. 'A prime site for development close to the town centre.'

'It's been years since you played asset-stripper,'

Richard remarked in surprise, while Bastien's personal staff and his security team boarded at the rear of the cabin.

Bastien had started out buying and selling businesses and breaking them up to attain the maximum possible profit. He had no conscience about such things. Profit and loss was a fact of life in the business world. Trends came and went, as did contracts. Fortunes rose and fell as companies expanded and then contracted again.

Bastien was exceptionally gifted when it came to spotting trends and making millions. He had a mind like a steel trap and the fierce, aggressive drive of a male who had not had a wealthy family to give him his breaks. He was a self-made billionaire, who had started out with nothing, and he took great pride in his independence.

But just at that moment Bastien wasn't thinking about business. No, indeed. Bastien was thinking about Delilah Moore—the only woman who had ever rejected him, leaving him tormented by lust and outraged by the frustrating new experience. His ego would have withstood the rebuff had she been genuinely uninterested in him, but Bastien knew that had not been the case. He had seen the longing in her eyes, the telling tension of her body when she was close to him, had recognised the breathy intimate note in her voice.

He could forgive much, but unquestionably *not* her deceitful insistence that she didn't want him. Fearlessly and foolishly judgemental, she had flung Bastien's womanising reputation in his face with as much disdain as a fine lady dismissing the clumsy approaches of a street thug. In reaction, Bastien's rage had burned, and now, almost two years on, it was still smouldering at the lack of respect she had demonstrated—not to mention her lies and her sheer nerve in daring to attack him.

And now fortune had turned the tables on Delilah Moore and her family. Bastien savoured the fact with dark satisfaction. He didn't believe she would be hurling defiance at him this time around...

'How is he?' Lilah asked her stepmother in an undertone when she spotted her father, Robert, standing outside in the backyard of her small terraced house.

'Much the same...' Vickie, a small curvaceous blonde in her early thirties, groaned at the sink, where she was doing the dishes with a whinging toddler clinging to one leg. 'Of course he's depressed. He worked all his life to build up the firm and now it's gone. He feels like a failure, and being unable to get a job hasn't helped.'

'Hopefully something will come up soon,' Lilah pronounced with determined cheer as she scooped up her two-year-old half-sister Clara and settled her down with a toy to occupy her.

When life was challenging, Lilah was convinced that it was best to look for even the smallest reason to be glad and celebrate it. Just then she was busy reminding herself that, while her father *had* lost his business and his home, their family was still intact and they all had their health.

At the same time Lilah was marvelling at the reality that she had grown so close to the stepmother she had once loathed on sight. She had assumed that

Vickie was another one of the good-time girls her father had once specialised in, and only slowly had she come to recognise that, regardless of their twenty-year age gap, the couple were genuinely in love.

Her father and Vickie had married four years earlier and Lilah now had two half-siblings she adored: three-year-old Ben and little Clara.

Currently Lilah's family were sharing her own rented home. With only two small bedrooms, a cramped living room and an even tinier kitchen, it was a very tight squeeze. But until the council came up with alternative accommodation for her father and his family, or her father found a paying job, they didn't have much choice.

The impressive five-bedroom home that her father and his wife had once owned was gone now, along with the business. Everything had had to be sold to settle the loans her father had taken out in a desperate effort to keep Moore Components afloat.

'I'm still hoping that Bastien Zikos will throw your dad a lifeline,' Vickie confided in a sudden burst of optimism. 'I mean, nobody knows that business better than Robert, and surely there's a space somewhere in the office or the factory where your father could still make himself useful?'

Lilah resisted the urge to remark that Bastien was more likely to tie a concrete block to her father's leg and sink him. After all, the Greek billionaire had offered to buy Moore Components two years earlier and his offer had been refused. Her father should've sold up and got out then, she thought regretfully. But the business had been doing well and, although tempted by the offer, the older man had ultimately decided that he couldn't face stepping down.

It was no consolation to Lilah that Bastien himself had forecast disaster once he'd realised that the firm's prosperity depended on the retention of one very important contract. Within weeks of losing that contract Moore Components had been struggling to survive.

'I'd better get to work,' Lilah remarked in a brittle voice, bending down to pet the miniature dachshund pushing affectionately against her legs in the hope of getting some attention.

Since her family had moved in Skippy had been a little neglected, she conceded guiltily. When had she last taken him for anything other than the shortest of walks?

Thoroughly unsettled, however, by her stepmother's sanguine reference to Bastien Zikos as a possible saviour, Lilah abandoned Skippy to pull on her raincoat, knotting the belt at her narrow waist.

She was a small, slender woman, with long black hair and bright blue eyes. She was also one of the very few workers still actively employed at Moore Components now it had gone bust. The Official Receivers had come in, taken over and laid off most of the staff. Only the services of the human resources team had been retained, to deal with all the admin involved in closing down the business. Engaged to work just two more days there, Lilah knew that she too would soon be unemployed.

Vickie was already zipping Ben into his jacket, because Lilah left the little boy at nursery school on her way into work.

It was a brisk spring day, with a breeze, and constantly forced to claw her hair out of her eyes, Lilah regretted not having taken the time to put her hair up long before she dropped her little brother off at the school. Unfortunately she had been suffering sleepless nights and scrambling out of bed every morning heavy-eyed, running late.

Ever since she had learned that Bastien Zikos had bought her father's failed business she had been struggling to hide her apprehension. In that less-than-welcoming attitude to the new owner, however, Lilah stood very much alone. The Receivers had been ecstatic to find a buyer, while her father and various resident worthies had expressed the hope that the new owner would re-employ some of the people who had lost their jobs when Moore Components closed.

Only Lilah, who had once received a disturbing glimpse of the cold diamond-cutting strength of Bastien's ruthlessness, was full of pessimism and thought the prospect of Bastien arriving to break good news to the local community unlikely.

In fact, if ever a man could have been said to have *scared* Lilah, it was Bastien Zikos. Everything about the tall, amazingly handsome Greek had unnerved her. The way he looked, the way he talked, the domineering way he behaved. His whole attitude had been anathema to her and she had backed off fast—only to discover, to her dismay, that that kind of treatment only put Bastien into pursuit mode.

Although Lilah was only twenty-three she had distrusted self-assured, slick and handsome men all her life, fully convinced that most of them were lying, cheating players. After all, even her own father had once been like that—a serial adulterer whose affairs had caused her late mother great unhappiness.

Lilah didn't like to dwell on those traumatic years, when she had begun to hate her father, because it had seemed then that he could not be trusted with any woman—not her mother's friends, not even his office staff. Mercifully all that behaviour had stopped once her father met Vickie, and since then Lilah had contrived to forge a new and much closer relationship with her surviving parent. Only now Robert Moore had settled down was his daughter able to respect him again and forgive him for the past.

Bastien, on the other hand, was not the family-man type, and he had always enjoyed his bad reputation as a womaniser. He was an unashamed sexual predator, accustomed to reaching out and just taking any woman who took his fancy. He was rich, astute and incredibly good-looking. Women fell like ninepins around him, running to him the instant he crooked an inviting finger. But Lilah had run in the opposite direction, determined not to have her heart broken and her pride trampled by a man who only wanted her for her body.

She was worth more than that, she reminded herself staunchly, as she had done two years earlier— *much* more. She wanted a man who loved and cared about her and who would stick by her no matter what came their way.

Being powerfully attracted to a man like Bastien Zikos had been a living nightmare for Lilah, and she had refused to acknowledge her reaction to him or surrender to the temptation he provided. Yet even now, two years on, Lilah could still remember her first sight of him across a crowded auction room. Bastien...tall, dark and devastating, with his glorious black-lashed tawny eyes.

She had been there to view a pendant that had once belonged to her mother and which Vickie, unaware of Lilah's attachment to the piece, had put up for sale. Lilah had planned to buy it back quietly at auction, preferring that option to the challenge of telling Vickie that she had actually been pretty upset when her father had so thoughtlessly given all her late mother's jewellery to his then live-in girlfriend.

And the first person Lilah had seen that day had been Bastien, black hair falling over his brow, his bold bronzed profile taut as he examined something in his hand while an auction assistant in overalls stood by an open display cabinet. When she had been directed to that same cabinet she had been hugely taken aback to see that Bastien had had her mother's very ordinary silver sea horse pendant clasped in his lean brown hand.

'What are you doing with that?' she'd asked possessively.

'What's it to you?' Bastien had asked bluntly, glancing up and transfixing her with breathtaking dark brown eyes enhanced by lush, curling black lashes.

In that split second he had travelled in her estimation from merely handsome to utterly gorgeous, and her breath had tripped in her throat and her heart had started hammering—as if she stood on the edge of a dangerous precipice.

'It belonged to my mother.'

'Where did *she* get it from?' Bastien had shot at her, thoroughly disconcerting her.

'I was with her when she bought it at a car boot sale almost twenty years ago,' Lilah had confided. although she'd been startled by his question, not to mention the intensity of his appraisal.

'My mother lost it in London some time around then,' Bastien had mused in a dark, deep accented drawl that had sent odd little quivers travelling down her spine. He had turned over the pendant to display the engraving on the back, composed of two letter As enclosed in a heart shape. 'My father Anatole gave it to my mother Athene. What an extraordinary co-incidence that it should have belonged to *both* our mothers.'

'Extraordinary…' Lilah had agreed jerkily. as disturbed by his proximity as by his explanation. He'd been close enough that she'd been able to see the dark stubble shadowing his strong jawline and smell the citrus-sharp tenor of his cologne. Her nostrils had flared as she'd taken a hasty step backwards and cannoned into someone behind her.

Bastien had shot out a hand to steady her before she could stumble, long brown fingers closing round her narrow shoulder like a metal vice to keep her upright.

Lilah had jerked back again, breathless and flushed, heat flickering in places she had never felt warm before as her gaze had collided with the tall Greek's stunning eyes.

'May I see the pendant before it goes back in the cabinet?' she had asked curtly, putting out her hand.

'There's not much point in you looking at it. I'm planning to buy it,' Bastien had imparted drily.

Lilah's teeth had snapped together as though he had slapped her. 'So am I,' she had admitted grudgingly.

With reluctance Bastien had settled the pendant into her hand. Her eyes had prickled as she looked at it, because her mother had loved the fanciful piece and had often worn it in summer. The pendant reawakened a few of the happier memories of Lilah's childhood.

'Join me for coffee,' Bastien had urged, flipping the pendant back out of her hand to return it to the hovering assistant.

Lilah had dealt him a bemused look of surprise. 'It would hardly be a-appropriate,' she'd stammered. 'Not when we're both going to bid on the same lot.'

'Maybe I'm sentimental. Maybe I would like to hear about where the necklace has been all these years.'

Bastien had dangled that unlikely assurance in front of her like a prize carrot and she had caved in to coffee, feeling that to do otherwise would be rude and unreasonable.

And so her brief acquaintance with Bastien Zikos had begun, Lilah recalled unhappily. Hurriedly she blanked out the memories of that short week she never, *ever* allowed herself to think about, far too well aware of how mortifyingly long it was taking for her to forget meeting Bastien Zikos. Yet she had never had any regrets about turning him down—not then and not since, even when the most cursory internet search of Bastien's name always revealed the never-ending parade of different beauties that it took to keep Bastien happy. Quantity rather than quality was what Bastien went for in women, she had often thought, while telling herself that she had made the only decision she could...even if he still hated her for it.

As Lilah walked through the factory gates, saddened by the lack of vehicles and bustle that had used to characterise the once busy site, her mobile phone rang. Digging it out, she answered it. It was Josh, whom she had gone to university with, and he was suggesting she join him and a few friends for a night out. Every six weeks or so they met up as a group, went for a meal and out to see a film. One or two of the group were couples, the others simply friends. Josh, for example, was recovering from a broken engagement, and Lilah's last boyfriend had dumped her as soon as her father's business had hit the skids.

'Tomorrow night?' Lilah queried, thinking about it and liking the idea, because evenings in her crowded little house were currently far from relaxing and the idea of getting out was attractive. 'What time?'

Her friends would take her mind off things, she reflected gratefully, and stop her constantly fretting about a situation she had no control over. Unfortunately for Lilah an instinctive need to fix broken things and rescue people and animals ran deep and strong in her veins.

From the main office on the top floor, Bastien watched Delilah Moore cross the Moore Components car park with laser-sharp attention. She was still the most beautiful creature he had ever seen, he acknowledged, angry that that should *still* strike him as being the case. There had been a lot of women in his bed since he had met Robert Moore's daughter, but none of them had held his interest for very long.

Bastien still saw Delilah in the same light as he had first seen her, with her silky black curling cloud of hair falling almost to her waist and her sapphire-blue eyes electrifyingly noticeable against her creamy, perfect skin. Even wearing worn jeans and scuffed biker boots she'd had that casual effortlessly elegant look which some women had no matter what they wore.

Then, as now, he had told himself impatiently that she wasn't his type. With a single exception he had always gone for tall curvy blondes. Delilah was tiny, and very slender—the complete opposite of voluptuous. He just couldn't explain what made her so appealing to him, and that annoyed Bastien because *anything* he couldn't control or understand annoyed him.

This time around, he would get close enough to see all her flaws, he promised himself grimly.

'The new boss is in the building!' carolled Lilah's colleague Julie as soon as she walked into the small office the two women shared.

Halfway out of her coat, Lilah froze. 'When did he arrive?'

'The security guard said it was barely seven... talk about an early start!' Julie gushed admiringly. 'Mr Zikos has brought a whole team with him—I think that's hopeful, don't you? He is seriously good-looking too.'

Lilah's coat finally made it on to the hook. Her slender spine was rigid. *'Really?'*

'Absolutely beautiful...like a male supermodel. Maggie made coffee for him and even *she* agreed,' Julie said, referring to the office cleaner and tea lady, a known man-hater, who was hard to impress. 'But Maggie said it isn't his first visit. Apparently he was here a couple of years back?'

'Yes, he was. He was interested in buying this place then.'

'You *knew* that? You've seen him *before*?' Julie exclaimed in consternation. 'Why didn't you mention it?'

'With all that's been going on, it didn't seem important,' Lilah muttered, sitting down at her desk and closing her ears while Julie lamented her lack of interest in the new owner of Moore Components.

A young man with a neatly clipped beard entered their office an hour later. 'Miss Moore?' he asked, stopping in front of Lilah's desk. 'I'm one of Mr Zikos' team—Andreas Theodakis. Mr Zikos would like to see you in his office.'

Lilah lost colour and tried and failed to swallow, scolding herself for the instantaneous fear that washed through her. Of course Bastien wasn't going to harm her in any way. Why did even the thought of him charge her with near panic?

As she mounted the stairs she breathed slow and deep to compose herself. Bastien would want to crow, wouldn't he? He had got the business at a knockdown price and the Moore family had lost it, exactly as he had predicted. Rich, powerful men probably liked to boast whenever they got the opportunity, she reasoned uncertainly. For, really, her brain cried, what did *she* know about rich, powerful men? After all, Bastien was the only rich and powerful man she had ever met.

He was using her father's office, and it felt exceedingly strange to Lilah to be entering such a familiar space and find her father absent. Her eyes flickered super-fast over Bastien without pausing, as she registered that no other person was to be present for their meeting. Was that a good sign or a bad one?

'Mr Zikos,' she framed tightly.

'Oh. I think you can still call me Bastien,' he derided, studying her while wondering how on earth she could look so good in a plain black skirt of indeterminate length and a shapeless camel sweater.

Curly black hair lay in tumbled skeins across her shoulders. It was still the same length. He would have been vexed had she had it cut shorter. But, no, it was unchanged, and there was still something strangely fascinating about that long, long black hair that had ensnared his attention the instant he first saw it. And something equally memorable about the striking contrast between her bright blue eyes and her pale porcelain-fine skin.

Forced to look at him properly for the first time, Lilah froze, willing her rigid facial muscles to relax, ensuring that she betrayed no reaction to him. It was an exercise she had become adept at using in self-defence two years earlier. Her breath rattled in her throat, as if she had been dropped unexpectedly into a dark and haunted house where she was surrounded by unseen threats.

Bastien stood about six foot four inches tall, a clear twelve inches bigger than she was, which meant she could easily get away with focusing on his blue silk tie. But the glance she had got at him as she'd entered the office was still etched on her brain—as if it had been burned there in lines of fire with a red-hot poker.

Whether she liked it or not, Julie had hit it right on

the nail: Bastien *did* have a supermodel look, from his sculpted high cheekbones, classically arrogant nose and strong jawline to his full, incredibly kissable lips. Uncomfortable warmth washed up over her skin and she reddened, gritting her teeth, because she knew that she was blushing and that he would notice. *Why* would he notice? Because Bastien never missed a trick.

'Take a seat, Delilah…' Bastien indicated one of the armchairs beside the coffee table in one corner of the spacious panelled room.

'It's Lilah,' she corrected, and not for the first time.

He had always insisted on calling her by her full name—that name with its biblical connotations, which had caused her so much embarrassment from primary right up through to secondary school.

'I prefer *De*-lilah,' Bastien purred, with all the satisfaction of a jungle cat who had been lapping cream.

Lilah sank down in the chair, her slender spine too rigid to curve into the support of the seat. Her entire attention was locked on to Bastien and she clashed unwarily with his truly spectacular eyes. Tawny brown, golden in sunshine, literally mesmerising and surrounded by the most fabulous velvety black lashes, she reflected dizzily, plunged into one of the terrifying time-out-of-time lapses of concentration and discipline which Bastien had frequently inflicted on her two years earlier.

'I can't think why you would want to see me,' Lilah told him quietly, just as the door opened and Maggie bustled in with a tray of coffee and biscuits.

Lilah jumped up and immediately removed the tray from the older woman's grasp. Maggie had chosen to work well beyond retirement and, although she would never have admitted the fact, Maggie now found it difficult to carry heavy trays.

'I would've been fine,' Maggie scolded.

Lilah settled the tray of fancy silverware and fine china which her father's secretary had kept for VIPs down on the table. Maggie departed. Lilah poured the coffee and sugared Bastien's before she had even thought about what she was doing.

'You can't think why I would want to see you?' Bastien queried, unimpressed by the claim. 'How very modest you are...'

Suspecting him of mockery, Lilah flushed and extended his coffee to him. He reached for the cup and took a sip of the black, heavily sweetened coffee, smiling when he discovered that she had got it right.

Striving to play it cool and composed, Lilah lifted her own cup and saucer—but that smile...oh, *that* smile...was flipping up the corners of his beautiful mouth, transforming his lean, dark forbidding features with an almost boyish grin. Helplessly she stared, sapphire-blue eyes widening.

'Today,' Bastien drawled lazily, 'you are a very influential young woman, because it is in *your* power to decide what happens next to Moore Components.'

Lilah kept on staring at him, literally locked into immobility by that astonishing assurance. 'What on earth are you talking about?'

CHAPTER TWO

BASTIEN STUDIED HER, inordinate satisfaction glittering in his dark deep-set eyes. He had waited a long time for this particular moment and it was giving him even more of a kick than he had hoped.

'I have a few options to put before you. The fate of Moore Components is now entirely in your hands.'

Lilah set her coffee down with a jarring rattle of china and leapt upright. 'Why the heck would you say something like that to me?' she demanded.

'Because it's the truth. I don't lie and nor do I backtrack on promises,' Bastien asserted levelly. 'I assure you that what ultimately happens to this business will be solely *your* responsibility.'

Still frozen in place, Lilah blinked rapidly while she battled to concentrate. 'I don't understand. How can that be?'

'You're not that naïve,' Bastien drawled with a curled lip. 'You *know* I want you.'

'*Still?*' Lilah gasped in astonishment at that declaration, because after all two years had passed since their last meeting, and even six months on she would have expected Bastien barely to recall her name, never mind her face.

The faintest scoring of colour had flared across Bastien's high cheekbones and he parted his lips, even white teeth flashing. *'Still,'* he confirmed, with forbidding emphasis.

Lilah didn't understand how that was possible. How could he still find her attractive after all the other women he had been with in the intervening months? It didn't make sense to Lilah at all.

It was not as if she was some staggeringly beautiful woman who regularly stopped men dead in the street. Admittedly she had never had a problem attracting men, but retaining their interest when she wasn't prepared to slide casually into bed with them had proved much more of a challenge. In fact, most men walked away fast sooner than test her boundaries, choosing to assume that she was either devoutly religious or desirous of a wedding-ring-sized commitment before she would share her body.

Lilah dropped back into the seat she had vacated, her brain buzzing with bewildered thoughts. How could Bastien's continuing physical desire for her have anything to do with the business and its prospects? And how could he still find her attractive when he had so many other more sophisticated women in his life? Was it simply the fact that Lilah had once said no to him? Could a male as clever as Bastien be that outrageously basic?

'I don't want to keep you all morning, so I'll run through the three options.'

'Three...options...?' Lilah queried even more uneasily.

'Option one—you choose to walk away from me,' Bastien extended grimly, shooting her a glance of warning that made her pale. 'In that event I sell the machinery in the factory and sell the site to a developer. I already have a good offer for the land and it would turn an immediate healthy profit…'

Lilah dropped her head, appalled at that suggestion. The town needed this factory for employment. The closure of Moore Components had already damaged the small town's economy. Shops and entertainment venues were suffering from a downturn. People were struggling to find work because there were few other local jobs, and many had already had to put their houses up for sale because they could no longer afford their mortgages.

Lilah was well-acquainted with the human cost of unemployment and had done what little she could in her HR capacity to offer her father's former workers guidance and advise them on suitable retraining schemes.

'Option two—you choose only to spend *one* night with me,' Bastien framed, impervious to the slight sound Lilah made as her lips parted on a stricken gasp of disbelief. 'I will then make the business function again for at least a year. It will cost me money and it will be a waste of time, because the factory requires sustained and serious investment to win and retain new contracts. But if that's the best I can get from you I'm prepared to do it…'

Lilah lifted her head and focused on Bastien's lean darkly handsome face in sheer wonderment. 'Let me get this straight. You are using Moore Components as a means of bargaining with me for my *body*?' she spelled out incredulously. 'Are you out of your *mind*?'

'Be grateful. If I *didn't* want you there would be

nothing at all to put on the table. But for you I wouldn't even have bothered coming up here. I simply would have sold the land,' Bastien informed her with lethal cool.

Lilah had great difficulty hinging her jaw closed again, because she was stupefied by the options he was laying out before her. 'You can't possibly want me that much,' she told him involuntarily. 'That would be crazy.'

'Obviously I'm crazy.' Bastien dealt Lilah a slow, lingering appraisal that began at her lush pink lips, segued down to the small pert breasts outlined by her sweater and glossed over her delicately curved hipline to her shapely knees and ankles. 'You have terrific legs,' he mused, fighting the sting of awakening interest at his groin with fierce determination.

Two years back Delilah Moore had kept him in a state of virtually constant arousal that had given him sleepless nights and forced him into cold showers. He was damned if he was going to let her have that much of an effect on him again! He wanted her and that was that—but their affair would be on his terms only.

Option two was probably the wisest choice for him, because once he had bedded her, her fascination would surely wane fast and he would tire of her as he had tired of all her predecessors. But although he was convinced that one night should completely exorcise her from his fantasies, he still didn't want to be forced to agree to that restriction.

Lilah yanked her skirt down over her knees, suddenly boiling up below her clothing, her whole skin surface prickling and reacting to his visual assessment with a rush of heat. He was such a very sexual male, she conceded in bewilderment. The atmosphere pulsed with astonishing tension and she hurriedly snatched her attention from him, recognising the swelling tautness of her nipples and the surge of ungovernable heat between her thighs as totally unacceptable reactions.

But she couldn't prevent those reactions—couldn't stop them happening around Bastien. On that level two years earlier Bastien had drawn her like a moth to a flame, because the wild, seething excitement he'd evoked in her had been incredibly seductive.

In a desperate attempt to regain control of her disordered thoughts, Lilah said with careful precision, 'I refuse to believe you're serious about this, Bastien. A man of your stature and wealth cannot possibly want a woman like me so much that he would make such a bargain.'

'What would *you* know about it?' Bastien cut in, whiplash-abrupt in that dismissal. 'I haven't reached option three yet.'

Outraged by his persistence, Lilah rose to her feet again. 'I refuse to listen to any more of this nonsense!'

'Then I sell this place today,' Bastien fired at her with cold finality as she walked towards the door. 'Your choice, your decision, Delilah. You're lucky I'm giving you options.'

Lilah was still and then spun round again, black hair sliding in a glossy fall across her shoulders. *'Lucky?'* she exclaimed in angry disbelief, her temper stirring as she thought about the contemptible offer he had made to her. Bottom line: Bastien Zikos was willing to do just about anything to get her into bed. Was she supposed to be *pleased* about that? Was it normal to feel as insulted as she did…as *hurt*? Why did she feel hurt?

'With my backing you can wave a magic wand here and be a heroine if you want to be,' Bastien imparted very drily. 'Option three—I do almost anything you want, up to and including employing your father as consultant and manager.'

That startling suggestion not only stopped Lilah's thoughts mid-track and froze her feet to the carpet, it also made everything else inside her head blur. For a split second she pictured her deeply troubled father restored to some semblance of his former confident, energetic self, able to earn again and provide for his family. What a huge difference that would make to Robert Moore!

'So *that's* what it takes to stop you walking out… you're a real Daddy's girl!' Bastien remarked with galling amusement. 'Are you ready to listen now, and stop flouncing around dramatically and asking me if I'm crazy? The answer to that is that I'm only crazy to have you in my bed…'

Colour blossomed below Lilah's skin and ran up to her hairline in a scalding surge. She could barely credit that he had said that without even a shade of discomfiture. But then she reckoned it would take something considerably more shocking than sex to embarrass a male as resolute and dominant as Bastien. 'All right…for my father's sake I'll agree to hear you out,' she conceded with flat reluctance.

'Then *sit*!' Bastien indicated the chair.

It occurred to Lilah that Bastien had spoken to her just then as she spoke to Skippy when the dog was playing up.

Raising a wry brow at his disrespectful mode of addressing her, she sat down again. 'Option three?' she reminded him succinctly.

'You become my mistress and stay with me for as long as I want you.'

'Keeping a mistress is an astonishingly old-fashioned concept,' Lilah remarked, to mask the reality that inwardly she was knocked sideways by that proposition.

Bastien shifted a broad shoulder in a careless shrug. 'In my world it's the norm.'

'I assumed sex slavery of that sort ended about a hundred years ago.'

'But then you don't have a clue what the role entails,' Bastien said drily, watching her while picturing her slender body sheathed in decadent silk and lace and diamonds purely for his private enjoyment.

The image gave him both a high and a hard-on.

'In return for your agreement to become my mistress I will set this business up and invest in it. As the owner of a network of companies I can easily provide contracts to keep the factory busy. I will instruct your father to rehire his former workforce. After all, skilled employees are difficult to replace. With my full financial support, virtually everything could go back to the way it was before Moore Components lost that crucial contract.'

Lilah was floored by those comprehensive assurances. Now she understood Bastien's jibe about her having the opportunity to play the heroine and wave a magic wand. *Everything back the way it was!* How many times in recent months had she longed for that to happen and for everyone to be content again instead of stressed, broken and unhappy? Countless times.

Bastien was a very powerful, enormously wealthy male, and perhaps for the first time she fully appreciated that reality—because she knew it would take thousands and thousands of pounds to get the factory up and running again, never mind build the business up to survive in the long term. It would be a hugely expensive challenge, but it would turn around the lives of so many people, Lilah reflected with a sinking heart.

'Like Tinker Bell, you're quite taken with the offer of a magic wand?' Bastien quipped with brooding amusement as he watched her expressive face intently. 'I suppose your response will depend on how much of a do-gooder you are. So far you're ranging fairly high in that list of good works now that you have your whole family living with you. You're keeping them too, aren't you?'

Lilah was furious that he should have access to such facts about her personal life, and the label of 'do-gooder' offended her. 'I'm *not* a do-gooder.'

'By my estimation you are,' Bastien countered drily. 'You've saved your wicked stepmother from living in emergency accommodation and you also raise funds for abandoned dogs and starving children.'

Lilah stood up again in a sudden motion. 'How on earth do you know so much about me?'

'Obviously I've kept an eye on developments here.'

'My stepmother is *not* wicked,' Lilah added uncomfortably. 'How do you know my family are staying with me? How do you know about the volunteer work I've done for the dog sanctuary?'

'I had to check you out before I came up here,' Bastien pointed out impatiently. 'If you'd got married or picked up a boyfriend since we last met there would have been little point in my approaching you. I don't like to have my time wasted.'

Lilah's chin lifted. 'I *did* have a boyfriend!' she bit out resentfully.

'Not for very long. He dropped you the minute your father's business went down.'

Angry words brimmed on Lilah's tongue, but she swallowed them whole because she wasn't going to sink to the level of arguing with Bastien over someone as unworthy of her defence as Steve, her ex-boyfriend.

Ironically, Bastien's reading of Steve's behaviour exactly matched her own. Steve had turned out to be very ambitious. He had started dating Lilah when Moore Components was thriving and had tried to persuade her father to take him on as a junior partner. It mortified her that Bastien should know about the revealing speed and timing of Steve's defection.

Rigid with self-control, Lilah lifted her head high. 'I can't believe that you really mean those options you outlined. They're immoral.'

'I'm not a very moral man,' Bastien told her without hesitation. 'I don't apologise for what I want and I always *get* what I want...and I want you. You should be flattered.'

'I'm not flattered. I'm shocked and disgusted at your lack of scruple!' Lilah told him angrily, her blue eyes bright with condemnation. 'You're trying to take advantage of this situation and play on my affection for my family.'

'I will use any advantage I have and do whatever I have to do to win you. Of course whether or not you choose to accept one of my two preferred options is entirely your decision,' Bastien pointed out, his wide, beautifully shaped mouth firming as he stalked fluidly closer to tower over her. '*You're* the glittering prize here, Delilah. Doesn't that thrill you?'

Lilah stiffened even more. 'No, of course it doesn't.'

'It would thrill most women,' Bastien told her drily, staring down at her with burnished dark golden eyes that sent an intoxicating fizz of awareness and frightening tension shooting through her every limb. 'Most women like to be wanted above all others.'

'I very much doubt that you're *capable* of wanting one woman above all others,' Lilah retorted with sharp emphasis. 'Women seem to be very much interchangeable commodities to you, so I really can't understand why you should have a fixation about *me*.'

'It's *not* a fixation,' Bastien growled, dark eyes hard, strong jawline squared.

'Oh, for goodness' sake—call a spade a spade, Bastien!' Lilah countered in exasperation. 'At least look at the lengths you're willing to go to to *make* me do what you want...does that strike you as *normal*?'

'Sexual satisfaction is extremely important to me,' Bastien parried, studying her with cool gravity. 'I don't feel any need to explain that or to apologise for it.'

Lilah felt like someone beating her head up against a brick wall. Bastien didn't listen to what he didn't want to hear. He went full steam ahead, like an express train racing down a track. He saw what he wanted and he went for it, regardless of reason and the damage he might do.

'Delilah... I would treat you well...' Bastien murmured huskily.

'What you've suggested...it's out of the question—*impossible*!' she exclaimed in a furious outburst of frustration. 'Not to mention downright sleazy!'

Bastien lifted a lean tanned hand and scored a reproving fingertip along the strained line of her lush lower lip. 'I am never, *ever* sleazy...' He positively purred. 'You have a lot to learn about me.'

Subjected to even that minor physical contact, she felt her whole skin surface break out in enervated goose bumps and jerked back a hasty step.

'What I've learnt today, just listening to you, is more than enough,' she stressed in biting rejection. 'You talk as if you're playing some amusing game with me, but what you're proposing is offensive and unthinkable. And nothing you could hope to offer would persuade my father to accept a job that would literally sell me to the highest bidder as part of the deal!'

Bastien scanned her flushed and furious face and the sapphire-blue eyes shooting defiant sparks at him. 'Only an idiot would suggest that you tell your father the truth and nothing but the truth,' he derided. 'All you would need to tell your family is that I have offered you your dream job, which will entail a lot of foreign travel and an enviable lifestyle.'

With a reflexive little shudder at that Machiavellian suggestion, Lilah snapped, 'My goodness, you have absolutely everything worked out!'

'But will you take the bait?' Bastien breathed in a roughened undertone. 'You have until ten tomorrow morning to make your decision and choose an option.'

'You haven't given me even *one* reasonable or fair option,' Lilah condemned bitterly.

'If you don't give me your answer tomorrow I *will* sell,' Bastien warned her with chilling bite.

Her narrow spine went poker-straight with the force of her resentment and her slender hands knotted into fists. It was far from being the first time she had been in Bastien's company and had longed to knock his teeth down his throat.

In the smouldering silence, Bastien released his breath in a hiss of impatience. 'It doesn't have to be like this between us, Delilah. We could discuss this over dinner tonight.'

Lilah flung him a shaken and furious look over her shoulder as her perspiring hand worked frantically at the doorknob. 'Dinner? You've got to be joking! Anyway, I'm already booked,' she fibbed, refusing to give him the idea that she sat in every night.

'To see who?' Bastien demanded, pressing a hand against the door to prevent her from opening it.

'That's none of your business.' Refusing to fight for control of the door, Lilah stood back and folded her arms defensively. 'Nothing I do is any of your business. You may own Moore Components, but that's the only thing you own around here.'

Dark eyes glittering brilliant as stars, Bastien flung the door wide for her exit. 'I wouldn't be so sure of that, *koukla mou*.'

Lilah hurried downstairs and straight into the cloakroom, needing a moment before she returned to work and faced Julie and her curiosity. She was shaking and sweating, and she held her trembling hands below the cold tap while snatching in a deep sustaining breath, praying for self-control.

Unfortunately Bastien had struck her on her weakest flank. The very idea that she could rescue her family from their current predicament had turned her heart inside out with hope and desperation. And what about all the other people whose lives would be transformed by the opportunity to regain the jobs they had lost? Jobs in a revitalised business which would be much more secure with Bastien's backing? All their former workers would be ecstatic at the idea of the factory reopening.

But Bastien Zikos had put an incredibly high price on what that miracle would cost Lilah in personal terms. It was too much to think about, she thought weakly, anger still hurtling through her, tensing her every muscle. How could he *do* that? How could he stand there in front of her and outline such demeaning options? A one-night stand…or a one-night stand which ran and ran until he got bored? Some choice! What had she ever done to him to deserve such treatment?

Her temples thumped dully—a stress headache was forming. She was stressed, out of her depth and barely able to think straight, she acknowledged heavily. Hadn't she felt very much like that when she was first exposed to Bastien's soul-destroying charm?

Of course that charm had not been much in evidence just now, during their office meeting, she conceded bitterly. It had, however, been very much in evidence when Bastien had taken her for coffee at the auction house two years earlier.

After a casual exchange of names and information

Bastien had taken out his business card to show her that his company logo was, in fact, a seahorse. The awareness that he also had a strong family connection to the pendant had made Lilah relax more in his company. Noting his sleek gold Rolex watch, and the sharp tailoring of his stylish suit, she had recognised the hallmarks of wealth and suspected that it was highly unlikely that she could hope to outbid him at auction.

She had teased him about the amount of sugar he put in his coffee and a wickedly sensual smile had curved his lips, sending her heartbeat into overdrive. Oh, yes. At first sight she had been hugely, hopelessly attracted to Bastien and had hung on his every word.

'You still haven't explained one thing,' Bastien had mused. 'If you value it so much, why is the pendant being sold at auction?'

She had explained about the jewellery her father had given her stepmother. 'Now Vickie's having a big clean-out, and I didn't want to risk upsetting her by admitting how I felt.'

'If you don't ask, you don't get,' Bastien had censured drily. 'Not that I'm complaining. Your delicate sense of diplomacy has worked in *my* favour. If the necklace hadn't gone on sale I wouldn't have known where it was. I've been trying to track it down for years.'

'I suppose you remember your mother wearing it?' she remarked.

'No, but I remember my father giving it to her,' Bastien had countered rather bleakly, his dramatic dark eyes veiled while his beautiful mouth had tightened unexpectedly. 'I was about four years old and I honestly believed we were the perfect family.'

'Nothing wrong with that,' she had quipped with a big smile, trying to picture him as a little kid, thinking that he had probably been very cute, with a shock of black hair and brown eyes deep enough to drown in.

'Irrespective of what happens at the auction tomorrow, promise that you will have dinner with me tomorrow evening,' he'd urged, and had invited her to his hotel.

'I'm still planning to bid,' she warned him.

'I can afford to outbid most people. Dinner?' he'd pressed again.

And she had crumbled, like sand smoothed over and reshaped by a powerful wave.

Bastien hadn't made the connection between her and Moore Components, and it had been a big surprise for both of them when her auction disappointment had been followed by an unexpected meeting with Bastien in her father's office the next day. Dinner at Bastien's hotel had been replaced by dinner at her father's home, to which she had been invited as well.

When a phone call had claimed Robert Moore's attention he had asked his daughter to see Bastien out to his car.

'If you're expecting me to congratulate you on your win, you're destined for disappointment,' Lilah had warned Bastien on their way down the stairs. 'You paid a ludicrous amount for that pendant.'

Bastien laughed out loud. 'Says the woman who bidded me up to that ludicrous amount!'

Lilah reddened. 'Well, I had to at least *try* to get it. Why are you seeing my father?' she had asked abruptly as they came to a halt in the car park.

'I'm interested in acquiring his business and he

wants some time to think my offer over. You work here. *You* could be my acquisition too,' Bastien had said huskily, sexily in her ear, making the tiny hairs at her nape stand up while an arrow of heat shot straight down into her pelvis.

Unsettled by the strength of her reaction to him, Lilah had stiffened. 'I don't think so. I don't think Dad will sell up either—not when he's riding the crest of a wave.'

'That's the best time to sell.'

Bastien had dealt her a dark, lingering appraisal that had made her toes curl even as her gaze widened at the sight of the limousine that had rolled up to collect him. She'd been impressed but troubled by the obviously large difference in their financial status and had resolved to look him up on the internet as soon as she got the time.

'I wish your father hadn't invited us to his family dinner.' Bastien had sighed. 'I was looking forward to having you all to myself at my hotel.'

Unease had filtered through Lilah. He was coming on very strong, and while initially she'd been delighted by that, she was unnerved by the suspicion that he might be expecting her to spend the night with him. An impulsive move like that would have been way outside Lilah's comfort zone.

But at the same time still being a virgin at the age of twenty-one had not been part of Lilah's life plan either. She just hadn't met anyone at university who had attracted her enough to take that plunge. Lilah didn't give her trust easily to men, and by the end of first year, after standing by and watching friends commit too fast to casual relationships that had ended in tears and recriminations, she had decided that she would definitely hold off on sex until she met a man who cared enough about her to be prepared to wait until she was as ready for intimacy as he was.

'Bastien's really into you in a big way,' Vickie had whispered in amusement after dinner at her father's comfortable home that evening. 'He watches your every move. And although I prefer men to be more grey round the edges, he *is* gorgeous.'

Before Lilah had been able to call a taxi, Bastien had offered to run her home. Within seconds of them getting into the limo Bastien had reached for her with a determined hand and kissed her with a hungry, sensual ferocity that had set her treacherous body on fire. She had pulled back, trying to cool the moment down, but Bastien had ignored her.

'Spend the night with me,' he'd pressed, his thumb stroking her wrist where her pulse was racing insanely fast.

'I hardly know you,' she had pointed out hastily.

'You can get to know me in bed,' Bastien had quipped.

'That's not how I operate, Bastien,' Lilah had murmured, reddening with discomfiture. 'I would need to know you really well before I slept with you.'

'*Diavelos*... I'm only here for another forty-eight hours!' Bastien had ground out incredulously, studying her as though she was as strange and incongruous a sight as a snowball in the desert.

'I'm sorry. I can't change the way I am,' Lilah had told him quietly as the limousine drew up outside the terraced house where she lived.

'You're my polar opposite. I don't get to know

women really well. To be brutally honest, sex is the only intimacy I want or need,' Bastien had breathed in a driven undertone.

'We're like oil and water,' Lilah had mumbled, hurriedly vacating his car and heading indoors, to heave a sigh of relief as soon as the door was closed behind her.

In the aftermath of that uneasy parting tears had burned her eyes and she'd been immediately filled with self-loathing. She was guilty of having woven silly romantic dreams about Bastien. Hadn't she just got what she deserved for being so naïve? He was only interested in a night of casual sex—nothing more. It wasn't a compliment…it was a slap in the face—and a wake-up call to regain control of her wits.

Although Lilah had initially been attracted by Bastien's stunning good looks, she had been infinitely more fascinated by his strong personality, and the seemingly offbeat way his brain worked. That same night she'd sat up late, looking Bastien up on the internet, and the sheer number of women she'd seen pictured with him had shaken her almost as much as his reputation for being a womaniser. Bastien Zikos slept around and he was faithless.

At first Lilah had been appalled by what she had discovered, but there had also been an oddly soothing element to those revelations. After all, what she had found out only emphasised that she could never have any kind of liaison with Bastien: he didn't do relationships…and she didn't do one-night stands.

Sinking back to the present, Lilah was dismayed to register that her eyes were swimming with tears. She blinked them back and freshened up, writing off her far too emotional frame of mind to the shocks Bastien had dealt her. She hated the way that Bastien always got to her—cutting through her common sense and reserve like a machete to make his forceful point.

'You were a long time upstairs with the boss,' Julie commented as Lilah dropped back behind her desk.

'Mr Zikos wanted to discuss his plans for the business,' she said awkwardly.

'Oh...*wow*!' Julie gushed, fixing wide, speculative eyes on Lilah's flushed and taut face. 'You mean he's planning to keep Moore Components open? He's not just going to sell up?'

Lilah cursed her loose tongue. 'No, his selling up is a possibility too,' she backtracked hastily, fearful of setting off a round of rumours that would raise false hopes. 'I don't think he's actually made a final decision yet.'

With a regretful sigh, Julie returned to work. But Lilah found that she could not concentrate for longer than thirty seconds. Aftershocks from her meeting with Bastien were still quaking through her.

He might as well have taken the moon down from the sky and offered it to her, she reflected in a daze. Her family were suffering—just like everybody else caught up in the crash of Moore Components. The little half-brother and half-sister so dear to Lilah's heart no longer had a garden to play in, and their more elaborate toys had been disposed of because there was no room for such things in Lilah's little house. Her father was suffering from depression and taking medication. The day the factory had closed the bottom had dropped out of his world. Without work, without his business, Robert Moore simply didn't know what to do with himself.

Lilah blinked back stinging tears. In spite of the troubled years, when her parents had been unhappily married, Lilah still loved her father very much. She had only been eleven years old when her mother had died very suddenly from an aneurysm. Her father had been very much there for her while she was grieving, but he was also a very hard worker, who had soon returned to work, slaving eighteen hours a day to build up his business.

Now, shorn of his once generous income and humbled, he felt less of a man—and at his age, with a failed business under his belt, who was likely to employ him? Although Lilah had told herself that she shouldn't be thinking about it, she could not resist picturing her father returning to work with a new spring in his step.

She blanked out the thought.

Was she really prepared to become a mistress?

Bastien's sex slave?

An extraordinary little chirrup of excitement twisted through Lilah and she was seriously embarrassed for herself. She was pretty sure Bastien wouldn't be expecting a virgin. But what did that matter? It was not as though she was seriously considering his sordid options, was it?

Still mentally far removed from work, she sank back two years again into her memories and recalled the flowers Bastien had sent her the morning after that family dinner and her rejection of what little he'd had to offer her. He had shown up on her doorstep the following evening as well, displaying a persistence that had taxed her patience. When he had tried to persuade her to join him that night for dinner she had lost her temper with him.

Why had she lost her temper?

Remembering why, Lilah paled and then flushed a painful pink. Utterly mesmerised by Bastien, she had already started falling for him. Being rudely confronted with the reality that he was a stud, who only wanted her for sex, had been hurtful and demeaning. *That* was why she had lost her temper. She had been angry with herself because somehow he had contrived to tempt her with that single erotically charged kiss and had made her question her own values. She had resented his power over her and she had flung her knowledge of his bad reputation in his teeth and called him a man whore.

Lilah was still secretly cringing from that memory as she walked home after work. Attacking Bastien had been wrong. He was what he was, and she was what she was. They were very different people. Insulting him had been ill-mannered, pointless and immature. His dark eyes had glittered like black ice, the rage in his stunning gaze filling her with fright. But he had done nothing, said nothing. He had simply turned on his heel and got back into his opulent limousine to drive away.

A few weeks later an unexpected gift had arrived for her at work. She had unwrapped an almost exact replica of the seahorse pendant Bastien had won at auction. The only difference between it and the original was that the new piece lacked the engraved initial As on the back. Only Bastien could have had it made for her and sent it to her. That he had given the pen-

dant to her in spite of the way she had spoken to him
had shocked Lilah, and made her feel as if she didn't
know Bastien Zikos at all. She had asked herself then
if she had imagined that dark fury in his eyes.

But now Lilah knew for a fact that she had not
imagined Bastien's rage, and she suspected that what
she was being subjected to was 'payback time' in his
parlance.

CHAPTER THREE

IN THE MIDDLE of the night, tossing and turning without sleep, Lilah crept out of bed and went downstairs to make herself a cup of tea.

Vickie was already there, seated at the kitchen table. 'Great minds, eh?' she framed round a huge yawn.

'You couldn't sleep either?' Lilah stated the obvious.

'It's the constant worrying that keeps me awake,' her father's wife opined ruefully while Lilah boiled the kettle. 'Some of the parents I was talking to at Ben's school said Bastien Zikos was at Moore Components today… I was surprised you hadn't mentioned it.'

Lilah stiffened defensively. 'I didn't see the point.'

'I hate asking you this…but I was thinking…maybe if you get the chance you could ask Bastien if he has an opening for your father anywhere?' Vickie said hopefully.

Lilah reddened. 'If I get the chance,' she echoed, feeling incredibly guilty for not telling the truth.

Bastien had been right on that score. No one would thank her for telling a truth that no one wanted to hear. And the truth was that she *could* wave a magic wand

and fix everything for everybody. How could she live with that knowledge and stand by doing nothing? How could she live with seeing her father slumped in a chair, staring into space? It was all very well to be furious with Bastien, to take offence and walk out. but at the end of the day she had to be practical. He had, after all, offered her a miracle.

Everything back the way it was.

Hanging on to her virginity at all costs seemed a little pathetic in such dire circumstances, didn't it? And, whether she liked it or not, she had always been attracted to Bastien. How could she hold out and justify herself when so many positive outcomes would result from her agreement? Bastien's interest in her would be short-lived as well: his past history spoke for him. He never stayed long with a woman. She would get her life back again quickly and probably never come back home, she acknowledged unhappily. When Bastien got bored with her she would look for a job in London and make a fresh start.

Lilah dressed for work with more care than usual, braiding her black mane of hair into submission and choosing a black pencil skirt and a silky cream blouse to wear.

The mere thought of finding herself in bed with Bastien brought her out in a cold sweat and turned her tummy over, so she refused to think about it. Sex was a rite of passage, she told herself impatiently. She was no different from any other woman and would soon become accustomed to it. No doubt practise had made Bastien most proficient in that department, and it was probably safe to assume that she wouldn't find sharing a bed with him too unpleasant. Of course she wasn't going to *enjoy* any of it either. Sex shorn of any finer feelings was a physical rather than mental exercise and she would detach herself from the whole experience, she told herself soothingly.

Detachment, after all, would hardly be a challenge when she hated Bastien with every fibre of her being. His options had taught her to hate him. Before yesterday he had simply been the womaniser who had once bruised her tender heart and whom she couldn't ever have. Now he was the ruthless lowlife forcing her to seal a bargain with her body as if she was a whore.

A little shudder racked her at that view and she breathed in slow and deep, strengthening herself for what lay ahead. She was about to make a devil's bargain, but she was darned if she would show an ounce of weakness in front of Bastien.

When she walked into the office, Julie gave her a curious appraisal. 'Mr Zikos has phoned down to ask for you already. I explained that you're never in before nine because you leave your kid brother at nursery on the way.'

'Thanks,' Lilah breathed, hanging up her coat with a nervous hand.

Bastien had said ten o'clock, but he was clearly jumping the gun. Of course he had no patience whatsoever, she reflected ruefully. He tapped his feet and drummed his fingers when forced to be inactive for any length of time. He was edgy, bursting with frenetic energy, always in need of occupation.

She smoothed her skirt down over her hips as she mounted the stairs. Her hands weren't quite steady and she studied them in dismay. Why was she getting

herself into a state? Hadn't she already decided that
sex would be no big deal and not worth making a silly
fuss over? It wasn't as though Bastien was going to
spread her across the office desk and have his wicked
way with her this very day...was it?

Her face burned, her stomach performing a somersault at that X-rated image. She wanted Bastien to
do the deed in pitch-darkness and complete silence.
She didn't want to have to look at him or speak to
him. She wished there was some way of having sex
remotely, without any need for physical contact, and
it was on that crazy thought that she entered what had
once been her father's office.

With a single gesture Bastien dismissed the team
hovering attentively round him and set down the tablet he had been studying.

'You've asked for me but it's not ten yet,' Lilah
pointed out thinly. 'It's only ten minutes past nine.'

Bastien straightened, brilliant dark golden eyes
lancing into hers in direct challenge. 'My internal
clock says it's ten,' he contradicted without hesitation.

'Your clock's wrong.'

'I'm *never* wrong, Delilah,' Bastien traded thickly,
his long-lashed gaze roaming over her as intently as
a physical caress. 'Lesson one on how to be a mistress: I keep you around to stroke my ego, not dent it.'

Lilah froze where she stood, wide sapphire eyes
travelling over him with a hunger she couldn't control. She scanned the exquisitely tailored designer suit
that delineated every muscular line of Bastien's broad-
shouldered, lean-hipped frame as he stood there facing
her, with his long, powerful legs braced. Something

clenched low in her body when she clashed with his gaze and her legs felt strangely hollow.

Her attention welded to his darkly handsome face, she stopped breathing, reacting with dismay to the treacherous stirrings of her own body. Her breasts swelled, constrained by the confines of her bra, while the sensation at her feminine core made her press her thighs together hard.

'I'm no good at stroking egos, Bastien,' she warned him.

Bastien dealt her an unholy grin. 'I've got enough ego to survive a few dents,' he asserted. 'Where do you think your true talents will lie?'

'You've taken my answer for granted, haven't you?' Lilah exclaimed. 'I haven't said yes yet, but you're convinced I will.'

'And am I wrong?' Bastien traded.

Her teeth gritted together. 'No, you're not.'

'So, are you going for option two or option three?' Bastien enquired lazily, leaning back against his desk in an attitude of relaxation that infuriated her.

Option three, option *three*, Bastien willed Delilah to tell him. That would be the most profitable option for him. He would sell the current site, relocate the factory to the outskirts of town and in doing so take advantage of several lucrative government grants aimed at persuading companies to open up in areas of high unemployment. For him it would be a win-win situation, because he would gain Lilah, an immediate profit to cover all outlay *and* a cost-efficient business.

'You have no shame, have you?' Lilah hissed, like oil bubbling on too high a heat.

'Not when it comes to you,' Bastien agreed. 'It's the only way I'm ever going to get you, because you're stubborn and contrary and you have a very closed little mind.'

'I am none of those things,' Lilah rebutted angrily.

'Stubborn because the minute we saw each other we were destined to be together but you immediately fought it. Contrary because you feel the same way about me as I do about you—instantaneous lust—but you deny it. And a closed mind because you believe a life of self-denial is innately superior to mine.' A wolfish smile slashed Bastien's lean strong face. 'I can't wait for the moment when you realise that you can't keep your hands off me.'

Lilah gave him a look of withering scorn. 'You'll get old waiting for that.'

Straightening up to his full commanding height, Bastien strolled forward, fluid as a predator tracking prey. 'Don't keep me in suspense. Option two? Or option three?'

'*Three*... Although I should warn you, you've picked the wrong woman.'

'Three...' Bastien's accent made a three-course meal of the word as he savoured it with immense satisfaction. 'In what way are you the wrong woman?'

Lilah shifted uneasily from one foot to the other. 'I haven't got the experience you'll probably expect,' she told him stiffly, deeply disturbed by his increasing closeness and fighting the revealing urge to step back out of reach.

'I've got enough experience for both of us,' Bastien purred, dark eyes flashing gold as he stared down at her. 'Are you trying to tell me that you haven't indulged that side of your nature very often?'

'Haven't indulged it at all,' she countered curtly, lifting her chin, standing her ground, refusing to feel embarrassed. 'I'm a virgin.'

Bastien actually backed away a couple of feet, his lean chiselled features setting into rigid angles of shock while his eyes flared more golden than ever below the thick canopy of his black lashes. 'Is that a tease?'

Lilah gave him a grim glance. 'No, it's not. I just thought I should warn you in case it's a deal-breaker.'

'Are you telling me the truth?' Bastien prompted in a roughened undertone, prowling closer again and circling her like a stalking panther. 'You're a *virgin*?'

Colour ran up below her pale cheeks but she held his fierce gaze. 'Yes.'

'If you're telling me the truth it's not a deal-breaker—it's the biggest turn-on I've ever had,' Bastien confessed, thoroughly shocking her with that assurance.

Bastien was disturbingly conscious that for once he was not uttering a mere soundbite for effect. He had never been with a virgin. When he was a teenager his partners had all been older, and when the age range of his lovers had begun to match his own maturity he had never dallied or even *wanted* to dally with a sexually innocent woman. For a start, he had never been attracted to young, immature girls. In addition he did very much like sex, and he had no time for those who would stick limits on a physical outlet he saw as both natural and free.

Yet something strange was happening to his views

while he looked at Delilah, because he was discovering that when those same limits were applied to her and her innocence he was happy with the idea…and even happier at the prospect of becoming her first lover. He didn't understand why he felt that way, because he had never been a possessive man, and nor had he ever been remotely unsure of his own skills in the bedroom and afraid of comparison.

A frown settled between his brows while he attempted to penetrate the mystery of his own gratification at her announcement—until the obvious answer came to him. What he found appealing had to be the sheer novelty of the experience she offered him…*of course* she would be something different, something new, something fresh!

'That's disgusting,' Lilah told him furiously. 'How can you admit something like that?'

Uncomfortably aroused by his thoughts, Bastien wanted to reach for her and demonstrate exactly how he felt, but he knew it wasn't the right moment. The nervous flicker of her bright blue eyes, her very restiveness, warned him that if he gave her sufficient ammunition she would take off in a panic like a hare bolting for its burrow.

'I will want you to sign a confidentiality agreement,' he told her levelly, sticking strictly to practicality. 'That's standard. It means that you will never be able to talk about our association in public or in private.'

Her nose wrinkled with distaste. 'I hardly think I would *want* to talk about it,' she said drily, fighting the nerves leaping in her stomach.

'In return I will purchase a suitable house for your father and his family.'

Lilah squared her slight shoulders. 'No, you will not. I don't want my family to be suspicious about my supposed job with you, and if you splash around too much cash they will definitely be suspicious. Give my father employment and he'll take care of his own family without any further help from *you*,' she told him with quiet pride.

'I'll want you to fly down to London with me tomorrow.'

Her eyes flew wide. *'Tomorrow?'*

'I'll call your father in to see me today and share the good news. I'll inform him that you're joining my personal staff. You can go home early to pack and you can dine with me at my hotel tonight.'

'I have a prior arrangement to meet friends.'

'To do what?' Bastien demanded impatiently.

'To eat out and see a movie.'

Bastien compressed his wide, sensual mouth. He wanted to tell her that in the near future she would do nothing without his permission. It was astonishing how much pleasure that belief gave him. But he didn't need to crack the whip right here and now, did he? She would be his soon enough and he would share her with no one—not friends, not family, no one.

Was that what could be described as a 'possessive' thought? His skin chilled at the suspicion. No, the thought was born of the reality that he had had to wait so long for Delilah that he wanted and indeed expected to receive one hundred per cent of her attention. He was not and never would be a possessive man, he assured himself with confidence. Even so, now that Delilah was officially set to become part of his life, in a way no other woman had ever been, he would ensure that she was protected by telling one of his security team to keep an eye on her from a discreet distance.

Lilah watched as Bastien unfurled his cell phone, stabbed out a number and spoke at length in Greek—short, staccato phrases that sounded very much like instructions.

'My driver will take you home now,' he informed her smoothly. 'And wait to collect your father and bring him back here to see me.'

Lilah hovered, because he made it all seem so bloodless and impersonal. Nothing she had said had changed his outlook about what he was doing. He neither regretted nor questioned his callous methods. He wanted her and he didn't care what he had to do to get her. The passion that had to power such an unapologetic desire for her body shook Lilah.

He closed a hand round hers and entrapped her without warning. 'Evidently I won't see you now until tomorrow, when we meet on my plane. It's probably just as well that you're seeing friends tonight. It takes the focus off us,' he pointed out with grudging appreciation. 'It will be more comfortable for all of us that way.'

'Certainly for you...if it keeps my father in the dark,' Lilah gibed.

'Do you honestly think I care about his opinion?' Bastien countered thickly. 'We're single adults. What we do in private is our business.'

Long dark fingers closed round her other hand, tugging her closer, fully entrapping her.

'Our business alone,' Bastien repeated thickly, lowering his arrogant dark head to hers and teasing along the tense line of her full lower lip with the blunt edge of his teeth, before soothing it with his tongue in a provocative caress that caught her unprepared and sent liquid heat to pool in her pelvis.

'We're at *work*, for goodness' sake!' Lilah protested in a rattled undertone.

'It's just a kiss,' Bastien husked, delving between her parted lips with his tongue and plunging deep with an unashamed hunger that roared through her like a bush fire.

Her knees locked and her legs swayed and she grabbed his forearms to steady herself, fingers clenching into the fabric of his suit jacket in consternation.

Just a kiss.

A little voice reminded her that in the near future she would have to give him a great deal more than a kiss. His mouth hardened on hers, hot and demanding, and a sensation like an electric shock tingled through her, awakening her body as nothing else had ever done. Her nipples pinched into tight buds of sensitivity; the secret flesh between her legs pulsed with sudden dampness. It was a wanting—a fierce wanting unlike anything she had ever felt before—and she was appalled by the response he was wringing from her treacherous body.

A lean hand clamped her spine to force her closer, and against her stomach she felt the hard swell of his erection even through the barrier of their clothing. A surge of burning heat that was very far from revulsion engulfed her and her face burned even hotter as he set her back from him with controlled force.

'I shouldn't start something I can't finish,' Bastien quipped.

Desperately flailing for something...*anything*...to distract her from the attack of self-loathing waiting to pounce on her, Lilah paused on her way to the door. 'Is it all right if I bring my dog with me tomorrow?'

'No pets. Leave the dog with your family.'

'I can't. My stepmother isn't comfortable with dogs. He's very small and quiet,' Lilah assured Bastien, lying through her teeth because Skippy wasn't remotely quiet once he got to know people.

Bastien frowned. 'Write down its details. I'll arrange for a specialist transport firm to handle the travel arrangements,' he pronounced after a considered pause. 'But once the animal arrives in France keep it away from me.'

'France?' she repeated in consternation.

'We're going to France the day after tomorrow.'

Lilah tottered back downstairs, shattered by the way she had succumbed to that single kiss. How could Bastien still have that effect on her? She hadn't been prepared for that. Perhaps naively she had assumed that her disgust at the unholy agreement he had offered her would protect her. But it hadn't.

Bastien had bought her acquiescence with a job for her father and the promised long-term prosperity of the reopened factory. Didn't he see how wrong that deal was? That reducing her body to the level of something to be traded like a product made her hate him? Didn't that matter to him?

But why should it matter to him? she questioned heavily as she informed Julie that she was leaving early. Bastien only wanted sex. He wasn't interested in what went on inside her head or how she felt about him. He didn't care... And neither should *she* care, she told herself defiantly. Being oversensitive in Bastien's radius was only going to get her hurt and humiliated. He wouldn't give her the kind of polite or gracious pretences that would allow her to save face. There would be no frills in the way of romance or compliments. He wasn't about to dress up their connection by making it about anything more than sex.

Later that same evening, in the wake of a whirlwind of embarrassingly untruthful explanations on the home front and a great deal of packing, Lilah emerged from the cinema with Josh—a tall, attractive man in his twenties, with brown hair and green eyes—and two other couples, Ann and Jack and Dana and George. There was nothing like a good fright or two to dispel tension, Lilah acknowledged wryly as she laughed at something Ann said about the horror movie they had watched.

'You're making a wise move on the career front,' Josh told her. 'Doing HR at Moore wasn't stretching you. Working for an international businessman will offer you much more experience.'

A shamefaced flush lit Lilah's face, because her friends had swallowed her lies about going to work for Bastien hook, line and sinker—just as her family had. 'I suppose so...'

'Very bad timing for me, though.' Without warning Josh reached for both her hands. 'You're leaving just when I was about to ask you out on a *real* date.'

'What?' Lilah's voice was shrill with surprise.

Josh grinned down at her, ignoring Jack's mocking wolf whistle. 'I mean, you must have wondered at least once what it would be like if we got together.'

Lilah grimaced, not knowing what to say to him. Because she never *had* wondered.

Josh edged her back against the wall behind her. 'Just one kiss,' he muttered.

Lilah stiffened, wondering why she felt like a stick of rock with 'Property of Bastien Zikos' stamped all the way through her. 'No, Josh,' she said, her hands braced against his chest.

But because she couldn't bring herself to actively push him away he kissed her, and she felt much as a shop window mannequin might have felt…absolutely nothing. Because while she liked Josh, and enjoyed his company, she had never fancied him.

'While you're away think about the possibility of *us*,' Josh urged, stretching an arm round her to guide her towards his parked car.

'I don't think so,' Lilah responded, wondering if there was a kind way of telling a man that you didn't fancy him in the slightest and knowing that there wasn't, and that the best response was probably for her just to pretend that absolutely nothing had happened.

'Awkward…' Ann mouthed, her eyes rolling with sympathy.

When Lilah walked back into her living room she was surprised by the expression of sincere happiness on her father's face. But she knew that even before she had reached home that afternoon Bastien had phoned her father, and the older man had already put on a suit by the time the car bringing his daughter home had arrived. When Lilah had gone out to meet her friends her father had still been out, presumably still with Bastien, which had worried Lilah.

'Everything all right, Dad?' she questioned anxiously.

'Better than that,' the older man assured her with vigour, and informed her that Bastien had hired him to act as manager at Moore Components—a role which he was very happy to take on.

'I'm beginning to understand how Bastien has become so very rich so fast,' the older man remarked in wry addition. 'He's very astute, and he spotted a break that would benefit Moore when no one else did.'

'What? *What* did he spot?' Lilah prompted with a frown.

'Bastien recognised that the council has recently rezoned the town's plans to open the door for further development. He's selling the current site for a *huge* amount of money and relocating the factory to the Moat Road, where he'll qualify for all sorts of lucrative government grants when he reopens for business. It's an incredibly smart move.'

'Good grief!' Lilah gasped, shock and temper bubbling up inside her at the belated awareness that Bastien had cut a very good deal with her in *every* way. Not only was he getting *her*, parcelled up like a gift, but he was also evidently on course to make a big profit too! And that realisation absolutely enraged Lilah.

CHAPTER FOUR

LILAH BOARDED BASTIEN'S private jet with her head held high. No, she wasn't about to show the shame she felt, and she wasn't anyone's victim—least of all Bastien's. This was *her* choice, she reminded herself doggedly. Bastien might have laid out those hateful options but *she* had made the choice, and she was still happy with what her sacrifice had achieved for her family.

Her father was managing the business he loved. For the moment he and Vickie would stay on in Lilah's little house, because it was affordable and within easy reach of Ben's school. Lilah thought her father and stepmother probably couldn't quite credit that life had changed for the better again. Having so recently lost everything, they were afraid of another disaster.

Lilah had had tears in her eyes when she'd parted from her little brother and sister that morning, for she had no idea when she would see them again. Did a mistress get time off from her role? Would she have any rights at all?

Bastien rested his arrogant dark head back to survey Delilah as she walked into the cabin. His mouth took on a sardonic curve when he saw her. She wore a drab, dated black trouser suit and had braided her hair again, concealing her every attraction to the best of her ability. But Bastien was hard to fool. She couldn't conceal the supple elegance of her delicate build or the healthy youthful glow of her fair skin and bright blue eyes, and when the jacket of her suit flapped back, revealing a sheer white shirt that hugged her small pouting breasts like a second skin, the fit of his trousers became uncomfortably tight.

Tonight, he thought impatiently, would finally rid him of the almost adolescent state of arousal she inflicted on him. A virgin, though... Was that really the truth? Didn't that deserve a certain amount of considerate staging?

Since when had he been considerate? Bastien asked himself irritably as Delilah attempted to walk past him towards the back of the cabin, where his staff were seated. His hand snapped out to close round her wrist and bring her to a halt.

'You sit with me,' he told her flatly.

Her full pink mouth tightened.

'Take off that ugly jacket. Let down your hair,' Bastien instructed.

Lilah froze. 'What will you do if I say no?'

'Rip off the jacket and yank out the hair tie for you,' Bastien traded without hesitation.

Warm colour flooded Lilah's cheeks and feathery lashes lowered over her eyes, because she was insanely conscious of his staff watching from the other end of the cabin. They were clearly wondering what she was doing on board and were now about to have their curiosity satisfied. She shrugged out of the jacket stiffly and reached up to tug at the tie anchoring her braid. Her hand was shaking as she loosened her hair.

Rage and mortification gusted through her as she dropped down into the seat beside Bastien, glossy black curls fanning in tousled disarray across her shoulders and brushing her flushed cheekbones.

'And just like that you look gorgeous again, *koukla mou*.'

'Is it going to be like this with everything? Your way or the highway?' Lilah pressed in a strangled hiss.

'What do *you* think?'

'That I once thought you were enough of a man not to need to control a woman's every move!'

His lean, darkly handsome features slashed into a sudden, entirely unexpected grin, his pride untouched by that crack. 'The trouble is...I *enjoy* controlling you.'

Lilah snatched in a much-needed gulp of oxygen. He sent her temper zooming from zero to sixty in the space of seconds. She had never considered herself quick-tempered until she met Bastien, but he literally set her teeth on edge almost every time he spoke.

'Why would you even want a woman who doesn't want you? Or is that what it takes to turn you on?'

That was a suggestion that deeply affronted Bastien, for the merest hint of aversion to him from a lover would have repulsed him.

He turned round to face her more directly, his dark eyes flaming gold as ingots, and closed a hand into the fall of her hair to hold her still. 'No, *you're* what it takes to turn me on...but, believe me, you can make very angry.'

'Is that a fact?' Lilah whispered tauntingly, tilting her chin, blue eyes gleaming.

In a searing movement of sensual intimidation Bastien crushed her soft mouth under his, driving her lips apart for the stabbing penetration of his tongue. She wasn't able to breathe, but then at that moment she didn't *want* to breathe. Her head was swimming, her body stinging with wild awareness, and a roaring hunger was awakening like a hurricane deep down inside her.

For a count of ten energising seconds Bastien thought about carrying her into the sleeping compartment and sating himself on her. But he would hurt her. He knew he was too hyped up for control. Besides, it was only a short flight to London and the jet would be landing soon.

He pulled back from her, positively aching from the throbbing force of his desire. 'You *do* want me,' he contradicted thickly, scanning her wildly flushed face and swollen, reddened mouth with satisfaction. 'You did from the first, *koukla mou.*'

Lilah whipped her attention away from him again and stared into space. *Well, you asked for that*, she told herself crossly, wondering why she always felt such a driving need to try to shoot Bastien down in flames. Unfortunately, in spite of all her efforts to ground him, he kept on soaring heavenward like a rocket.

Even so she was being confronted by a truth that she couldn't bear to examine. From the very first glimpse she had got of Bastien she *had* wanted him, and the hunger he had awakened in her was both primitive and terrifying. It truly hadn't mattered who he was or even what he was like, because her body had instantly seethed with a life of its own, wanting to connect with his, and her brain had swum with new and disturbing erotic images.

She hadn't known attraction could be that immediate or that powerful, and had certainly never suspected that it could overwhelm all restraint and common sense. Even worse, she was painfully aware that, had Bastien employed a more subtle approach and less honesty, he most probably would have succeeded in seducing her into his bed.

The cabin crew served drinks, the glamorous blonde stewardess syrupy sweet and persistent in her determination to serve and flirt with Bastien at the same time. He ignored her behaviour as if it wasn't happening, neither looking directly at the woman nor responding to her inviting chatter.

'Where are we going?' Lilah asked once the jet had landed.

'I'm taking you shopping, and tomorrow we head to Paris. I have a business meeting there.'

'Shopping?' she queried in surprise.

Bastien shrugged a broad shoulder and said nothing. Lilah caught the stewardess studying her with naked envy and thought, *If only you knew the truth.*

But what *was* the real truth? Lilah asked herself as the limo whisked her and Bastien through the crowded streets of London. She had given her word and Bastien had already delivered on his promises, which meant that he owned her body and soul for the foreseeable future. And that interpretation cast her as a complete victim, Lilah acknowledged ruefully—until she admitted the reality that one glance at Bastien's exquisitely chiselled features and tall athletic physique reduced her to a melted puddle of lust and longing. He was incredibly attractive—and, taking into account his reputation as a legendary womaniser, a very large number of women agreed with her.

They were met at the door of a world-famous store and conveyed upwards in a lift, surrounded by a posse of attendants composed of a stylist, a personal shopper and sales assistants. Clearly Bastien had already stated his preferences, and they were shown into a private room where he was ushered into a seat. Lilah hovered, watching the approach of a tray of champagne, and then she was steered into a changing room, where an astonishingly large selection of clothing awaited her.

Surely trying on loads of clothes for Bastien's benefit wasn't the *worst* thing that could have happened to her? But if making her model the clothes he wanted her to wear was a deliberate ploy to annoy her, he had played a blinder. The demeaning concept of swanning around in clothing personally picked by Bastien set her teeth on edge.

With a flush on her cheeks, she stepped back into the room clad in a blue silk dress that clung to her like cling film.

Bastien kicked back in his comfortable chair, very much in the mood to enjoy himself. His burnished gaze rested on Delilah and the oddest sense of contentment settled over him. Amusement tilted his handsome mouth when she teetered dangerously in the very high heels she clearly wasn't accustomed to walking in. The dress was rubbish: far too revealing. The only place Delilah would be encouraged to show that amount of flesh was in his bedroom and nowhere else.

He moved a dismissive hand and awaited the next

outfit, a pale pink jacket and skirt that was cute as hell against her cloud of blue-black hair and bright blue eyes. There might not be much of her, Bastien conceded, but what she lacked in curves she more than made up for in class, and with a delicacy that he considered incredibly feminine. The first time he had seen Delilah she had put him in mind of a flawless porcelain doll—until he'd noticed how expressive her face was: an ever-changing fascinating vista of what she was feeling and thinking. And what he liked most about her face was that he could read it as easily as a child's picture book.

'I'm not modelling underwear for you,' she warned him in a biting undertone.

Disconcerted, Bastien froze and lifted his arrogant, dark head to meet her bright eyes head-on, finally recognising the blaze of anger banked down there. 'Not a problem,' he assured her lazily. 'We'll save that show for the bedroom, *glikia mou.*'

Lilah's cheeks blazed with sudden livid colour. 'No, that's not me,' she parried abruptly. 'If that's what you want, you've picked the wrong girl!'

'You're perfect for me,' Bastien assured her levelly.

'Well, that's not a compliment I can return,' Lilah replied tartly. 'After all, it's obvious that we're a match made in hell. You want a dress-up doll that does exactly what's it's told and I won't do that.'

Bastien rose lithely to his feet and looked down at her from his commanding height with unreadable dark eyes. 'That's not what I want.'

'You want all the imperfections airbrushed away. You want obedience. Clearly you want a woman with submissive traits, and yet I don't have a submissive bone in my body! In fact, I'm more likely to *argue* with people who make unreasonable demands,' Lilah shot back at him in angry frustration. 'You're the king of unreasonable demands, Bastien. So, what are you doing with *me*?'

'You're misinterpreting everything I've ever said to you,' Bastien told her drily.

'Am I?' Lilah rolled her bright blue eyes, unimpressed by that accusation. 'You're such a control freak that you even want to choose the clothes I wear.'

'That's untrue,' Bastien incised. 'You're more like a jewel I want to see polished up and placed in the right setting. I don't want to see you wearing cheap clothes... I want to see you shine—'

'Bastien!' Lilah broke in helplessly, hopelessly confused by his attitude. He only wanted to have sex with her. He had been brutally honest about that reality. What did the clothes she wore have to do with a hunger that basic? Why on earth did he care what she wore?

She had paraded around for his benefit in one outfit after another. A vast wardrobe was being assembled for her use. She was stunned by that reality as well. For goodness' sake, was Bastien planning to keep her for the rest of her life—and his? How would she ever wear even a quarter of these clothes while she was with him? This was a male who was famed for barely lasting a month with one woman. Yet she had been equipped with countless wardrobe choices—indeed, everything a woman could conceivably want for every possible occasion and every season. Late afternoon had already stretched well into evening to encompass the shopping trip.

'We'll go back to the hotel now for dinner,' Bastien proposed, as if no dispute had taken place.

Lilah returned to the changing cubicle and selected a skirt and top from the rack to put on. She was being torn in two. On one level she wanted to fight Bastien, but on another she wanted to give him what he wanted to keep him happy. After all, how much was her own pride really worth when she could still clearly recall her father's renewed energy and hope?

What Bastien had given could easily be taken away again, she reflected fearfully. By giving her father a job, Bastien had revitalised the older man's drive and confidence. She should be grateful, she told herself urgently, but it was no use—she was too idealistic for such practicality. Unlike Bastien, she wanted sex to come packaged with romance and commitment.

Bastien took her back to an exclusive hotel and a very spacious suite. There were two bedrooms, and in the doorway of the first, Bastien paused to say, 'This is your room. I like my own space.'

Relieved by the news that she would not have to share a bedroom and surrender *all* privacy, Lilah watched as the hotel staff carted in the boxes and bags containing her brand-new wardrobe as well as a sizeable collection of designer luggage.

Bastien turned to grasp the phone extended to him by one of his personal assistants. Lean, strong face intent, he began talking urgently in French while raising an impatient hand to summon his team. As he spoke he strode to the desk in the large reception room, where a laptop had already been set up for his use.

His attention had drifted away from Lilah at supersonic speed. She watched his staff move into action, unfurling phones and tablets to follow Bastien's instructions. One name was mentioned repeatedly— Dufort Pharmaceuticals.

She kicked off her high heels and switched on the television in the far corner of the room. The fancy evening meal she had expected to eat in Bastien's company did not materialise. Instead, about an hour later waiters arrived with trolleys of buffet food to feed staff more interested in standing upright to eat than sitting down.

'Delilah!' Bastien called across the length of the room. 'Eat...you must be hungry by now.'

'Starving,' she admitted, padding over to him barefoot to grasp the plate he extended, daunted by the sheer size of him when she stood next to him without her shoes.

'A promising business deal has come up,' Bastien confided, studying her casually tousled hair and teeny-tiny bare toes, admiring the lack of vanity that allowed her to relax to that extent in his presence. She didn't care about impressing him, and he respected her innate sense of self-worth.

'I guessed that...' Lilah hid her amusement, delighted not to be the sole focus of his attention.

Ebony brows pleating, Bastien watched Delilah curl up on the sofa to return to the reality show she was watching. She was simply accepting that business came first for him without either taking offence or angling for a greater share of his attention. Yet, watching her relax back into the sofa and start eating with appetite, Bastien wondered if *he* should be the one taking offence—because it really wasn't a compliment that she should be so unconcerned by his preoccupation.

Becoming bored after an hour, Delilah switched off the television and crammed her feet back into the shoes she had kicked off to stand up. It was too early for bed and she was restless.

'Where are you going?' Bastien asked as she moved towards the door.

'For a walk. I need a break.'

Delilah was stepping into the lift when, to her surprise, one of Bastien's security team joined her.

'Is Bastien scared I'm going to run away?' she gasped in frustration, recognising the young man.

'I'm afraid you're stuck with me.' Her companion sighed. 'My instructions are not to let you out of my sight.'

'What's your name?' she asked.

'Ciro.'

'I'm Lilah,' she responded with a rueful smile, knowing that it wasn't fair to take her irritation out on Ciro, who was only guilty of doing his job.

A pianist was playing in the low-lit bar on the ground floor. Sitting down, Lilah ordered a drink. Ciro retreated to a table by the wall and left her in peace. Wishing she had thought to tuck a book into her bag, Lilah decided to catch up on her phone calls instead.

She rang her father first. Robert Moore talked non-stop to his daughter about Bastien's plans for the business and the advantages of the new location Bastien had picked for the firm. Lilah followed up that call with one to Vickie, learning that her dog, Skippy, had been picked up on schedule by a transport firm that morning.

She was replacing her phone in her bag when a

blonde woman sat down without warning in the seat opposite her. Lilah looked up in disconcertion.

'You're staying here with Bastien Zikos, aren't you?' the woman pressed with a smile.

Lilah's brows pleated. 'Why are you asking me that?'

'I'm Jenny Gower and I write for the women's page on the *Daily Pageant*,' the blonde told Lilah cheerfully, setting a business card down in front of her. 'That's my number. Feel free to call me any time you'd like a chat. Bastien's a real favourite with our readers and we like to keep up to date with his latest ladies.'

The woman was a reporter, Lilah realised in dismay. 'I've got nothing to say to you,' she said uncomfortably.

'Don't be shy. We pay generously for even little titbits.'

Without warning Ciro appeared at her elbow and intervened. 'Lilah…you're talking to a journalist.'

Lilah stiffened. 'We're not actually talking. I was just about to leave.'

And with that last word Lilah finished her drink and left the table.

'Mr Zikos loathes gossip columnists,' Ciro warned her with a grimace. 'I'll try to avoid mentioning the fact that you were approached.'

When Lilah returned to the suite Bastien was in the act of dismissing his staff for the night. 'I was planning to come down and join you,' he informed her.

Lilah flinched and coloured, focusing on Bastien with her heart in her mouth.

Annoyance flared in Bastien when he recognised the apprehension flashing in her gaze. Women didn't shrink from him; they *wanted* him. She must've been telling the truth about her inexperience, he concluded grimly. Only ignorance could explain such an attitude. It was surely past time that he showed her that she had nothing to fear from him.

'Would you like a drink?' he asked lazily, strolling closer.

'No, thanks,' she said jerkily.

Bastien crossed the room and scooped her right off her feet. Loosing a startled gasp, she wriggled like an electrified eel, strands of coconut-scented hair brushing his cheek as she moved her head back and forth.

'Relax,' he urged.

'Are you *kidding*?' Lilah exclaimed.

'You said you were a virgin. You didn't tell me that you were a hysterical one,' Bastien derided.

Lilah froze in his arms as though she had been slapped. She *was* overreacting, she acknowledged ruefully. Obviously Bastien was going to touch her, so his move shouldn't have sent her into panic mode.

'I'm *not* hysterical,' she protested, dry mouthed.

'You could've fooled me,' Bastien traded, settling down in an armchair with her slim body still firmly clasped to his broad chest.

'You startled me...you *pounced*,' Lilah condemned.

'And I'm not about to apologise for it,' Bastien husked, running down the back zip on her top and tugging it off her arms in one smooth movement.

'Oh...' Lilah gasped again, shocked to find herself stripped down to her bra without ceremony.

Bastien splayed a big hand across her narrow midriff to hold her in place while his mouth moved urgently across the pale skin at the nape of her neck.

Her heart hammered inside her tight chest and a tiny uncontrollable shiver racked her when his teeth grazed and nipped along the slope between her neck and her shoulder. It was a fiercely erotic assault, subsequently soothed by the skim of his tongue.

Her eyes flew wide, her pupils expanding as quiver after quiver of response gripped her. Suddenly even breathing became a challenge. Bastien closed his hands to her waist to lift her and turn her to face him, bringing her down again with her skirt hitched and her legs splayed either side of his hips.

His tongue plunged against hers in a deep, marauding kiss that made her tremble. Her bra felt too tight and the ache stirring in her pelvis was powerful enough to hurt. He kept on kissing her, forcing her lips apart with urgency and drawing her down on him so that she could feel the hard thrust of his erection between her spread thighs.

'Bastien… I—'

Dark golden eyes accentuated by a canopy of black velvet lashes held hers and silenced her. He truly had the most stunning eyes. Her mouth ran dry. Her mind was as blank as an unpainted canvas because she was reeling from the intensity of what he was making her feel.

She didn't even realise he had flicked loose her bra until he ran his hands up over her pert breasts to make actual skin-to-skin contact. Her usual alarm about her lack of size in the breast department had no time to develop, because his hands were already curving to the small pale mounds. With knowing fingers and thumbs he roughly tugged and chafed the pale pink sensitivity of her straining nipples. His touch sent hot tingles of longing arrowing through her limp body, heat and moisture gathering at the pulsing heart of her.

'You have such pretty breasts,' Bastien said thickly, bending her back over his supporting arm to capture a swollen stiff bud between his lips and torment it with attention. 'And so very sensitive, *koukla mou...*'

Her breath see-sawed back and forth in her throat while he rocked her over his lean, powerful body, ensuring that on every downward motion her tender core connected with the hard swell of his arousal. The tightening sensation in her womb increased to an unbearable level. Long fingers skated over the taut fabric stretched between her legs, where she was excruciatingly sensitive. He eased a finger below the lace edge of her panties. Excitement roared through her as he stroked and rubbed the tender bud of her clitoris. Rational thought vanished, because her body was greedily craving every new sensation, living from one intoxicating moment to the next.

As he rimmed the tiny wet entrance to her body with a teasing fingertip and at the same time let his carnal mouth latch hungrily on to an agonisingly tender nipple, Lilah's every nerve ending went into screaming overdrive.

'Come for me, Delilah,' Bastien told her rawly.

And then there was no holding back the explosion of excitement that had risen to a high Lilah could no longer suppress. Within seconds she was crying out, shuddering and convulsing with the wild surge of pleasure Bastien's expert hands had released. Exhausted and drained in the aftermath, she let her head drop down against his shoulder, barely able to credit that her body could react so powerfully that it still felt as though she was coming apart at the seams. He smelt of expensive cologne, testosterone and clean musky male, and at that moment—astonishingly—it was the most comforting scent she had ever experienced.

The strangest sense of protectiveness crept through Bastien while Delilah clung to him. He licked his fingers, her unique taste adding another layer to his fierce arousal. He wanted more—so much more that he knew he dared not let himself touch her again until he had cooled down. Unfortunately he had never been a patient man, and he knew his own faults.

He stood up, cradling her slight body in his arms, and carried her through to her room, where he settled her down on the bed.

'I'll see you in the morning.'

Conscious of the cool air hitting her bare breasts, Lilah crossed her arms across her body with a defensive jerk and looked up at Bastien in astonishment as he switched on the bedside lamp. That was it? He wasn't joining her in the bed to finish what he had started?

Hot colour surged in her cheeks as she collided with glittering dark golden eyes. 'But…'

'Tonight was for you, not for me,' Bastien told her wryly, striding back to the door and then coming to a halt to glance back at her with a blindingly charismatic smile that mesmerised her into staring. 'You know the weirdest thing…?'

His lean, darkly handsome features were pure fallen angel in the shadowy light. 'No…' she whispered, almost hypnotised by the flawless perfection of his sculpted features.

'What we just did…' he mused, with a self-mocking

curve to his beautiful mouth. 'That has to be the most innocent experience I've ever shared with a woman.'

As the door thudded shut on his exit Lilah's brows lifted almost as high as her hairline. *Innocent?* How could such shattering intimacy be in any way innocent? What on earth was he talking about?

Her body was still aching and quaking as though it had come through a battle zone. She slid off the bed and staggered dizzily into the en-suite bathroom, challenged to place even one foot accurately in front of the other. There she studied her tousled reflection in disgust. Her hair was messy, her mascara smeared and she was half-naked.

With a groan of shame she stripped off the skirt and panties and stepped into the shower. But even beneath the cleansing, cooling flow of water her body tingled and burned with new awareness in the places Bastien had touched.

Lilah shuddered—and *not* in disgust—at the thought of him doing it again. That acknowledgement alone was sufficient to keep her tossing and turning half the night.

CHAPTER FIVE

'COULD I HAVE a quiet word, sir?'

Manos, Bastien's head of security, approached him as he was still working, close to midnight. The older man seemed uncomfortable.

'It relates to Miss Moore…'

And within the space of minutes Bastien's even-tempered mood had been destroyed by the information Manos put in front of him.

Having initially assumed that Delilah was simply another employee, Manos had only belatedly realised that the news that she had been seen consorting with another man might be of interest to Bastien.

Bastien was shocked. And then furious with himself for *being* shocked. After all, how many times had a woman let him down? Lied to him? Ripped him off? Faked emotions to impress him? Too many times to count, Bastien conceded, tight mouthed with cynicism, his lean, starkly handsome bone structure rigid. But as far as he was aware not a single one of his lovers had ever *cheated* on him.

Forewarned is forearmed, Bastien told himself forbiddingly. And if Delilah had been with another man as recently as the night before, he no longer wanted her, did he? Damn Security for not following her home to establish exactly how the evening had concluded!

Frustration building at this incomplete picture of events, Bastien clenched his fists, plunged upright and decided to go out. The frustration was fast becoming rage, in a vicious tide that came with a bitter backwash.

A virgin? Of *course* Delilah was not a virgin! How likely had that claim ever been? Obviously she had made up that story in an effort to make him feel guilty while she played the poor little victim. And he didn't do victims any more than he did relationships, did he? Delilah Moore was toxic for him. Hadn't he suspected as much two years earlier? When had he ever wanted one particular woman that much? Any hunger that particular wasn't healthy.

Bastien headed for an exclusive nightclub to find another woman for the night. He had to prove to his own satisfaction that he was not remotely concerned by what he had learned about Delilah. She was not special in any way, he told himself furiously, downing his third drink in fast succession. She was like every other woman he had ever met: immediately... *easily*...replaceable.

In the club, Bastien was surrounded by beautiful women eager to attract his attention. He waited for one to give him a buzz, studying a blonde and deciding she was too voluptuous. A brunette who had eyes that were too close together. A redhead who laughed like a hyena. Another wore a hideous floral dress, and yet another had enormous feet.

Delilah's were the very first female feet Bastien had ever actually noticed, he acknowledged abstractedly. She had very small feet, with teeny-tiny toes and nails like polished pearls.

He settled into his fourth drink and wondered first of all why he was thinking about feet and then why he was still on his own. Why the hell was he suddenly being so fastidious? *Any* attractive woman would do. Hadn't he always believed that? He did not, *could* not, still want a woman who had cheated on him.

So what was he planning to do about Delilah?

Bastien registered that he wanted to confront her, and that strange urge deeply unsettled him. After all, he had always avoided high drama, and he had never, ever argued with the women who'd shared his bed. Why would he argue when women who annoyed him were instantly banished from his life, never to hear from him again?

He would send Delilah back up north, forget about her, cut his losses....

When the bedroom door opened abruptly Lilah was jolted awake. She sat up. Light was flooding the doorway to silhouette a powerful male figure. Instantly she knew it was Bastien, and instantly she was apprehensive.

The light was snapped on, momentarily blinding her, and Bastien strode in. His lean bronzed features were clenched ferociously hard, and his eyes, dark as eternal night, glittered above high lancing cheekbones. Her tummy performed a nervous dance and she backed up against the pillows with her knees defensively raised.

'I want a word with you.'

Bastien sent the door behind him thudding shut and her throat closed over convulsively.

A faint whiff of alcohol assailed her nose; he had been drinking. For the first time Lilah was appreciating that she knew very little about Bastien Zikos—basically only what she had read on the internet, none of which was reassuring. Did he drink a lot? Was he drunk now? Was he violent? Was such random temperamental behaviour the norm for him?

'Stop looking at me like that...' Bastien growled in frowning reproof, studying her from below the thick canopy of his black lashes.

Clutching the duvet to her with a nervous hand, Lilah breathed out. 'Like what?'

'As if you're scared!' Bastien grated accusingly. 'I have never hurt a woman in my life.'

A tentative half smile stole some of the tension from Lilah's triangular face. 'You just walked in... You startled me... I was fast asleep,' she explained, struggling to excuse herself rather than tell him the truth.

And the truth was that Bastien *was* scary. He was very tall, very muscular, much larger and stronger than she was in every way. Moreover, although he had the hauntingly beautiful face of a fallen angel, his dark eyes currently had a piercing, chilling light that utterly intimidated her.

'I want you to tell me where you were and who you were with last night,' Bastien bit out harshly, taking up a brooding stance at the very foot of the bed. 'Don't leave anything out.'

'I was out with a group of friends,' Lilah almost whispered, wondering why on earth he could be demanding such an explanation. 'We went for a meal and then to the cinema.'

'Do you normally kiss your male friends and then climb into a car to go home with them at the end of the night?' Bastien asked grimly.

Her eyes widened and flickered in dismay, colour warming her pale face. 'How do you know there was a kiss?'

Bastien was watching her face, recognising the embarrassment and the sudden flash of resentment there but seeing not a shred of guilt. 'I had one of my security team watching you last night. He lost track of you after you got into the guy's car.'

'Oh...' It was the only thing Lilah could initially think to say, because she was hugely disconcerted by the idea that someone Bastien employed had been following her round before she'd even left her home town. How dared he invade her privacy like that? 'You had no right to have anyone watching me.'

'From the moment I let you into my life I had that right. Did you spend the night with him?'

Battling to keep her temper over that far-reaching declaration of his rights over her, Lilah swallowed hard. 'No, I didn't. Josh dropped me straight home. There was one kiss, Bastien, nothing more.' She frowned at him, dismayed by the depth of his distrust. 'He's never kissed me before, and I wasn't expecting it. He was just trying it on.'

'You didn't try to stop him.'

'He's a friend and we had an audience.' Lilah grimaced. 'I didn't want to make a big scene of rejecting him in front of everyone. It would have made us all feel horribly uncomfortable.'

Bastien studied her, torn between belief and disbelief. His lean, strong features remained hard and set, his tawny eyes veiled by his lashes. The silence lay there, thick as a swamp between them.

'You were too generous. You're mine now,' Bastien told her in a raw, gritty undertone. 'I will not tolerate any other man touching you.'

'Bastien...I don't want anyone following me around, spying on me.'

'It goes with the territory. It's for my peace of mind and your protection.'

'I don't need protection.'

'That's my decision,' Bastien decreed, snapping off the light in a sudden movement that made her flinch.

'Bastien...?' Lilah whispered.

A powerful silhouette, he hovered. 'What?'

'Sometimes you really, really annoy me.'

'That cuts both ways.'

Bastien studied her slight figure in the bed and then strode into the room to flip back the duvet and scoop her up into his arms.

'What are you doing?' she gasped in consternation as he strode into the room next door to hers.

Bastien thrust back the sheet on his bed and settled her on the mattress. 'I want you where I can see you,' he told her curtly.

'You told me that I was getting my own room,' she reminded him breathlessly.

'For what remains of tonight, I've changed my mind.' Removing his jacket, he cast it on a chair, a lean, strong band of muscle flexing below his shirt. 'I'm going for a shower,' he extended, without any expression at all.

Lilah curled up in a ball on one side of the bed, too tired and wrung out to agonise or argue. So that was that? There was to be no further discussion?

Bastien had assumed that she had slept with Josh last night. Did he believe that she hadn't? Did she care whether he believed her or not?

He was so…so…*volatile*. She hadn't been prepared for that—had assumed that deep down inside he was cold as ice and detached. She had been wrong. In addition, only a few hours ago she would have been overcome with embarrassment at the prospect of facing Bastien again. At least she would've been until Bastien himself had dismissed what they had shared as 'innocent', which had certainly clarified matters as far as she was concerned.

Years of standing back and protecting herself while other people dabbled in sex had, she had decided ruefully, made her prudish and naive. As far as Bastien was concerned nothing worthy of note had yet happened between them. Why else would he have called an episode that had shocked her 'innocent'? And if *he* wasn't disturbed or embarrassed by it why should *she* be?

The arrival of a lavish breakfast tray awakened Lilah the next day. She glanced at the dent in the pillow next to her own and marvelled at the reality that she had fallen asleep with Bastien beside her and, in spite of his presence, slept like a log.

She was tucking into a chocolate croissant and covered in crumbs when Berdina, one of Bastien's personal assistants, arrived to tell her that Bastien was in a meeting and that after a brief appointment with

Bastien's lawyer she would be flying to Paris with Bastien in a couple of hours.

While wondering why she was to meet with a lawyer, Lilah packed her new wardrobe and picked out a stylish electric blue coat and fine dress to wear. These designer clothes were props, to support the role that she was being well paid to play, Lilah told herself firmly. Bastien was reopening Moore Components and re-employing the workforce—including her father. That was her payoff. That was why she was with Bastien in the first place.

She needed to remind herself of that reality on a regular basis. There was nothing complicated about their agreement. Bastien had made it all completely straightforward, hadn't he? He wanted her and he had worked out exactly what it would take to persuade her to surrender to his demands. He had proved that she had a price, and she doubted she would ever be able to forgive him for being right about that.

When she emerged from the bedroom the lawyer was waiting to present her with the confidentiality contract that she had agreed to sign.

The older man settled the slim document on the table and Lilah sat down to read it. He drew her attention to various clauses and handed her a pen. It was fairly standard stuff, and after adding her signature she passed the document back.

Porters had arrived to pick up her luggage, and she vacated the hotel in Berdina's company.

'We're lunching with François and Marielle Durand in Paris,' Bastien informed Lilah the instant she sat down opposite him on board his sleek, opulent jet. He wore a charcoal-grey suit, superbly tailored to his lean, powerful frame, and his white shirt framed his strong bronzed jaw.

'Who are they?' Lilah asked curiously.

'Marielle is an ex, now married to François. Including you in the arrangement will make it a more relaxed meeting,' Bastien opined with smooth assurance as coffee was served.

His admission that Marielle Durand was a former lover sent Lilah's interest hurtling into the stratosphere.

'This is for you...' Bastien tossed down a credit card on the table between them. 'While I'm taking care of business this morning you will go shopping, and I'll pick you up when it's time for lunch—'

Lilah studied the credit card with a sinking heart and pushed it away several inches. 'I don't want to spend your money,' she told him tightly.

'I didn't give you a choice. Spending my money goes with the territory and I expect you to do it,' Bastien decreed, flicking the card back towards her with the tip of a forceful finger.

Lilah reminded herself that she didn't have to buy anything and put the card in her clutch bag for the sake of peace. It had not escaped her notice that Bastien's staff watched her every move, visibly curious about her connection with their employer. That interest implied that, from the outside at least, her relationship with Bastien appeared unusual in some way.

She lifted her chin and collided unexpectedly with Bastien's smouldering dark golden eyes. Her temperature rose and her heartbeat thundered, the tip of her tongue sliding out to moisten the dryness of her full lower lip. She was helplessly recalling the expert stroke of Bastien's fingers over the most intimate part of her body and reddening to the roots of her hair.

'*Se thelo*… I want you…' Bastien breathed thickly.

Lilah couldn't have found her voice to save herself. Hot colour inflamed her pale complexion, her eyes widening she gazed back at him, taken aback by his candour.

A long, tanned forefinger skimmed down the back of her hand where it rested on the tabletop. 'I've never waited as long for any woman as I've waited for you. Of course I'm hot for you. Last night only whetted my appetite, *koukla mou*.'

As he touched her Lilah tore her gaze from his and yanked her hand back out of reach. 'You weren't *waiting*,' she told him with tart emphasis, before she could think better of it. 'Over the past two years you've been with one woman after another.'

A winged ebony brow climbed. 'Keeping count, were you?' Bastien quipped.

'Why would *I* care what you do?' Lilah traded, hot cheeked.

'I don't want you to *care* about me in any way,' Bastien countered without hesitation, his stunning dark eyes welded to her expressive face. 'This is sex, nothing more.'

Lilah lifted a delicate brow. 'What else could it be?'

Walking through the airport in Paris with Bastien, she was disconcerted to move beyond the barrier and suddenly find a phalanx of cameras aimed at them. Dismay gripped her, because the last thing she wanted was to be publically outed as Bastien Zikos's latest 'hottie'.

In an effort to lessen that risk she stepped away from Bastien and endeavoured to act more like an employee than a lover. The cameras continued to flash regardless. Questions were shouted, asking who she was in both French and English. They, like the photographers, were ignored.

Her colour fluctuating, Lilah climbed into the limo outside the airport accompanied by Berdina, who was to act as her guide on the shopping trip, and Ciro, who was with her for security. By that time Lilah was worrying that her family or her friends would see photos of her with Bastien in the papers and become suspicious that she was doing more than simply working for him.

But once the affair was over would that really matter? she asked herself ruefully.

The car whisked them to the Avenue Montaigne, where a whole range of designer shops were located.

While Berdina's attention was elsewhere Lilah looked up Marielle Durand on her phone. Photos of a slender exquisite blonde cascaded across the screen and Lilah swallowed hard. Marielle had been a famous model before her marriage.

Her thoughts abstracted, Lilah prowled through Louis Vuitton, Dior and Chanel and browsed, before obeying the letter of the law in Ralph Lauren and flourishing Bastien's credit card to buy Bastien a new tie. He couldn't complain now, could he? She had bought something.

Bastien joined her at noon. 'Where are your shopping bags?' he demanded.

Lilah extracted the small package from her clutch and handed it to him. 'For you.'

Bastien frowned at her. 'For...*me*?'

'You said I had to spend your money, so I did.'

Bastien unwrapped the gold silk tie and studied it in astonishment. 'You bought me a tie?'

'I won't need anything new to wear this century, after the amount of stuff you bought in London,' Lilah pointed out.

'That wasn't the point of the exercise,' Bastien traded harshly. 'The point is that, for once, I wanted you to do *exactly* as you were told.'

'Sorry, sir, I'll have to try harder,' Lilah quipped.

'Have you always found it this hard to follow instructions?'

'When *you're* issuing them...yes,' she admitted ruefully.

'You should *want* to please me,' Bastien told her as blue eyes bright as sapphires met his critical gaze.

With her dark hair framing her triangular face and her eyes sparkling above her neat little nose and her full rosy mouth, she looked amazingly fragile and feminine—as well as fizzingly alive.

'Why?'

'It puts me in a better mood.'

While Lilah tried to imagine Bastien's moods influencing her in any way, the limo nosed back into the traffic.

The Durands lived in an imposing eighteenth-century townhouse on Ile Saint-Louis. A maid ushered them into an airy salon, where introductions were performed and drinks were served.

Keenly aware of Marielle Durand's scrutiny, Lilah struggled to relax. Marielle was even more beautiful in the flesh than she had looked in her photographs, and Lilah was surprised to realise that the other woman was English.

Bastien surprised Lilah by closing his hand over hers to keep her close while he chatted to François. The conversation was solely in French, until Marielle addressed Lilah in English and asked her about her home town. Relieved not to be forced to stumble out any more stock phrases in her schoolgirl French, Lilah relaxed a little over the light lunch that was being served.

Over a glass of wine, the beautiful blonde invited Lilah to walk round the garden with her.

'How long have you been with Bastien?' Marielle asked with unconcealed curiosity, as soon as the men were out of earshot.

'Only a few days,' Lilah admitted wryly. 'Am I allowed to ask when you…?'

'Years and years ago—soon after I first made my name in the modelling world. He was probably my most exciting affair,' the other woman confided with an abstracted laugh. 'I adore my husband, but I've never felt anything like the excitement I once felt around Bastien. He's a heartbreaker, though, too damaged to ever trust his heart to one woman and settle down.'

'Damaged?' Lilah queried with a frown.

'Oh, I don't know any details, but I've always been certain he must come from a challenging background. No man's that hard to hold, and no man finds it that impossible to trust a woman without good reason,' Marielle opined. 'He was too complicated for me.'

And then Lilah made a discovery that disconcerted her: she *liked* complicated—actually *enjoyed*

the challenge of wondering what made Bastien tick.
He was like no other man she had ever met. Incal-
culably clever, impatient, volatile and unpredictable.
He was an unashamed workaholic, evidently unful-
filled by the huge achievements he had already made.
What had made him like that... *Who* had made him
like that? What drove him? And why did she care?

'You charmed the Durands very effectively,' Bastien
pronounced on their journey back to the airport. 'You
don't have a jealous bone in your body where I'm concerned, do you?'

'Why would I?' Lilah parried, quickly overcom-
ing her surprise at that unexpected stab. 'I can't think
you'd welcome a possessive woman.'

That was certainly true, Bastien acknowledged
grudgingly, and yet when he had glanced out through
the patio doors standing open to the sunlight to see
Delilah smiling and laughing, seemingly on the very
best of terms with Marielle, he had been surprisingly
riled by Delilah's complete indifference to his past
history with the beautiful blonde.

The faintest colour warmed Lilah's cheeks, because
although she had not been jealous or possessive she
had felt uncomfortable in Marielle's company—and
positively nauseous at the knowledge that Bastien had
been sexually intimate with her hostess.

'Where are we going now?' she asked, purely to
change the subject.

'I have a chateau in Provence...'

CHAPTER SIX

THEY LEFT THE airport in a rough terrain vehicle, with Bastien at the wheel and his security team following in another car.

The glorious Provençal light was beginning to fade, softening hard edges with shadow. They drove through rugged hills with deep gorges and fertile valleys. The hilltops were scattered with picturesque fortified villages with narrow meandering streets and sleepy shuttered houses. As the landscape grew increasingly spectacular the land became lusher. Ancient vineyards cloaked the sloping hills with ranks of bright green vines, while orchards of peaches, pears, nectarines and cherries flourished on stone terraces.

'Did you inherit the chateau from your family?' Lilah finally asked, unable to stifle her curiosity because Bastien had not offered a shred of further information.

'I'm not from a rich family,' Bastien told her drily. 'My mother was a waitress born in an Athens back street. My father is a small-time property developer who is, admittedly, married to a very wealthy woman. Regrettably, he was never married to *my* mother.'

'Oh…' Lilah responded after an awkward pause.

'When you mentioned your father giving your mother the sea horse pendant, and you thinking that you and your parents were the perfect family, you gave me a very different impression of your background.'

'What I meant was that back then I was still young enough to be ignorant of exactly what their relationship entailed.'

'And what *did* it entail?'

'My father, Anatole, is married to another woman. My mother was his mistress. She once admitted to me that she deliberately chose to become pregnant with me because she believed my father would divorce his wife for her if she gave him a child,' Bastien volunteered in the driest of tones. 'Unhappily for her, her scheme failed—because my father's wife had already conceived my half-brother, Leo, who is only a few months older than I am. My mother was extremely bitter about *that* development.'

'And she *told* you that?' Lilah pressed in consternation.

His beautifully shaped mouth quirked. 'Athene wasn't the maternal type, and she never did overcome her resentment at having the responsibility and expense of a child she no longer had any use for.'

Lilah compressed her full lips, the skin around her mouth bloodless from the force of will it took for her to remain silent in the face of what he was telling her. She was shocked, but she didn't want to admit it, sensing that Bastien would ridicule her revulsion at his mother's callous candour. But no child should know he was unwanted, she thought painfully. No child should have to live with the demeaning knowledge that he had only been conceived to be used as a piece of emotional blackmail in his mother's battle to win a wedding ring from his father.

'No comment? I felt sure you would have several moralising remarks to make.'

'Then you were wrong. I know that all children don't grow up in a picturebook-perfect world,' Lilah breathed tautly. 'Otherwise my father would have loved my mother and stayed faithful to her...'

'He *wasn't*?' Bastien shot her a disconcerted look from frowning dark eyes. 'You're very close to your father. I naturally assumed...'

'My parents weren't happily married. There were always other women in my father's life, and constant upsetting scenes in my home. He didn't love my mother. They'd been together since they were teenagers, though, and everyone expected him to marry her—so eventually he did,' she proffered ruefully. 'It was a long time before I understood that succumbing to that social pressure had made him feel trapped in their marriage. He's a different man with my stepmother.'

'Did your father's infidelity contribute to your judgemental view of me as a "shameless man whore"?' Bastien shot at her, throwing her completely off balance.

Lilah flushed to the roots of her hair at having her own insult flung back at her two years after the event and when she'd least expected it. 'Of course not... However, you *are* a womaniser, Bastien.'

'But *not* a man whore. I have never been unfaithful to a lover,' Bastien asserted levelly. 'I have never taken indiscriminate sexual partners either. While my values may not be the same as yours, I *do* have standards.'

Mortification had claimed Lilah and it was eating her alive. She closed her hands together tightly on her lap. 'I lost my temper that night. I shouldn't have made such personal and disparaging comments to someone I barely knew,' she conceded, hoping that her admission would close the subject.

'Is that an apology?'

Lilah breathed in so deep that her narrow chest swelled.

'I mean,' Bastien mused, and his deep, dark, Greek-accented drawl was as rich as molasses, 'I did only ask you to dine with me and spend the night. I didn't assault you or abuse you.'

Lilah lost her battle with her temper and flung her hands up in a violent demonstration of exasperation. 'All right...all *right*... I'm sorry with bells on! Are you satisfied now?'

Bastien stole an amused glance at the glittering brightness of her eyes above her pink cheeks. 'What would a virgin know about a man whore's lifestyle anyway?' he derided.

Staring rigidly out through the windscreen as the vehicle turned between tall stone pillars to drive down a lane lined on both sides with very tall stately trees, Lilah rolled her eyes. 'Maybe I read a lot of raunchy books...'

Amused against his will, Bastien bit out a rough-edged laugh. She was in the wrong and she knew it—but she still wouldn't back down the way other women did with him. He enjoyed her stubborn streak and the challenge of making her toe the line.

Lights came on as Bastien parked and killed the engine. 'Welcome to the Chateau Sainte-Monique.'

Wall lamps in the form of iron lanterns illuminated the old building, accentuating the warm honey-coloured stone of the façade and the very Provençal violet-blue shutters at the many windows. Gravel interspersed with formal beds of flowers and trees ornamented the frontage.

Lilah climbed out of the car and accompanied Bastien to the entrance. 'So, when did you buy this place?'

'About three years ago. The owner was an elderly countess, whom I met during the course of a land development deal. The first time I saw the chateau I made her an offer, but it was months before she finally agreed to sell. The renovation took another year. I come here when I want to relax and when I can work from home. I stayed here all last month,' Bastien admitted smoothly.

A middle-aged man in a crisply ironed white shirt and bow tie opened the door and greeted them with a smile.

'Stefan and his wife, Marie, take care of everything here,' Bastien informed Lilah after making an introduction, and a lean hand resting at the base of her spine guided her indoors.

The interior was breathtaking. The hall had a chequerboard black-and-white marble floor and surprisingly modern furniture. A huge stone staircase curved up from the ground floor.

Their luggage was being brought in behind them, and Bastien was heading for the stairs, when Stefan opened a door and a familiar little bark of eagerness froze Lilah in place. Stefan grinned as a brown, silky little bundle of flying flapping ears and wriggling body flew at Lilah with a noisy burst of excited barking.

'Yes...yes, I missed you too,' Lilah admitted, crouching down to scoop up the miniature dachshund. She separated him from one of the beloved squeaky toys he liked to carry around in his mouth and attempted to calm him before she put him down again.

As the dog snatched up the toy again and hurtled across to Bastien, Lilah warned him. 'Just ignore Skippy. He'll get the message and leave you in peace...that's what Vickie always did with him. She prefers cats.'

Skippy nudged the toe of Bastien's shoe with his nose, his beady little eyes pleading. Bastien sidestepped the animal to stride on up the stairs, and Lilah watched in dismay as Skippy hurtled in his wake. Stefan moved forward to intercept the little dog, seemingly aware that his employer was not animal-friendly.

Lilah followed Bastien upstairs into a spectacular atmospheric bedroom furnished with a mixture of antique and contemporary pieces. Oyster-coloured silk festooned the windows and tumbled down in opulent swathes from the wrought-iron crown holder above the big bed.

'This is an amazing place,' Lilah whispered, impressed beyond words by the splendour of her surroundings.

'The maids will unpack for you. I'll see you downstairs for dinner in an hour,' Bastien imparted as a man brought in her luggage and two young women in uniform arrived to move the cases into the dressing room visible through an open door.

Lilah hovered uncertainly.

'Dress up…' Bastien lowered his handsome dark head to murmur huskily in her ear. 'Dress up for dinner so that I can enjoy *undressing* you later, *glikia mou.*'

Banners of self-conscious colour brightened Lilah's porcelain-pale complexion as she turned her head to stare up at him. She collided with brilliant dark eyes that glittered like stars in the low light—stunning eyes, ringed by spiky lashes of velvet black. She was mesmerised. He curved long flexible fingers to the side of her face and brought his mouth crashing down on hers.

That kiss was a taste of heaven and a taste of hell in one package. It was heaven because she couldn't get enough of that hot, hungry mouth on hers and hell because she hated the response she couldn't suppress. He released her, staring down at her for a split second in silence, and then swung on his heel and walked out.

Lilah drifted into the marble bathroom, her fingers creeping up to brush her tingling swollen lips, shame and guilt rising like a dark, choking cloud inside her. It would be cruel if he made her *like* having sex with him, she thought wildly. Or would it? Surely that could only be foolish pride talking?

Her rational brain scolded her for the melodrama Bastien could somehow infuse into her very thoughts. Common sense told her that simply accepting that their intimacy was inevitable would make the experience much more manageable for her. After all, she wasn't a masochist, was she?

Sex was supposed to be enjoyable, she reminded herself. But from listening to friends talk about their experiences she knew it often wasn't that great. Once she had done the deed with Bastien she would probably wonder what all the fuss was about, she reflected wryly, because, after all, sex had to be the most ordinary pursuit in the world.

Stripping, she went for a shower, retrieved her cosmetics to do her face and finally returned to the bedroom wrapped in towels. In the dressing room she flicked through the formal wear now hung for her perusal. *Dress up*, Bastien had urged. Humour sparkling in her eyes, she pulled a ballgown from the rail and fanned it out on the bed. It was over the top and theatrical, rather like the chateau, and when she had modelled it she had noticed Bastien's dark golden eyes blaze like banked-down fires.

Bastien stood in the hall, watching Delilah descend the stairs with the glossy grace and dignity of a queen. The dress was amazing—a glistening sheath in peach that hugged her slender body to just below the waist before it flared out into thousands of layers of net that swept the stone steps. Her black hair tumbled in a mane down her back, strands rippling round her triangular face to highlight her bright blue eyes. The tightening swelling at his groin was so instant he didn't even question his reaction.

He stretched out a lean-fingered brown hand to greet Lilah as she reached the foot of the stairs, his arrogant dark head thrown back, smouldering dark golden eyes locking to the full pink pout of her lush mouth. He closed his fingers round hers.

'In that dress you take my breath away,' he told her. Her mouth ran dry as she met his gaze and her small breasts swelled below the skin-tight bodice as she gulped in oxygen. She hadn't expected that blunt compliment, didn't know how to deal with it.

He walked her through an airy salon, with an ancient stone carved fireplace and sleek blue sofas, out on to a tiled terrace where a candlelit table awaited them.

'I'm really hungry,' Lilah confessed as a manservant moved forward to pull out a chair and lingered to whisk a napkin across her lap.

'You should enjoy the meal. Stefan's wife, Marie, is my cook, and she was a chef in a Michelin-starred restaurant in Paris before they came to work for me,' Bastien remarked while the wine was poured.

'You have a huge staff here...you live like a king,' Lilah commented helplessly as soon as they were alone.

'I do when I have the time to enjoy the chateau—which is rarely,' Bastien qualified drily. 'When I'm travelling on business I eat out or cook for myself.'

'You can *cook*?' Lilah said in surprise.

'Of course I can. I'm not spoilt. I've never been spoilt. But I do appreciate the best things in life.'

'Is your mother still alive?' she asked abruptly as the first course was served.

Bastien studied her in silence, black brows drawing together in a frown. 'You're very curious about my life.'

Lilah shrugged her lightly clad shoulder. 'Why wouldn't I be?'

Bastien set down his glass. 'My mother died in a car accident when I was a child and I had to go and live with my father.'

Lilah toyed with the artfully presented courgette flowers topping the tiny onion tart on her plate. 'And how was that?'

'Hideous,' Bastien admitted grimly. 'Anatole's wife, Cleta, hated me on sight. I was the living proof of her husband's infidelity. As for my half-brother... Leo was an adored only child and suddenly I turned up. Naturally he resented me. But there were some advantages to my new home,' he conceded, his dark eyes veiled with mystery, his beautiful mouth compressing.

'Such as...?' The sliver of onion tart Lilah had selected was melting in her mouth.

Bastien frowned at her continuing interest. 'It was a fresh start for me in many ways. I was able to see Anatole regularly and I went to a much better school.'

'Obviously you're close to your father,' Lilah commented, relieved to hear that hint of indulgent warmth in his dark drawl when he referred to his parent, because really it was brutally obvious to her that Bastien had been cursed by the most utterly miserable childhood.

'Yes. I'm very fond of Anatole. He may have been a push-over for the wrong women, but as a father, when I needed him, he was the very best,' Bastien stated with quiet pride.

Relief filled Lilah that there had been someone loving in Bastien's life, and she wondered why the idea of nobody having cared for him as a child should disturb her so much. His answers to her questions, however, had given her a certain insight into what had made him so tough and unyielding.

'But that's enough about my life, *glikia mou*,' Bastien continued, smooth as glass. 'Tell me about Josh Burrowes.'

Thrown off balance in her turn, Lilah stiffened, her spine straightening. 'There's nothing to tell. We were on the same course at uni. He's one of my friends.'

Bastien lounged back in his seat as their plates were cleared and the main course served. 'But obviously Josh wants to be something more. You should've told him the truth.'

Lilah's delicate bone structure tightened. 'I gave my friends the same story you suggested I use with my family. I said you'd offered me a job.'

Bastien rested his shimmering dark gaze on the voluptuous promise of her pink lips as she savoured the tender lamb on her plate. 'But you should have come clean for Josh's benefit and told him that you are *mine*.'

Her small white teeth gritted as if she had trodden barefoot on a stone. 'I am *not* yours, Bastien.'

'You *are*,' Bastien purred in immediate contradiction, his accented drawl vibrating through her slender taut frame. 'I know it every time I look at you. No hunger this powerful is one-sided.'

Lilah concentrated on her meal, deeming silence the most diplomatic response. She was very, *very* attracted to him, she admitted inwardly, but no way did she owe him that amount of truth.

As she studied him a snaking curl of warmth stirred low in her pelvis and something tightened even deeper inside her, making her shift uneasily in her seat. The hard, masculine lines of his compellingly beautiful face and the suppressed ferocity of his stunningly intense eyes welded her attention to him.

The first time she had seen Bastien she had known

that she had never seen a more beautiful male specimen, and in the two years that had since passed that
fact remained the absolute truth. Bastien was gorgeous. She knew it and he had to know it too.

Perspiration beaded her short upper lip, and as a
member of staff stepped up to the table to refresh their
wine glasses she finally dragged her attention from
Bastien and breathed in deep.

'Stefan's wife is a fantastic chef,' she remarked,
after savouring the first mouthful of a roasted pear
dessert served with chocolate sauce and then pushing the plate away in defeat. 'But I can't find room
for another bite...'

'Coffee?' Bastien prompted.

'No, thanks...' Lilah tensed as he rose fluidly out of
his seat and strolled, jungle-cat-graceful, towards her.

'I react like a teenager around you,' Bastien murmured thickly. 'I can't wait one minute longer.'

Lilah pushed her hands down on the table-edge and
levered herself upright, the layers of her dress spilling out round her in peach abundance. *Time to pay
the piper*, she thought crazily.

Bastien didn't immediately touch her. Instead he
lowered his dark head and circled her mouth almost
teasingly with his own, touching delicate nerve-
endings that screamed with awareness to send pulses
of heat shooting down through her. Her head swam a
little...her knees wobbled.

With a guttural sound low in his throat, Bastien
swept her up in his arms.

'I was so angry with you last night when I heard
about you kissing Josh,' he told her unexpectedly as
he carried her up the stone staircase, contriving that

feat as easily as if she weighed no more than a child. 'Don't let another man touch you in any way while you're with me.'

Her senses still drowning from that extraordinarily intoxicating kiss, Lilah looked up at him with dazed blue eyes and blinked. 'Not much risk of that.'

'Why not? You're a beauty. I saw it... *Josh* saw it,' he grated in harsh reminder.

'But you see things in me that I don't,' she muttered uncomfortably, thinking of the conventionally beautiful fashion models he generally took to his bed.

In comparison, *she* was an aberration. Each and every one of her predecessors that she had seen had been tall, blonde and classically lovely, with Marielle the perfect example of that ideal. Lilah, however, was small and kind of skinny. She had certainly been way too skinny and small in the bust and hip department for any of the boys to look at while she was at school, at an age where having curves had seemed so very important.

'I know that I want you,' Bastien spelt out. 'Everything else fades in the face of that.'

'Everything?' Lilah questioned in disbelief.

'Everything...' Bastien husked, breathing in the coconut scent of her shampoo, the faint aroma of the cosmetics she had applied, the fragrance that was uniquely and alluringly hers. And those eyes, he savoured, those sapphire-blue eyes that shone like jewels...

He settled her down on the bed in her room, and the hunger driving him spooked him more than just a little as he looked down at her. That hunger would fade as soon as he'd had her, he told himself cynically, and in all likelihood even the sex would be a disappointment. How could it be otherwise when she had no experience? She couldn't possibly be a truly sensual woman, his rational mind assured him. No truly sensual woman could have stayed untouched as long as she had. She might light up when he looked at her, move in his arms as though she were a sensually aware woman, but it was unlikely that she would have much to offer.

He plucked off her shoes, resisting a decidedly warped urge to stroke those tiny feet of hers. Her virginity was unsettling him, Bastien decided, desperate to suppress the strange thoughts and reactions assailing him. But if she was telling him the truth—and he had to believe it *was* the truth—she would be more his than any other woman had ever been. And for some peculiar reason he liked that idea, he acknowledged in bewilderment. He *really* liked that idea.

'What are you thinking about?' Lilah whispered awkwardly as he ran down the zip on her dress.

'Sex. What else?'

'So I asked a stupid question…deal with it,' Lilah cut back without skipping a beat.

Above her head, an unholy grin slashed Bastien's firmly modelled mouth. He eased the dress off a slight white shoulder and rolled the sleeves down her slim arms, completely attuned to the rising tempo of her breathing.

'I'm not going to harm you,' Bastien breathed with husky assurance. 'Not in any way.'

'I've heard it can hurt,' Lilah told him stubbornly.

'You make the prospect of having sex with me

sound like some form of medieval torture,' Bastien growled.

'I'm going to shut up now. Zipping my mouth,' Lilah spelt out jerkily.

Bastien tugged off the dress and tossed it in a careless heap on the carpet.

'I saw the price tag on that dress, Bastien. You can't treat it like that…it's indecent!'

Bastien flung back his handsome dark head and laughed out loud. 'I thought you were zipping it? Keep quiet…you're making me nervous.'

'What have *you* got to be nervous about?' Lilah demanded in wonderment.

She was finding it a huge challenge not to simply dive below the sheets. There she was, with her body on display, skinny as a rail, clad only in little pale pink lacy pieces of lingerie, and she was being forced to pose like some pantomime seductress on a silk-clad bed. Goosebumps rose on her exposed skin.

Bastien slid a hand into his pocket and withdrew a jewel box. 'This is for you.'

Lilah sat up and took the opportunity to hug her knees, covering up her all-too-bare body as best she could. 'I don't want gifts, Bastien.'

'You will wear it to please me, *koukla mou*. The first time I saw you I wanted to see you in diamonds.' Bastien flipped open the lid on an exquisite shimmering diamond pendant on a chain. He removed it from the box and clasped it round her slender neck.

Taken aback, Lilah didn't move a muscle as he put the pendant on her, feeling the diamond settle cold and heavy against her chilled skin. Bastien stepped back from the bed to remove his jacket and unbutton his shirt, but the whole time his attention was fixed to her.

Lilah met dark golden eyes, tawny as a lion's, and her skin blazed as though he had set her on fire, all sense of being cool in temperature and cold with nerves instantly evaporating. Beneath his bronzed skin he flexed washboard abs and well-developed pectoral muscles, which made her stare for a second or two. He was what a friend had once described as 'built'—powerfully masculine in every way.

She glanced away as his long, tanned fingers reached for the waistband of his trousers, cursing her shyness, her awful self-consciousness with her own body, never mind his. He tossed some foil packets down by the bed, and the nape of her neck prickled.

He came down on the bed still in his boxers, and with the flick of a finger unfastened her wispy bra and pulled it away. She felt her nipples bead, tightening into pointed peaks, and then all of a sudden, or so it seemed to her in her heightened state of nerves, he was laying her down against the pillows and touching those agonisingly sensitive buds with his mouth and his fingers.

A little shudder racked her, and then another. Sensation was breaking through her defences as her breasts tingled and swelled, responding to his attention.

'At least put out the light!' she exclaimed.

'You're beautiful. I need to look at you.'

'I don't want you looking,' she gritted between clenched teeth.

'Close your eyes and pretend I'm not,' Bastien suggested.

Sniping back at him became an impossibility while he was tracing a trail down her slender body with his mouth—kissing here, licking there, discovering the areas of her midriff that responded to his blatant teasing with wild enthusiasm and then slowly shifting down to more intimate areas. His fingers tugged at the waist of her knickers and she stopped breathing. She felt his breath on her...*there*...where it shouldn't be. He found the most achingly sensitive place of all with his clever fingers, and her hips jerked and her breath hitched and she closed her eyes, blocking out the bedroom while becoming even more insanely aware of Bastien's every move.

'You're really practised at this, aren't you?' Lilah commented gruffly.

'We're not about to pursue that subject.'

'No... *Oh!*' A strangled exclamation broke involuntarily from her lips as he stroked his tongue across the little nub of nerve-endings at the apex of her thighs.

With a strangled groan, Bastien came up over her again and crushed her parted lips under his, his tongue plunging only once, but deep, into the moist interior of her mouth, somehow igniting a ball of heat in her pelvis. Startled blue eyes flew wide and clashed with gold circled by lush black lashes.

'Oh...' Bastien said for her, with a wolfish grin that made her tummy flip in a somersault.

Feeling like a child who had foolishly stuck her hand in the fire, Lilah closed her eyes again circumspectly. He punished her by returning to his former activity, his fingertips grazing the inside of her slender thighs, where she had never been touched, and every single point of contact tingled and fired hot, like a burn. He used his mouth on her clitoris and it felt unbearably good, with sensation firing through her on all cylinders as the little tickles and prickles of uncontrollable pleasure mounted and she could no longer stay still. Her neck extended and her hips shifted and rose.

Bastien was touching her so gently. She had not imagined that he could be gentle in bed—had, in truth, been braced for passion, aggression and impatience. He slid a finger into her tight sheath and then another...tender, subtle, tormentingly pleasurable. Her blood was pounding in her veins, her heart was racing, and her whole body was damp with perspiration because everything she was feeling had swiftly become so shockingly intense.

She gave up on the losing battle to resist and opened her mouth on a gasp of reaction. Indeed, she was all reaction now, as waves of response coursed through her in an unstoppable tide. Every tiny caress and exploration he executed engulfed her in another wash of sensation. A tight feeling nestled at the heart of her and she shifted impatiently up towards Bastien, fighting the hollow sense of tortured frustration he had awakened without even fully grasping what it was.

'Bastien!' she exclaimed.

Burnished golden eyes assailed hers. 'Tell me you want me.'

'You know I do!' she flared, with a bitterness she couldn't hide.

'You always did, didn't you?' Bastien grated.

'What do you want? A trophy?' Lilah gasped.

'You *are* my trophy,' Bastien told her, his skilled fingertips moving with expert precision at her tender core and setting off a chain reaction inside her.

The mushroom of heat penned inside Lilah suddenly surged up, with a force that blindsided her and overflowed. Out of her control, her body bucked and twisted and convulsed as the paroxysms of a powerful climax rippled through her slender frame.

Bastien ripped open a foil packet with his strong white teeth. He didn't want to hurt her, he didn't want to harm her in any way, but now she was as wet and receptive as she would ever be. He dragged a pillow under her to tip her hips up more and settled between her spread thighs.

The pleasure Bastien had meted out was like a powerful drug that took time to wear off. Lilah was still in a daze when she felt the pressure of Bastien's entry stretching her tender flesh. Apprehension made her stiffen, a heartbeat before the sharp sting of his full possession made her catch her breath on a huff of dismay. He withdrew, hooked her legs higher and thrust into her yielding body again. This time there was no pain—only the amazing sensation of his fullness inside her.

'It's not hurting,' she told him in relief.

A sheen of perspiration dampened Bastien's lean, handsome features—for such care, such temperate precision, had not come without cost. '*Se thelo*…you feel unbelievable, *hara mou*.'

He rolled his hips in a wicked snaking motion that sent extraordinary sensation flooding through Lilah's pelvis, and her eyes went wide with surprise. As he began to move, the first jolt of excitement careened through her without warning, and then the heat and pressure at the heart of her began to build again. It was a little like hitching a ride on a comet, she thought dizzily, with new responses released and overwhelming her.

Hunger sank talon claws of need into her very bones. Her heart slammed against her ribcage. Her body thrummed and pulsed with rippling darts of pleasure that only stoked her rising hunger. And then the intensity climbed to an unbearable height and pushed her over into the intoxicating grip of wave after wave of sweet, drowning pleasure.

It was over…it was done, Lilah reflected in a daze, crazily conscious of the crash of Bastien's heart against hers, the brush of his hair against her cheek, the dampness of his big, powerful body against hers, the sheer weight of him and the incredible intimacy of their position. Well, she had no complaints, she conceded thoughtfully. In fact, he had made the experience amazing.

In the process of rebooting, after the longest, hottest climax in his considerable experience, Bastien breathed again. He rolled off her and caught her back into his arms, pressing a kiss to her brow without even thinking about it…

And then the thinking kicked in hard. What the hell was he doing? What the hell was he playing at? He didn't *do* touchy-feely—never had and never would. True, she had just given him a pleasure he was finding hard to match in his memory, and he already knew he wanted her again. But it was in the way an alcoholic knew he wanted a drink.

The comparison jarred, but it worked its magic, and Bastien pulled away from the strangely tempting pleasure of having her small, slender body lying against his. He sprang out of bed and headed for the bathroom.

'I'm a restive sleeper and I prefer my own space,' he told her carelessly. 'I'll be sleeping in the room next door.'

Lilah could feel herself freeze with regret and discomfiture. Yet such separation was what sex without caring was like, she scolded herself. It was a bodily thing—not a mental thing. Bastien didn't feel any deep connection with her. He had satisfied his lust for the moment and that was that: he had leapt out of bed and straight into the shower. She could already hear it running.

Had she expected a warmer conclusion to their intimacy?

Well, if she had expected that she was an idiot. After all, wasn't this exactly why she had lost her temper with Bastien two years back? He had only offered sex when she had wanted more, and that had hurt—hurt her pride, hurt her heart too. Wasn't it time she was honest about that? She had started falling for Bastien Zikos the first moment she'd laid eyes on his fallen angel face and stunning eyes.

Of course she hadn't known him in any way, so it had been infatuation rather than love, but his magnetic attraction had called to her on every level. And resisting it, recognising that he could only make her unhappy, had cut deep and filled her with disappointment. But it was the truth and it remained the truth, Lilah conceded ruefully. Bastien skated along happily on the shallow side of life, taking pleasure where he chose, discarding women whenever he got bored... and now she was one of those passing fancies—a sexual whim.

She shifted in the bed, and the ache between her

thighs made her wince and grimace. Once she had said no to Bastien, and evidently that had put a price beyond rubies on her head because he wasn't used to the word *no* and evidently couldn't live with it.

Stop thinking these negative thoughts—stop it, she screamed inside her head, shifting on the pillow as if to clear it. It would be better to concentrate on the positive—think of the factory up and running again, her father back in his office and her little half-siblings secure because their parents were no longer worried sick about how to pay their bills. That was a *good* picture, she told herself soothingly.

And what about all Moore's former employees? Her father had mentioned that he'd be calling a meeting on site today, to discuss the relocation of the factory and the planned reopening. That news would make a lot of people very happy.

Indeed, only a very sad, total loser would sit feeling sorry for herself when she was surrounded by so many positive reminders of what sacrificing her pride had achieved. And she *wasn't* a loser, she told herself angrily, and she *wasn't* going to make a big dramatic deal out of what couldn't be changed. So she had had sex with Bastien—that was all it had been and she could live with that reality.

Sliding out of bed, she walked naked into the dressing room and extracted a robe, knotting the sash at her waist with impatient hands.

As she walked back towards the bathroom, Bastien emerged from it, lean bronzed hips swathed in a towel. Crystalline drops of water sprinkled his hair-roughened chest and his thick black hair curled back damply from his brow.

Seeing her out of bed, he frowned. 'I thought you'd be sleeping.'

'No. I need to shower.' To wash his touch and the memory of it away, Lilah thought frantically, colliding with smouldering golden eyes framed by velvet dark lashes and feeling her heart skipping an entire beat. A shadow of faint black stubble accentuated his hard masculine jawline and his beautifully modelled sensual mouth.

As Delilah attempted to sidestep him, Bastien shot out a hand to enclose her wrist and force her to a halt again. 'You were amazing, *glikia mou*,' he husked.

Mortification drummed up hot below Lilah's skin, but she lifted her tousled head high. 'It wasn't as bad as I thought it would be,' she admitted prosaically, tugging her wrist free to continue on past into the bathroom.

Taken aback, Bastien blinked. How to damn with faint praise, he reflected grimly, thrusting open the communicating door between the bedrooms to stride into his own. And how very typical of Delilah to sting him like a wasp.

Well, what else had Bastien expected from her? Lilah asked herself as she washed. Compliments?

She had told him the truth, even though she knew that she hadn't been strictly fair. He could have been more selfish and less careful with her in bed. To give credit where it was due, he *had* made an effort not to hurt her. Unfortunately his consideration in that respect could not eradicate the ugly fact that Bastien Zikos had blackmailed her into his bed. Yes, she had made the choice to accept his unscrupulous deal, but he could not expect her to start treating him like a much-appreciated and personally chosen lover, could he?

Lilah fell into an exhausted sleep, but Bastien was awakened by a phone call at an ungodly early hour of the following morning and given the kind of news that wrecked both his day and his mood.

CHAPTER SEVEN

'DELILAH!' BASTIEN GRATED from the doorway. 'Get up—I need to talk to you...'

Wondering what she had done to deserve such a rude awakening, Lilah opened her eyes only wide enough to peer at the pretty miniature alarm clock adorning the bedside cabinet. It was barely seven in the morning.

Blinking rapidly, in an effort to get her brain functioning again, she swallowed back a yawn and struggled to focus on Bastien's tall, powerful figure by the door that appeared to communicate between her room and his. 'What's wrong?' she asked sleepily.

'We'll discuss it when you get up,' Bastien framed darkly, glittering dark eyes settling on her with chilling distaste. 'I'll see you downstairs in five minutes.'

Exasperated, Lilah rolled her eyes. In mega-bossy mode, Bastien infuriated her—and she refused to be ordered round like an unruly schoolgirl. On the other hand, something bad had clearly happened, and he evidently thought she was involved in it in some way—because why else would he have looked at her as if she had just crawled out from under a stone? Even so...he expected her downstairs within *five minutes*? In his dreams!

Scrambling out of bed, she went into the dressing room and searched through innumerable drawers to find her own humble clothing, from which she selected denim shorts and a simple white tank top to deal with the early-morning heat she could feel in the air. Following a quick shower and the application of a little light make-up, Lilah stalked downstairs in flat canvas shoes, ready for whatever Bastien might choose to throw at her.

With a noisy scrabbling of his claws on the hallway tiles, Skippy hurled himself at Lilah's knees. Stefan informed her that Bastien was waiting for her in his study and directed her down a corridor. Breakfast, he added helpfully, would be served out on the terrace.

Bastien was lodged by the window of a large, imposing book-lined room with his broad back turned towards her. Muscles flexed beneath the taut, expensive fabric of his jacket. He swung round, and she was irritated that she immediately noted that his dark designer suit acted as a superb tailored frame for his wide shoulders, narrow hips and long, powerful thighs.

Hard, dark golden eyes zeroed in on her, and involuntarily, Lilah paled at the intensity of that tough, questioning scrutiny.

Mouth curling, Bastien scanned her appearance in the worn shorts and casual top, neither of which had featured in her officially sanctioned new wardrobe. The adolescent outfit combined with her long, tumbled hair and only a touch of make-up made her look very much like a teenager. Admittedly, though, an incredibly pretty teenager.

Pretty...an old-fashioned word which didn't belong in his vocabulary, Bastien reflected in exasperation at his lack of concentration. *Hot* would be a more appropriate word, and from the top of her curly dark head down to her pert breasts, tiny waist and slim sexy legs and the very soles of her tiny canvas-shod feet, Delilah looked amazingly hot.

He tensed, reluctant to embrace that thought, but his body was already doing that for him, reacting with libidinous enthusiasm to her presence.

'What's this all about?' she asked in apparent innocence.

In answer, Bastien crossed the room and lifted his tablet from the desk top. *'This!'* he bit out wrathfully.

Lilah moved closer to stare at the British newspaper headline depicted on the screen.

Dufort Pharmaceuticals to join Zikos stable?

'I still don't know what you're talking about,' Lilah pointed out, although she had the vaguest recollection that she *had* heard that company's name mentioned during Bastien's deliberations with his staff that first evening in the hotel in London. Unfortunately, since she had not really been listening, she had not the foggiest idea why Bastien was so annoyed.

'Someone leaked confidential information to the press that night in London...and I believe it was *you*!' Bastien breathed with raw emphasis.

Lilah's spine snapped straight as an arrow, her blue eyes rounding with disbelief as she tipped her head back to look him in the eye. *'Me?'* she spluttered incredulously. 'Are you nuts?'

His cool, sculpted mouth hardened. 'You're the only person who left the suite during my discussions with the team that evening. According to my sources, someone tipped off the press halfway through that evening. The bodyguard accompanying you saw you making several phone calls. You also had contact with a journalist.'

Her soft mouth had fallen open in shock, because she could barely credit what she was hearing. How dared he accuse her of being some sort of business spy when he had shared a bed with her the night before? How *dared* he?

Her colour rose even higher when she recalled that he had actually slept apart from her, and she replied curtly, 'I can't believe you're serious. Why would you suspect me of stealing confidential information? Why would anyone want to leak it?'

'The tip that I'm planning to buy Dufort Pharmaceuticals is worth hundreds of thousands of pounds on the open market.'

'But I didn't leak it. I didn't discuss it with anyone,' Lilah remonstrated. 'Why would I have? Apart from anything else, I'm not interested in that information and I wasn't really listening to what you and your staff were talking about... I was watching TV.'

'You were present throughout. You heard *everything*,' Bastien reminded her obdurately.

'At least four members of your staff were present as well! Why are you picking on *me*?' Lilah demanded in a furious counter-attack.

'I have absolute faith in my personal team.'

'I'm delighted to hear it, but obviously your faith is misplaced in at least *one* of them,' Lilah pointed out thinly. 'Because I can assure you that *I* didn't sell any information about your business dealings to anyone.'

'I don't trust you,' Bastien admitted harshly, because he had looked at the evidence from every angle and the conclusion that Delilah had sold the information made the most sense.

Lilah set the tablet back down on the table. 'Well, I'm not playing the fall guy, here, so you have a problem. I suggest you stop wasting time suspecting me of doing the dirty on you and search out the real mole. Why would you suspect me anyway? I've got too much to lose in this situation.'

'How?' Bastien gritted, unimpressed, and particularly outraged because he had wakened to the phone call forewarning him of the press release with a powerful craving to enjoy her small slender body again.

'You gave my father a job, which means a lot to him. I wouldn't do anything to jeopardise his continuing employment,' Lilah argued vehemently. 'I'm not an idiot, Bastien. If I betrayed your trust you wouldn't stick to our agreement.'

His hard mouth set into a grim, clenched line, Bastien said nothing. He could not count on her loyalty. She was a woman, not an employee, and she might well want to punish him for the choice he had offered her. That gave her a good motive, and she had certainly had the opportunity that night to pass on news of his acquisition plans for Dufort Pharmaceuticals.

Worst of all, the damage was done now that the facts were out in the public domain. Either he paid through the nose to acquire a company which was no longer the bargain it had been or he decided to back off altogether.

'You have cost me a great deal of money,' Bastien told her harshly.

'You don't *listen*. You haven't listened to a single word I've said in my own defence, have you?' Lilah accused, her eyes flaring an almost other-worldly blue with suppressed rage. 'But I'll say it one more time… *not guilty*. I didn't gossip about your business plans or pass them on to anyone who could profit from knowing about them. I made two separate phone calls after leaving the hotel suite—one to my father and the other to my stepmother. On neither call did I mention your business discussions. The journalist who approached me was a gossip columnist, *not* a financial reporter…' Her voice trailed off as she studied his lean, darkly handsome face, which was shuttered and forbidding. 'You're *still* not listening to me…'

Seething resentment was flaming up through the temper which Lilah was struggling to keep under control. Her hands closed into punitive fists. Even before she had answered his charges she had clearly been judged and found guilty, which was hideously unfair.

'Tell me, do you distrust *all* women or just me?' she slammed.

'Women are very clever at establishing a man's weaknesses and playing on them,' Bastien countered.

'And your only weakness is protecting your profit margins?' Lilah folded her arms defensively and breathed in slow and deep. 'What you really need, Bastien, is a proper challenge.'

The lush black lashes enhancing his gorgeous eyes

lifted, to reveal glittering dark gold chips full of stark enquiry. 'Meaning…?'

'All bets are off between us until you find out who *did* betray your trust and you clear my name.'

'*Diavelos*…what are you trying to say?' Bastien demanded curtly.

'No sex until you sort this out,' Lilah told him in the baldest possible terms. 'I refuse to sleep with a man who thinks I'm some sort of thief and fraudster.'

Dark colour accentuated the exotic line of Bastien's supermodel cheekbones. 'That is *not* what our agreement entails and nor is it an accurate version of what I said to you.'

'Stuff the agreement!' Lilah flung back at him wildly. 'You can't make the kind of accusation you just made and then act like it shouldn't make a difference to me. You check out every employee who was there that night, and anyone else who knew about your interest in that company, you find out who sold you down the river…and then you *apologise* to me.'

Bastien sent her an incredulous glance, dark eyes flashing the purest gold, pride and anger etching taut hard lines into his lean, darkly handsome features. 'Apologise?'

'Yes, you *will* apologise—even if it *kills* you!' Lilah launched at him full volume, all control of her temper abandoned in the face of such wanton provocation. 'You have deeply insulted me, and I refuse to accept that kind of treatment. And, by the way, you can keep this…' Digging the diamond pendant out of her pocket, Lilah set it down on the table. 'I didn't ask for it, I don't appreciate it, and I will not wear it again unless you apologise to me!'

'Are you finished?' Bastien demanded wrathfully. 'I don't *do* apologies.'

'Fortunately it's never too late to learn good manners!' Lilah stated without hesitation, before turning on her heel with Skippy following close behind like a shadow.

She walked out to the shaded terrace for the breakfast Stefan had promised her.

She was trembling when she collapsed down limply into a seat by the table, but she didn't regret a word she had said to Bastien. She had to be tough to deal with him or he would roar over her like a fireball and burn her to ashes in his wake. Bastien had questioned her integrity, and Lilah was proud of her integrity. She was no angel, but she didn't lie, cheat or defraud, or go behind people's backs to score or make a profit, she thought angrily.

It shook her that he could misjudge her to such an extent even after they had become lovers. And that she should even *have* that thought warned her that she was still being very naïve about the nature of their relationship. Their bodies had connected—*not* their minds. Bastien did not know her in the way she had always assumed her first lover would know her. But did that excuse him for assuming on the flimsiest of evidence that she would sneakily sell confidential information about his business plans?

She was already convinced that Bastien did not hold a very high opinion of women—at least not those who shared his bed. She shuddered as she remembered the cold, heavy feel of that brilliant glittering diamond at her throat the night before. Did he believe that expensive gifts of diamonds would excuse bad behaviour? Had other women taught him that?

Nibbling little bites of a chocolate croissant and sipping fresh tea, Lilah tried to be realistic about Bastien. He was incredibly good-looking and incredibly rich…and incredibly good in bed, she affixed, hot-cheeked. For many women his wealth alone would be sufficient to excuse almost all character flaws. Not that it would bother Bastien that *she* was unwilling to overlook those flaws, Lilah reflected ruefully, because Bastien was only interested in sex.

And every time she came back to that salient fact it was like crashing into a solid brick wall, which concluded all further speculation.

Having eaten, she asked Stefan for a bottle of water and went off to explore, with Skippy bouncing in excitement round her feet. She could not contemplate sitting around in the chateau submissively, as if she was waiting for Bastien to vindicate her or justify her very existence.

The gardens surrounding the chateau were typically French and formal, lined with precise low box hedges and sculpted topiary set off with immaculate paths, weathered urns and gravel. She balanced like a dancer to walk the edge of an old stone fountain, sending shimmering water drops down into the basin below.

From above, Bastien watched her from a window in the huge first-floor salon. Delilah was larking about like a leggy child, while repeatedly throwing that damned stupid squeaky toy for her even sillier yappy little dog. Delilah outraged his sense of order—

because he did not like the unexpected, and in every
way she kept on tossing him the unexpected.

He was willing to admit that she was not behaving like a guilty woman. At the same time he knew
women who could act the most legendary Hollywood
stars off the screen. His own mother had always put
on an impressively deceptive show for his father, who
had adored Athene to the bitter end.

But while Anatole had been easily fooled Bastien
had always had a low opinion of human beings in general, and he preferred hard truths to polite lies and social pretences. He had also learned that the richer he
became, the more people tried to take advantage of
him, and he was always on the watch for false flattery and sexual or financial inducements.

In fact, when anyone injured Bastien he hit back
twice as hard to punish them and teach them respect.
He was not weak. He was not foolish. He was not forgiving. That had been his mantra growing up, when
he had had to prove to his own satisfaction that he was
stronger than the feeble but kindly father he loved. No
woman would ever make a fool out of Bastien Zikos
as his mother had made a fool out of his father.

His mother, Athene, had ridiculed his father, calling him 'Mr Sorry', because every time Anatole had
visited his mistress and his son he had invariably been
grovelling and apologising for something, in a futile
effort to keep the peace in the double life of infidelity
he led. That was why Bastien was unaccustomed to
making apologies of any kind. To his way of thinking,
apologies stank to high heaven—of weakness, deceit
and cowardly placation.

But at that precise moment Bastien was shocked

to acknowledge that he had not thought through the likely consequences of choosing to confront Delilah immediately about the newspaper leak. Shouldn't he have kept his suspicions to himself until he had established definitive proof? Why the hell had he lost his temper with her like that? Loss of temper meant loss of focus and control, and invariably delivered a poor result. That was why he never allowed himself to lose his temper. Yet on two separate occasions now he had gone off like a rocket with Delilah. Naturally she was playing the innocent and offended card— what else could she do?

'I'll check out every member of your team,' declared Manos, his chief of security, in receipt of his employer's instructions. 'I'm aware that Miss Moore had the opportunity, but somehow she doesn't seem the type.'

'*Is* there a type?' Bastien asked drily, his attention locked to the sway of Delilah's shapely derrière in those tight, faded shorts and the slender perfection of her thighs below the ragged hems.

His fingertips tingled at the idea of trailing those shorts off her slender body and settling her under him again. He cut off that incendiary image and hoped she wasn't planning to leave the grounds dressed in so provocative an outfit.

His strong white teeth gritted. His continuing sexual hunger for Delilah had made her important to Bastien in a way he utterly despised. If she realised how much he was still lusting after her she would use it against him—of course she would. He much preferred the immediate boredom that usually settled in for him after a fresh sexual conquest. He needed to move on, he told himself urgently. He needed to move on from Delilah Moore in particular...*fast*.

The morning flew past while he worked, furiously trying to counteract the damage done by this morning's news report. He went downstairs for lunch and discovered that he had the terrace all to himself, Delilah having opted to have a simple snack in her room. His teeth gritted again and he studied Skippy, lying in a panting heap in the shadows. She had evidently roved far enough around the estate to totally exhaust the dog, which admittedly had pitifully short, stumpy legs.

After a moment's contemplation of the miniature dachshund's lolling pink tongue, Bastien emptied some fruit out of a bowl and poured water into it before putting it down for the animal. Skippy lurched up and drank in noisy gulps. After trotting back indoors, he reappeared with his squeaky toy in his mouth and laid it tenderly at Bastien's feet...where it was ignored.

Full of restive energy, Lilah paced her room. Was she supposed to be a prisoner at the chateau? She refused to sit around and wait as if she had no existence without Bastién to direct her every move.

Recalling the pretty little village of Lourmarin, which they had passed through shortly before their arrival, she decided that what she really needed was an afternoon of sightseeing. Having washed the dust off her canvas-shod feet, she pulled on a white sun dress and sandals before heading downstairs to find Stefan and ask if it was possible for her to visit the village.

Within minutes a car drew up outside to collect

her, and she skipped down the steps, smiling at Ciro as he slid in beside the driver.

Bastien was disconcerted when he discovered that Delilah had left the chateau. He hadn't expected that. Frustration at the childish avoidance tactics she was using on him coursed through him, and he had Manos check with her driver. He set out for Lourmarin in a short temper.

What *was* it about Delilah? She was a lot of trouble, demanding so much more effort and attention from him than other women did. *Why* was he allowing her to wind him up? And why did he still want her, regardless of how much she annoyed him?

It was market day in Lourmarin, and Bastien's disposition was not improved by a lengthy search for a parking spot.

When he tracked Delilah down he heard her laughter first, and even that contrived to annoy him— because two years had passed since *he* had last heard her laugh. In addition, although he hated gigglers, there had always been something incredibly infectious about Delilah's giggles. He saw her seated on a café terrace, her white dress spilling round her, black hair framing her animated face as she laughed and chattered to Ciro, at one point even touching the younger man's arm with a familiarity that set Bastien's teeth on edge.

Ciro, not surprisingly, wore a slack-jawed expression of masculine admiration.

'Delilah...'

The sound of that deep, dark drawl banished the pleasure of Lilah's sun-drenched surroundings and stiffened her spine as much as if a poker had been attached to it. She lifted her head and fell into the smouldering golden sensuality of Bastien's intent scrutiny. His dark-fallen-angel face was grim, but nothing could detract from the sheer beauty of it, nor the mesmeric potency of his gaze.

'Been looking for me?' she quipped, setting down her glass of wine. 'I doubt that your presence here is an unlucky coincidence.'

In answer, Bastien reached down to close a hand over hers and used that connection to literally lift her upright out of her chair. 'Thanks for looking after her for me, Ciro. We're heading home now.'

'You're making me feel like I shouldn't have gone out,' she whispered thinly as he walked her away.

'No, what you shouldn't have done is flirt with Ciro,' Bastien told her drily.

'I wasn't *flirting* with him!' Lilah snapped back in irate protest, practically running to keep up with his long stride as, with one strong hand gripping hers, he cut through the clumps of pedestrians and dragged her in his wake. It didn't help that almost two glasses of wine had left her head swimming a little...

'He should know better than to get that close to a woman who's mine,' Bastien added grittily, hanging on to his temper by a hair's breadth and ready to grab her up into his arms and bodily carry her back to the car at the first sign of rebellion.

'I'm *not* yours!' Lilah fired back at him with ringing vehemence. 'I simply agreed to sleep with you until you got bored...that's all!'

As that startling statement rang out, Bastien watched curious heads swivel in their direction and compressed his sensual mouth. 'You're shouting.

Would you like a megaphone to share that confession further afield?' he demanded in a tone of incredulous reproof.

'I wasn't shouting,' Lilah hissed with a furious little shrug of her slight shoulders, her bright blue eyes remaining defiant. 'I was merely pointing out the basic terms of our agreement. It was a devil's bargain but I've stuck to *my* side of it. The least I deserve from you in return is respect and consideration.'

'When do *I* qualify for some respect?' Bastien enquired with honeyed scorn.

'When you do something *worthy* of respect,' Lilah slammed back without hesitation.

Unlocking the Ferrari, Bastien scooped Delilah up and stowed her in the passenger seat, impervious to her vocal complaints. He wanted to shout at her. For the first time since his childhood, anger and frustration had reached a peak inside him and he actually wanted to shout. Evidently Delilah really was toxic for him, challenging his self-discipline and making him react in unnervingly abnormal ways.

'And why are you dragging me back to the chateau anyway?' Lilah queried truculently as he swung in bedside her. 'You should be avoiding me like the plague right now.'

In slow motion, Bastien twined his fingers slowly into her long black hair to turn her face up while his other hand framed a delicate cheekbone to hold her steady. The crash of his mouth down on hers felt as inevitable to him as the drowning heat of the summer sun in the sky.

Lilah jerked, as if he had stamped her with a burning brand. Her hand rose of its own volition and delved

into his luxuriant black hair, fingertips roaming blissfully over his well-shaped skull. Hunger coursed
through her like a hot river of lava, scorching and
setting her alight wherever it touched.

She had never felt hunger like it. In fact, it was as
if Bastien's lovemaking the night before had released
some dam of response inside her that could no longer be suppressed. The resulting ache between her
legs and the sheer longing to be intimately touched
physically hurt.

Long fingers eased below the hem of her dress and
roamed boldly higher.

In a sudden movement Lilah pulled back and
slapped her hand down on top of Bastien's to prevent
him from conducting a more intimate exploration.
'No,' she told him shakily.

Bastien swore long and low in Greek, the pulsing
at his groin downright painful. He wanted to yank her
out of the car, splay her across the bonnet and sink into
her hard and fast. He gritted his teeth, rammed home
his seat belt and drove out onto the narrow twisting
road that snaked down the mountain.

The screaming tension inside the car made Lilah's
mouth run dry. It was his own fault. He should never
have touched her, she thought piously, pride making
her ignore the hollow dissatisfaction of her own body.
But then *every* time Bastien touched her he shocked
her, she conceded grudgingly, because somehow he
always made her desperate to rip his clothes off.

Mortified, she dragged her attention from him and
stared out of the car, mouth swollen and tingling.

Manos was waiting for Bastien when he returned.
Delilah took the opportunity to race upstairs.

Bastien did not want an audience as he learned that preliminary enquiries had revealed damning facts about one of his personal staff. Andreas Theodakis had taken a smoke break that evening in London, and had been seen using his phone out on the balcony. Furthermore, a colleague had volunteered the news that Theodakis was a gambler. Bastien knew then in his gut that in all likelihood Andreas had tipped off the business press about the Dufort Pharmaceuticals deal.

'I should have confirmation for you one way or another by the end of tomorrow,' Manos concluded.

Bastien had a stiff drink and brooded over the information. No way was he saying sorry when Delilah had made such a big deal of him humbling himself. Indeed, he cringed at the prospect.

He dined alone at his desk, burying himself in work—as was his habit when anything bothered him.

A scrabbling noise made him glance up from the screen, and he frowned at Skippy, who must have sneaked in when Stefan had delivered Bastien's meal. The miniature dachshund was engaged in using a briefcase on the floor as a springboard to the chair on the other side of Bastien's desk. Skippy made it up on to the chair and then with a sudden tremendous leap reached the desk top, whereupon he trotted towards Bastien, his long ears flapping, and dropped his squeaky toy beside Bastien's laptop.

With a sigh, Bastien scooped up the dog before it skidded off the desk and broke its legs, and settled it on the floor. Then, lifting the toy with distaste, he flung it—sending Skippy into a race of panting pleasure.

'I will only throw it once,' he warned the animal.

Unable to get back to work, he walked out onto the balcony and groaned out loud as he paced in the warm evening air. His muscles were stiff.

Banishing Skippy, who was showing annoying signs of wanting to follow him, Bastien went down to the basement gym in an effort to work off some of his tension. A marathon swim, followed by a long, violently cathartic session with the punch bag, sent Bastien into the shower.

All he needed was a good night's sleep and a clear head, he told himself urgently when he was tempted to approach Delilah. He did not need or want *her*...

Lilah sat up late in bed, reading, and fell asleep with the light on, wakening disorientated at around three in the morning. On her way back from the bathroom she thought she heard someone cry out, and she went to the window and brushed back the curtain to look down at the moonlit garden below. Nothing stirred... not even the shadows.

When the sound came again she realised that it had come from Bastien's room, and she crossed the polished wooden floor to listen behind the communicating door with a frown etched between her brows.

The sound of a shout galvanised her into opening the door. Bastien was a dark shape, thrashing about wildly in the bed, and choked cries interspersed with Greek words were breaking from him.

There was no way on earth that Lilah could walk away and leave him suffering like that. He was having a nightmare, that was all, but it was clearly a terrifying one.

She hovered uncertainly by the side of the bed,

and then closed her hand firmly round a sleek tanned muscular shoulder to shake it.

'Wake up, Bastien…it's just a dream,' she told him gently.

CHAPTER EIGHT

ARMS FLAILING AND eyes wild, Bastien reared up and closed a hand round her throat, dragging her down to the bed on top of him as he struggled to focus on her.

'Bastien...it's Lilah!' she gasped, in stricken dismay at the effect of her intervention. 'You were stuck in a bad dream. I was trying to wake you up.'

'Delilah...' Bastien framed dazedly, shifting his tousled dark head in confusion, his eyes glittering dark as night in the faint light emanating from her room. He blinked. 'What are you doing in here?'

'You were having a really bad nightmare,' she repeated as she levered herself away from him and settled on the empty side of the bed. The dampness of perspiration sheened his lean dark features and he was still trembling almost imperceptibly. 'What on earth has got you that worked up?'

'I put my hand round your neck... Did I hurt you?' Bastien demanded, switching on the bedside light and tipping up her chin to examine the faint red fingermarks marring her slender white throat. '*Diavelos*, Delilah... I'm sorry. I could have seriously injured you. You should never have come near me when I was like that. I'm very restless. That's why I always sleep alone.'

'I'm fine… I'm fine… I was worried about you,' she admitted.

'Why the hell would you be worried about a guy who doesn't treat you with respect or consideration?' Bastien prompted grimly.

'I was really concerned about you,' Lilah countered, ignoring that question because she could not have answered it even to her own satisfaction. 'What on earth were you dreaming about?'

His lean dark features were shuttered. 'Believe me, you don't want to know.'

In an abrupt movement that took her by surprise, he pulled her backwards into his arms. Little tremors were still running through his big powerful frame.

Lilah released her breath in a bemused hiss. 'Try to relax,' she urged him, aware of the shattering tension still holding his muscles taut in his big body.

'Don't try to mother me, *glikia mou*,' Bastien growled warningly, resting back against the pillows and breathing in slow and deep before exhaling again. 'That's not what I want from you.'

'Well, you're not getting anything else,' Lilah warned him bluntly.

At that tart response unholy amusement quivered through Bastien's lean, powerful frame and he laughed out loud.

'So, what was the dream about?' she prompted again.

In the low light, Bastien rolled his eyes and laced his fingers round her abdomen as she relaxed back against him. 'I was getting beaten up… It's something that happened when I was a child.'

Taken by surprise, Lilah twisted round in the circle of his arms and lifted her head to look directly at him. 'When you were a *child*?'

'I walked in on my mother, in bed with her drug-dealing boyfriend. She didn't intervene. She was terrified that I would accidentally let it drop to Anatole that she had other men because Anatole paid all our bills.'

Lilah frowned down at him in disbelief. 'For goodness' sake—what age were you?'

He shrugged a broad shoulder. 'Five…six years old? I really don't remember. But I almost died because Athene didn't take me to hospital until the next day—and then not until she had coached me to say that I'd fallen down the stairs.'

'Damaged'—that was how Marielle Durand had labelled Bastien. And for the first time Lilah truly saw that in him, recognising the angry defensive pain in his eyes. His mother had neither wanted nor loved him, and by the sound of it had been a cruel and selfish parent.

Lilah recognised his discomfiture under her continuing scrutiny and she looked away, twisting round to give him back his privacy. Her eyes were smarting with tears, though.

As a teenager she had felt so sorry for herself when her father had been bringing a string of different women home for the night and she'd had to occasionally share the breakfast table with strangers. In retrospect, though, she was realising that she could have suffered much worse experiences, and that no matter how much her father's sex-life had embarrassed her he had always looked after her and loved her.

Bastien had not been so lucky.

'I don't know why I told you that,' Bastien breathed in a harsh undertone.

'Because I'm very persistent when I want to know something,' Lilah declared, with deliberate lightness of tone. 'And because you're shaken up.'

'I don't *get* shaken up,' Bastien asserted predictably.

'Of course not,' Lilah traded, tongue in cheek.

Without warning Bastien sprang off the bed, carting her with him.

'What—?'

'I need a shower,' he ground out.

'I'll go back to—'

'You're not going anywhere,' Bastien contradicted, striding into the en-suite bathroom and straight into the spacious shower with her still in his arms.

'Bastien…what on earth…?' she exclaimed in angry disbelief as he elbowed a button and warm water cascaded down on her from all directions, instantly plastering the nightdress she wore to her body.

Bastien knew he was acting like a mad man, but he was on automatic pilot and he didn't care—because his hunger for Delilah at that moment was overwhelming. He hauled her dripping body up against him and closed his mouth hungrily to the luscious soft pink enticement of hers, long fingers stroking her wet hair back from her face.

Lilah's hands closed over his broad shoulders, clenching there to steady herself as the hot, demanding intensity of the kiss took her by storm. His tongue delved deep into the moist interior of her mouth, plundering a response from her.

She recognised the force of his need, suspecting that Bastien was not in control the way he usually was. Rather than dismaying her, that suspicion excited her beyond bearing—because Bastien was generally so controlled that he unnerved her. In fact, the unashamed passion he was unleashing now was much more to Lilah's taste, and it went to her head even more strongly than the wine that afternoon.

Her hands skimmed down over his lean, strong torso. She could feel the hard urgency of his erection against her midriff, and before she could even let herself think about what she was about to do she had dropped to her knees. The warm water teemed down, somehow separating her from the world and from all the anxious self-judgement that kept her from experimenting. For the first time ever she felt free to do simply as she liked. As she liked and as she wanted. And she was proud of that inner spur of passion for the first time.

Slender fingers roved up over Bastien's hair-roughened muscular thighs, and she was smiling at his sudden ferocious tension as she bent her head—all woman, all feminine power.

Bastien groaned, threw his head back against the tiles and arched his hips to facilitate her, making no attempt to hide his pleasure as she worked magic with her mouth and her tongue and her agile fingers.

His potent reaction gave Lilah a high. For once she was in charge, and what she lacked in experience she more than made up for with creativity and enthusiasm.

Allowing himself to be out of control in any way

was a dark and seductive novelty for Bastien. And when he could no longer withstand the hot, all-encompassing pleasure of her mouth, he bent down and hauled her up to him, bracing her against the tiles as he hitched up her nightdress and clamped her slim thighs to his waist. He plunged into the glorious tight wet heat of her body with a raw groan of masculine pleasure.

Still tender from her first experience the night before, Lilah felt every inch of Bastien's smooth hard length as he surged inside her. Her arms wrapped round his neck for support, her head falling back as he withdrew and surged deep again. Excitement engulfed her in a heady rush, her heart slamming inside her chest, her breath hitching and breaking in her throat.

So sensitive was she that as Bastien increased the tempo and hammered into her the pleasure swelled to an almost painful intensity. The rising heat within her finally soothed the hollow ache of tormenting hunger, and she gasped and moaned in delight. Her hips writhed against the cold tiles as she reached a climax too powerful to restrain and it swept her over the edge, sending intoxicating explosions of blissful sensation rippling through her quivering length as she sagged in Bastien's powerful hold.

By the time she had floated down from that dizzy peak of satisfaction Bastien was trailing off her sodden nightdress and wrapping her in a towel.

'You didn't say sorry...this wasn't supposed to happen between us...' Lilah mumbled in limp reminder as she reclaimed her wits.

'I jumped to conclusions. I was wrong. It appears that one of my staff *was* responsible for the leak to the press,' Bastien shared with taut reluctance as he grabbed up another towel to fold it round her dripping hair.

'Told you so,' Lilah remarked ungraciously.

'I lost my temper with you. I don't *do* that,' Bastien growled half under his breath in explanation. 'When anger is in control, mistakes are made.'

'So you're saying sorry?' Lilah whispered, weak as a kitten as he laid her down on the soft firmness of his bed and pulled a sheet over her cooling skin.

Bastien didn't answer. He didn't do apologies, but he was quite happy for her to assume that he had apologised. He was intent on her, still worked up in an unsettling way he didn't understand. She made him feel alive, crazily *alive,* and for some reason he hadn't had enough of her yet. One taste of her had only made him hunger for more.

He framed her face with long dark fingers, rejoicing in the silky softness of her skin and the rosy purity of her features. He savoured her swollen pink mouth with his own, revelling in the taste of her and the thundering race of his heartbeat as the hunger raged through him again like a tempest.

Bastien kissed with the same wild potency with which he made love, Lilah reflected dizzily, and the pulse of heat was awakening in her pelvis again as his tongue tangled with hers and flicked the ultra-sensitive roof of her mouth in a teasing assault that made her push up against him. Desire shimmied through her like an electrical storm, lighting up every place he touched, from the peaks of her straining nipples to the infinitely delicate damp flesh between her thighs.

'I still want you, *glikia mou*,' Bastien grated, and his stunning dark golden eyes were bright with lingering wonder at that anomaly as he ran his mouth down hungrily over the sweet mounds of her small breasts, licking and tasting and nipping to make her slim body writhe frantically.

As he reached the heart of her arousal and dallied to torment her with every carnal caress he had ever learned she gasped his name over and over again, and he very much liked the sound of his own name on her lips.

Lilah had not believed he could make her want him again so soon, when her body was still heavy with fulfilment, but somehow he'd pushed her to the raw, biting edge of feverish need again, and the first plunge of his powerful male heat inside her felt gloriously necessary.

Her spine arched, wild torrents of joyous sensation cascading through her quivering body as he pushed back her thighs and rose over her, pounding into her tight depths with driving hunger. She thrashed under him, every nerve-ending electrified by the pagan rhythm of his hard thrusts and the inexorable climb towards another climax. When it came, she hit a peak and shattered like glass, shocked by the white-hot intensity of excitement exploding inside her.

She fell back against the pillows, utterly drained of energy, while Bastien groaned long and low and shuddered with pleasure.

Bastien drank in the scent of Delilah's shampoo as he struggled to get his breath back. Her silky hair had the sweet fresh perfume of a summer meadow. Her arms were still wrapped around him and he lifted his tousled dark head to drop a brief but appreciative kiss on her brow.

'You're an unbeatable cure for a nightmare, *glikia mou*,' he husked with wicked amusement, rolling free of her to head for the bathroom.

The minute he arrived there he realised too late what was missing. He had not used a condom—not that last time or the time before it in the shower.

It was a very dangerous oversight that chilled Bastien and made him want to punch something hard in angry self-loathing. The shower beat down on him while some of the worst memories of his life engulfed him and he shuddered, knowing what he must do, knowing that this time around he would not dare to walk away and simply hope for the best.

Delilah needed to know that, whatever happened, her future and that of any child she had would be totally secure.

A towel knotted round his lean brown hips, he strode back into the bedroom and proceeded to disconcert Lilah with what she deemed to be inappropriate questions.

'Why on earth are you asking me such things?' she demanded tautly, her colour high from embarrassment.

'We've had sex twice without a condom,' Bastien told her grimly. 'I'm regularly tested and I'm clean, so there is no risk of an infection. I'm merely trying to calculate the odds of conception.'

Lilah's whole body turned cold at the threat of an unplanned pregnancy. She hadn't noticed the lack of contraception—had been as lost in passion as he must have been. That acknowledgement stung, because she knew how important it was to take precautions and protect herself from such consequences.

Ashamed that she could have been so reckless and immature as to overlook such necessities, she answered his questions about her menstrual cycle and watched his frown steadily darken.

'Obviously you could conceive. You're young, fertile…naturally there's a good chance.' His beautiful mouth compressed hard. 'We'll get married as soon as I can get it organised.'

'Married?' Lilah parrotted in a strangled shriek, sitting up in bed with a sudden jerk, her eyes awash with disbelief as she stared back at him.

His unfathomable dark eyes glittered. 'You need to know that whatever happens I'm there for you, and a wedding ring is the only security a man can offer a woman in that situation.'

'People don't rush off and get married simply because of a contraceptive oversight,' Lilah whispered shakily. 'That would be crazy.'

'I know exactly what I'm doing. My first child was aborted when I was only twenty-one,' Bastien explained, shattering her with that flat statement of fact. 'I refuse to risk a repeat of that experience.'

Lilah was poleaxed. 'But…but I—'

'So we'll get married. And if it transpires that we have no reason to *stay* married we'll get an equally quick divorce,' Bastien assured her smoothly, as though such a fast turnaround from marriage to divorce would be the most natural development in the world.

'But we can't just get married on the off-chance that I might be pregnant,' she muttered incredulously.

'If you have conceived we'll be married and you'll be less tempted to consider a termination,' Bastien pointed out with assurance. 'We don't need to publicise our marriage in the short term, or drag anyone else into our predicament. We'll have a private wedding.'

Stunned, Lilah flopped down flat again, exhaustion rolling over her like a hefty blanket. It was all too much to take in. The shocking revelations of his past and the sheer impossibility of their future.

'We'll argue about it in the morning,' she countered in a daze. 'You're thinking worst-case scenario.'

'No, I've already *lived* the worst-case scenario,' Bastien contradicted with an edge of derision. 'And that was losing the child I wanted because the woman concerned decided that she didn't.'

Lilah winced, recognising the edge of bitterness in his dark deep drawl. She wondered who that woman had been, while marvelling at how much Bastien was revealing about himself. He had a deep, sensitive side to his nature that astonished her. For the first time she wondered what it had felt like for him—a man who wanted a child with a woman when the woman did not feel the same. Her heart ached for him. Clearly he had grieved that loss, but he had also interpreted the termination as a personal rejection and a humiliation, which struck her as even more sad.

Without comment she watched him stride lithely back to his own room, utterly unconcerned by his nudity. But why would he be concerned? an inner voice asked. When you were *that* perfectly built and physically beautiful you had to be aware of the fact.

She stretched out in the big bed, wondering why

she wished he had stayed…wondering why what he had told her had left her feeling bereft and unsettled.

Had he loved the woman who had chosen not to have his child? Why did it bother her that Bastien might once have cared deeply for another woman? Evidently back then Bastien had not been quite as emotionally detached and untouchable as he was now. He had cared…he had been hurt. Why did that touch something deep down inside her and wound her? It couldn't be jealousy… It couldn't possibly be jealousy.

She didn't care about Bastien in the smallest way, Lilah assured herself agitatedly. Bastien Zikos was simply the man she'd slept with to fulfil her side of their agreement to be his mistress. That was all he wanted from her. And all she had ever wanted from him was that he reopen the factory and re-employ her father.

Honesty urged Lilah to admit that she *was* lying to herself. Two years earlier, when she had first met Bastien, she had very quickly begun developing deep feelings for him—but his sole reaction to *her* had been superficial and sexual. And nothing had changed since then, she reminded herself doggedly. Even if she was pregnant—even if she agreed to marry him—nothing would change between them. If she hadn't got to Bastien on a more meaningful level when they first met it was extremely unlikely that anything more would develop the second time around.

But how dared he simply assume that if she had conceived she would automatically want to consider a termination? He had no right to make that assumption—no right to try and take control of that decision either.

Too tired to lie awake agonising about what might never happen, Lilah ultimately dropped off to sleep.

The next morning that entire conversation with Bastien about getting married seemed surreal to Lilah. She was still deep in her bemused thoughts when she went downstairs for breakfast.

Bastien watched Delilah cross the terrace, a lithe, slim figure in a turquoise playsuit that showcased her tiny waist and long slim legs. She looked very young, with her black curls rippling loose round her shoulders. He watched her sit down and settle anxious sapphire-blue eyes on him.

Clad in tailored cream chinos and a black T-shirt, Bastien was casually seated on the low wall bounding the terrace, with a cup of coffee in his hand. His bronzed sculpted features smooth shaven, his lean, powerful body fluidly relaxed, he exuded poise, sophistication and an absolute charisma which stole Lilah's breath from her lungs.

A tiny muscle low in her pelvis clenched and her face coloured hotly as she became uncomfortably aware of the damp flesh between her thighs.

'I've been thinking, and I believe you're worrying about something that's unlikely to happen. It's not always that easy to get pregnant,' Lilah told Bastien quietly, keen to distract him from looking at her too closely because Bastien was far too astute at reading women. 'It took my stepmother months to conceive.'

'I'm not about to change my mind about marriage as a solution, Delilah,' Bastien warned her, secretly amused and impressed that she lacked the avaricious streak that would have made many women grab at

the chance to marry him. 'While the arrangements
are being made—there's a lot of paperwork involved
in getting married in France—we'll continue here as
normal. My lawyers are drawing up a pre-nup as we
speak—'

Lilah poured her tea and groaned. 'You're really
serious about this...'

'It may not seem immediately obvious to you in our
current relationship,' Bastien remarked in a roughened
undertone, watching her nibble at a croissant with un-
conscious sensuality and gritting his teeth as he hardened in response, 'but if you do prove to be pregnant I
have a lot to offer as a husband and a father...'

Who was she? Lilah immediately wanted to know.
Who was the evil witch who had made Bastien feel
worthless at the age of twenty-one when he had been
little more than a boy?

'I know that, Bastien,' she said quietly. 'Who was
the woman who had the termination?'

Bastien grimaced. 'This long after the event, there
is no need for us to discuss that.'

Lilah tilted her chin. 'If you want me to marry
you in these circumstances I have a right to know
the whole story.'

'Her name is Marina Kouros. She's the daughter
of a wealthy businessman.'

'Greek?'

'Yes. She hung out with my half-brother, Leo. I
knew she had a thing for him, but he saw her only
as a friend.'

Lilah winced when he described that connection.
'Complicated...'

'Nothing I couldn't handle at the time, I thought.

I was very confident with women even at that age,'
Bastien admitted bleakly. '*Too* confident, as it turned
out. Of course I was infatuated with Marina. We had
a one-night stand but I wanted more. I didn't see it at
the time, but she was using me to try and make Leo
sit up and take notice of her.'

'You were *brothers*. It was wrong of her to come
between you like that,' Lilah opined.

'To be fair, Marina didn't intend to cause trouble,
and Leo and I have never been close. I also know
why she went for the termination behind my back,' he
admitted tautly. 'I was illegitimate and penniless—
hardly a winning package for a wealthy socialite. Unfortunately when Leo heard the rumours that I had got
her pregnant she lied to save face with him and pretended that I had bullied her into the abortion clinic.
He's held that against me ever since.'

'That's *so* unfair,' Lilah breathed angrily.

Bastien shrugged a broad shoulder. 'Very little in
my life has been fair,' he derided softly. 'That's why
I prefer to make my own luck and my own fortune.
I don't owe anyone anything and that's how I like it,
glikia mou.'

'But *I* would prefer not to risk having an unnecessary marriage and divorce in my relationship history,'
Lilah told him quietly. 'I think we should wait and see
if we have anything to worry about first.'

His dark golden eyes hardened. 'Not this time.'

'Even if I have conceived I don't think I'd choose
a termination,' Lilah added.

Bastien sprang upright and set down his coffee cup,
an aggressive edge to his movements. 'We'll do this
my way. We'll get married.'

Lilah stood up. 'It's not the course of action I would choose, Bastien.'

'I don't care. This is an amendment to our original agreement,' he declared without hesitation. 'Deal with it.'

Lilah turned away from him, angry and stressed.

'You'll have a few days to think your position over,' Bastien told her. 'I have to make a trip to Asia, to check out some trouble at one of my manufacturing plants.'

Taken aback, Lilah turned. 'How long will you be away?'

'About a week.'

Lilah had a second cup of tea while Bastien talked on the phone in a foreign language. *Deal with it*, he had told her. An amendment to their original agreement? Was he *threatening* her? Would continuing refusal to marry him on her part be treated as a breach of that agreement? Did she dare push it?

What, after all, *was* she planning to do should Bastien's fears prove correct and she found herself pregnant? Her skin turned clammy with anxiety. If she was pregnant she would want Bastien's support every step of the way, she reflected ruefully. Maybe, just maybe, she was fighting the wrong battle…

CHAPTER NINE

IT WAS A beautiful dress. Exquisitely simple in shape, it flattered Lilah's slender figure, with long tight lace sleeves, a boat-shaped neckline and a slimline skirt. Her wedding gown, she acknowledged in lingering astonishment as she studied her reflection. It was her wedding day, and she still couldn't believe that she was actually about to marry Bastien Zikos.

The whole of the previous week had been taken up with marriage-orientated activity. Accompanied by one of Bastien's personal assistants, a fluent French-speaker, she had undergone an interview at the local *mairie*—the mayor's office, where the ceremony would take place. A whole heap of personal documents had been certified and presented on her behalf to fulfil the legal requirements, and forty-eight hours later, following a meeting with a lawyer at the chateau to protect her interests, she had signed a pre-nuptial agreement. Bastien had made liberal provision for her in the event of a divorce, offering a far more generous settlement than she thought necessary.

'Look on it as compensation,' Bastien had advised her on the phone, when she had protested the size of that settlement. 'You didn't want to marry me, but you're doing it.'

It wouldn't be a *real* marriage, she told herself soothingly as she clasped the diamond pendant round her throat. And wasn't that just as well? Bastien had been away for seven days and she had missed him almost from the moment of his departure. How was that possible? How could she miss the male she had believed she hated, who had persuaded her into a morally indefensible sexual relationship?

Lilah walked to the window and breathed in slow and deep, struggling to calm herself. She had *not* become attached to Bastien, and she had *not* fallen for him. She was just wildly attracted to him. She had also begun to understand him better as she'd come to appreciate his tough childhood and the experiences which had made him the hard, aggressive character that he was.

She wasn't *excusing* anything he had done, was she? No—she remained fully aware of Bastien's every flaw, and was therefore completely safe from getting attached to him, she assured herself soothingly.

A knock sounded on the bedroom door. It was time for her to leave. Manos smiled at her as she emerged from the room, rich fabric gliding in silken folds round her legs. Bastien had had a whole rack of designer wedding gowns sent to her and she had been taken aback, having assumed that they would be bypassing all such frills.

'No, this should look like a normal wedding,' Bastien had decreed.

Yet how could it look or feel normal when neither of them had any family members present?

Lilah felt absurdly guilty that she was about to get married without her father's knowledge.

Bastien was waiting in the hall. Clad in a superbly tailored pale grey suit, he looked breathtakingly handsome. When she met his long-lashed dark golden eyes her heart thudded and her pulses quickened, and she could feel heat rushing into her cheeks.

'You look fantastic,' he husked, closing a hand over hers as she reached the bottom step.

'When did you get back?'

'At dawn. I slept during the flight,' he shared, just as Stefan presented Lilah with a small bunch of flowers and she thanked him warmly.

They came to a halt in the stone front doorway as a photographer stepped forward to capture them on film.

'I wasn't expecting him,' Lilah admitted out of the corner of her mouth.

'This is not a moment we can easily recapture,' Bastien declared.

'But who's going to be interested?' she whispered helplessly.

'Our child will be interested in our wedding day,' Bastien countered.

'But…' Her lips clamped shut on a rush of denial as the photographer asked her to relax and smile.

She was convinced that there wasn't going to be a pregnancy, or a child, but she could see that Bastien had already decided otherwise.

A limousine whisked them to the *mairie*, a sleepy creamy stone building sited behind the war memorial in a small village. It was a civil ceremony, conducted by a middle-aged female official. Lilah held her breath as Bastien slid a gold ring on to her finger and she performed the same office for him, albeit more clumsily, all fingers and thumbs in her extreme self-consciousness as she thought about what the gesture actually meant: Bastien was her husband now.

When they emerged back into the sunshine the photographer was waiting, and she laughed and smiled, suddenly grateful that the unsettling ceremony was over and she could forget about it.

She was climbing back into the limo when a sports car shot to a sudden halt at the other side of the road and a woman called, *'Bastien?'*

Bastien stepped back from the limo and swung round as a lithe blonde scrambled out of the sports car and ran to greet him. She wore only a chiffon wrap, which was split to the waist at either side to show off her fabulous legs and brief leopard print bikini pants.

Lilah smoothed her gown over her knees and watched as the blonde kissed Bastien on both cheeks and he returned the greeting. The woman chattered, her slim hands moving expressively in the air. Very French, very chic, Lilah conceded, deliberately looking away from the encounter. Bastien's dealings with other women were none of her business.

Her tummy flipped, her chin coming up. No, that couldn't be true *or* acceptable. She was Bastien's wife now, and that had to make a difference.

'Who is she?' Lilah enquired when Bastien finally joined her and the limo moved off again.

'Chantal Baudin—one of my neighbours,' Bastien divulged carelessly.

'You've slept with her…haven't you?'

The instant those provocative words leapt off Lilah's tongue she was shocked by them, because she hadn't even known that that question was in her head.

'On several occasions over the years since I bought the chateau,' Bastien revealed, as cool as ice water in tone. 'She's a model.'

'What else would she be?' Lilah traded drily, while colour flared over her cheekbones like a revealing banner, because she felt as though an evil genie had taken over both her brain *and* her tongue.

'We were ships-that-pass-casual,' Bastien qualified very quietly. 'Not that that's any of your business.'

Lilah's shot a stubborn look at him, sapphire-blue eyes bright and defiant. 'Oh, it's my business *now*,' she assured him without hesitation. 'For as long as you remain married to me you have to be a one-woman man.'

A line of colour flared over Bastien's exotic cheekbones and his dark golden eyes smouldered. 'That sounds suspiciously like a warning.'

'It was. Do you expect *me* to stay away from other men?' Lilah asked dangerously.

'Of course,' Bastien breathed, in a harsh uncompromising undertone.

'Well, let's not be sexist about it—the rule cuts both ways. While we're married, your wings are clipped,' Lilah pronounced with satisfaction.

'Presumably you intend to ensure that the sacrifice of my sexual freedom is worth my while?' Bastien purred, black lashes dropping low over his gaze.

Lilah clashed with expectant dark eyes, brilliant as stars in a black sky, and her tummy performed a somersault while damp heat gathered at her feminine core. She shifted uneasily on the seat, uncomfortable with the potent physical effect Bastien had on her. Even when he annoyed her he could still make her want him. One glance at those high cheekbones and those stunning eyes and she melted into a puddle of longing.

Lunch awaited them on their return to the chateau. The table had been set with white linen, lace and rose petals, and Lilah stiffened in dismay when she saw it because it was very bridal and romantic. But the meal was superb, and Bastien's businesslike account of how he had dealt with the problems at his Asian manufacturing plant relaxed Lilah again.

Bastien studied Delilah, ultra-feminine and lovely, in a dress that merely enhanced her petite proportions, wondering if she was pregnant. He wanted a child, he acknowledged. Perhaps it was simply that he was *ready* for a child and for a change in lifestyle. But would he have felt that way with any woman other than Delilah?

'I should get changed,' Lilah murmured over coffee.

'*I* want to take off that dress.'

Lilah coloured. 'It's the middle of the day, Bastien.'

'My libido is not controlled by the clock. In any case, we're newly married and anything goes,' Bastien pointed out smoothly as he rose from his chair.

But Lilah refused to think of them as a married couple, thinking it wiser to regard their current relationship as simply an extension of their original arrangement. In other words, barring the ring on her wedding finger, she was still Bastien's mistress and his desired entertainment between the sheets. It would be very unwise, she thought, to start thinking of herself as occupying any more important or permanent role in Bastien's life.

Lean brown fingers closed over hers and she walked upstairs with him, her slender body taut with anticipation. She listened to the faint buzz of his mobile receiving messages and suppressed a sigh. Bastien never, ever switched his phone off, and it set her teeth on edge.

Bastien glanced at his phone and frowned when he saw the text. Chantal was making a nuisance of herself. He had told her that he was not alone at the chateau and she should have taken the hint that he wasn't available. Perhaps he should have mentioned that he had just got married, but why telegraph that news when there might be no need to do so? After all, if Delilah *hadn't* conceived he would soon be alone and free as a bird again, he reminded himself. And that was what he wanted, wasn't it? What he had always wanted: freedom without rules or ties.

Obviously he still had to get Delilah out of his system. Surely one more week would do that? Although he grudgingly admitted to himself that he did not *like* the prospect of parting with her. Why did the thought feel like a threat?

And then the sure knowledge hit him like a bombshell, blowing apart everything he had believed he knew about himself. He didn't *want* to let Delilah go. He wanted to *keep* her.

Struggling to rationalise that aberrant urge, he ran down the zip on her dress very slowly and eased her smoothly out of its concealing folds. Her porcelain-pale skin showed to advantage against the defiantly unconventional scarlet bra and panties she sported.

For some reason he had expected to find her wearing blue underpinnings, in line with that old bridal rhyme about something old, something new. He scanned her slender legs, but there was no garter to be seen either.

'Something blue?' he queried.

'It wasn't a real wedding, so I didn't see the point of bothering with tradition,' Delilah explained cheerfully.

Exasperation and annoyance shot through Bastien, who had assumed that she would be more sentimental. 'It felt real enough to me.'

'It's not real when you've already planned the divorce *before* you get married,' Delilah told him with vehement conviction.

'No man of my wealth marries without a pre-nup. And I won't be divorcing you if you're carrying my child,' Bastien pointed out, lifting her up to seat her at the foot of the bed, while wishing she would stop talking about divorce.

'I just don't think that it's very likely…that I'll be pregnant,' she extended, feeling insanely bare in her flimsy underwear while he remained fully dressed.

'Time will tell,' Bastien traded, easing off her silk sandals. 'And I do have an entire week to concentrate on getting you pregnant.'

Her bright blue eyes flew wide. 'What on earth do you mean?'

'Now that we're married it would be silly to start taking precautions again,' Bastien pronounced.

'Not to *my* way of thinking. If there is a decision still to be made on that score I don't think I want to *plan* to have a baby with a womaniser,' Lilah told him tartly.

Bastien shrugged free of his jacket and pitched it on to a chair before tugging at his tie. Whatever it took, he was determined to keep her. 'If you give me a baby I can promise that you'll be the only woman in my life.'

Lilah was hugely disconcerted by that offer, coming at her out of nowhere. 'You want a baby that much?'

But only with *her*, Bastien completed inwardly. She had first-rate qualities which he had noticed from the first. She wasn't greedy, dishonest or manipulative, like so many of the women he had known. In addition she was loyal, and kind to those she cared about, and she was a curiously attractive combination of downright old-fashioned sensible and mulishly spirited. Add in her looks and sex appeal and Delilah Moore-Zikos inhabited a class all of her own...

Not that he was planning to share that high opinion with her, though. Particularly not when she talked as though she was indifferent to both him and the prospect of a baby. But he didn't believe that. Like him, Delilah tended to hold back, judging a situation before she bared her soul or committed to a path of action.

Having reached his decision at a speed which slightly stunned him, Bastien curved long fingers to her slim shoulders. 'I want a baby with *you*.'

'But that pre-nup—'

'*Thee mou*...think outside the box,' he urged. 'I will settle down with you if you give me a child.'

Lilah went pink. 'And why would you think that I would be interested in *that* outcome?'

Bastien elevated an ebony brow. 'Aren't you?'

'Are we bargaining again, Bastien?'

Lilah was so tense she could hardly breathe. The unthinkable was happening: Bastien Zikos, the legendary womaniser, was offering her fidelity and a real marriage.

'Negotiating?' he countered.

'I may not even be able to *get* pregnant,' Lilah countered with quiet practicality.

'If and when that happens we'll deal with it, *glikia mou*,' Bastien told her levelly. 'I don't expect an easy ride. Nothing worthwhile is ever easy.'

Her heart swelled like a balloon inside her chest at that forthright opinion, which perfectly matched her own. Tears lashed the back of her eyes and she blinked them back furiously to focus on the beautiful burnished golden shimmer of his gaze.

'In that case, I'll… I'll give it a go,' she responded jerkily, afraid of the way she was laying herself open to getting hurt again, but desperately wanting to give him another chance.

Another chance to smash her heart to smithereens? Another chance to walk away from her without a backward glance and console himself with other women? How likely was it that Bastien could settle down into marriage? Did she dare risk bringing a child into so potentially volatile a relationship? And why was she even considering doing so?

Stealing a glance at his lean, darkly handsome face, she felt her breath hitch in her throat. The freedom of choice was suddenly cruelly wrenched from her, along with much of her pride. The reason she so badly wanted to give Bastien another chance was that she had fallen hard for him two years earlier and had struggled to fight feelings almost stronger than she was. Sadly, now that she was actually in Bastien's life and wearing his ring on her finger, she was weaker, more open to hope and dream fulfilment and love.

And that was the most basic truth, which she could no longer ignore or deny. She *loved* Bastien Zikos— had fallen like a giant stone the very first time he had settled those gorgeous dark eyes on her and smiled.

'You look so serious,' Bastien censured as he trailed off his shirt to reveal the torso that starred in her every fantasy. He was so wonderfully well-built, and he worked at staying fit—a reality etched in the lean hard sheet of roped muscle framing his pectoral muscles and abdomen.

Lilah's mouth ran dry. He brought his mouth down on hers, nibbling sexily at her full lower lip, swiping the upper with the tip of his tongue to gain entry to the intimate space beyond. A ball of heat mushroomed inside her when his tongue flicked against her own. Her hands spread on his chest, fingertips grazing hair-roughened skin and smoothing down to feel him jerk with sensitivity when she found the hard thrusting length of him.

With a hungry groan he lifted her up and brought her down again on the bed, arranging her over him with careful hands.

'I want you,' Bastien growled, dark eyes shooting golden sparks over her warmly flushed face.

'You sound so aggressive,' Lilah scolded as she obediently bent forward for him to unclasp her bra.

'It's been a week.' He swore bitterly. 'An endless, frustrating week.'

Strong hands pulled her down to him, to enable

him to close his lips round a pouting pink nipple. He hauled her close to him and rolled her over.

'Didn't *think* I was going to get to stay on top,' Lilah muttered with helpless bite.

His broad chest rumbled with amusement. 'Some day very soon...but not today,' he agreed in a roughened undertone.

Employing every sensual skill he had acquired, Bastien worked his way down over Delilah's slim squirming body, revelling in each sound that revealed her enjoyment. As her hips bucked in climax and she cried his name he smiled and flipped her over, lifting her up on to her knees.

He slid against her damp flesh to tease her, and then when she complained in frustration he sank into her, hard and deep.

Lilah moaned, her head still swimming and her body still sensitised, floating on the aftermath of extreme pleasure. Extraordinarily conscious of Bastien's every slight movement, Lilah felt her heart race and her pulse quicken with exhilaration. Intense excitement controlled her as he ground his hips into hers, quickening his pace until all she was conscious of was the wild, feverish climb of pleasure. As the ascent to satisfaction consumed her spasms of potent sensation coursed through her quivering body and then rose to an irresistible peak, leaving her thrashing in explosive convulsions of delight.

'I'll never move again,' she whispered limply in the aftermath.

'I'll move you,' Bastien husked, turning her round in the circle of his arms, his breath fanning her cheek, his body hot and damp against hers.

The scent of his skin enveloped her and she smiled up at him.

'I do hope you appreciate that you're not getting out of this bed for the rest of the day?' Bastien purred. 'But I'll make up for it tomorrow. I'm taking the rest of the week off. You will have my full attention, *kardoula mou.*'

Lilah rubbed her face against a broad brown shoulder, gloriously relaxed and feeling amazingly happy. She loved him, and he was with her, and his entire attention was on her. For the moment that was enough. And for the first time she didn't feel like Bastien's mistress—she felt like his wife, and it felt good.

A week after their wedding day Lilah woke suddenly during the night to register that Bastien had got out of bed and was pacing naked while he spoke Greek into his phone, his lean strong features stressed and taut. He waved a hand to silence her when she mouthed a query and she had to be patient, even though she didn't *feel* patient, lying back against the pillows and wondering what had happened to put that look of concern on his beautiful face.

So much had changed between them in the course of a week. Bastien had let down some of his barriers and was sharing a bed with her every night. Only once had he had another bad dream, and wakening to find her leaning over him had put more exciting pursuits into his mind, she recalled, her body heating at that wickedly erotic memory.

By day they had explored the chateau grounds before ranging further afield. They had gone to a jazz concert in the vineyards near Vaison-Ventoux-en-

Provence. They had strolled round vibrant markets, walked through narrow cobbled streets to enjoy coffee in shaded squares with softly flowing fountains. The hilltop villages were wonderfully picturesque, and the views spectacular.

He had bought her a gorgeous leather handbag in a workshop, and laughed heartily at the colourful pottery hen she had bought for Vickie, questioning that she could really *like* her stepmother and still buy her such a thing.

On several evenings they had dined out in local restaurants, although truthfully they had yet to eat anywhere that could compete with the superb food Marie served at the chateau. Some nights they made love until dawn…some afternoons they didn't get out of bed until the need to eat drove them out. His insatiable hunger for her was mercifully matched by hers for him, and with his encouragement Lilah had become more adventurous.

The only little niggle at the back of her mind, that had prevented her from totally relaxing, was the question of how Bastien was likely to react if she *didn't* prove to be pregnant. After all, was it really her he wanted, or was he merely giving way to a long-suppressed desire to become a father?

He could become a father with almost any woman, couldn't he? Lilah didn't like to think that her being in the right place at the right time was all that had prompted Bastien to seek a more lasting relationship with *her*. In any case, in another few days she would know whether or not she had conceived. And even if she had it was perfectly possible that she would still never tell Bastien that she loved him for fear of making him feel trapped, she thought ruefully.

'What's wrong?' she asked as Bastien cast aside his phone and paced restively back across the room.

'That was my brother, Leo,' he explained grimly. 'My father's in hospital in Athens with a suspected heart attack. Leo says there's no need for me to go, because he'll keep me posted, but...'

'Naturally you want to be there,' Lilah slotted in.

'But equally naturally Leo and his mother don't want me there.'

'How is *that* natural?' Lilah pressed, immediately defensive on Bastien's behalf. 'Anatole is as much your father as your brother's.'

'I may have lived with my father's family for years, but I was never part of that family,' Bastien pointed out drily. 'I'm never a welcome visitor. Leo's mother Cleta—my father's wife—hates me.'

Lilah compressed her lips. 'After the number of years that have passed since your mother's death, and the years you lived in her home with Anatole, that's very definitely *her* problem—not yours,' she pronounced with conviction. 'Don't let *anyone* make you feel as though you don't have the right to see your own father. You're his son too.'

The fiery gleam that illuminated Bastien's dark eyes only accentuated the worried frown stamped on his lean bronzed face. 'I do want to see him. We'll fly out as soon as I can get it organised.'

CHAPTER TEN

BASTIEN AND LILAH drove straight to the hospital from the airport. Lilah hung back a little as they entered the waiting room, because at first glance it seemed to be filled with people. Anatole was still having tests, and only close family would be allowed to visit him. The target of a slew of stares as she entered the room, Lilah flushed and acknowledged that she might be married to Bastien but she did not *feel* like a member of his family.

A small, curvy older woman, improbably dressed in a purple brocade evening coat and matching dress, and more diamonds than Lilah had ever seen outside a shop window, shot a look of derision at Bastien. 'How *dare* you bring one of your whores to the hospital?' she spat.

The very tall black-haired male standing to one side of this shrew stiffened and said something in Greek, while Bastien curved a strong arm to Lilah's tense spine.

'May I introduce my wife, Delilah? This is Cleta Zikos, my father's wife…and my brother Leo and his wife, Grace.'

'Your *wife*?' the pretty redhead exclaimed in an

unmistakable English accent as she surged forward. 'When did you get *married*?'

'Recently,' Lilah responded, grateful that Leo's wife seemed warm and friendly in comparison to his brother, who seemed stunned by the news, and Anatole's sour-faced wife, who had merely grimaced, making it clear that any attachment of Bastien's— married or otherwise—was not welcome.

Annoyance rippled through Lilah at the disturbing awareness that after his mother's death Bastien had spent *years* living in Cleta Zikos's home. Evidently Cleta had never tried to treat Bastien as a stepchild, but had preferred to despise him for the reality that his late mother had been her husband's mistress.

Bastien's brother, Leo, stepped forward to congratulate them. 'Never thought I'd live to see the day,' she heard him quip, half under his breath.

Apart from their similar height and build, the two men did not look obviously related. The awkwardness between them was apparent as they engaged in stilted chat, slipping into Greek, presumably to discuss their father's condition.

Grace settled a hand on Lilah's sleeve and urged her over to some seats at the far wall. 'So, tell all, Delilah,' she urged. 'Leo was convinced that Bastien would stay single for ever.'

'Everyone but Bastien calls me Lilah,' Lilah shared with a rueful look.

'We are both married to very stubborn individuals,' Grace said with a grin. 'Neither one of them gives an inch in a tight corner.'

Lilah glanced up as another woman arrived and

Cleta Zikos rushed up to welcome the tall, shapely brunette with a flood of Greek.

'Who's that?' she asked her companion.

'Marina Kouros—an old friend of the family.'

Bastien's first love, Lilah registered, her heart performing a heavy thud inside her chest.

Clearly Bastien had had good taste, even at the age of twenty-one, because the lively chattering brunette was a classic beauty. She watched Marina stiffen and pale, her animation taking a dip when she belatedly appreciated that Bastien was present. She didn't smile at him and he didn't smile at her. They exchanged a stiff nod of acknowledgement, but Lilah fancied that Bastien looked at his former lover longer than was necessary, and a twist of green jealousy shivered through her.

What was that old cliché about a man never forgetting his first love? Her attention roved down to Marina's hand, which bore no rings, indicating that the woman was still single.

'I propose that you, me and Marina take a break for coffee at our home,' Grace suggested. 'None of us are going to be allowed in to see Anatole anyway. Cleta, I would invite you, but I know you won't leave the hospital until you've seen your husband.'

'I'll pick you up later,' Bastien told Lilah quietly, clearly content for her to depart.

'I'd be happy to stay,' she told him.

His dark golden eyes skimmed her troubled face. 'I don't need support, *hara mou*.'

That was a matter of opinion, Lilah reflected ruefully, avoiding Cleta's haughtily resentful glance and Leo's cool, curious regard. In such company Bastien stood very much alone, and she hated that it was like that for him. But then in such a dysfunctional family circle he had *always* been alone, she thought unhappily. Bastien was still treated like the illegitimate son—the outsider to be resented and kept at a distance.

Not unnaturally, Bastien had eventually learned to live like that—never getting too close to people, steering clear of messy human emotions as best he could because he had seen far too many unpleasant displays of turbulent emotion while he was growing up.

'How do you get on with your mother-in-law?' Lilah asked Grace as the three women stepped into a lift.

'I don't see much of her. Her life revolves round Anatole. She's a bit of a cold fish,' Grace volunteered with a grimace.

Lilah pressed her arm against her breasts. They were sore, aching and tender, but she occasionally suffered from such discomfort before her menstrual cycle kicked in. On the other hand, she was already late... She was planning to do a pregnancy test the following morning, but was convinced it would be a waste of time because she just couldn't imagine that she would be pregnant.

She rested back against the wall of the lift, feeling incredibly weary, and noticed that Marina was staring at her.

'I was surprised to hear that Bastien had got married,' she admitted baldly.

'He rushed me into it,' Lilah responded coolly, studying the woman whose one-night stand with Bastien almost ten years earlier had caused such lasting and damaging repercussions.

'He must've been scared of losing you,' Grace opined.

'Very little scares Bastien,' Lilah said wryly, thinking of how she and Bastien had started out at daggers drawn, and of how quickly her feelings had changed.

Obviously she had no resistance when it came to Bastien. Love had been softening her up for a serious fall from the beginning, she reckoned ruefully, feeling nausea stirring in her tense tummy because she felt so ridiculously uncomfortable in Marina's presence.

Lilah was experiencing a volatile cocktail of jealousy and resentment, and telling herself that she was not entitled to those reactions wasn't helping. She hated knowing that Marina had once shared a bed with Bastien, hated the fact that Bastien had wanted Marina first, and hated even more the reality that Marina could have had him but had instead chosen to throw him away, while at the same time lying about him to poison his relationship with his only sibling.

'You're very quiet,' Grace commented in the limousine.

'I napped during the flight but I'm still very tired,' Lilah confided with an apologetic smile.

'When did you first meet Bastien?' Marina asked.

'Over two years ago.'

'He's quite a guy,' Marina remarked, in a tone that Lilah took exception to because it oozed intimacy to her sensitive hearing. 'A lot of women will envy you.'

Including you? Lilah wondered, thinking that the brunette might well have come to live to regret rejecting Bastien once he had become rich and successful, and as such much more socially acceptable.

It dismayed Lilah that she should feel so angry with Marina and so very protective of Bastien.

Leo and Grace lived in a palatial town house. A nanny brought their daughter, Rosie, to meet them. The toddler was adorable, and Lilah relaxed in little Rosie's presence—but only until she began wondering how Bastien would react to her not being pregnant. After that disappointment would he still want to stay married to her? Or would that single disappointment be sufficient to knock the gloss off his belief that he wanted to keep her as his wife? Rich, powerful men didn't deal generously with disappointments because they met with very few.

A chill ran down Lilah's spine as she sipped her tea and tried to think cheerfully of returning to the life she had left behind.

'I was hoping that you and Bastien would join us for dinner some evening while you're in Athens,' Grace shared. 'Break the ice a bit.'

'I think it would take an ice pick,' Lilah confided ruefully.

'Bastien's not the family type. He's a natural loner,' Marina remarked.

Lilah stiffened angrily and her bright blue eyes sparked. 'Bastien might be closer to his brother if *you* hadn't soured their relationship by lying about what happened between you and Bastien ten years ago,' Lilah condemned, the stream of recrimination racing off her tongue before she could even stop to think about what she was saying.

In response to Lilah's outburst the most appalling

silence spread. Marina had turned the colour of ash, and Grace was staring at Lilah in wide-eyed consternation.

'I… I don't know what to say,' Marina responded, and as a deep flush highlighted her cheeks her guiltiness was obvious to Lilah.

'But I do. Delilah…time for you to leave.'

A deeply unwelcome voice sounded from behind the sofa she was sitting on. Lilah's head swivelled and she focused on Bastien in shock. The fact that he had heard what she had said to Marina was stamped on his lean darkly handsome face and in the threatening golden blaze of his eyes. She had embarrassed him by prying into his past and he was absolutely furious.

Her cheeks warm, she stood up and encountered a sympathetic glance from Grace.

'I'm sorry. I put my foot in it…trod where I shouldn't… whatever you want to call it,' Lilah muttered in a rush as soon as she was in the car with him.

'We'll discuss it when we get back to the apartment.'

'How's your father?' she asked.

'They think he's had a minor heart attack. He's going to have to change his lifestyle—eat less, exercise more,' he breathed curtly. 'Cleta's staying with him. I'll go back to see him later.'

Lilah stole a glance at his grim bronzed profile and cursed the misfortune that had led to Bastien overhearing her attack on his former lover. She knew she was in the wrong. She should have minded her own business. Should never have embarrassed Grace like that in her home. And now Bastien was furious with her.

She gritted her teeth, angry that she had spoken on impulse and without sensible forethought, but not sorry that she had told Marina what she thought of her behaviour.

His apartment was a penthouse, furnished in contemporary style and full of airy space, glass, metal and stone.

Lilah slung her bag down in the main reception room and sat down heavily. 'Say what you have to say,' she urged apprehensively, her nerves worn to a thread by the enforced wait.

Bastien settled burning golden eyes on her. 'What the *hell* got into you? I told you something private and you used it as a weapon to attack Marina. It was none of your business. You embarrassed me and you embarrassed Grace.'

'Well, if I embarrassed Marina, I'm not sorry,' Lilah fired back. 'She deserved what I said. And I didn't specify what I was talking about in any way, so I doubt if I embarrassed anyone.'

'Is that all you've got to say to me?' Bastien raked back at her rawly. 'You dug up something very confidential from my past. I can't *believe* that I even told you now. I should've known a woman couldn't be trusted.'

'Oh, don't throw any of that prejudiced nonsense at me!' Lilah warned him, equally rawly. 'It just got to me when Marina walked in all smiles and charm, acting as if she was a friend of the family.'

'She *is* a friend!'

'Not of yours, she's not!' Lilah flung back feelingly. 'She's caused a whole lot of trouble between you and your brother and you shouldn't have let her lies stand unchallenged. Your pride makes you your own worst enemy, Bastien!'

'I can't believe we're even having this conversation. Nothing that happened between Marina and I or Leo and I is anything to do with you. Where the hell do you get the nerve to interfere?'

'Maybe...just maybe...I was trying to do something for you.'

'You had no right to upset Marina like that.'

'*Marina?*' Lilah gasped as if he had punched her, because she was suddenly desperately short of breath, pierced to the heart that he should be more concerned about his former lover's feelings than about her.

'Yes—Marina,' Bastien repeated curtly. 'Of *course* she was upset. I saw her face. She knew instantly what you were referring to. You can't have thought this through, Delilah.'

Lilah was wounded by the angle the conversation had taken and fighting to hide the fact from him. Bastien was standing there, all lean, powerful and poised and devastatingly beautiful, and he was defending another woman to her face. He was *her* husband but he wasn't on her side.

Her tummy flipped, leaving her struggling against a sickening light-headed sensation.

'The termination caused Marina considerable distress,' Bastien delivered in a grim undertone. 'She made her choice, but I don't doubt that the decision cost her. That's the main reason why I didn't persist in arguing my case with Leo. Marina doesn't deserve to have that distressing experience raked up again. So she lied and played victim to look more sympathetic in

Leo's eyes? OK…that was wrong. But *Leo* is the one who chose to believe her story and disbelieve mine.'

Belated guilt pierced Lilah and she felt more nauseated than ever. On one score Bastien was correct. She had not thought through the implications of what she was throwing at Marina. But she was not a naturally unkind or unfeeling person. She knew she should never have referred to so private a matter. She had been cruel, and the shame of that reality engulfed Lilah like a suffocating blanket.

She blundered upright, desperate simply to escape Bastien's censorious gaze and lick her wounds and her squashed ego in private.

She swayed as the room telescoped around her in the most disturbing way. Her head was swimming and her skin was clammy and cold. Not a sound escaped Lilah's lips as blackness folded in behind her eyelids and she flopped down on the rug in a faint.

For a split second Bastien stared at Delilah, who had dropped in a heap on the rug, and then he plunged forward to crouch and gather her up, his brain obscured by the most peculiar fog of something that felt like panic but which he refused to acknowledge as panic. He wasn't the panicking type—never had been, never would be.

He dug out his phone to ring his brother's home and ask for Grace. Leo, mercifully, asked no questions, but Grace more than made up for that omission.

Grace told him quietly and succinctly what to do and Bastien followed her instructions, furious that he had once disdained to take a first aid course, assuming he would never feel the need for such training.

By the time he'd come off the phone and was carrying Delilah down to the main bedroom she was showing signs of recovery. Her lashes fluttered, her head moved, and a faint hint of colour began to lift the drawn pallor of her complexion.

Only then did Bastien dare to breathe again. He smoothed a shaking hand over Delilah's brow to brush back her tumbled dark hair. He had never felt so scared in his life. That knowledge shook him up even more. He had shouted at her, condemned her. And why had he done that?

Maybe I was trying to do something for you, Delilah had said, and the sheer shock value of those words was still reverberating inside Bastien. When had anyone *ever* tried to do anything to improve his life? When had anyone *ever* tried to protect him from the consequences of his own behaviour?

Delilah had been trying to *protect* him.

He swallowed hard. He didn't need anyone's protection. Nobody had protected him as a child or as an adolescent—neither his mother nor his father—and Bastien had learned never to look to other people for support. But Delilah had blundered headfirst into a difficult and delicate situation in a clumsy and futile attempt to straighten out his non-relationship with his only sibling.

Admittedly he had noticed how his wife had pokered up by his side when she'd seen how the Zikos family treated him. Delilah, he registered in a daze, *cared* about him—in spite of the methods he had used to ensnare her, in spite of all the mistakes he had made.

He snatched in a ragged breath and studied her in wondering appreciation.

'My goodness—what happened?' Lilah mumbled, blue eyes opening to fix on Bastien's lean darkly handsome face. 'Did I faint? I've never done that in my life! I'm *so* sorry.'

'You were upset—and when did you last eat?' Bastien pressed, pushing her back against the pillows when she tried to get up. 'Lie there for a while. Are you feeling sick?'

Lilah grimaced. 'Only a little... It's fading.'

'I'm really sorry I shouted at you,' Bastien said abruptly, a lean brown hand closing over hers, and he was astonished at how easily the apology emerged.

'You weren't shouting.'

'I'm not in a good mood. I was stressed about Anatole and feeling guilty about him,' Bastien admitted, disconcerting her with that confidence. 'I love my father, but I've never been able to respect him, and... and that makes me feel like a lousy son.'

Lilah squeezed his fingers uncertainly. 'No, I think it means you're adult enough to appreciate that he's not perfect and love him anyway...which is good.'

'Do you have a comforting answer for *everything* bad that I feel?' Bastien groaned, searching her anxious features with appreciative golden eyes.

'I doubt it, but you were right about Marina. Dragging that up was cruel... I'm afraid I didn't see it from her point of view, only yours, and I also felt jealous of her, which was even less excusable.' Lilah loosed a heavy sigh. 'I'm ashamed of myself for being so insensitive.'

'You were thinking of me and of my relationship with Leo,' Bastien said. 'But why on earth would you feel jealous of Marina? It's nearly ten years since I was with her—when we were both young and foolish.'

Lilah breathed in deep. 'I'm jealous of anyone you've ever been with. There—I've said it. I've got a possessive side I didn't know I had.'

'Like me,' Bastien cut in unexpectedly. 'I am irrationally jealous when it comes to you, and I've never been like that with any other woman. I couldn't even stand seeing you laughing and chattering with Ciro.'

'*Seriously?*' Lilah prompted, wide-eyed at that confession.

'I've been acting like a madman since I got you back into my life. Unfortunately for you I like my life much better with you in it. In fact, simply waking up in the morning to find you beside me makes me happy,' he bit out with bleak reluctance.

'It...it does?' Lilah was hanging on his every word, wondering why he was talking in such a way. 'Are you still going to be happy if I'm not pregnant?'

'*Diavelos*...what difference should *that* make?' Bastien was bemused. 'If it's not meant to be it's not meant to be and we'll handle it...that is if you want to stay with me...'

Lilah lifted up off the pillows and wrapped both arms round his neck, burying her face against his shoulder, drinking in the familiar scent of his skin in a storm of relief that felt both emotional and physical.

'Of *course* I want to stay with you.'

'There's no "of course" about it,' Bastien countered wryly as he unhooked her arms and gently settled her back against the pillows. 'I railroaded you into my bed and then into marriage, employing every piece of blackmail I had to put pressure on you.'

Lilah treated him to a troubled appraisal. 'I know…
I know you're extremely imperfect and that you've
done dreadful things. I know you manipulated me.
But… I still love you. I shouldn't, but I can't help
loving you…'

Bastien's throat thickened as if he had been slugged
in the vocal cords. 'I don't deserve your love.'

'No, you don't.' Lilah was quick to agree with him.
'But it seems I love you anyway.'

'Which is fortunate, because I'm not going to turn
perfect any time soon, and it's probably best that you
see all the flaws upfront—so that you know what
you're getting in me,' Bastien told her uncomfortably.

Both of his hands closed slowly round hers to hold
them in a grip of steel.

'But I love you too—so much more than I ever
thought I could love anyone. In short, I'm absolutely
crazy about you…so crazy I thought it was *normal* to
waste two years plotting and planning to acquire your
father's business and gain enough power over you to
acquire you as well.'

Lilah blinked rapidly. '*Crazy* about me?'

Bastien lifted one hand to his mouth and kissed
it almost awkwardly. 'Can't-live-without-you crazy,'
he extended in a driven undertone. 'It doesn't matter
if you're pregnant or not pregnant, or even if you can
never get pregnant. I just want and *need* you in my
life to make it feel worthwhile.'

'Even though I go interfering in things that are
none of my business?' she whispered, scarcely able
to believe what she was hearing, while her heart was
taking off inside her like a rocket ship.

'That was just you, taking a typical caring approach to sorting my life out,' Bastien informed her forgivingly. 'You know, in my whole life nobody has ever stood up to defend me or try to protect me until you spoke up today. And when I thought about that… *that* was the crucial moment when I finally realised how much I love you and why.'

Lilah was gobsmacked. 'It *was*?' she whispered.

'I've probably been in love with you since you called me a man whore and slammed that door in my face two years ago…' Bastien groaned. 'I've certainly been pretty much obsessed with *you* ever since then.'

'Obsessed while sleeping with other women?' Lilah derided gently.

'And I couldn't settle for five minutes with *any* of them. Don't blame me for that when you weren't willing to take a chance on me back then.'

Moisture stung the backs of her eyes and she blinked rapidly. 'I wasn't brave enough to dream that something more lasting might come from what seemed to be a very shallow sexual interest.'

'Ouch…' Bastien groaned again, looking pained. 'The minute I had you in my life everything changed, *hara mou*. You make me feel things. And when you're not around… I feel dead, as if I have nothing to look forward to or work for.'

A tear trickled down Lilah's cheek. 'Oh, Bastien…' she mumbled in a wobbly voice. 'You're making me cry. I love you so much, but I'm terrified you'll wake up some day and feel trapped.'

'Every woman who came before you made me feel trapped or bored. You do neither.'

His dark golden eyes burnished with warmth and appreciation, Bastien leant down and claimed a kiss—

a slow, deep kiss that said everything he couldn't find the words to say. She was the woman he hadn't even known he was looking for, waiting for. Her image had been locked in his head for two long years, ensuring that no other woman could please or hold him.

The kiss wakened Lilah's body, sending little tingles into her tender breasts and down into her pelvis. The sound of a doorbell could not have been less welcome to either of them.

Bastien lifted his head. 'I'd better see who that is... Don't get up.'

Lilah slid her legs off the mattress as soon as he had left the room and sped back to the main reception room to reclaim her bag. On her return she passed through the hall, and realised that their visitor was Leo.

When Bastien frowned at her, for being out of bed without permission, Lilah smiled valiantly at both men and muttered, 'I'm going back to lie down, Bastien.'

In fact, she took her bag straight into the en-suite bathroom and removed the pregnancy test she had purchased some days earlier. She had to know one way or the other, she reflected ruefully. Had she not been so fearful that their relationship would be damaged by a negative result she believed she would have done the test sooner. But Bastien's assurances had removed that worry. Furthermore, that fainting fit had roused Lilah's suspicions, because she had never fainted before.

The couple of minutes she had to wait for the result of the test seemed to last an unnaturally long time. When she finally straightened from her seat on the

side of the bath she froze, because she saw the result
straight away. It had an electrifying effect on her and
she wrenched open the bathroom door to yell.

'Bastien? *Bastien?* We're *pregnant*!' she gasped
from the bedroom doorway, reddening in dismay
when she registered Leo's presence, because she had
totally forgotten that Bastien was not alone.

Leo was startled enough by her announcement to
break into a grin. He gave Bastien a very masculine
punch on the arm and wrenched open the front door
for himself, departing at speed to leave them alone.

'Pregnant?' Bastien queried with a frown of uncertainty. 'But I thought you were convinced that you
weren't.'

'The symptoms were misleading,' Lilah told him
primly. 'Well? You're not saying anything... What do
you think? How do you feel?'

'I think I'm in shock. I'm a husband, and now
I'm going to be a father, and...' Bastien's beautifully
shaped mouth slanted into a wide, brilliant smile as
he moved towards her. 'I couldn't be happier.'

Lilah padded towards him. 'Even though it's not
what you originally signed up for?'

'I signed you up in an open-ended contract...or
didn't you notice that? I *never* promised to let you
go, and believe me, I won't now,' Bastien warned her.
'You're my wife, and you're going to have my baby,
and I'll never let either of you go.'

'We won't want to be without you,' Lilah swore,
rising on tiptoe to close her arms round him. 'I love
you so much, Bastien.'

Bastien stared down at her with wondering pleasure. 'I know—and I don't know why.'

'Because you're very loveable,' she pointed out.

Bastien was still bewildered, but he decided that it would be insane to question a miracle. He had done everything wrong and she had forgiven him. She cared about him—*really* cared. When had anyone ever truly cared about him?

His eyes suspiciously bright, Bastien lifted his wife with reverent hands and laid her back down very gently on the bed. 'You need to rest,' he said with conviction.

'No, I need *you*,' Lilah countered, her hand snatching at his to keep him close.

Bastien hung back a step. 'If I join you on that bed, I'll—'

His wife grinned at him, her heart racing, body thrumming. 'Do you think I don't know that? I'm throwing down a red carpet and a welcome mat.'

'In that case...' A wolfish smile tilted his beautiful mouth and he shed his jacket with fluid grace, all power and satisfaction. 'Your wish is my command.'

'Since when?' Lilah quipped, unimpressed by that unlikely claim.

'Since you told me that you love me.'

'I do...' Lilah sighed, breathing in the scent of him like an addict.

Bastien smoothed her hair back from her cheekbone, his burnished dark golden eyes brilliant. 'I really do love you, Delilah...'

Lilah put her sultry mouth to his and slow-burning heat rose inside her, as potent as the happiness she was barely able to contain. Her future was filled with Bastien and the promise of a family, and she was overjoyed by the knowledge.

EPILOGUE

Three years later

LILAH SMOOTHED DOWN her print sundress and studied the sapphire and diamond eternity ring Bastien had given her to celebrate their son's birth. Nikos was a lively toddler, with a shock of black hair and his mother's bright blue eyes. He was also a wonderfully affectionate child, and revelled in the attention he received from his father, who was determined to give his son a secure and loving childhood.

So much had changed during the past three years. Their home base was a London town house, but whenever they needed some downtime from their busy lives they flew out to the chateau in Provence.

The big house was the perfect base for family get-togethers, and Lilah's father, stepmother and siblings were regular visitors. Robert Moore was still running Moore Components, which had gone from strength to strength, expanding to facilitate the number of orders it was receiving.

Within weeks of Anatole's heart attack Bastien and Lilah had celebrated a second wedding in Provence—

a church ceremony, attended by all their family, and followed by a lively party at the chateau.

For a while afterwards Lilah had worked with Bastien as one of his PAs, and that had enabled the couple to spend more time together—particularly when he was travelling a lot. Since their son's birth, however, Bastien had consolidated the various elements of his business empire to enable him to travel less and spend more time with his family.

Grace and Leo had also become steady visitors. It had taken a long time, but Leo and Bastien had finally bonded as the brothers they were. Marina had told Leo the truth about the termination, and Leo had come to see Bastien to mend fences the same day on which Lilah had discovered she was pregnant.

Prompted by Grace and Lilah, who got on like a house on fire, the two families had enjoyed several vacations together, both on Leo's yacht and at the chateau.

Following his heart attack Anatole had lost a good deal of weight, in order to improve his health. He adored his grandchildren, and was a regular visitor to both London and Provence, but his wife, Cleta, almost never accompanied him on those visits. The pleasure Anatole received from seeing his sons finally treat each other like brothers had touched Lilah's heart.

'Sorry I'm late...' Bastien groaned from the doorway, already in the act of peeling off his shirt to head for the shower. 'Nikos and Skippy caught me on the way in and I've been playing ball. Leo has taken my place, even though Rosie has told us that kicking balls is "a stupid boy thing".'

Lilah laughed, because Grace's daughter was ex-

tremely clever for her age and often amused the adults
with the things she came out with.

She crossed the room to help Bastien unbutton his
shirt. 'Happy birthday,' she told him softly. 'Fancy
some company in the shower?'

'Is that my birthday present?' Bastien asked hopefully.

Lilah stripped off her dress where she stood, reaching round to unhook her bra. 'No, it's just a surprise.
You've been away for three days and I missed you.'

'Missed you too,' Bastien groaned, dropping his
shirt to reach for her warm slender body. 'You'll get
your hair wet.'

'I'll put it up...'

Lilah moaned under the urgent onslaught of his
passionate kiss, sensible matters like her appearance
dwindling in importance when it came to reconnect-
ing with Bastien.

'I told Leo we'd be a while,' Bastien confessed.

'Fancied your chances, did you?'

'Always, *hara mou*,' Bastien husked, fighting free
of his clothes without once letting go of his wife.

And the passion that never failed to enthral them
when they had been apart reigned supreme until they
lay in the lazy aftermath, wrapped in each other's
arms and catching up on stray bits of news while simply revelling in being together again.

'I love you,' Lilah sighed.

'I love you more,' Bastien murmured, ever competitive.

* * * * *

LET'S TALK
Romance

For exclusive extracts, competitions
and special offers, find us online:

- facebook.com/millsandboon
- @MillsandBoon
- @MillsandBoonUK

Get in touch on 01413 063232